SCION

S.L. BHYRAPPA

Sahitya Akademi Award and Saraswati Samman Winner

Translated from the Kannada original *Vamshavriksha* by

R. Ranganath Prasad

THORNBIRD

NIYOGI BOOKS

Published by
NIYOGI BOOKS
Block D, Building No. 77,
Okhla Industrial Area, Phase-I,
New Delhi-110 020, INDIA
Tel: 91-11-26816301, 26818960
Email: niyogibooks@gmail.com
Website: www.niyogibooksindia.com

Editor: Vibha Chakravarty Kumar
Design: Shashi Bhushan Prasad
Cover: Pinaki De

ISBN: 978-93-91125-02-8
Publication: 2023

Printed at: Niyogi Offset Pvt. Ltd., New Delhi, India

PREFACE

From the author's original preface:

While I penned this novel, I cogitated as to what 'Literary Pursuit' was. There were those subconscious ideas in my mind that directed my creativity. I retrieved them, and scripted them in conceptual clarity in an essay titled 'Literature and Perception of Values.'

From a speech of his:

But this novel transcends all that rubric, and is simply the depiction of a certain spatio-temporal Indian eidos.

TRANSLATOR'S NOTE

In relating the thoughts of the characters in this novel—and his other novels as well—it is typical of Dr. S.L. Bhyrappa to script contiguously within a single sentence the seemingly disparate thoughts as they occur in their minds. Though the constituent parts of this 'Stream of Consciousness' are almost complete semantically, they are mostly incomplete syntactically, except possibly the last in the series. While translating sentences thus structured, care has been taken to strike a balance between retaining the 'stream' per se and splitting it into several sentences with a view to ironing out impediments to comprehension. I have ensured that the former instances are sustainable within the ipseity of English language, wherefore there shall neither be confusion in the minds of the readers nor loss of import.

Also typical of the literary narrative of this author is synthesis of actuality, author's take, and characters' thought/speak[1] in the same sentence. Here, too, I have been selective in retaining such script per se. Wherever retained, it is not at the cost of comprehension. I am aware that such structuring is not legit, but I feel it to be kosher here for two reasons:

1 The three types of literary expressions distinctly defined in Indian poetics.

One, this is not a work of science, and two, it serves to impart aesthetic experience to the reader in the manner the original successfully endeavours to.

Strictly, a novel should have no accoutrements like glossary, for it would be breach of relish to take a break for referring to them. But this story is set in a traditionally and culturally rich milieu of the Indian way of life. Hence, a glossary of philosophical and cultural terminologies (to the exclusion of contextually comprehensible ones) pertinent to the Indian tradition has been appended at the end of the book.

CHAPTER 1

1

Just as music ascends gradually on taking off at a low tempo, and just as the tempo of the sonic eventually culminates in the dynamic impetus of the rhythm, the tranquil river Kapila, for once, kept on swelling till she attained her utmost motive potency. The great flood of 1924 sent her course haywire in Nanjangud (pronounced nun-jun-good). Kapila's colour, which used to be a soft white, was now a daunting blood red. As if seized by madness, Kapila surged ferociously while at the same time intensifying her expanse for five days in a row, putting the people of Nanjangud into consternation. Her vehemence seemed to stem from her volition to thoroughly cleanse her bed. Nobody had a clear idea as to the number of casualties, collapsed buildings, and families that turned destitute in her wake. The people of the town cursed the river for the havoc it wreaked on them, but Srinivasa Srotri did no such thing. Chanting a mantra that proclaimed all water to virtually be the sacred Ganga, Yamuna, et al., he had ceremoniously immersed himself in it by the sill of the main door.

After the flood receded, his neighbours abandoned their wrecked houses and gradually moved to new houses in a colony upward from the shores of the river, as a result of which the school lane, the Narayana-Rao precinct, and the market street around the temple—which exist even to this day—forfeited some of their prominence. But for Srinivasa Srotri, it was mentally an impossible task to simply abandon his traditional ancestral house and relocate to a novel one. The water that inundated his house was just about ankle-deep. His eight-year-old son Nanjunda, wife Bhageerathamma, and the resident housemaid Lakshmi told him that he better abandon the house, but he did not heed them. *Just because of our mother going wild for once, should we disregard the fact of her tending to us all through hitherto, and turn our backs on her?* He continued to dwell in that same house on Palace Road. He asked the women to shift to the upper floor and start the kitchen fire there.

The flood receded. Akin to the serene resonance that lingers much after the tempo of music tapers out, the flow of the river reverted to its normalcy. As if it were typical of her existence, the river adhered to a practice of surging in June and July every year, and remaining composed at other times. The areas assailed by the flood were being badly ravaged, year after year. Alas, it wasn't the river that was ravaged!

A few years passed by. Srinivasa Srotri's son Nanjunda Srotri grew up. He moved to Mysore to pursue his higher studies. He wed Katyayani, whom his parents wholeheartedly doted on. Soon, the newlywed couple became parents to a baby boy. When this child was six months of age, Nanjunda Srotri drowned in the floods of Kapila in June that year. He was adept at swimming. And this young man's arms and limbs weren't weak either. He was tall like his father, with longish arms. His forehead was palm-wide. He was muscular, and of clear skin. But who can put up with the fierceness of a river that overflows? He hadn't gone to swim in that swelling river. He had cautiously descended the steps of the Manikarnika deck to bathe when he slipped into the water. All his efforts at getting to the shore failed. Those on the banks called out to him. He, too, yelled. But he was anon sucked into a whirlpool. Nobody got to see the corpse. Lackeys searched for it on both the shores of the river up to T-Narasipura. No sign of it. The flood receded after five days of his oblatory—so it seemed—demise. The post-funeral rites were performed on the banks of that very river.

Six months passed by.

2

Which of the two is graver—the agony of doting parents who have lost their lone son in his prime, or that of a wife who lost her loving husband in her twentieth year? It is nigh impossible to assess the intensity of one from the metric of the other. Owing to the death of her lone son, Bhageerathamma became old within the month. She was at a loss regarding whether to grieve at the death of her son, to lament at the widowhood of her young daughter-in-law, or to rend her entrails at the sight of her infant grandson's intermittent chuckling. She just kept on weeping. When memories of her son assailed her, she would go pick up her grandson. Tears would ooze much more. Her daughter-in-law, who would be nearby, would revert to sobbing. Shoring up her own fortitude, the elderly lady would approach her daughter-in-law and placate her. The infant, though, would keep up with his giggling, oblivious of joy or sorrow. In fact, it was the infant who placated both the women—the grandmother and the mother!

One afternoon, Katyayani was seated beside the cradle in the room on the upper floor. The baby was asleep in the cradle. Her mind had retracted, as would a land snail into its shell, and was thoroughly regarding the incidents that dotted her married life. She was just two years into the marriage. A husband whom she had liked much and who loved her much, distinguished parents-in-law, an infant that lit up the entire house as would moonlight—a family that any woman would live contentedly in. Her father-in-law's virtuosity and in-depth scholasticism in Vedas and sāstras had engendered respect for the family in the minds of the people. Her husband's ever-radiant face and lovingness never failed to mesmerize her. 'What else do I need,' she had told herself in exuberance. One day, six months ago, Kapila had wrecked her happy family. The quantum of tears that she has shed since is no less than that of the waters that Kapila swamped the earth with. At times, she would take to cogitating about life. But she wasn't erudite enough to comprehend much.

Katyayani hadn't graduated past intermediate. She had read what the novelists and essayists had expounded on life. She felt that none of them was capable of delineating the cause of her adversity.

She heard footsteps scaling the staircase. She craned her neck to look; it was her father-in-law. She put down her sight and began rocking the cradle, unmindful that it might jolt the baby from his sleep. Srotri was lost in thought even as he climbed the stairs. He didn't look in the direction of his daughter-in-law. He headed straight to the other room on that floor. That room was his library, wherein were many manuscripts of birch bark, printed books, and some books that he had made copies of. Stored in a shelf was homemade ink prepared by charred finger millet; and pens too. Laid out on the floor beneath it was a full-size tiger hide mat to sit on, and on it was placed a bolster against a wall to lean on. A foldable book-pedestal stood across from the bolster. It held an open book. For over 30 years, he has been spending quality time here to pursue Vedas, sāstras, Purāṇas, *dharmaśāstra* and Āyurveda. From the day of the demise of his son until the funeral rites were consummated, he has not been there—not even for a few months after that. He would keep company with his wife and daughter-in-law, consoling them. He has now resumed his routine. His wife would always be with the resident housemaid Lakshmi. The senior lady of the house would reminisce her son and simply weep. Lakshmi, who was of the same age as her mistress, grieved silently. Infrequently, Srotri would look for a pretext to accost his grief-stricken daughter-in-law. The young Katyayani would be in a state of eternal grief in the memory of her husband. But she did not witness her father-in-law shed a single tear. She knew that he wasn't stone-hearted. All the same, the depth of his fortitude was beyond her comprehension.

The baby would be asleep until five in the evening. Seated by the cradle or elsewhere, Katyayani would be doused in her insurmountable bereavement. 'Kiddie,' someone seemed to call out to her from afar, but it was actually her father-in-law close behind. Katyayani turned in the direction of the call. Srotri, who was headed towards the staircase, retraced his steps towards her and sat by a pillar near her. She stood up. 'Sit child,' he said. Muted, Katyayani complied. She wasn't at all inhibitive in talking to her father-in-law. Ever since she stepped into this house as its daughter-in-law, the cordiality between them was that of a father and a daughter. But since her husband's death, she hardly spoke to anyone. Srotri asked, 'Kiddie, are you reciting Bhagavadgīta as suggested by me?' She neither lifted her head nor gave any reply. After two minutes when he asked the same again, she said, 'I tried reading it, but I am not able to understand anything. I can't concentrate even.'

'Irrespective of how much is comprehensible, you should keep reading it. You will be able to grasp it by and by.' After a minute's silence, she said, 'The philosophy discussed in Bhagavadgīta is beyond me. No Vedanta has the potential to mitigate my grief. What is the point in reading it?'

Smiling in melancholy, Srotri said in a tone of consolation, 'It is true that we alone have to put up with our sorrows. No treatise, nobody can relieve us of it. But from these treatises, you will get to know the paltriness of our sorrow vis-à-vis the happenings in this vast world. Then it becomes a tad easy to rein in our grief. So, please evince some interest in studying it.'

While Srotri said this, the child in the cradle woke up. He started crying. 'Console him and bring him to me,' Srotri said, and walked down the stairs. Katyayani picked the infant up from the cradle and started breastfeeding him. Reclined on his mother's lap, as he helped himself to his sustenance, the baby went silent. While feeding him, she would reminisce about her husband, and embrace the baby firmly to her chest. She would derive a semblance of relief.

When his belly was full, the baby began his play. Tugging at her necklace with his nails and gazing at his mother's face, he smiled. For once, he chortled so volubly as to be heard from every nook and corner of the house. Hearing that, the grandfather called out from below, 'Cheeni.'

Katyayani took him into her arms and climbed down the staircase. Grandpa, who was pacing in the living downstairs, collected him, positioned him on his shoulders and took him to the cattle shed in the backyard. Katyayani headed for the kitchen. Her mother-in-law was attending to the cooking. Katyayani entered and simply stood there. Noticing her, the elderly lady said, 'Kiddie, you shouldn't resort to solitude. The more you are reticent, more will the mind delve into those worries. Keep me or Lakshmi company. Keep chatting about something. Consign the kitchen waste to the manger in the cattle shed, or feed horse gram juice to the calves, or attend to some other work.' She turned to the earthen stove and added pigeon pea gram to the boiling water. She placed a vessel on another stove to prepare curry, and lightly doused the fire of the stove where the rice was almost done. 'Keep a watch on the flame. If pigeon pea bubbles up, call me in the puja chamber. I will make arrangements for his puja and join you soon. It is time for his evening puja and he will be here any moment.' Assigning some simple jobs to her daughter-in-law, Bhageerathamma headed to the puja chamber.

3

By the time Srotri was through with his *sandhyāvandana* and puja, it was 8 pm. Taking with him the vessel that contained the oblatory water of the *sandhyāvandana*, he went to the backyard to dispense it into the bed of a plantain tree. On his way back to the puja chamber, Katyayani called out to him, 'Dr Sadashiva Rao from Mysore is here. He is seated in the living room.'

'When did he arrive?'

'About two hours ago. You had just started on your *sandhyāvandana* then.'

Foregoing any more recitation of Veda-mantras, Srotri placed the vessels in the puja chamber and exited. Dr Sadashiva Rao was about 35 years of age, and of average build. He wore spectacles, and a good part of his hair had turned white. He was not very keen on dress. Seated on a chair in the living room, he was engrossed in a Sanskrit book. It was only when Srotri drew his attention vocally that he pulled his eyes away from the book. 'I am told that you came quite some time back. Sorry to have kept you waiting.'

'A senior, you should not say so. I have no other work. I am visiting here at leisure.'

Srotri sat on a chair and said, 'I'm curious to know the progress of your book.'

'It has been published by a London publisher. I am here to give you a copy.' He took out a printed English book titled *Dharmic Foundations of Ancient Indian Polity* from his bag and gave it to Srotri humbly. It was a 100-page book, and the layout was fine. Srotri took it and turned the cover page. The Canarese autograph on the title page read 'With my respects, to the venerable Sri Srinivasa Srotri–Sadashiva Rao'.

'That reverence is incommensurate,' said Srotri.

'In a sense, you are the guide for this dissertation. I have learnt from you much of what has gone into it. You have clarified quite some doubts of mine. I have even stated so in the preface.'

Srotri was not very conversant with English language. He could just about attend to some transactions—writing a bank cheque, writing addresses on postal covers, etc. 'You have penned such a voluminous work. I truly cannot read it fully. My daughter-in-law would,' he said. Placing the book in the topmost bookshelf in the living room, he handed

Dr Rao a towel and said, 'Come, wash your feet. Let's have supper first, and then we shall discuss it all leisurely.'

Seated on the floor in the passage between the kitchen and the puja chamber, they supped; Bhageerathamma served the food. When he had helped himself to a few morsels, Sadashiva Rao suddenly asked, 'Nanjunda Srotri is not to be seen. Where is he?'

Though disturbed for a moment, Srotri said calmly, 'Let's speak after we are done with this meal. I will tell you everything.'

Dr Rao was a teacher to the deceased son of Srotri. He taught history when junior Srotri was pursuing his BA. He got to meet the senior Srotri through this pupil of his, and went on to benefit from his scholasticism. Srotri's words engendered some doubts in Rao's mind. When he had arrived in the evening, Katyayani had greeted him at the door; he had attended her wedding. On his few visits since, he had talked to her some. She had responded with no inhibition whatsoever. But today, head hung, she had just asked him to be seated, telling him that her father-in-law had just started on his evening puja, and that he would be done in about an hour. She'd receded into the house thereafter. Her face was not clearly visible at that dusky hour.

After supper, they both returned to the living room, and sat facing each other with the betel-nut case between them. Srotri said, 'I have quit chewing betel. You have it, please.' Rao then garnished four leaves for himself. While chewing them, he asked, 'Why, Nanjunda Srotri is not in station?'

'No, Kapila took away your pupil. He slipped into the river last June. He never got ashore,' Srotri said in a calm tone.

Dr Rao was shocked at the news. He could not get himself to believe it. He just kept looking at Srotri, who resumed in the same composed tone. 'The fate of your pupil afflicts you much. But everything has to be taken into stride. There is his wife and one-year-old son. You should wish for his child to merit a teacher like you. Well, what plans have you? One with such acumen as yours should discourse on the life of our ancestors for the benefit of upcoming generations. Pray, isn't it about a year and a half since you visited here last?'

Rao held Srotri's character in great esteem, alright. But he could never have imagined that he could remain so composed despite his heart being heavy from the sorrow of his son's untimely demise. Gathering from his words that Srotri was not inclined to discuss his son's ill fate, Rao said, 'This work has brought me great success. Scholars from European countries have written to me in praise of it. But I am not content with just this one work. While I researched on the topic of *Dharmic Foundations of Ancient Indian Polity*, I got to know that *dharma* served as the basis for all the peoples of ancient India. It engendered a desire in me to delineate the cultural heritage of this nation from as far back as historians can perceive, till now. The content is so copious as to call for its publication in five volumes, and I am confident of penning it over 25 years. Just as with this book, I need your guidance and blessings for that tome as well.'

While they were deep into this conversation, Katyayani brought two beds there and laid them closely. After placing rugs on both beds, she placed a copper urn of drinking water and two glasses, and exited. They kept up with their discussion even after retiring.

Rao resumed, 'Many have written about the history of this country. But those are all political histories. One or two works have dwelled on its cultural history. But my view is something else. Serving as a brace for the constituents of Indian culture viz. art, polity and daily life of the people, the *dharma* undercurrent has been flowing incessantly—sustaining them all. It can be seen that the constitution of culture mutated when such creeds as Brahminism, Buddhism and Jainism attained their zenith. The reason for this land's cultural edifice to thrive without suffering any significant impairment despite the concurrent regnancy of these three creeds prior to the Moghul invasion is that the core essence of these three creeds came from the same source. My research shall be pivoted on the effect of Islam on our cultural foundation, and as to the dimensions it is assuming in modern times. To that end, it is necessary to study *dharmaśāstra*, philosophies, literature, etc. of this land we call *Bhārat*. By now I have done quite some study. Henceforth, I will have to study a few treatises in your company. In this pursuit, there is none other than you who can help me.'

They continued to discuss through midnight. Srotri was interested in knowing about the modalities of penning such a tome, and the hindrances that such endeavour was susceptible to. Rao explained. 'Such research requires a lot of time. If one or two assistants are available, the researcher should consider himself fortunate. Many source books will not be available in our domicile. We have to go discerning them in libraries across the length and breadth of the country. It also calls for visiting places of historical significance and getting firsthand information. And for all this, there is the need for finance. I have sent a set of my published works to Maharaja Krishnaraja Wadiyar, with a humble letter of appeal apprising him of my proposed project. His secretary has written to me that I am appointed to see His Highness this coming Monday at 3 pm. I think His Highness may help.' Srotri was intently listening. It was 2 am when they slid into sleep.

4

As usual, Srotri was up at 4 am and headed for the Gundala stream that flowed at a distance of a 100 yards behind his house. As it was the second fortnight of the lunar month, the moon was absent in the sky, but planet Venus was shining bright. The stars that smiled from across the sky triggered his imagination to perceive eternity. In the serene dawn, he strode beneath those stars, went through his morning ablutions and came inside the cattle shed. The cows affectionately rose as he neared the shed. He caressed their dewlaps by turns, checked which cow had consumed how much grass, shifted them outdoors, and by the time he entered the house, Bhageerathamma was up and about. Taking hold of a dhoti and an urn, he exited, passed by the temple and headed for the Manikarnika deck. Kapila flowed calmly à la the octave *ṣaḍja*. By the time he bathed in the river, washed his soiled dhoti, collected water in the urn and returned home, crows were heralding dawn. Bhageerathamma had bathed, cleaned the puja chamber, drawn raṅgoli, and had laid out the puja paraphernalia.

It was 8 am when Dr Rao woke up. It was his usual hour; he would have retired at 2 am the same day! On getting up, he found a chair and was seated when Katyayani appeared there and said, 'He is performing puja. You better bathe now and join him. I have kept the hot water ready.'

After bathing, Rao posted himself at the door of the puja chamber. Concluding the puja, Srotri gave him the *ārati* and *tīrtha*. Rao was to return to Mysore that same afternoon. As Srotri was not used to having breakfast, only Rao was served the same. Taking leave of Rao at 11 am, Srotri went out for a while and returned soon after. After lunch, when Rao took leave, Srotri held before him a tray containing betel, areca and coconut—the usual hamper given to guests—and said, 'Please accept this.' Rao looked, and was intrigued when he noticed an envelope therein. Gathering that there were currency notes, Rao stepped back and said, 'I will accept the hamper as a mark of your blessings, but I know what that envelope is, wherefore I won't take it.'

Srotri said in a gentle voice, 'You have set out to pen a tome. That project needs all the money it can get. God has blessed this house with a little more than just sustenance. For what purpose may the surplus be utilized other than such? Please accept.'

'Still, I will seek a different sort of support from you, not this.'

'Who am I to support? Whenever you feel like it, please visit here without hesitation. Now, you must accept this. This is neither for your personal effects, nor is it *me* that is giving it. The money deserves to be expended for such work. If the donor were a miser and is parting with money reluctantly, or if he is donating by putting his wife and children to misery, or if he is donating ill-earned money, such money should not be accepted—notwithstanding that it shall be expended for dharmic activities. Here's another of those subtleties of *dharma*: you will be defying *dharma* if you refuse this.' Srotri smiled.

Rao became very inhibitive, and vacillated even as he accepted the tray. Before leaving by the afternoon train, he formally took leave of Bhageerathamma and expressed a few words of consolation to Katyayani. When the train left Nanjangud station, he checked the envelope out of curiosity. He was dumbstruck. There were 10 notes of 100 rupees! Even before the train reached Mysore, he had decided on the investment portfolio—for 200, buy a fine new typewriter; for 300, buy books that were not available in the library of the university here, and use the balance for research travel.

CHAPTER 2

1

Though he was awake by 9 am, Dr Sadashiva Rao had not exited his bedroom. He was going over the notings he had made in a book yesterday night. He was not in the habit of having coffee in bed. He would have coffee or breakfast only when his wife gave him. He never went asking for it even if he was hungry either. In the book that he was currently reading, there were many sections he could not come to terms with. He desired to delineate them in his work so as to lay bare their flaws. While his mind was engrossed in imagining how life was two millennia ago, he felt a cold palm on his head. He looked. Holding a cup of castor oil in her left hand, his wife had poured some on to her right palm and was massaging his head. His face creased from irritation. 'Nagu, what are you up to this morning?' he asked.

'Should I state it verbally? Can't you see for yourself? Go tie just a towel around your waist soon. I will anoint your entire body too,' said Nagalakshmi.

'It is enough to rub it on my scalp. Answer me. Why did you take to this first thing this morning? I have some work to attend to. Can you think at all?'

Smiling, Nagalakshmi said, 'You store many, many books in your memory. You have on your fingertip information as to how many aged elephants were in the war troop of some obscure king. Can't you remember something told by your wife yesterday night? Recall what I told you yesterday night.'

Try as he might, he was unable to recall. He had memorized all that was discussed in that 300-page book that he had read overnight till 3 am. Nagalakshmi smiled teasingly and said, 'You cannot recall. Will the likes of you be attentive to their wives' needs? Let it go. Today is your birthday. I had told you that I would give you an oil bath and prepare pudding. Don't you get riled up at me for anointing you. Get up, wrap yourselves in a towel and wait for me in the bathroom.'

While applying castor oil to his back in the bathroom, Nagalakshmi said, 'You will not peer into the mirror even while combing your hair. Have you noticed that your hair have turned fully grey? Today, you have turned 35. Oldie so soon! That aside, do you know your wife's age?'

Rao permitted himself to a smile. 'Whatever it is, it is less than 35.'

'Very smart. For one who pays no attention to his wife, will her age matter? I am two months elder to Raja. He turned 25 last fortnight. Now tell me what my age is.'

'Two months more than Raja's age.'

'To hell with your cleverness. At least tell me how much younger to you I am.'

'You are younger to me by two months less than exactly how much Raja is younger to me.'

Nagalakshmi gently squeezed his nose with her unctuous fingers and said, 'I will not spare you if you do not recall even this much. Let the oil percolate some. Keep massaging yourself. I will put some pigeon pea gram to simmer, and bring you coffee. I will not give anything to you to eat until you bathe and prostrate before God.'

Nagalakshmi went into the kitchen. She had mopped the house clean the previous night, and had drawn rañgoli at select spots. She had dusted the puja chamber and laid out the puja paraphernalia. She only had to go through cooking as fast as she could. It was already 10 am. By the time rice and vegetables were cooked and pulse was half-cooked, her four-year old son Prthvi, who had gone to play in the neighbouring house, returned and proclaimed, 'Ma, I am hungry.'

'Today is papa's birthday. Lunch will be served only after his oil bath. If you are hungry, here, help yourself to this,' she filled his shirt pocket with a fist full of rice flakes. The lad jogged away to resume playing. When she went to the bathroom after she was done with the dishes, Rao wasn't there. She went to his study to check. Squatted on an old gunny bag that was laid out on the floor, he was making notes from the book he had read last night. Nearing him, Nagalakshmi said, 'Get up. Ye shall read all the 364 days. One should indulge the wife and the children on their birthday. Bathe and lunch. Rest if you want. Let's watch the play *Vasantasena* this evening. Lakshmibai is playing the lead role.'

'Let's watch it if time permits. Let your words rule today, er...' as if he recalled something, he asked, 'What time is it now?' Looking at the wall clock, Rao said, 'Oh, it is 11:30 am. Come, bathe me quick. I have to see His Highness at 3 pm.'

'Is it? You didn't share it with me. What for?'

'I didn't? Think I forgot. I have recorded it in my diary. Come on, bathe me.'

'Is recording in the diary the same as sharing it with the wife? Well, can I read your English diary at all? I am a dunce, a village girl, daughter of Kunigal Ramanna.' She yanked him by his arm and led him to the bathroom. Pouring jug-fulls of steaming water over him, she scrub-cleaned his head, back and entire body. Later, while performing the puja, she got him to prostrate before God. She then gave the sacraments to him and to her son. By the time all three had lunched, it was 1:30 pm. Washing the plates and stashing away the remaining food, when she entered Rao's study with betel, areca and lime in a tray, she found that he was dressed to the hilt! Even in that hot summer he had on a coat, a black tie and a turban, and was putting on his shoes. Taken aback at his headstart, she asked him, 'Why leave so early? Shouldn't you partake of betel in my company at least today! Wait, let me garnish one for you quickly.'

'No, Nagu, it is already 1:45. His Highness will make his appearance at exactly 3. If I consume betel, I will have to brush my teeth for I cannot exhibit my stained teeth before him.' He got up to leave. Placing the tray on the table, Nagalakshmi neared him, held both his hands in hers and said, 'Look in my eyes.' When he complied in letter and spirit, she said in a tone succulent with affection, 'Go on and see him. The puja I just performed will augur well for you. His Highness will surely facilitate your proposal.'

2

When Dr Sadashiva Rao was 10 years of age, his mother, who had just given birth to a baby boy, passed away. His maternal uncle, Kunigal Ramanna, had fostered them both. Two years after the death of his mother, his father went the same way. There was no estate to be inherited from his father. Sadashiva Rao was 10 years elder to Nagalakshmi, his uncle's daughter. She was just a kid of five when Sadashiva Rao moved to Mysore to study high school while staying at an orphanage there. His brother Raja and Nagalakshmi were the same age. They would together play tag, hide-and-seek, hopscotch, etc.

Rao finished his MA at the age of 24, and began his career as a history lecturer in Maharaja College. He almost immediately began studying for his PhD. Ramanna kept pestering his nephew to wed Nagalakshmi. Fourteen at that time, the tall and presentable Nagalakshmi had turned maidenly. She was of fine disposition, and was adept at household chores. But, poor girl, she was not erudite enough to graduate past middle school. Her parents held that there was no point in her pursuing academics, and she shared their view. Studious ab initio, Sadashiva Rao had given no thought to marriage or his would-be bride. He just heeded uncle's words. The wedding was consummated and Nagalakshmi joined him in Mysore. Raja followed her so as to pursue his studies in Mysore. Even now Nagalakshmi's camaraderie with Raja is much more than with her husband. It can't be said that Sadashiva Rao does not love his wife; he does love her. Was there any such thing as loving one's own wife with full cognition and application! Characteristically, he was engrossed in his studies, research and manuscription. Prthvi was born six years into the marriage.

Ramanna had passed away four years ago; and a year later, his wife too. Nagalakshmi's brother and his wife looked after their ancestral agricultural lands in the village.

After securing his masters in English literature, and having served as a lecturer in the very college that he attended, Raja landed a scholarship to pursue higher studies in England. That was two years ago, and ever since he sailed to Oxford, Nagalakshmi was bored from absence of company. By nature, she was a chatterbox. Her studious husband would forget himself when visiting in a library. On returning home, he would stick to his study and be engrossed in his reading and writing until the wee hours! He didn't even have the time to write to his brother overseas. Nagalakshmi would write to him, and Rao would just write the address on the envelope in English and post it. By now, Raja was through with his studies at Oxford, and was bound to his homeland on seas. He was likely to disembark in Mumbai in a day or two.

After her husband left to meet His Highness, Nagalakshmi had no work to do; her daily chores weren't much either. Her husband had consented to take her to the theatre that evening, and she was quite excited about it. *How much time would the meeting with His Highness take up? In consonance with his status 'His Highness', he would wind it up with just a few words. Why wouldn't he share with me that His Highness had invited him for a meeting? Well, would he share anything at all with me! He and his writing were everything; nothing else was important.*

It is 5, and he was not yet back. Nagalakshmi summoned her son who was playing in the neighbouring house, and attended to dressing him up, and herself too. She wore a fine sari. Wasn't it her husband's birthday today? The birthday boy himself was indifferent about it, but how could she be so. 'Amma, papa isn't here yet. No theatre?' Prthvi asked. 'Wait, he will be here any moment,' she said, but she was as apprehensive herself. He wasn't back even by 6. She posted herself at the main door. In 10 minutes, a postman walked up to her, obtained her signature, and handed her an envelope. Inside was a telegram of just three words, and she could gather that it was signed 'Raja'. And though she could gather the import of the three words, viz. 'Arriving Tuesday evening', she was not confident. *Whom to ask? Raja, who would write letters in Canarese, why has he sent this telegram in English? Should he too mock at my ignorance of English?* 'Let him arrive, I will take him to task,' she resolved.

When Rao returned at 8 pm, he saw the telegram and said, 'Raja will arrive tomorrow evening.'

'So, I have understood it correctly, right?' asked Nagalakshmi in delight.

'Yes, you are smart. Once Raja is back, get some tuition from him and brush up your English. Then you can assist me.'

'Yeah, only that remains to be done! I know very well that education is not in my good fortune. Well, so much for today's theatre. Raja returns tomorrow. Let us all go watch it the day after. Fill me in on what His Highness ordained.'

'I had earlier sent him that book of mine. He has read it. I was told that he was appreciative of it. He ordained that full support be accorded to my proposed tome.'

'Was it with this proposal that you met with him? And why should you keep me in the dark about it all?'

'My clogged mind missed it. It is getting late. Go see if the kid is hungry.'

Nagalakshmi went looking for Prthvi.

3

Sadashiva Rao went to the railway station to receive his brother. Immediately on alighting, Raja prostrated at his brother's feet. When they were home, one look at him, and Nagalakshmi was ready to remark, 'Your complexion has brightened a bit, but you have gone down bodily.'

'There wasn't a Nagalakshmi there to cook for me. I even thought of wedding a local to run the kitchen and tend to my belly, but I abstained from doing so thinking that you might not approve of it.'

'As if you heed my every word! Sit, help yourself to a glass of lemon juice.' She held out a tray of treats.

Two friends of his were visiting, and Rao was chatting with them in his study. Prthvi had forgotten about his uncle. 'Unca, unca,' he, who would earlier so jump in joy at the sight of his uncle, now kept his distance from the 'stranger'. When Raja had left for England, Prthvi was two years old, and it was he who humoured the kid at all times. He was a darling with kids, all and any. He asked his sister-in-law, 'Nagu, tell me, how have you spent these two years? Brother's book is well received in England. Does he converse with you at all, or is he lost in his writing as before?

'Is his nature amenable to change?' she doused the flame of the earthen stove some.

'Yet, with a doting wife alone at home, wouldn't one be encouraged to chat some with her?'

'Go and ask that of him. Now, tell me, what did you do in England. You had written that you watched quite some theatre. How was it?'

Raja's area of exclusive interest was theatre, the stage. While pursuing his BA at Oxford, he had found time to watch English theatre and participate in study circles to quite an extent. He had even befriended some thespians. He had got himself acquainted with the improved make-ups and mechanized stage accessories. He went on relating everything to her. She could not grasp it all. But she was wont to intently listen to whatever anyone related to her, notwithstanding her inability to comprehend it fully. Raja was a chatterbox, too; and hence, they were compatible. Nagalakshmi said, 'The SSS theatre has camped in this town.

They have been enacting *Vasantasena* for 15 days now. The entire town is converging there. Lakshmibai has acquitted herself well in that title role, I was told. We had plans to watch it yesterday. By then we received your telegram. We then thought of watching it today along with you.'

Laughing, Raja said, 'Nagu, you are lying. You just said that he never talked to you much. Now you say that you both had planned to go to the theatre together.'

'Oh, God! Yesterday was his birthday, so I insisted that we watch that play. Promising to return by evening, your brother went to see His Highness, and returned only at 8. By then, I had received your telegram.'

After seeing off his guests, Rao came into the living room. Not knowing what subject to broach, he looked at his brother and said, 'The climate of England seems to be favourable to you. You have become more hale and hearty than before.'

Raja replied smiling, 'Nagalakshmi just said that I have withered. You certify me as better than before. Between you two, who is right?'

'I. I am right.' Nagalakshmi intervened.

'Yes,' Rao conceded.

While they were having supper, Rao asked, 'Have you read my book?'

'Not just read it, I was witness to the critical acclaim it earned too. When they got to know that I was the author's brother, the history professors of Oxford befriended me. I got to know that you have plans to pen a tome. What is that all about?'

'Who told you?'

'A bulletin by Mademoiselle Nagalakshmi and Co.'

'Yes. I have big plans. Sri Srinivasa Srotri of Nanjangud has blessed me with good luck, and has donated 1,000 rupees. Yesterday, I saw His Holiness and appealed to him. He has assured to support me as well. For six months now, I have been writing to the university authorities. Once, I even met the Vice Chancellor. The tenor of his words was thus: 'You are a lecturer. Delivering lectures just about does justice to your pay grade. What have we got to do with your monograph?' Research calls for study travel. What with financial support, they are not even inclined to provide me enough leave for my research. I have pinned all my hopes on the support of His Highness.'

Reminiscing the encouragement afforded to scholars and researchers in the Western universities, Raja said, 'It is this state of affairs of the universities of this country that is causing many scholars to relocate to the West. If you submit the book you have just penned to Oxford or Cambridge, and make out a project report as to your proposed tome, they will support in all ways just on the potential of that published book of yours. He, who has set out to pen the history of India, shall land greater resource material and facilitation in England.'

Nagalakshmi intervened, 'If he goes to England, he will forget his family and stay there permanently.'

'Ye fear not. If such scholars move there, stay arrangements will be made for their family as well. Besides, if brother left you back, what will he do for his victuals? Without the curry prepared by you, he will consume no cereal whatsoever. Serve some gravy of the curry for my curd-rice, please.'

'Aren't you adept at mesmerizing speech,' she picked up the ladle to serve the gravy.

Rao was immersed in thoughts about the renowned library of the British Museum and the universities of Europe.

4

In a matter of just one day, Prthvi got accustomed to his uncle again. When they left for the theatre, he stuck to him. Though Rao wasn't very enthusiastic about watching the play, he still joined them. They walked the distance from Chamarajapura to Shivarampet. It was the times when the Sangeeta Sahitya Samrajya troupe mesmerized theatre connoisseurs, and they all—educated or otherwise—watched its shows. Even before they arrived at the gate of the auditorium, Raja was accosted by many acquaintances, greeted, and was enquired after his good health. When a few senior professors spotted Rao with family, they approached him and said, 'Back to life. Congratulations.' In the chairs-section, Rao sat with Raja to his left and Nagalakshmi to his right. Prthvi climbed up on his uncle's thighs. When it came to theatre, Raja's interest had graduated from pedantry to appraisal. He was not merely an enthusiast who had come just to watch a play.

Rao's mind was redolent of scholasticism. He had read the play *Mṛcchakaṭikam* long back from the viewpoint of historical research. His mind was now filled with the milieu of that era viz. civilization, life, social circumstances, etc. Awe from curiosity rent the minds of just two—Nagalakshmi and Prthvi. This was the first time that she had gone to watch theatre in the company of her husband. When she was still young, she had watched *Shanimahatma*, *Danashurakarna* and other plays in Kunigal. The roles therein were essayed by select villagers locally. The stages there were not as well appointed as this. Besides, she had heard much about this play from the women in the neighbourhood. Prthvi was asking his uncle what those pictures on the screen were. When the musical ensemble of harmonium, violin and tabla rendered the auspicious *Rama jayatu Srirama sunama,* signalling the commencement of the show, he craned his neck and began watching with bated breath. Nagalakshmi experienced horripilation from excitement.

Charudatta and Vidushaka came on stage in the first act. The king's brother-in-law Shakara, who came chasing Vasantasena, said, 'Hey Vasantasena, you are burning my heart like a wildfire, you are driving away my sleep at night, but now you run unmindful that you will trip. Now you become my captive just as Kunti became Ravana's captive. I will now kidnap you just as Hanuman kidnapped Subhadra, the sister of Vishvavasu.'[1] Hearing this, the entire audience burst into laughter. Overcome with billowing laughter, Nagalakshmi

1 These statements are of an ignoble character from the classical play Mṛcchakaṭikam (listed here). He cites characters from the epics as simile, but he makes a comical mélange of them. Kunti and Subhadra are characters in the epic Mahabharata. Rāvaṇa and Hanuman are characters in the epic Ramayana. Viśvāvasu is an imaginary character from a classical literary work.

placed her hand on her husband's and said, 'Look, he calls himself the brother-in-law of the king. Isn't he a dunce?'

Rao was lost in thought. At all times in history, the ward of the authorities shall merit benefaction despite their being dumb. The wife squeezed his hand again. 'Seems like you are not watching the play.' 'No, no,' he said, 'the play is fine.'

Shakara kept up with his raving and ranting. 'I can hear the haroma of her garland. But my nose being doused in darkness, I am unable to clearly shee the shound of her hornaments.'

Once again, the audience was swept away by a wave of laughter; Nagalakshmi was too. But the recurrent gag would not amuse Dr Rao's inquisitive mind.

During the interval, Raja asked his sister-in-law, 'They are performing fine, right?'

'Very fine. Who is the actor in Shakara's role?'

'It is Nagendra Rao. The Charudatta role is donned by Subbaiah Naidu. Notice how well he sings.'

In Act III, while carving a chink in the wall of the house of Charudatta for committing thievery, Sharvilaka said, 'These burnt bricks have to be hauled out. The bricks here are shaped differently—lotus-shaped, sun-shaped, half-moon shaped, well-shaped, broad one, swastika-shaped, and jug-shaped—seven types in all. I will haul them out pristine so that the people witnessing it tomorrow shall be dumbstruck.'

This episode failed to sustain Nagalakshmi's interest. She reflected that it was unbecoming of a robber to be so very unhurried. To Rao though, the details seemed curious. *If in those times they could think up designs of bricks that would strengthen a structure, what would the level of architectural advancement of those peoples be? Are these details discussed in Śilpaśāstra viz. the science of sculpting? If yes, what is the date of Śilpaśāstra? This deserves to be studied in particular detail.* He made notes in his mind.

Raja noticed that though the stage setting was simple vis-à-vis that in England, the impact herein was tremendous. Prthvi had slipped into sleep long back. Nagalakshmi watched the play intently throughout. When she saw capital punishment pronounced on Charudatta, she wept. Eventually, when she saw Charudatta exonerated, and that he was united with his family, her mind swelled with delight. Nevertheless, a fleeting thought occurred in her mind as to how his wife would put up with a rival wife. When Rohasena would not stop wailing unless he was provided with a golden toy cart, Nagalakshmi glanced at Prthvi who was sitting on Raja's thigh. It was 4 in the morning when the play ended and they were back home.

One week thence, Rao received a post from a high up authority of the university. Not only was he promoted from Lecturer to Assistant Professor, the university had undertaken to provide him an endowment of Rs 500 per annum for penning his proposed tome, a cabin exclusively for him in the university library, and leave of absence whenever he had to go on a study tour.

'Appeal to His Highness has borne fruit,' said Raja. Rao wrote a letter to His Highness' secretary, expressing his gratitude.

CHAPTER 3

1

Sadashiva Rao has been on tour the last one month. He had, by now, visited all the historically significant sites in India. He had undertaken this tour to refurbish his memory, and toured South India extensively. After visiting Kanyakumari, Tanjavur, Madurai, Chidambaram and Mahabalipuram, he went to the cave temples of Ellora via Hyderabad. After beholding the grand achievements of Ellora over three days, he visited Devagiri and Aurangabad. He had arrived in Ajanta now.

Among his travel paraphernalia were a moderately weighing hold-all, a trunk for clothes, water-bag, a camera suspended by the shoulder, khaki trousers to go with the dust of the journey, a hat for protection against sun, binoculars to get a bird's eye view of the environs from a vantage point, pen, pencil and sheets of paper. He stayed in a room in a guesthouse in Fardapur near Ajanta caves, and visited the caves daily for study. On day one, he stationed himself outside the caves and regarded the forlorn environs all round. He saw the same through the binoculars and made a note thus: 'The hill is horseshoe-shaped, and the caves are carved atop. There is a hill opposite of this; rather, it seems like the valley has merged into a single hill. There are no facilities whatsoever for human dwelling here. Why did the Buddhist bhikṣus build these cave temples amidst this forest? That the rock of the hill is suitable for building temples is one reason. But a more profound reason strikes me. The bhikṣus needed to undertake their meditation in seclusion, wherefore they chose this forlorn hill to build temples for pursuit of their life's goal.'

Another note: 'These caves were lost to mankind from the seventh century CE till 1819; to those who dwelled in the surrounding areas too! The theory, that a few British Army Generals deserve praise for eventually bringing to light this intriguing achievement of mankind's history, is not tenable. Owing to the prevailing political situation of the peoples, and for possible reason of religious conversion, the proximate inhabitants would have lost faith in the caves. For reason of this, it would not have been possible for them to maintain these temples in good condition. The English historians' conceited accounts are nothing but delusions of one-upmanship. Weren't there people in America before Columbus set foot on it? There is evidence to the existence of Hindu idols in America well before him. Peoples of the world knew of America even before Columbus.'

On the second morning of his visit there, Rao posted himself in the unfinished cave No. 24, and was inspecting it closely when an elderly couple came up to him. The man appeared to be more than 60. He wore white trousers and shirt, and carried an umbrella. He was of dark complexion, and was of good build. His wife seemed a little over 50. She wore a pure white sari, and by the way she had worn it, Rao surmised that she was a Sinhalese. The man neared Rao and said, 'Excuse me. You seem to be a researcher. Why is this cave in such dilapidated condition? Seems like some unskilled stonemason dug it up and left it at that, doesn't it?'

Rao said, 'This is an unfinished cave. We can speculate three phases in the excavation process of Ajanta caves. First, unskilled stonemasons must have dug up an expanse. This was probably done by the farmers as a dharmic act. In the second phase, skilled chiselers would have carved semi-manifest pillars, idols, etc. as per the instructions of the sculptor. In the final phase, accomplished artists would have attended to the intricate works and given the temples their consummate form. All this would've taken up quite a few decades. There would have been some political upheaval at the time this cave went through the first phase. Or the peoples' faith would have undergone change. Patronage would have suffered. Alas, this one stands unfinished.'

The man explained the same to his wife. From the language he related in, Rao was now sure that they were indeed Sinhalese. He had some more questions, and Rao gave all the answers. They both were introduced to each other. The elderly man said, 'We have been observing since yesterday. Noticing your industry, my daughter said that you were a researcher. We are staying at the same guesthouse that you are staying at. You just haven't noticed us. We are from Kalutara in west Ceylon. My name is Jayaratne. My daughter is a student of history. She returned home last year after her BA at Cambridge. She is in some previous cave, making notes.'

Rao introduced himself. It was 11 am by then, and they were both spent. Jayaratne asked, 'Do you have to go to your guest house for lunch?'

'No, a waiter is bringing it here.'

'He will bring ours too. He will be here any moment. He had brought it here at the same time yesterday. Come, let's sit there.'

They headed towards cave No.12, and soon they saw a woman heading in their direction. Aged about 26, she had worn her sari in Sinhalese style too. Her round face dazzled with erudition. She had drawn her complexion from her parents. Diamond studs shone in her ears. She had sparkling eyes, and she carried a notebook and pencil in her hands. Even as he reflected that she could be the elderly man's daughter, Jayaratne introduced her to Rao. 'This is my daughter, Karunaratne. Child, as you rightly noticed, he is a researcher. He apprised us about these caves quite a bit. His name is Sadashiva Rao.'

They greeted mutually. Karunaratne said nothing immediately. She seemed to browse her memory for something. A little later, she asked, 'Are you Dr Sadashiva Rao?'

'Yes.'

'Then it is you who has authored the book, *Dharmic Foundations of Ancient Indian Polity*! I have not yet got my copy of it. But I know all about the critical acclaim it has received. I am happy to meet the author of such a work.'

Jayaratne said, 'Let's sit some place. We are aged, and spent.'

All four of them lounged in the shade of the entrance of cave No.10. Then Karunaratne asked, 'I think that you have seen all this before. So, what could be the reason for you in undertaking a detailed study now? Planning a new book?'

'Yes. I have planned to pen a massive work of about five volumes.'

'May I know what the title is, and what perspective you have in mind?'

Just then the waiter of the guesthouse walked up to them. He was carrying a basket on his head. The taxing trek in the sun sent down streams of sweat from his forehead; his shirt was soaked in sweat too. Putting down the basket, he asked, 'Saheb, will you all lunch together? Wait, I will bring water in 10 minutes.' He took hold of a big tin drum and headed for the valley below.

2

Millet roti, dal curry, rice and curd—the Maharashtrian cuisine was tasty. Besides, they were all famished. While they lunched, they got more acquainted. Jayaratne was a Buddhist of the Mahayana sect. He ran quite a big business in Kalutara. In a village 15 kilometres from there, he had a rubber and pepper farm. His son looked after the farming. A devout Buddhist that he was, he had undertaken this tour of all the

Buddhist sites in India. His daughter was there for a different purpose. She said, 'Though it is true that I am touring to keep my parents company, I have my own special interest in this. I desire to study Sinhalese culture in the background of Buddhism. I have visited all the historical places in my country. I have collected quite a lot of information. But I cannot undertake penning this exposition without guidance. Nonetheless, I spend all my leisure time in collecting whatever and however much information I can get.'

The waiter served food to everyone. Karunaratne's mother did not eat the roti. It was clear to everybody that she did not like the dal either. She had to do with the rice in curd. Jayaratne ate two rotis; he had artificial teeth. Karunaratne and Rao had their full quota. While they were polishing off their meal, Jayaratne said, 'There are both the Hinayana and the Mahayana sect caves in Ajanta. I am not saying this just because I belong in the Mahayana sect. In the Hinayana caves, absent will be Buddha idols. Notwithstanding the copiousness of the peripheral sculpting in a temple, we get to feel that it is an abode without a Lord. In the temples of the Mahayana sect, there will be the idol of the Buddha, peace personified, in *dharmachakra-mudra*. We, who step into the temple, also get to feel the promise of protection and reassurance.'

Rao said, 'True. It is said that Hinayana is the first phase in the development of history of Buddhism. It was a de novo era when the effulgence of Buddha's thoughts held forth. Per the dictum "everything shall culminate in naught", even reverence towards a guru is preposterous. But just dictums do not cater to the desires and aspirations of the people. It eventually culminated in worshipping the very Buddha! Some historians opine that this is an influence of Hinduism wherein idolatry is exuberant. Though this is true, that alone is not the cause of the rise of the Mahayana sect. There isn't a religion that does not engage in worship. If it is not restrained by embargo and strictly enforced, every religion will gradually take to idolatry in one or other form.'

By then they were done with lunch. After everybody had washed their hands, the waiter gave them arecanut and aniseed. After packing up the plates and vessels, he asked the elderly man, 'Saheb, is it okay for the vehicle to be here at 5 pm?'

'Okay.'

The waiter left. The foursome continued to be seated to relax some more. Karuna's mother reclined on a rock. Her father leaned against a wall and stretched his legs. She asked Rao, 'Are you done with your notes for now?'

'No. Why?'

'I am curious to learn the modality of your jottings. I am yet to thoroughly study cave No.1. Are you free? It will be helpful if you can explain to me personally about the aspects that I cannot grasp yet.'

'I, too, am yet to make notes of that cave. Come, let's go together.'

'Pa, we will be in cave No.1. Come over after you have rested,' she told her father. By then he was half asleep and snoring mildly.

The sun burned. Rao wore his hat. Pulling the *pallu* of her sari over her head, Karuna followed him. As they entered the cave, they asked the lights attendant to illuminate select idols and pictures with the floodlight. Karuna said, 'There is no need for us to make separate notes. You dictate and I will script. I will give you a copy of it tonight without fail.'

For a while they studied the pictures and the idols in the sanctum sanctorum. Karuna took to noting down what Rao dictated. 'The Buddha idol of huge proportions in the sanctum sanctorum is in the *dharmachakra-mudra.* The placement of the index finger of the right hand at the tip of the little finger of the left hand that this mudra entails only means that he is enumerating each and every aspect of his preachment to his protégés. Depending on the illumination pattern, the face of this idol depicts varied essences. If the flood light were beamed upward from the *dharmachakra* on which the Buddha was seated, his face will appear as peace personified. If the light were beamed from the left, a gentle smile lights up Buddha's face. If the light were beamed from the right side, the face will seem replete with earnestness. This idol bears testimony to the towering achievements in the art of angulate sculpting.'

As Rao related detailed description of the pictures in that cave, Karuna kept on scripting—the one wherein the prince listened to the preaching of the hermit, he bathing, he chatting with his wife, *padmapani-bodhisattva*, etc. She made notes of the culture, values of life, etc. as could be guesstimated on the basis of common things of daily life, the ornaments, the hairstyles, body contours of men and women, etc. that could be gleaned from the pictures.

Jayaratne turned up at cave No. 1 at 5 pm. The attendant had departed after providing lighting service up to the time limit. Rao was using his torch to look into the minute details and dictating notes. Entering, Jayaratne noted, 'Seems like you have made notes about the contents of the cave fully. Cry a halt now. The cart has arrived, and is parked downhill. The driver awaits us here.'

As dusk was descending, it was getting harder for them to look into the fine details. They wound up for the day and followed Jayaratne out. Trekking downhill in the murkiness of the receding sun, when all four had boarded the bullock cart, Jayaratne said, 'We had never visited cave No. 26 before. There is the Buddha's Mahaparinirvana. The sculpture is about 25-feet tall. He sleeps there in anticipation of his final moments. We both were there all the while now.'

Rao was spent. He tried to sit relaxed by leaning against a railing of the cart. But there wasn't enough space to stretch his legs, considering the number of occupants. Karuna was spent too. Still, she moved closer to her father and made comfortable space for Rao. The cart swayed them as it rolled.

3

Jayaratne had plans to leave the next day, but his daughter insisted that they stay on for two more days, for she had discovered the utility of the notes that Dr Rao would dictate about Ajanta. Over the next two days, they both visited all the prominent caves and made copious notes, on the basis of which they could weave the cultural milieu of the bygone era. While in the caves, Dr Rao would continue to stand while observing and dictating notes. Karuna, too, would be on her feet. Well-versed in shorthand as she was, she could take notes speedily, and recorded three books full of them that day. The Sinhalese family finalized their travel plans, and decided to leave the next day by bus to Jalgaon, and onward to Delhi. Rao had plans to go to Aurangabad and return home via Pune. After staying in the headquarters for a month, he planned to tour again—this time North India.

The guest house at Fardapur had, in fact, become the familial home to the four of them. As their quarters were opposite of each other, Dr Rao and Jayaratne would chat for a while after supper. Despite learning much about Buddhism from the historian, Jayaratne's quest still remained unquenched. While those other historians would just recount the chronological events, the sagacious Rao would delineate the history from the viewpoint of the intrinsic dharmic predisposition of the times. As Rao had to catch an early bus in the morning, Jayaratne asked him to get some sleep, and went back to his room. Rao did not go to sleep immediately. The Ajanta that he was leaving back had filled his mind in all its historical resplendence. For four days now, he was a denizen of a different era. Tomorrow, he would reclaim his citizenship of the modern era.

It was 9 pm. Moonlight that permeated the environs of that forlorn place had made a dreamland of it akin to the Ajanta cosmos. He surmized that it was the odyssey of the Buddhist bhikṣus and artists that gifted them this agreeably tranquil destination, and inspired them to mould the rock and infuse life into it. Instead of watching a patch of moonlight framed by the window, he thought of basking in the whole of it. Pacing about hundred steps away from the guest house, he sat on a boulder there. The fatigue from having been on his feet all day long in the caves was out of his mind. His mind became buoyant in that moonlit night. Clear before his eyes was the history of ancient India that he had endeavoured to delineate. The protracted cultural tradition of several millennia sailed past in his imagination like the radiance of that moonlight. He needed to identify the pivot on which his proposed discourse would radiate around; he could now perceive that pivot clearly. But what is the starting point of this cultural tradition? Is it omniscient like the Vedas? Or is it 2000 years BCE as opined by the historians? Or 3000 years BCE? Could we assess the history of the era of cultural tradition of mankind through the eyes of anthropologists? Rao was fully lost in contemplation.

'He, who has to catch the first bus tomorrow morning, is still awake! What thoughts are you lost in?' It was Karuna walking up behind him. Rao looked back. She neared him, sat close to him, and asked, 'Hope I haven't disturbed your stream of thought.'

'No. Sit.'

'I came to report to you that the notes are three books full. It is impossible to make a copy of it here. If I give it to you, you may find it difficult to decipher my handwriting. Besides, I have taken down quite some of it in shorthand. We will be back in our hometown in about one month. I will type it and post it to you. Don't get anxious. I will send it without fail. Okay?'

Harboring some doubt, Rao went silent for a few minutes. Then he said, 'You very well know how much I need this. Don't forget to send it. God, you have delivered me to an alien!'

'I pray to that same God to remind me of this stranger,' she smiled.

They fell silent. Rao's mind was still rooted in his musings. After five minutes of silence, Karuna asked, 'I want to ask something. Are you in a mood to speak?'

'Ask away.'

'Historians of every nation endeavour to segregate historical time into classical era, modern era, pre-historic era, date of commencement of history, etc. But I think that no nation's history will give out clues as to the transmutation in the eons it has passed through. Right?'

Piqued, Rao said, 'I have been thinking on these lines, and lo, you bring up the same! Vis-à-vis history, the term Yuga viz. era is of no metrical relevance on the time scale. The ways of a civilization shall be in consonance with the value systems that are ingrained into the minds of the peoples therein. At times, these values endure for centuries, even millennia. The details of the progress in arts, literature, ethics of life, material development, etc. that they achieve during the currency of a given block of period may be identified, but no fundamental change shall be witnessed therein. They are merely permutations of a given set of values of life. It is when the fundamental values of a people clearly morph that a new era begins. Then history, too, assumes a new form.'

'How do historians identify this changeover phase?'

'Calls for deep insight. He, who identifies just the outward changes, is no historian. The dynamism deep in the soul of a people and their life-values are noted not just by history; art, literature and philosophy capture them in their own ways too. In this sense, the difference between history and literature is not any significant. While history records the dynamics in the soul and the life-values of an entire people, literature does it at the level of individuals—real and/or fictitious. Works of historians and littérateurs that identify apocalyptic shifts in the soul of the people and their life-values stand out as great by heralding a changeover phase. *Mahabharata* is one such. It belongs in the "epic" genre, and epics encompass literature, history and philosophy.'

Karuna went silent for about 10 minutes, cogitating Rao's words. After all, she had pursued higher studies in history at Cambridge. Though she had acquainted herself with many theories as to the characteristics of history and what the domains of their inquiry were, she didn't know if this theory of Dr Rao was among them. A doubt arose in her mind about the view held by Rao: 'You hold that history should diametrically identify the era of mutation of values, state the cause therefor, and delineate the impact thereat. A historian, who takes to delineating on the era of mutation of values, in effect ends up judging the values. May he commit it? From this standpoint, is history progress-oriented evolution or mankind's afflictions from retrogressive hibernation?'

'To aver that history is ever progress-oriented will mean that the culture of our ancestors is inferior to ours. If we hold that other view, it will mean that we are inescapably headed for decadence. Noticing the classification of *yuga*s (eons) into Krtayuga, Tretayuga, Dvaparayuga and Kaliyuga—in that order—we may be coerced into thinking that history is retrogressive as indicated by gradual dilution in values through those eons. But Kaliyuga isn't the culmination. After this, the *yuga*-cycle restarts each time. Krtayuga sets foot.'

'Which means there is no cessation of this loop?'

'Just as it is impossible to perceive the genesis of history of mankind, it will be imprudence in the same measure to mark its terminus. In this unremitting loop, values may flag at times; they may brace up again. Viewed thus, mankind's history may be said to be God's pastime! Therefore, historians have to put themselves on guard when they take to passing judgment on values.'

Karuna said measuredly, 'We have spent four blissful days in Ajanta. Your insightful statement is made in this tranquil locale that makes us forget debating and counter-debating. I get to feel that it is credible. Will you please do me a favour?'

'What favour can I possibly do?'

'It has been one year now since I returned from Cambridge. There is no facility in my place to pursue higher studies. I desire to land a teaching career or research fellowship in a university in Colombo in the upcoming academic year. If I write to you seeking clarifications in these matters, will you respond?'

'Surely, I will, to the best of my knowledge. You have to pardon me at times when my mood plays truant.'

When it was past midnight, moonlight dimmed and there were signs of the moon heading for the horizon. They went to their respective rooms. Before Rao said goodnight, she said, 'I will see you once again tomorrow before you leave.'

They exchanged their addresses the next morning. Karuna's parents brought together their palms in greetings and bade a cordial farewell to Rao. While he boarded the bus, Karuna shook her hands and said, 'I will send the notes. It is my good fortune that I, too, shall have a copy of it.'

CHAPTER 4

1

It was June–July and, as usual, the impetuous Kapila took to her erratic ways. But in this year's flood, there were no casualties. The city municipality of Nanjangud displayed 'SWIMMING PROHIBITED HERE' boards along the shore of the river. One month had passed since Nanjunda Srotri's first death anniversary was observed. Though it was impossible to refill the dent in the family caused by his death, the intensity of bereavement had abated with time. The baby had permeated the hearts of his grandparents. The one-and-half-year-old Cheeni had inherited his father's looks and contours. When he smiled, displaying the four incisors that had grown by now, it would seem as though Nanjunda was reborn in his son.

Srotri would place him on his shoulders and romp around. Twenty-seven years ago, he had done the same with his son Nanjunda. 'Taddy, taddy,' that kid would prod him, and tug at the shining knot of jet-black hair at the back of his father's scalp. The 24-year-old Bhageerathamma would snap her fingers to humour the child. The maid Lakshmi would intercede and carry away the child to the garden in the backyard. Srotri was now 55 years old, his hair had greyed, and the sumptuous tuft of hair was replaced by a small, sparse shock. Nevertheless, the grandchild tugged at it and prodded him, 'Gampa, gampa.' His daughter-in-law Katyayani would behold the sight from a distance and smile.

All day long, the baby would be with his grandparents and Lakshmi. Occasionally, he would accost his mother. At night, he would always sleep in the company of his mother. To Katyayani, who would embrace her son as she lay in bed, the irretrievable phase of propitious conjugation with her husband would keep surfacing in her mind. Her husband Nanjunda Srotri was gentle-mannered. He was loyal to his parents. But the elderly couple never domineered over him or their daughter-in-law. They had no daughters; Katyayani had arrived in their house as if to make good that paucity. Srotri would often speak in lighter vein in the company of his son and daughter-in-law, and laugh heartily. Whenever a theatre camped in their town, he would urge them to go watch the play. By and by, he initiated his son to the household, and rescinded to a religious life, spending much of his time in puja and study of the scriptures. It was much prior to his son's death that he visited his farms at Hejjige, Devarasanahalli, Arasinakere and Kalale; it was exactly three years ago. He had trained his son in managing the farms as well as running the household. He, who had retired from family affairs, found himself reluctantly giving it all a fresh start. He took to the routine of visiting the farms at harvest time, extracting his share from the sharecroppers, paying land taxes, etc.

Katyayani's heart would brim up at the love and care showered by her parents-in-law, and also at the memory of her husband. She would keep reminiscing the incidents that dotted her married life: the pleasantry, the conjugal indulgence, he getting mad at her, she awaiting him at the door with anxiety whenever he got delayed at the farm, etc. Sleepless, when she rolled over, her mother-in-law asked, 'Sleep won't come, child?'

'Comes, amma.' Though that reply would be given, the mother-in-law knew that it was untrue. She now recalled every detail of she tending to her son. 'Look child, as a kid he resembled Cheeni. He would wake up overnight and start playing in the cradle. I had to stay awake and keep him company. Else he would start complaining. Your father-in-law would retire to the room upstairs.' Katyayani knew why her father-in-law retired to the room upstairs, letting his wife and child retire downstairs. 'He would play all night. And slip to sleep at dawn. That is the time when I would wake up, bathe and make arrangements for your father-in-law's worship rituals. At times, when I could not stay awake, I would wake Lakshmi up, put him in her care and retire. Later, I and Lakshmi took to sharing a room.' She would then sigh in exasperation and start weeping, 'We stream our bloods, conceive them and tend to them. Turning a blind eye to all that, God takes them away.'

'Control yourself, amma. What can we do?' Now it would be Katyayani's turn to console her mother-in-law. After a while, reminiscing her father-in-law who slept in the living room, she said, 'Amma, we are the vacuous ones. We keep lamenting even one and half years after his death. Papa alone is the stolid one. When he got news that his son had drowned, he dashed there. We, too, went there soon after; there was no sign of his son. The way he consoled us and brought us back home! I took to crying and fell by the pillar in the living room. You fell unconscious in this room. Papa said, "Lakshmi, look after her. Sprinkle some water on her head," and came near me. I, too, was losing consciousness fast. He sat by me, put my head on his thigh and said, "Child, it is in such circumstances that we should shore up our fortitude. God does so in order to test us." In my despair of the moment, his words seemed vain. He said it solemnly alright, but what composure! I opened my eyes and looked at him. I was shocked that a father who had just lost his only son could say so. If we had his fortitude, we could put up with any difficulty, right?'

'True. Still, to that degree! When grief assails, one should cry. It is cathartic. For the past one and half years, we have been silently crying in our hearts; we are not to weep in his presence. But if we weep in his presence and he weeps too, that would be a great relief, won't it?'

By then, the sound of snoring was heard from the room. Bhageerathamma kept up the conversation with her daughter-in-law. 'Look, Lakshmi sleeps sound. When he was a small kid, it was she who always carried him and romped around to amuse him. She used to take him to school. She loved him as if he were her own son. When he drowned in the river, she cried too. Just as he did to us, I think your papa had sermonized a few words of Vedanta to her as well. She just reined in her grief, and took to her chores! Isn't she the better one? As you said, we should learn to put up with sorrows and joys alike.'

By then, Katyayani's eyes had pulled up. At times, the kid who slept beside his mother would wake up and start crying. So that it didn't disturb her daughter-in-law, Bhageerathamma would take him away and feed him the milk that she would have kept handy. If his crying did not cease, Srotri would call out from the living room, 'Bring him here.' Seeing his grandfather's face in the dim light, the boy would stammer 'Gampa, gampa' and hasten to near him. Srotri would ask his wife to go get some sleep, and would take the child to the garden in the backyard, pace around, and show him the twinkling stars. After a while, the kid would fall asleep on his shoulders. He would tread carefully indoors, put him on his bed and put a shawl over him. If he felt like sleeping, he would retire. Else, he would go to his study upstairs and light the lamp.

2

By the time he turned two, Cheeni could be contained by none. Though Lakshmi always kept an eye on him, he would give them all the slip and walk out into the street. One day, he went up to the temple, and not knowing the way back, he kept doing the rounds within the precincts of the temple, weeping. By the time the temple oboists recognized him and took him home, Srotri had searched the entire street and Lakshmi had looked for him on the banks of the Gundala stream that flowed behind the house. Then on, they started keeping both the exit doors shut so that he could not go out in the scorching sun during afternoons.

Once, in the month of March, he went missing. There was no trace of him till 4 in the evening. Srotri got anxious thinking he'd have gone to the river. He rushed to the Manikarnika deck. To the east, where the Gundala stream flowed into Kapila, Cheeni was building a frog hutch on the sand bed along with the shepherd boys his age. When he spotted his grandfather, he neared him and said, 'My hutch is biiig,' gesticulating the same by opening up his arms wide. For having played in the sun all afternoon, he was perspiring profusely. When he felt thirsty, he helped himself to the water in the pits in the river bed four times. Lifting him up, Srotri returned home. Incensed, he reprimanded the ladies of the house that they did not look after the kid well. He even admonished the kid, 'If you go out of the house, I will tie up your legs.'

Cheeni, who slept beside his mother, took to laboured breathing by about 10 at night. Placing her palm on his forehead, Katyayani sought the attention of her mother-in-law. 'Amma, he is running fever, look.' Checking him, Bhageerathamma brought Nilgiri oil and started massaging his forehead, neck and foot. Srotri, who was resting in the living room, got wind and came to check. Cheeni was asleep. 'Let's give him medicine tomorrow morning,' he said and exited.

Next morning, Srotri had to go to Kalale. Cheeni's fever had remitted too. Instructing that he be administered the Kasturi tablet, Srotri bathed, had his lunch and left. Up and about, Cheeni began romping around. Bhageerathamma and Katyayani both stood relieved that their anxiety of yesterday night was no more. The elderly lady went into the kitchen. Asking her mother-in-law to keep watch on him, Katyayani left Cheeni there and went to wash clothes by the well in the backyard. When she came back in, Cheeni was not there. He was missing already! Anxious, Katyayani went looking about. By then, Lakshmi entered the house from the backyard with Cheeni in tow and reported, 'On my way back after herding the cattle to the pasture, I saw him playing in the water in the Gundala stream.'

In summer, the Gundala stream flowed to one side of the bed, and the water is just ankle-deep. There is no danger whatsoever of even children drowning in it. The women of the house sealed both the exit doors of the house once again. But by 3 in the afternoon, Cheeni was running temperature again. By the time Srotri was back in the evening, the temperature was high. The kid's eyes had gone red, his face had swelled and he was partly unconscious.

Srotri immediately brought the village physician, Venkatachala-pundit. After checking his pulse, the pundit said, 'Typhoid. Fever may persist for 21 days. You should be careful. I will administer medicine. No fear for life.'

The pundit's assessment was right. Fever did not abate. He didn't gain back full consciousness either. Whenever his grandpa called out to him, he would mumble something as if he heard something from afar. He could sense nothing else. He neither wept nor smiled. Lost to his house, his grandfather, grandmother, mother and Lakshmi, he just sailed on in a subconscious state. There was only the laboured breathing. The kid's body became so weak it appeared unable to bear even the strain of breathing.

The agony persisted till the twelfth day; then it got worse. Nobody in the house was sure if the kid would recover at all. But nobody expressed it verbally. On the night of the fifteenth day, the breathing became spasmodic. Eyes that had remained closed due to fever, now just about parted, only to reveal lack-lustre eyes. Face had lost its vitality too. Bhageerathamma, who was beside the kid at all times, called out to her husband. Srotri darted and checked the kid's hands and feet; his feet were getting cold, and sweat beads appeared on his forehead. Breath continued to come out in spasms. It was time for everyone to shed hope of salvaging the child. But Srotri lost no hope. He asked Lakshmi, who stood anxiously nearby, to fetch the pundit immediately. He then asked his wife to get him cowpat ashes.

He started rubbing the ash on the feet of the kid, coaxing him to get warm. He rubbed some on the hands too. Finally, he applied Nilgiri oil on the emaciated chest of the kid, and resigned to anticipate the pundit's arrival. Katyayani could grasp the situation. She could stand there no more. She headed straight to the kitchen. She could not control her grief anymore; she started sobbing. She then cried aloud. Sounds outside the house indicated the arrival of the pundit. Srotri told his daughter-in-law, 'Child, it will serve no purpose to cry in such circumstances. Go receive the pundit and bring him straight here.'

Arriving, the pundit felt the pulse. He asked for the chafe-slab. He took out a tablet and chafed it on the slab one and half rounds in honey, collected it on a finger and had the kid lick it. The kid had neither the strength nor the consciousness to lick it. Knowing well that it would mix with the saliva and go down the throat, the pundit smeared it all on the kid's tongue. Could well be the effect of rubbing the ash on the feet, it began picking up temperature. Fever remained stable; it didn't increase. The pundit stayed there for two hours, handed one tablet and said, 'I will leave now. Smear one and half chafing of this tablet in honey on his tongue every two hours. I will visit again at dawn tomorrow.'

After the pundit left, Katyayani consoled herself and neared her son. Bhageerathamma shed no tears, but her face was like one who had suffered a cardiac arrest. Lakshmi neared them, sat and said, 'Sheenappa, I will take the child into my lap. Please give him carefully.' Srotri, who was deep in some thought, said, 'No, let him stay in my lap.' He then turned to his daughter-in-law and said, 'Bring the timepiece that is in the living room here. I have to give him medicine every two hours. Remind me timely. None of you know the manner in which to chafe one and half rounds of it. I will chafe it and have him lick it.'

Bhageerathamma brought a copper vessel containing the water of Kapila with a copper spoon in it. So as to put the kid into a more comfortable position, Srotri slightly loosened his limbs. Srotri was a man of robust physique; he had to hunch over to pass through doorways. Even at an age nearing 60, he was fit as a fiddle. He would easily tread more than 20 miles on foot daily. His face was broad and his eyes had an expressive sparkle to them. Unmindful of the baby in his lap, he filled his right palm with a spoon full of water from that vessel, and reciting the mantra—'He that reminisceth God Vishnu is sanctified within and without', he sprinkled it thereabouts. He then—as he would often do during his daily puja and at other religious occasions—relayed three spoons full of water to his lips through his right palm consecutively, and sipped each of them by uttering synonyms of God Vishnu. That done, he held the knot of his *yajñopavīta* (sacred thread) with the fingers of his right hand, and began reciting the Gāyatri mantra in his mind.

Katyayani's eyes were glued to the child's face. Bhageerathamma and Lakshmi were watching Srotri. These two felt sort of reassured.

3

Srotri lived the *sanatana* way of life. As per his unwavering belief, man would marry to start a family life, family life was a means of discharging one's destined duty in this world, and procreating was for taking further the genealogical tree of the lineage. He who passes on without procreating leaves this world by terminating his lineage, thereby leaving a void. The very existence of an individual is a debt inherited, and can be repaid only by procreating.

He had utmost faith in his lineage. He held the belief that 'Srotri lineage' was synonymous with the 'Sruti' viz. Veda. Just as it is impossible to measure the timeline of our lineage-founding sages, so is identifying the antiquity of a given extraction. Nobody can fully fathom the antiquity of a lineage that goes farther unto the past than man's comprehension. Yet he was of the conviction that an individual's esteem and pride were derived via his lineage. I, Sri Srinivasa Srotri, belonging in the Kāṣyapa-*gotra* of the ancestral triad Kāṣyapa-Āvatsāra-Naidhṛva, adhering to the Āṣvalāyana tenets, and pursuer of Rigveda, prostrate before thee, oh God—he would daily recite this extraction of his during *sandhyāvandana*; he would derive a sense of exaltation each time. He would go about his routine with the effervescent awareness that if he were to fail to tread that exalted ancestral path, he would be bringing disgrace to the entire lineage.

After carrying out the wedding of his son, he had resigned to a retired life. Consequent to the sad demise of that son, he pegged all his hopes on his grandson. He resumed his transactional living and looked forward to his grandson starting a family. In his life, he never stooped to such base aspirations as greed and desire. Nevertheless, he considered himself entitled to aspire for abundance so that his household didn't wither, for he wanted his grandson—

who would eventually start his family—to inherit it. When his father Nanjunda Srotri Sr passed away, Srinivasa Srotri was 18 years of age. He had just entered wedlock. It was a miracle that the ailing senior Srotri lived on that many years! The ailing man passed away soon after his son's wedding was consummated, as if he had witnessed what he was in anticipation of. Srinivasa Srotri's mother had passed away four years previously. Being the lone son to his father, he inherited some property. And the property yielded more than for his effects. Neither had Srinivasa Srotri amassed more property nor had he squandered any fraction of the inheritance. Except for some buffer that he held in a bank account for contingencies, he would judiciously expend all his annual harvest for charitable causes in the name of God: food for all at the annual car festival of the temple, help seekers, honorarium to scholars and musicians, subsistence to the farmers during famine, etc.

Even though he had assumed detachment in life since his early years, he could not remain composed when the lone inheritor of his lineage—his grandson—slept limp in his lap, death staring at him. His mind, which was engaged in the recitation of Gāyatri-mantra, could not adhere to its metric with undivided devotion. His afflicted mind supplicated that Gāyatri-mantra alone shall save the kid. How shall non-pretextual devotion go into a prayer that is benefit-seeking? Srotri, who never prayed for benefits, was now praying for the life of his grandson at this midnight hour...when a day is past and the next day is born.

After Bhageerathamma lost her son, her grandson had become the focus of her motherly love. Regarding him as her son, she had reverted to her postnatal days. If he, too, were to slide into oblivion, who would be the recipient of her motherly love? 'God, what punishment are you perpetrating on us, for what sin of which birth of ours?' she would say, and spill her hands before God.

For the widowed Katyayani, forgetting the auspicious moments with her husband can just not be forgotten. She had been through poverty ever since her childhood. Her father, Srikanthaiah, was a lawyer in Srirangapattana. Her mother breathed her last when Katyayani was eight. Her father had married again, and though he loved his daughter, nobody ever gave mother's love to her. She travelled daily by train to Mysore and successfully earned her intermediate. She had also earned the reputation of being a student of keen intellect. Ensuring that the Srotris were a decent family, Srikanthaiah had given his daughter in marriage to Nanjunda, who was then pursuing his BA. After the wedding, he wrote an exam but didn't get through. He was preparing to write it again when he passed away, leaving behind his parents, wife and son.

When her husband passed away, there seemed to be no future for her. Now, she realized that her future was not non-existent; rather, it was obscure. There were her in-laws, there was this son, he was to grow, get educated, become a man and start a family of his own—were all these milestones not her future also? Until now, she had turned a blind eye to this future canvas. Unfortunately, such realization dawned on her at a time when she was about to forfeit that canvas even! The kid that slept on his grandpa's lap was breathing heavy. Before another bout of cry erupted from within her, she exited from there hurriedly, went into the kitchen and wept to her heart's content.

Another being that belonged in that house was Lakshmi. Lakshmi's parents worked as domestic help in this house in the time of Srotri's father. When Lakshmi was 15, Srinivasa Srotri financed her wedding. But her husband was murdered four years into their marriage. Widowed Lakshmi returned to the Srotri's. By then her father had passed away too. She had lost her mother at birth. Since then, Lakshmi had become a family member and partook in all the joys and sorrows of this house. She had tended to Nanjunda Srotri as a kid, and now she was tending to his young son. She was sensitive enough to grasp the tribulations of Srinivasa Srotri's mind. Now, this family was at the threshold of losing its last link. She knew how to put her life at stake and serve it. She was also aware that she did not have the faculty of checking fate. But she had faith in the Gāyatri-mantra recitation by Sheenappa. Among all, it was she who put up with all this with a sense of spiritual unaffectedness.

4

Nobody slept the whole night; all faces in the house were devoid of gleam. Eyes were like those of goats. The pundit arrived at 6 in the morning, checked the kid's pulse, his legs and hands, and said, 'Danger has passed. Only fever remains. Pulse is even. Feet and hand are warm. Today is the sixteenth day. Fever will relent five days from now. Take courage.'

'Truly pundit-ji?' Bhageerathamma asked sceptically. 'Yes mother, Lord Nanjundeshvara's blessing,' the pundit reassured her. Advising that the kid be given curdled milk and some tablets, the pundit left. Srotri shifted the boy to a bed, asked Katyayani to keep watch, and went to bathe.

Though the high fever stung unabated over the next five days, his breathing had normalized. The curdled milk that was fed intermittently went past his gullet. Everyone felt relieved. On the twenty-first day, the temperature abated and he regained consciousness over the next few days. His first word on regaining consciousness was 'Gam…pa…'.

Katyayani, who was near him, called out to her father-in-law in the puja chamber. Abandoning his worship, Srotri rushed, checked the kid's forehead and said, 'Cheeni!' The child uttered nothing more. But his face revealed he had heard his grandpa's call. Seeing her son return from the brink of death, Katyayani's eyes welled up. Noticing, Srotri said, 'Child, just as we accept joy, so should we accept sorrow. Leaving our minds at the mercy of the fervour of emotions will not help in any way.'

Katyayani could hear nothing of it. She came close to her child and held his hand. For one month thence, Srotri himself looked after the kid's nutrition. He was regularly helping him to the Ayurvedic tonic and medicinal jam that the pundit had given him.

CHAPTER 5

1

On Raja Rao's return from Oxford, the art activities of his college underwent revamping. He was the president of the theatre association of the college prior to leaving the shores. He would get his pupils enact the best of plays; the plays he taught and produced on stage received greater acclaim. Consequent to his pursuing higher studies overseas, his colleagues regarded him in high esteem too. It was four months since his return from England when a famous British Shakespearean troupe toured India. Four plays were scheduled to be played in Mysore. Quite naturally, the responsibility of receiving the troupe at the railway station, stage arrangements, audience bookings, introducing the troupe and its members to the audience on the first day and other such tasks devolved onto Raja. He was fascinated by such work too. All the shows in Mysore turned out to be a grand success. After the last show, the manager of the troupe invited Raja Rao on stage, gave him a bouquet, thanked him for his helpfulness and profusely praised his knowledge of stage design. Raja Rao's esteem gained on some more.

The principal of the college, too, desired that the college should progress in extracurricular activities. Not only did he make available a large room for use of the theatre association, but also gave instructions that arrangements be made to enact one play every month in the open-air auditorium in the front yard of the college building. Raja Rao produced a benefit show and procured screens, sceneries and other effects out of the proceeds.

Raja was never seriously studious. True, he was an erudite one, but he had no desire to shore up his scholasticism or pen books like his brother did. He would write some plays for producing them for the theatre association of the college. They would be successful too. But he never went to the extent of publishing them in print. He was aware that their value as literature was meagre. After his return from England, he had penned two mono-act plays. He was capable of mingling with all, capable of starting a conversation with people disposed every which way, and go on sustaining their interest. He could effectively introduce personalities on stage, make even vote of thanks interesting, and more. His pronunciation of the English language was akin to that of the British, and as fluent. He became the darling of the students.

Sadashiva Rao concluded his tour of north India. Now, he was making preparations for penning the first volume of his tome. There was that well-equipped cabin earmarked for him at the university. There were tables, chairs, an armchair, a fan, bookracks, and all other facilities. He had purchased his own typewriter, but he was not adept at typing. Though Raja was good at it, but because he was not interested in it, he would not help out his brother in typing. Now that Rao was an Assistant Professor, his salary was more. Raja was earning too—no money crunch whatsoever. Since Raja's return, Rao stood relieved of the household effects. He hadn't taken it much to his mind hitherto too. Nagalakshmi would manage it to the best of her abilities. At times, she would seek advice on sundry matters: 'Kid is running fever. Which doctor shall we take him to?' 'The bedspread of your bed is torn. Come, let's get a new one.' Rao would accompany her to the physician's. Twice a year, he would inevitably accompany her to the market for sundry purchases. Teaching alphabets to Prthvi, buying saris for his sister-in-law, refilling writing ink and other stationery for his brother—all these responsibilities had devolved onto Raja now.

Rao would rise at 9. After bathing, he would silently lounge for a while under the sun in the balcony. At 10, he would have breakfast in the company of Raja and then go to college. He was required only to lecture for a total of less than four hours a week. If he wasn't in the mood to lecture, he would tell his pupils so, and confine himself to that cabin of his in the library. Reading some chapter in some book; making notes about the lifestyle of peoples of a certain period of history based on descriptions in a certain book; reading every paper and book written by oriental scholars and making notes; visiting oriental research institutions and making copies from birch manuscripts; writing to overseas scholars, whom he knew personally or thorough correspondence, and seeking their clarification in certain doubtful matters—the gamut of his deskwork was as vast as the history of India itself! At 3, the attendant would bring him some snacks and coffee from the restaurant. That done, he would drown himself in his work again. At 7:30 pm, he'd return home. Having slogged it out from morning till dusk, he would remember nothing of anything or anybody, wherefore he would converse with none. He would simply recline in the armchair in the balcony. There would be a holiday break here and there when he would chat with Nagalakshmi and Prthvi, and eat sumptuously. Else, he would silently munch on some food and retire to his study. The study room in his house brimmed with books—his own, and borrowed from the library and elsewhere. His study would go on unto the small hours—2, 3, sometimes 5 am! Getting up at 9, he would bathe, have breakfast and go to the library; he would go there even on Sundays. He was given a duplicate key to the library.

2

One Sunday afternoon, Prthvi ran fever. Irritated by it, he turned adamant. 'Unca, take me to papa.'

'No, kiddo. When papa comes home in the evening, he will be with you. Now sleep silently,' Raja consoled him. He was adamant for some time, but the heat of the fever took over and he slid into sleep. Raja sat on the cot by Prthvi's head. After she was done with cooking food, Nagalakshmi came there and sat on a chair by the cot. Looking at her son and at Raja, tears came to her eyes. She started crying. Lifting his head, Raja saw her and said, 'Why cry for just a simple fever? Let's take him to the doctor this evening. It's a mild fever, it will subside.'

'That is not why I wept,' Nagalakshmi wiped her tears with the *pallu* of her sari.

'Why else then?'

'Fever comes and goes. The kid longs for his "papa". Can't he stay home now at least?'

'He doesn't know of Prthvi's illness. When he left this morning, Prthvi was okay. So, he proceeded to his workplace as usual.'

'"Proceeded as usual!" Isn't it as simple as that for you? Why should he work on Sundays even? He hasn't even an iota of affinity towards his wife and child.'

Raja fell silent. He knew better than to incite his incensed sister-in-law. Nagalakshmi continued from where she left off. 'It has been 11 years since I wed him. "Nagu, Nagu", he would accost his newlywed bride back then for a few days. He soon forgot her. When he pursued his PhD, she was entirely forsaken. He took to writing another book and sent her into oblivion for five years. Now this monster of an epic has found its way into his head. It is a multi-volume work I was told, and he would be done with it in *just* 25 years. Until then, he needs none of us. By then, I will be 50. Pray, what the birth star of this bloke is! When his proposal came,

Thippa Jois of our village had compared our horoscopes and remarked, "Deadly combination!"'

'Why? Are you both at loggerheads now, and taken to quarreling? Even if you pick up a brawl, brother would just keep his cool without countering.'

'Let's say he has other options! "*Can wield a rifle, but not a ladle*", the saying goes. You know everything, but choose to underplay. One specimen is your brother, one is you!'

Raja suppressed a smile and fell silent. It was no news to him that his brother, who had taken to pen an epic-size anthropological work of the Indian nation, hadn't given quality time to his wife and child; to him—Raja—either. But Raja hadn't taken it personally. He knew the amount of work that the scholars of England would engage in. He also knew that his brother's conviction could not be sustained without unwavering perseverance. He asked his sister-in-law, 'Then, are you not for brother penning that tome and earning scholarly fame? If he merited veneration as an able scholar, will you not be happy?'

'Why wouldn't I be happy? Have I once objected to his literary pursuits? But why ignore one's wife and child?'

'Alas, such is the way of scholars. It is not just brother who is so. The ones I have seen in England are also thus. Their ilk is sparse in this country; the likes of brother are exceptional.'

'If you knew that the scholars of England are also thus, then you would know what their wives do too.' She was still simmering.

'Their wives have no such issues, for...Let go,' he trailed off. He had noticed in England that the wives of the scholars were learned enough to assist their husbands in their research work. They assisted their husbands by making notes, maintaining the library, proofreading, etc. They would work as their husbands' personal secretaries. The wife of the professor who tutored Raja did so too. Obviously, there would be much to communicate between them. Besides, without the wife's assistance, the husband's scholastic achievements would register no progress. So, there was no reason whatsoever for the wife to get disillusioned, bored even. The system there was entirely different. One felt free to select one's spouse according to one's likes, dislikes and life goals. Down the line if they discovered that they were not compatible any more, they would part without ill will, and look for new partners. Raja did not venture to judge whether the ways of that country were right or of this.

He was aware of the intellectual divide between his brother and sister-in-law, and that his sister-in-law could in no way complement or supplement her husband in his scholarly endeavours. Post wedding, when she moved to Mysore along with him as he wanted to pursue his academics, he had attempted to tutor her in the English language. He aspired to somehow see to it that she pursued post-matriculation academics. His brother had encouraged him too. But she evinced no interest whatsoever. She did not even realize the need for it. 'Academics is not in my fate. Besides, why do I need it?' she had said, silencing them both.

Piqued at his silence, Nagalakshmi picked up from where he let off. 'Why are you silent?'

'Nothing at all. Scholars like my brother are the same everywhere. Just as you do, their wives put up with their husbands too.'

'Is that factual? That aside, you are as educated as your brother too. Why can't he communicate with me like you do?'

He could only humour her. 'I am a chatterbox. Besides, I have not undertaken to script any magnum opus. My main focus is to direct plays. And conversation is the stock-in-trade there. Shall I take to writing a book?'

'Man! Stick to your theatre. Never graduate to be a writer.' Then, as if she recalled something, she said, 'Aren't you 25 now...why not give a thought to marriage? I will get company at home.'

'No marriage for me. I am happy now. I bring a wife and just as you do to my brother, she would admonish me, "You have time to give to the theatre, but you don't have some for me? Don't I merit to be beheld even as much as you watch the curtain?"'

Prthvi was simmering the whole day. At 5 in the evening, Raja took him to the doctor and got him medicines. It wasn't an acute ailment. The physician told him that the fever would subside by tomorrow and the boy would be alright.

When Rao was home at 7 pm, Raja was not in. Immediately on his arrival, Nagalakshmi ranted away, 'Is it inevitable to work Sundays even?'

Determining the tone of her voice, Rao chose to keep mum. When she asked the same question again, Rao said, 'When an incensed person asks a question, though a patient reply is given, it will fuel the inquisitor's ire further. The effect will be the same even if the reply were incensed too. So, isn't it wise to remain silent?'

She took hold of his hands, led him to the room where the boy was sleeping and said, 'He is running fever since afternoon.'

Placing his palm on the his forehead to check the temperature, Rao asked, 'Wasn't Raja at home?'

'He was. Who else would care? He took him to the doctor and brought the medicines. But shouldn't you, the father of the child, be doing that?'

Rao said nothing. He simply sat by the head of the child. After looking intently at her husband's face for two full minutes, Nagalakshmi said, 'Can't think of something to do other than simply sitting?'

'What shall I do? Raja has brought the medicines. You are taking good care of him.'

'My fate!' Nagalakshmi took to sobbing. Rao felt embarrassed. Getting up, he neared her, sat beside her, ran a palm over her back and said, 'I can understand your weariness, Nagu. Well, henceforth, I will be home sooner.'

She was content at that. In two minutes, she pepped herself up, held her husband's shoulders with both hands and said, 'I will not object to your studies. But if your pursuit comes at the price of my company, how can I put up with that?'

There was the sound of the main door thrown open, indicating Raja's arrival. Nagalakshmi went into the kitchen.

That night Rao asked Nagalakshmi to rest, and checked himself from sliding into deep sleep so as to keep a watch on his son. The fever was already abating.

Nagalakshmi didn't sleep either. The couple slept with the kid in between. Rao initiated an affectionate conversation with his wife. The topics ranged from the royal-jasmine flower in their front yard and the Hyderabadi pigeon pea gram that Raja had brought this month, to the traits of the new maid who had reported today for duty in the neighbouring house. Rao kept grunting comprehension in spot-on accord. By 11 pm, she slipped into sleep. The child, too, was asleep. It wasn't retiring time for Rao though; he got up gently and went to his study.

3

Two months after Rao returned from Ajanta, a registered-post from Karuna was delivered to his address. He retrieved the contents only to see the typed matter in excess of 60 pages. It was the notes that they had prepared in Ajanta. Rao read it fully. It was scripted in good language and the matter was appropriately chronologized. Though he had dictated unambiguous accounts to her for jotting down, it was improbable that his extempore narration would be in any chronological order, given that he kept moving from one spot to another and had related everything in the spirit of conversation. Karuna had thoroughly reviewed it, and had presented it as a formal essay. There wasn't even a single typographical error. The uniformity of impression of the letters on the paper indicated that it was the work of a skilled and experienced person.

With it, she had enclosed a letter too:

> On returning here, I visited the library of the Colombo University. I browsed through the four volumes of *Ajanta: The Colour and Monochrome Reproductions of the Ajanta Frescoes Based on Photography* by Dr Ghulam Yazdani. Its narrative is just factual description. There wasn't any historical value analysis as is typical in your work. I got to know the importance of these notes as I went about typing them. Even if this were revised and published as a booklet, the literary world will heartily welcome it. If you permit, I will attend to it to the extent possible by me and send you a revised version.
>
> I am moved by your concept of history. I now feel that it is appropriate to pen my proposed book *Sinhala Culture in the Backdrop of Buddhism* from this viewpoint enunciated by you. Your resolve to script the cultural history of India is sublime. I pray to God to bless your enterprise. My parents always reminisce about you. They have asked me to convey their respects to you.

Rao was appreciative of this young lady who, though belonging to a different country and only a recent acquaintance through all of three days, had evinced much interest in his research. He read the typed notes once again. He felt that it could be developed into a publishable monograph just as she had suggested. Yet, without paying any more attention to it, he just inserted it in a file. He wrote a letter to Karuna, expressing his gratitude for her act of reviewing the notes, typing them, and remembering to dispatch them as committed.

Rao had collated all the information necessary for scripting the first volume of his tome. He also proposed to commence writing it in about three months' time. He had corresponded with the British publisher of his last work, and had contracted with them to publish his proposed series too, in recognition of which, the publishing company had undertaken to give him a decent amount of royalty.

The first volume was to begin with a chapter titled 'The Genesis and Basis of Indian Culture'. The viewpoint that would be discoursed in that chapter was to diametrically relate to the content of all the five volumes. He had ready the draft outline of the chapter, and would give it final form soon. By then, he received another letter from Karuna.

> I read your work *Dharmic Foundations of Ancient Indian Polity*. I had read a critical appraisal of it earlier. I could never have known that it was a work of such high credentials. The purpose of this letter is not to congratulate you. I am a midget that is not entitled to congratulate a colossus of a writer that you are. I come to you with a request. I desire to

> work for my proposed work *Sinhala Culture in the Backdrop of Buddhism* entirely under your guidance. I would like to have this as my PhD dissertation and publish it later. If you consent, I aspire to undertake this research under your guidance. My parents and brother have consented to this too. Please accept me as your pupil. I will start from here the moment I receive confirmation from you.

It was a matter of pride for university professors to have such educated research scholars under their tutelage. Though the thought flashed in Rao's mind as to whether it was convenient for a lone female to relocate to such a distant place for pursuing research, he recalled that she had lived two years in England alone to pursue academics. He wrote to her that he had no reservations whatsoever in her pursuing research under his guidance, and that she may plan her travel according to her convenience.

One afternoon, Nagalakshmi was standing by the royal-jasmine plant in the front yard of her house when a tonga came to a halt near the gate. A dark-complexioned young woman wearing a white sari alighted, neared her, and asked in English if it was Dr Sadashiva Rao's residence.

Nagalakshmi could understand that much. 'Yes,' she said in Canarese, but Karuna could not understand it. She then said something else in English, which Nagalakshmi could not understand. Karuna was about to leave when Raja arrived there and took it over from Nagalakshmi. Soon, he invited the visitor inside, made her comfortable, and asked his sister-in-law to prepare coffee. After she had coffee, he asked if she had had her lunch.

'Yes,' she said, 'on alighting from the train, I went to a hotel, bathed, lunched, and left for here.'

'Had you informed my brother of your date and time of arrival?'

'I had. He had responded to it too.'

'He must have forgotten. He is so much into his research that he tends to forget everything. Let me take you to his office at the university library.'

On the way, Raja and Karuna got more familiar. Inclined on the armchair, Rao was placing a remark in red ink in the left margin of some notes. On the table were manuscript sheets, pen, pencil and tens of books left open. The entire room was brimming with books. Though the scorch of the afternoon had not yet subsided, Rao seemed to have forgotten to turn on the fan. When he spotted Karuna, he withdrew his stretched legs, got up a bit and greeted her. 'Welcome. Come. I totally forgot your travel plans. When did you arrive?'

When she and Raja were seated on the chairs there, he asked, 'Are your parents keeping well?'

'They are doing fine. They have conveyed their *namaskaras* to you.'

Rao's mind was still deep in what he was presently reading. He did not know how to take the conversation further. He simply sat. The silence made Karuna a bit uncomfortable. Sensing it, Raja chose to break the impasse. 'You have come to a faraway land.'

'Nah. How far after all?'

'The distance isn't much between Sinhala and India. If it were distant, was it possible for Ravana to kidnap Seeta without a break in the journey?' said Raja.

Karuna laughed at his remark. Rao was drawn into the conversation. He said, 'The sage-author of *Ramayana* must have known Sinhala. Though he has called Ravana a demon, he has praised him for being an exalted sage devoted to the Vedas. Both these lands belong in the same cultural milieu.'

'Brother, instead of enquiring after her well-being on undertaking such a long journey, you give her sermons on history!' Raja remarked.

Realizing his lapse, Rao asked, 'Where are you staying?'

'In a hotel.'

'There is no need for you to stay in a hotel. You should have come straight to my house. Even now, you take my brother along, collect your baggage, check out of that hotel and go straight to my house. Tomorrow, you shall apply to the university for registration of fellowship. In a few days, lodging arrangements can be made for you in the women's hostel.'

After Raja and Karuna left from there, Rao went back to his reading. After checking out, Karuna accompanied Raja back to his house and reached there at 7 pm. Raja introduced his sister-in-law viz. Karuna's guru's wife to her. When Karuna brought her palms together in greeting, Nagalakshmi did the same. While cooking, Nagalakshmi looked for an opportunity to speak to Raja. 'Instead of marrying and starting a family life, why should women go this far?'

'Why, to pursue academics. She has been to England, and is as educated as I am. Now, she is here to pursue higher studies under brother. What do you think of my brother?'

'Is he just that—a *brother* to you? Is he nothing to me?' she asked as a matter of pride.

'Ask that of him,' said Raja as he exited. And till his brother was home at 8, he kept the guest in cheerful company. Most of their conversation revolved around England and the common ground of their academic pursuits there.

CHAPTER 6

1

Despite of the doting in-laws, the charming child and other comforts at home, Katyayani found life boring. The grief from widowhood was not as intense as hitherto. Now and then, she would converse gaily with her in-laws. She would play horseback, hide-and-seek, tag, etc. with her child. Still, she found it difficult to kill time. Sweeping the house and the front yard and drawing *raṅgoli* was her share of household work. By then, her in-laws would have bathed; her father-in-law would have deputed himself to the puja chamber, and her mother-in-law, the kitchen. Lakshmi would attend to the rest. Katyayani would be done with her daily chores when she had bathed her kid, dressed him in fresh clothes, bathed herself, washed everyone's clothes, and hung them by the clothesline. Then on, she had to virtually push time. At times, her mother-in-law would invite her for a game of dice. But Katyayani was not interested in it.

A little after her husband was dead, Katyayani's father had taken her to Srirangapattana. A stepmother, just about eight years elder to her, and a ritualistically austere father, wholly unlike her father-in-law, had put her to discomfort there. There was a stark divide between her father-in-law's traditionalism and her father's orthodoxy. While Srotri endeavoured to fathom the quintessence of *dharma* that would lend direction to his deeds, lawyer Srikanthaiah religiously adhered to the peripheral zing of *dharma*. Though he had implicitly made known his opinion that his widowed daughter tonsure her head as was customary, Srotri had taken no notice of it. After only a few days, she had returned to Nanjangud. At times, she alone would clear the litter in the beds of plants and trees in the garden in the backyard. She would de-weed the leafy-vegetables nursery. She would irrigate the entire backyard. The jasmine and royal-jasmine creepers therein yielded bountiful aromatic flowers. She would irrigate these plants well. But whenever she slogged in the backyard, memories of her husband would return. Back then, they would together irrigate the jasmine creeper. The creeper had grown luxuriously, and had spread its vines wide in a canopy. When she was closeted therein to harvest the flowers, he would rib her many a time. Though she would sneer at him, it was pleasurable to her. These memories would haunt her whenever she went to the backyard.

The vegetation in the backyard was now a resplendent green. The paddy fields to the back of her house that were barren until recently since last harvest were once again a comforting green. To be barren always was neither the way of nature, nor was it so ordained. But she would sigh in exasperation that her life that had wilted shall remain so forever. But whenever she set eyes on her child, her mind would swell. But she was capable of handling much more than tending to a kid. If, per chance, Srotri passed by while she slogged it out in the garden, he would offer a word of consolation, 'Why slog it out in this sun? Go indoors, child.' Whenever she thus basked in her father-in-law's affectionate concern, a new cheerfulness would advent in her grieving life. At times, her college days would surface in her memory. She would shuttle daily from Srirangapattana to Mysore in train. Her teachers had appreciated her as being a student of keen intellect. While in senior intermediate class, she had donned the role of Savitri in the play *Savitri-Satyavan* enacted by the girls, and had essayed the role so effectively that the audience wept. She that had, on stage, saved Satyavan from being withdrawn by the God of death. Yama had, in her real life, taken her husband two years into marriage. As she entered wedlock before she could finish her intermediate, she had to discontinue it. But she never lamented it. She didn't think of collegiate academics as higher than meriting such parents-in-law as the Srotris, and a husband like Nanjunda Srotri.

A new thought flashed in her mind. Many girls from Nanjangud traveled to Mysore to attend college. Why couldn't she do the same and pursue BA? Behind this aspiration, another hope surfaced in her mind. Her husband could not take his exams the first time. When he wrote them the next year, he'd failed in some subjects. He took to studies with a resolve to clear them all in the third year. His parents, too, aspired that their son earn a BA degree. But fate had willed otherwise. His books were in that cupboard on the first floor.

Katyayani went up the stairs and looked inside the cupboard. All his books—Sanskrit, English, history—were all neatly stacked. All were hard bound, and on the front cover was the name N.S. Nanjunda Srotri. It was she that had written the names on some books. Beside his name, he had written 'Kaatti', and it still bore evidence to her act of erasing it.

Her desire to attend college and pursue education steeled more and more by the day. And though she doubted that her father-in-law would grant her wish, deciding to get over with it, she discussed the matter with him one day. He said, 'Child, why compromise on timely nourishment and travel daily that much distance? To what end? Just be comfortable at home. When he grows up, let Cheeni pursue higher education.'

'He would surely have completed his BA by now. We had to face this fate. If I do it in his name, I will get some solace,' she said and went silent.

It was not in Srotri's nature to disregard any matter whatsoever. He was witness to his daughter-in-law's insipid life of late. He reflected that the diversion of college education would augur well for her. Still, he told her, 'I had asked you to recite the Bhagavadgīta. Instead of going for formal academics, take to reciting the Bhagavadgīta. You shall get peace of mind. Then on, read the Upanishads. I will regularly tutor you after my daily worship. It is one thing if we were constrained economically. God has given us enough for our basic needs. If you ask my opinion, for the likes of you it is better to recite the Bhagavadgīta than attend college.'

When Srotri deployed the words 'for the likes of you', he had done it with no emphatic intent. Nevertheless, it pricked Katyayani's mind and brought tears to her eyes. Not getting to know the real reason for her tears, Srotri was moved by them and placated her, 'But if you so desire, you are free to pursue academics. Why shed tears in disappointment?'

Wiping her tears, Katyayani said, 'I tried reciting the Bhagavadgīta. But interest does not sprout. What shall I do? I tried reading his books in the cupboard upstairs. I have developed a liking to them.'

'True, child. Time decides everything,' said Srotri and went silent.

2

One afternoon, Katyayani was asleep with her kid on the upper floor. Bhageerathamma, Lakshmi and Srotri were in the living room on the ground floor, chatting. Bhageerathamma said, 'College! After all that she has undergone? What does she know about the ways of this world? She proposes and you dispose. Why won't she just stay indoors and look after the kid?'

Srotri was convincing her. 'Age is on her side. How may she keep herself engaged all day at home? Let her attend college for a year or two.'

'Am I not pained at her ill fate at such a young age? If she had got her head tonsured, there would have been much work for her viz. cleaning the puja chamber, drawing raṅgoli, cleaning the idols frequently, preparing wicks for the oil lamps, cotton festoons for the portraits of Gods, regular recitations, etc. Time would just fly. You stood by her saying that she was a modern-day girl. True, I was for it too. But how does it become tenable if she says she is bored?'

Lakshmi intervened, 'The reason Katyamma wants to attend college is to take it further from where her husband had left it, isn't it? She does it in his name, and not for her sake. Let her enroll. What have you got to lose?'

Recalling that her daughter-in-law was set to earn the BA degree that her son should have achieved, Bhageerathamma fell silent. Her silence accorded half the sanction. Noticing it, Srotri said, 'Who would take a liking to get a young widow tonsured? But I would say that it is appreciable if assumed voluntarily by her. Such an unfortunate woman should not be coerced into adhering to such practice, but should rather be left to realize on her own that her presentability and adornment is henceforth indecorous of her, for the *persona designator* of such benefaction is no more.'

Presently, there loomed in the doorway the shadow of a caller. Lakshmi went to check. It was Dr Rao. When Lakshmi announced accordingly, Srotri approached him with folded hands and greeted him. 'Welcome. Isn't it one and half years since I last saw you? Please come inside.'

Carrying the big leather bag, Rao entered the living and sat on a chair. Srotri brought a glass of churned buttermilk from the kitchen and gave it to Rao. 'Will you have something to eat?'

'Not for another two hours at least. I left home immediately on having lunch,' said Rao.

For a while they exchanged pleasantries. Rao related the generous ways of His Highness. Later, Srotri asked, 'You know I am curious to know about the progress of your tome.'

'I am here just to share that. I have made a draft of the first few chapters of the first volume. The first of those chapters is of prime significance, and I have called it *The Genesis and Basis of Indian Culture*. I want to discuss some aspects therein.'

'Okay, but first freshen yourself. Wasn't it too hot outside?' Srotri led Rao to the bathroom. Washing his face and feet, Rao returned to his chair and made himself comfortable. He then retrieved a set of typed sheets from his bag.

'Let's go to my study. I am getting old, and of late my memory suffers. If we have to refer to some treatise, it will be handy there,' said Srotri and led the way. While they scaled the stairs, Katyayani was climbing down, carrying her child. The kid had just got up from sleep. Seeing her, Rao enquired, 'How are you?'

'I am doing fine. When did you arrive?' she enquired as courteously.

'A few minutes ago,' responded Rao as he carried on up the stairs.

Entering Srotri's study, they both sat on deer-hide mats, facing each other. Glancing through the pages in his hand, Rao said, 'I have broached the subject of my work with the doctrine *The Genesis and Basis of Indian Culture are the Omniscient Vedas and Upanishads.* The various strains of culture that shall be delineated in the subsequent chapters shall have their justification in the Vedas and the Upanishads. Idolatry, serpent worship, nature worship, etc. that the later historical periods brought up are regarded by some European scholars to be ethos imported from uncivilized cults, and not innate to the Vedas and the Upanishads. If we concede to this reasoning, then the very premise of my discourse will become unfounded. What is your opinion?'

Given the gravity of the query, Srotri regarded it for a while and then said, 'Why should we give in to the supposition that idolatry is inferior and uncivilized? Why can't serpent worship, tree worship and such practices be considered decorous? We can glean three levels of worship from the Vedas: elemental worship (say fire), worshipping the Gods representative of the elements (Agni, the fire God) and worshipping the omnipotent God (the ultimate one to whom the worship is perceived to accrue through the form of Agni). Elemental worship, viz. idolatry, performed without perceiving its overarching significance, does not merit distinction. Worship of nature that takes cognizance of such exalted meaning is enunciated in the very Vedas.'

They kept up their discussion till 7 in the evening. Intermittently, Rao was making notes in his notebook. Srotri cited from the three Vedas copiously from memory. At times, he would have Rao look into certain pages of Sanskrit books.

Exiting his study at 8, Srotri bathed and entered the puja chamber. Rao went to the living room and kept ruminating about the discussions. Having had supper at 9, they returned to the study upstairs and resumed their discussion. Past midnight when they came down and slept in the beds laid out in the living room, Srotri shared with Rao about his daughter-in-law's desire for academic pursuits. Rao endorsed it. 'It will do her good. What would she do at home other than whiling away time?'

'That is right, but my wife is objecting. She is apprehensive about college life.'

'Whatever the environ, the virtuous will sail through. Those who are prone to go wayward will go that way anyway. College is not an undesirable place. Am I not in one?'

Rao's words went well with Srotri. He said, 'When will the college reopen after the summer vacation?'

'In a fortnight's time. Send her on the 24th of the month. I will be in my cabin at the university library. She need only apply for admission on that date. The classes start sometime later.'

Srotri steeled his determination.

3

Vasanti, the daughter of Dr Sripada Rao residing at Market Road, had finished her junior BA last year, and was to attend senior BA this year. When she heard that Srotri's daughter-in-law had enrolled for the same college she attended, she visited her to ensure. Katyayani was happy that some company for daily commuting was available close by. The Srotri couple felt relieved too. Rao had posted an enrollment form so as to reach Srotri well before the 24th. Having filled it, Katyayani took her father-in-law's signature in the space meant for 'Guardian'. Then, as instructed by her mother-in-law, she placed it before the idols in the puja chamber, prostrated before God, kept the form safely in a bag and got ready to leave.

Since that morning, Katyayani was feeling excitement and incomprehensible anxiety all at once. A thought flashed in her mind as to what she would be achieving by being away from such a good home a large part of each day and attending college. Even as she lunched, she kept cogitating as to why she should pursue academics at the cost of being away from home from 9 to 6:30, and at the cost of forfeiting precious time with her lovely kid. That day, she was lunching alone. For two years henceforth, she would lunch alone. While her thoughts rolled on thus, Cheeni who was playing outside came in and asked her, 'Amma, why a'h you eathing withouth me?'

Bhageerathamma, who was serving food, said, 'She will go to Mysore to attend college, kiddo.'

'Why you go college?' She could not think of an answer to the child's question. Vasanti arrived in Srotri's house at 8:45 am. Katyayani prostrated at the feet of her mother-in-law first, and then at the feet of her father-in-law, and sought permission to leave. When she stepped out, Cheeni started crying, 'Don'th go amma, thake me also with you.' He tugged at her sari. Srotri picked him up and consoled him, 'Amma will return in the evening. You stay in the house, kiddo.' Reassured, Cheeni told his mother, 'Come back choon.'

On the way to the railway station in the company of her friend, Katyayani's mind was heavy from some incomprehensible apprehension. The railway station was just five minutes away by foot. At 9 when she sat in the ladies' compartment of the train that rolled in from Chamarajanagar, tears came to her eyes. 'Don't worry much,' consoled Vasanti. As the train rolled on, Katyayani felt that it was taking her away to some strange destination. The thought that she would be returning home by the same route this very evening did not register in her mind at all. The Chamarajanagar-Mysore train was a train of only few cars, and it chugged along leisurely. The drizzle of June set in, and Kapila was gaining inflow. As the train crawled over the Dalavai bridge, she could see the expanse of the east-flowing river on both sides of the bridge. Half a mile yonder was the steadfast turret of the temple of the presiding deity, Nanjundeshvara. To the left of the temple were the steps leading to the bathing deck of the river. It was in this very zone, two years ago, that the champion of her vermilion had neutralized her life by drowning. That was June too. That year, the monsoon had set in early and the water inflow was much more than now.

By then, the train had rolled some more. Past Kambalimutt, it gained on speed. Vasanti engaged Katyayani into conversation. They were not friends; they just about knew each other. Their friendship awaited reinforcement from an entire year's co-commutation. So that she would not disturb the fragile sentiments of Katyayani, Vasanti took to chatting about college life. 'What subjects will you opt for?'

'History, English and Sanskrit.'

'A queer combination! Why did you think up one?'

Katyayani gave no reason. Those were the subjects her husband was pursuing when alive. And those were the books in his collection. Of course, the reason for her opting for those subjects was not just the availability of books. Now she said matter-of-factly, 'Doesn't matter what subjects I study. It is just a diversion for me. My passing or failing the exams is of no consequence.'

Even before the train rolled into Kadakola, the Chamundi hill came in view to the right. Firm and lone, the hill reached up to the skies, and Katyayani had developed a certain unfathomable attraction towards it. She had been there with her husband on two occasions. She had looked at the town, villages, tanks and fields around from the peak. More than these, what sustained her attraction to it was its altitude and stateliness. But now, the clouds of June obscured its peak and shoulders. Its stateliness would not be fully revealed in this partial view as it did in clear skies. She kept looking out the window. The hill kept changing its position. The hill that was to the right of the train presently came to the fore of the train, and the train came to a halt. South Mysore station was here.

Two minutes later, they alighted at Chamarajapura station and walked to college. Very many students from Nanjangud and thereabouts alighted in that station. Arriving at the college, Vasanti took Katyayani to the girls' lounge and said, 'You said you had to see someone.'

'Dr Sadashiva Rao.'

'Oh, that person! He is well-known to all. But those that have actually met him are not many. As a matter of fact, I haven't met him either.'

'I was told that he will be in his exclusive cabin in the library.'

'Come, let me take you to the library. Meet with him, and whatever the amount of time you spend there, make yourself available in the girls' lounge by 5 pm. The train arrives in Chamarajapura station at 5:30.' They then reached the main door of the library. Vasanti asked the attendant there to show Katyayani to Dr Sadashiva Rao's cabin, and left.

4

Gently pushing the flap door shown by the attendant, Katyayani entered. Seated on a chair at a table, Dr Rao was dictating something to a dark-complexioned woman of about 26, clad in white sari and seated across from him; she was taking notes in shorthand. In between, Rao would peer into some sheets of paper on his desk. The room was brimming with books, and one entering the cabin immediately felt hot despite a ceiling fan running. For about 10 minutes, neither of the two noticed her. Though the thought occurred to her that she had better leave, but that would be improper, and she continued to wait. Five minutes later, Rao took to reading one from a stack of papers on his desk. The lady seized the interval to limber out the ache in her neck. It was then that she noticed her. She drew Rao's attention, 'You have a visitor.'

Rao looked in the direction of the door. For two full minutes, he could not recognize her. Taking off the spectacles from the ridge of his nose, he looked again. Embarrassed, Katyayani hung her head. After one more minute, Rao got up from his chair and said, 'Come, come. Oh, today is the 24th. How long have you been waiting? If you do not draw my attention, I will be unto myself, letting you to be unto yourself! Come here.'

By then, the woman drew a chair close. When Katyayani was seated, Rao introduced the ladies to each other. 'She is Ms Karunaratne. She is from Sri Lanka. She has done her BA at Cambridge in the UK, and is a research fellow here.' Then pointing to Katyayani, he said, 'I always keep telling you about a mentor of mine, Sri Srinivasa Srotri. She is his daughter-in-law. She has enrolled for an undergraduate course in our college.'

After they both greeted each other, Dr Rao turned to Katyayani. 'Let me have your application form.' Verifying it, he said, 'History, Sanskrit and English, the very same subjects that Nanjunda studied. I, too, am an unfortunate one that lost a good pupil. Now I don't teach BA classes. An erstwhile pupil of mine, Mr Honnaiah, will be your history lecturer. Some sessions of optional English is handled by my brother. I think for Sanskrit, it is Narasimha Shastri.' He struck the bell on his desk; he attendant appeared. 'Go to the college and bring Raja Rao along,' he said, then turned to Katyayani and asked, 'At what hour will you leave house daily?'

'Quarter to nine.'

'Quarter to nine. And it will be 6 or 7 by the time you return. My house is nearby in Chamarajapura. Go to my house daily for a quick lunch during lunch break at 1:30 pm.'

'No. I will pack a light lunch. And I have company of some girls from my town.'

'Bring it nevertheless. But give it to me here and have your lunch in my house,' he laughed loudly. 'Never hesitate. You belong in this house too.'

Karuna could not gather why Dr Rao laughed loud. She could only pick up a few English and Sanskrit words from their exchange. Rao explained it to her. By then, Raja arrived. Rao introduced Katyayani to him, 'You know Nanjunda Srotri, right?'

'Of course, I do. We were classmates. He was studying English for his senior BA. I was studying for the same paper for my Honors second year.'

'Okay then,' Rao turned to Katyayani, 'You give him the application form and the fee amount. He will post you a card well in time, informing you of the date of commencement of classes. Until then, you don't have to attend college. Now, go visit my house along with him.'

'No, I...,' Rao cut her out, 'You have never visited our house. Shouldn't you get acquainted? Besides, your return train is in the evening.'

Katyayani handed over the application form and fee money to Raja. Before they left, Karuna asked Raja, 'What is your maiden play for this year?'

'*Chandragupta Maurya*. I'll make it very dramatic and get your fellow historians to swear that it is all false.' He exited, laughing, with Katyayani in tow. While they walked together, Katyayani felt squeamish. So as to rid her of her inhibition, he asked, 'What subjects have you opted for?'

'History, English, Sanskrit.'

'Fine choice. History is my brother's forte. The other two belong in the domain of literature. May I understand your choice as affinity towards literature?'

She said reluctantly, 'A bit.'

'A bit and a few more bits add up to much. When the classes commence, borrow books from the library and cultivate a reading habit. Have you read Canarese novels?'

'I did, two years ago. Now, no.'

They arrived at the gate of Raja's house. Nagalakshmi knew about the Srotris. When Raja introduced Katyayani to her, she felt moved. While Nagalakshmi was still reflecting on the plight of Katyayani, Raja asked Katyayani, 'What time did you leave from home this morning?'

'Quarter to nine.'

'Well then, lunch now. My sister-in-law will serve you cold rice.'

Nagalakshmi was thinking of preparing some snacks, but now insisted that she have lunch. Inevitably, Katyayani complied. After lunch, Raja said, 'You must have your lunch here on a daily basis. The house is very close to the college.'

Katyayani was surprised by the synchronicity of the brothers' minds. She was sure that their offers were a result of their genteel, and that they had entered into no such pact between themselves. Retiring to an inner room, Nagalakshmi and Katyayani chatted for long, and both took a liking to each other. When it was time for Katyayani to leave for college, Nagalakshmi said, 'Come here daily for lunch. Any time convenient to you is okay with me. Even some rice in buttermilk will be helpful. This house is yours too.'

Raja wanted to go to the college too. He said, 'Come along. I will take you to the college. I have to go for watching the rehearsal of a play.'

Katyayani was greatly relieved at the cordiality shown by Rao's brother and wife. The apprehension that had occupied her mind as she left her house in the morning eased. Though, while returning to the college, she felt a bit comfortable with Raja, she didn't initiate a conversation. Leaving her at the girls' lounge, he walked away. Katyayani went in and settled in a chair. Barring seven to eight girls—all strangers—there was no one else there. Vasanti was not yet there. She was getting eager to go home early. A few times, she walked up to the door in anticipation of Vasanti's arrival but there was no sign of her. It was still 2 in the afternoon. Sure that she would turn up before 5, Katyayani went in and reclined on a rattan chair. Her mind was filled with memories of her husband. 'Where did he lounge when he attended college before? Like I do now, did he get eager to go home soon too?' When she was lost in these thoughts, Vasanti turned up.

CHAPTER 7

1

Karuna's arrival in Mysore galvanized Rao's manuscription. Before writing the next chapter, he would relate it to her. Listening to it intently, she would pose questions about aspects therein about which doubts arose in her mind. 'Good that you brought it up. This deserves to be dealt with in the book circumstantially,' said Rao, as he made note of one of them. She had truly strengthened his hands, for she had gained hands-on experience as to what book in the library contained what information, what books would be needed for the present, how to retrieve them, etc. Many a time Rao would dictate to her based on his notes. She would take it in shorthand, type it in her hostel, and make it available next morning. She wouldn't just type as dictated; she would cleanse it of the colloquial jargon, and shuffle sections with a view to chronological perfection. The new typewriter that Rao had purchased was now with her in the hostel.

Besides her eligibility as a research fellow, Dr Rao's recommendation was instrumental in Karuna getting an exclusive room for herself in the women's hostel. She got accustomed to the hostel food, but for her breakfast, she had made her own arrangements for bread and milk. She would have lunch at 10 am and go to the library. She would wind up for the day at 7 in the evening, until which time she would attend to her studies, prepare notes and do other works assigned by Rao. She would have some snacks in the afternoon in the company of Dr Rao in the library. She would attend to her thesis writing during night-time. Even before she moved here, she had collated quite a lot of information for her thesis. Only, she didn't know how to expound on them and appoint it within the template of a dissertation. After deliberating on it with Dr Rao over a couple of months, she could determine the core around which her dissertation was to evolve. Now, only the scripting remained, and she was confident of successfully going about it. She, therefore, accorded priority to her guide's tome. She thought it her good fortune to partake in the production of this epic work that her mentor had taken up as his life's mission, and she applied herself fully to that work.

When the scripting of the first volume began, Rao found himself removed from the transactional world about him. Even when he returned home late in the evening at 8, he had no interest in any household matter whatsoever. The aptitude to speak would be triggered only if someone asked him about his research. Else, not only would he feel it unnecessary to speak, he would find it impossible to.

'What is the progress in compilation?' Raja would enquire at times.

'Half of the first volume is done.'

'When would it be done completely?'

'The manuscript would be ready in about six months.'

The length of their discussion in this matter could simply not be in excess of the shortest 'Act' among the plays Raja knew of; he would not be interested in prying deep either. History was not his area of interest anyway…his mind would be occupied in some play or some other extracurricular activity. When at home, he would chat lively with his sister-in-law or play with Prthvi. It was not in his nature to sit reticent in seclusion.

One night Rao was home at 8, and Raja was not yet back. Prthvi had turned adamant for some reason and was troubling his mother. Raja would take him for a ride on his bicycle every evening. Today, Raja was delayed for he had to direct a play. On seeing his father, Prthvi began pestering him to take him on a bicycle ride. Slumping himself into an armchair, Rao summoned him and seated him on his thigh. But Prthvi was not to be silenced. 'Take me on a bicycle ride,' he tugged at the sleeve of his father's shirt and started crying. Not only was Rao drained from his day-long work, he could not think up any words that would comfort his son. His mind fully immersed in reconstructing the overall cultural history of this nation, it was but natural he couldn't think of words that could comfort his son. He wanted to be left alone, wherefore he said, 'Don't you make fuss, sonny. Go to your mother.'

As if she were in anticipation of this response from her husband, Nagalakshmi darted out of the kitchen and said,

'*Go to your mother! Go to your mother!* Who tends to him all the while—his mother or you? When, for once, the kid asks for a small favour, what would you lose if you heeded him? I would have joined you if you so wished.'

There wasn't enough energy left in Rao to counter his wife. All he wanted was to be left alone for an hour or two, so he could recoup for his overnight reading or writing into the small hours. He just looked at her once and remained silent. Nagalakshmi was disappointed. Eventually, she asked, 'Why should he always say *amma*. Is he just my kid? Isn't he yours too?'

Still, Rao chose not speak. Fully aware of human disposition, he was sure that a debate with an incensed person would only incite the anger further, wherefore he stretched himself in an armchair. As if to herself but in a voluble voice, Nagalakshmi said, 'After these many years into marriage, no interest in the wife, no concern for the kid! Keep it up. If perchance I am dead, you will then learn to lament my absence.'

Rao was annoyed at that remark. He said, 'Why mouth bad omen? Come here.' The kid had by then gone silent on hearing the voluble tirade of his mother. Nagalakshmi neared him and asked, 'What?'

'Come, sit here,' he showed her to the arm of the chair he was sitting in.

'It is okay. *One beseeched to be called for a banquet* goes the saying,' she stepped back one. The kid, too, walked up to his mother. Rao fell silent once more.

After five minutes, Nagalakshmi walked up to her husband, and sat on the arm of the chair he was seated in and said, 'You go to the extremes in everything. Why can't you have an oil bath every Sunday? Go look at yourself in the mirror, you look so emaciated of late.'

'My book is swelling,' Rao smiled.

'Book! Book! What of wife and child, you are neglecting yourself too! Mad about the book only. I think realization will dawn on you only with my death.'

'Why mouth inauspicious portends?'

'What else may I do? Do you ever ask after my troubles? Do you speak to me for a while even once in a week? Do you ever take me out? If you have no need for me, why should I live on?' Her eyes welled up. Rao's heart thawed. 'Get up. Let's go for a walk,' he got up himself. She said, 'It is already half past nine. Raja will be here any moment.' At that very moment, the bicycle bell was heard at the main door. Getting up from where she sat, she said, 'On waking up tomorrow morning, you should take a well-oiled head bath.'

'Not tomorrow. I have much writing to do. Some other day,' he said as Raja rolled in the bicycle. Nagalakshmi sighed at the futility of all her reconciliation efforts. As if he was in anticipation of his uncle, Prthvi ran up to him and stepped on the pedal.

2

Next morning at 10, Rao was in his cabin in the library and dictating to Karuna. Five minutes into taking down the dictation, she said, 'Sir, I think you are out of moods.'

'Why?'

'I feel your narration is not coherent.'

'It is okay. Just take down the notes,' Rao continued dictating.

Karuna checked Rao again five minutes later and said, 'Sir, you are really disoriented. You have erred at many places. Instead of saying "India's Purāṇas" you said "*Kalidasa's plays*"! Instead of saying "culture of India" you said "Babylonian civilization"!'

'Is it?'

'Shall I read out what you dictated?'

'No need. I admit. My mood is really off,' said Rao, leaning back in his armchair and added, 'You attend to your thesis. I am unable to concentrate.'

Karuna exited the room and went looking for some books in the library. Rao got up from his usual chair and slumped in an armchair. He was disturbed since yesterday night after Nagalakshmi had picked up a quarrel with him. Her words 'I think realization will dawn on you only with my death' were resonating in his ears. Why did she speak so tersely, like never before? He could not think of any reason. He had resolved many a time that he should give her some quality time and communicate properly with her. But the mammoth task on hand gave him no leeway. His living and research forfeited their separate identities, so much so that such routine acts as nourishment and rest were imperatives that belonged in his subconscious existence, and adhered to their own clocks. If he forcefully insulated his mind against the profound task on hand, and took to deliberate twosome with his wife even for an experimental duration of time, he would feel that he had taken to a new living by sacrificing a good living.

Karuna re-entered half an hour later with a load of books, shot a glance at him and said, 'Sir, you are reclined on that chair in śūnya-mudra. You need a few days' rest. You are pushing the clock. Man's brain is no machine. You go home.'

Rao took a liking to Karuna's words of solace. He asked, 'What will you do?'

'I have scripted some last night. I will review it.'

'Let's go dawdle for a while.'

She mused on his proposal for a moment and said, 'This is India!'

'So what? Get going. I think there is a train to Kannambadi at noon. Let's return by evening. My better mood will not return any sooner.'

Locking his cabin, Rao exited with Karuna. They walked past the college mound, hired a tonga on Viceroy Road, and went to the railway station. They entered a third-class car for there was no second-class car in that train. When the train chugged along, Karuna said, 'I desired to see Brindavan.

I couldn't find time all these months. Thanks to your bad mood, I could make it today!'

By the time the slow-speed train went past Belagola and rolled into Kannambadi station, it was 12:45 pm. Alighting, they made a beeline to a restaurant. After snacks and coffee, they strolled a bit and sat under the shade of the trees beyond the fruits garden. Rao's mind completely distanced itself from the cultural history of India. For one that had confined himself to the constricted poorly lit cabin where fresh air was scarce, the open space with abundant natural light and air was a refreshing relief. The roar of the nearby waterfall resounded in the nearby pool like a pair of *tanpura* tuned to high pitch. Birds glided playfully in the high sky. Rao, who was silently watching all this, asked Karuna, 'In about a year your research will conclude, and you will be awarded PhD even. What will you do on returning to your hometown?'

'That is my anxiety as well!'

'Continue to research, in a different discipline. Or if you ruminate with conviction, a new vista will open up in the same discipline; it leads you thus forever. It all depends on your ability and conviction to research.'

'I am not at all confident of continuing with research on my own.'

'Never give in to such thinking prima facie. The work you are doing now for your PhD will equip you with methodologies of research. The real work has to happen then on.' As if recalling something, he added, 'Or, if you so desire, collect your reward, go to your hometown, marry and be happy. If you get a spouse who is similarly disposed, you may pursue research together.'

Karuna voiced a protest so as not to be heard by him, and sighed. He heard the sigh and asked, 'Why, don't you hold belief in marriage?'

'I do.'

'Then?'

Karuna did not reply. Changing the topic, Rao asked, 'How was interest in historical studies and research kindled in you? Any relative of yours has been into it and has served as a model?'

Now Karuna shed all hesitation and opened up. 'In my family the only one who took studies seriously is me. Since my grandfather's time, the family has been into business. Prior to that, we were peasants in a village called Pelpola, very close to the town. I have been in that village. We have rubber plantations and pepper vines there. But the family concentrated more on business. My brother studied BA in a college in my town; and me too. Aspiring to continue higher studies, I did my MA in Colombo. That was when interest in serious study was kindled in me. There was a professor called D'Silva. He was very keen on learning, but not disposed to research. When I studied under him, I got addicted to books. I read much more than the stipulated curriculum. It was then that I took to studying the genesis and growth of Buddhism. Though all my family members are Buddhists, none of them know much about it. I would visit all the Buddhist places in Sinhala, read all writings available about them, and make notes. While pursuing my MA in Colombo, I acquainted myself with Sanskrit and Prakrit. Without familiarizing oneself with these two languages, who can learn about Buddhism; rather, learn about Indian history? Then I was awarded scholarship for pursuing higher studies at Cambridge.'

Rao listened to her in rapt attention. Karuna continued, 'At Cambridge, I learnt about methodology of study. But it was from you I learnt methodology of research. If I had not met you, I would not have penned this book. When I perceive in my mind's eye your dedication to research, my mind scales impossible heights that I cannot fathom! I hadn't got to know what my life was about, and as to how my soul may identify my deepest aspirations and endeavour to achieve them. After I came here, you made my soul see it.'

Rao was delighted on hearing Karuna's words. Nobody had hitherto praised him in person as unreservedly and as unaffectedly. Scholars had written to him in praise of his works, they had published scholastic reviews about them, but none had expressed veneration as one would in a guru. All the more, the person regarding him thus now in person was a Cambridge-educated young female scholar. In a glee that he could not himself place, and in a sort of inexplicable semblance of affliction, Rao said, 'Karuna, scholasticism and the path of researchers is akin to a devil's life. It calls for forgetting everyone and dousing oneself in one's own avocation. Can you fully forego marriage?'

The blood drained from her face. Her sparkling eyes narrowed from shyness. Composing herself, she said as if she recalled something, 'A marriage proposal had come up too. My brother was into coconut export business, in which he had a partner his age. They were buddies, and he had visited our house a few times. I was 20 then, and was pursuing my BA. He had just completed his BA and had started that business. On one of his visits, he expressed right in my presence his desire to marry me. I didn't express any inclination. My family thought that it was my natural shyness. My brother was hopeful that this proposal would materialize. That man was truly mad for me. Eventually, I expressed my desire to move to Colombo to pursue my MA. My parents would not let me go before the marriage was consummated, but they had to relent when I turned adamant.

The man waited in anticipation that I would consent on completing my MA. After returning from Colombo, I could clearly see my future path. I realized that there was no compatibility whatsoever between my studiousness and his calling. I wrote to him stating that he mustn't harbour any hope. He wrote back to me, beseeching that he could not live without me, and that he would not hinder my academic pursuits in any way. True, he may not have hindered my academic pursuits, but on what common ground could we have come together? The path I had chosen for my emancipation was totally alien to him. So was his business, money, gold and silver to me. Determining that there was nothing common between two aliens, I categorically warded him off. I did so for the benefit of both. I then left for Cambridge. After being in hope for some more time, he found another bride two years ago.'

She fell silent. When she dodged that proposal each time, she would in fact be pained. Many a time, her mind would oscillate. Her resolve to stay clear of it would be encumbered by many possibilities: *how much will this madness for studies endure? Would it not be indiscretion on my part to hang on to such madness at the cost of a marriage proposal by a family friend, a handsome man of good social standing, and who is beseechingly soliciting my love? How could love that would serve as a bond between us affect my studiousness? Is it impossible to strike a balance between the housewife's calling and my studies?* But her resolve had finally won. Nevertheless, when she got news of his wedding two years ago, she had shed a tear, not knowing why. But then, she had composed herself, attended his wedding along with her brother and wished him good. She didn't share this with Rao.

3

For about half an hour, nobody spoke. Rao was reflecting on her determination. She had decided on her goals even before a marriage proposal came up in her life, and had chosen her path accordingly. But it had not happened so in Rao's life. Though he had identified his goal prior to his marriage, he had not given a thought as to the need for compatibility between them—goal and marriage. His wedding happened when he was concurrently both—a mature individual in the matter of studiousness, and an adolescent in the matter of conjugal life. He was introspecting on this.

Twice, Karuna attempted to say something, but thought the better of it. Rao asked, 'Seems like you want to say something.'

'Nothing at all.'

'It is okay to tell me. Don't hesitate.'

'Nothing really,' she said, but after a few seconds she came out with it. 'Your personal matter.'

'There can be nothing personal about me. Ask away.'

'You will always be deep in study. Your wife is not educated. Are you both compatible?'

'Why ask?' he asked in a calmness he thought fit to impose on himself.

Noticing it, Karuna said, 'Nothing really. I wanted to know if your example will serve to doubly ensure that my decision to rescind on my brother's friend's marriage proposal was right.'

Rao smiled and said, 'In this matter, the pupil seems to be wiser than the mentor.'

'How so?'

Subconsciously, Rao spilled all the details of his marriage. Karuna was listening intently.

When Sadashiva was orphaned and became a member of his uncle's family, he was a boy of 12. This studious boy was at the forefront among his classmates in studies, and he came out with flying colours in his lower secondary exams.

He could get accommodation in Tataiah's orphanage in Mysore. He got enrolled in Marimallappa high school. In fact, it was Tataiah who taught him in high school. He had given Sadashiva history articles by Macaulay, Johnson, etc. from his own collection. The intelligent boy was sure of his goals by the time he did his BA. When he successfully completed his MA with history as a major subject, he landed himself a teaching job in the very college from which he had graduated.

Nagalakshmi was his uncle's only daughter. She was 13 by then. The fresh MA graduate, the boy whom his uncle had tended to as family—his nephew—was 23. When this uncle said, 'Shivu, wed Nagu,' the boy did not resist. The girl had grown tall and maidenly. Her long plait, and the way she wore jasmine strings to match her plait's luxuriance, made her very presentable. She was adept at household work too. Rao had never thought about marriage or about the kind of woman he wanted for a wife. All he knew was that marriage was imperative after finishing academics and landing a career. While in college, there weren't many female classmates. For reason of being a resident of an orphanage, he hadn't spoken even once to the few that were there either. All he did was read the books suggested by the professors, make notes and memorize the topics.

Post his uncle's proposition, when he first went to his house, Nagalakshmi would move about in the house so carefully as not to be seen by him. But he, who was a family member in that house, was free to move about inside out.

Her womanhood that was just about blossoming did not fail to attract his eyes and mind. The luxurious jasmine string that she wore in her plait left a trail of aroma in her wake. And while she attended to her chores, the chime of the many glass bangles she wore on her wrists would be music to his ears. Rao consented to his uncle's proposition.

Post wedding, they moved to Mysore. Raja, too, moved with them. By then Raja had studied two years in a high school in Kunigal. Initially, Rao would always stay glued to his new wife. His professor goaded him with a passion for PhD. That professor was to retire in two years, wherefore Rao had to inevitably complete his thesis by such time. Raja would look after the household. And this adept wife would run the household on a tight budget without pushing her husband financially. What else does one need? He plunged into research. In two years, he became Dr Sadashiva Rao. Before retiring, the professor said, 'For a university professor, it would not suffice to stay contented with just a PhD. A true teacher is one who engages in research all his life. You take to writing another book.' By then Rao's PhD thesis was published. He was consumed by the contentment and glory of scholastic writing. He embarked on his next work. He worked on it incessantly for five years and completed it successfully. Though he had sired Prthvi in this nine-year period, his life goals, his routine, and his mental state had morphed drastically. Household had become the responsibility of Nagalakshmi and Raja, and Dr Rao had submitted himself entirely to research.

Rao finally came up with his notion as to the essence of marriage. 'Whatever type of spouse you wed, the physical attraction that ensues is short-lived. The likes of me are destined to solitary living all their life.'

Listening to the details of her guru's life with attention and sympathy, Karuna interrupted him. 'It need not inevitably be so. I have noticed this at Cambridge. My professor's wife would partake in the intellectual activities of her husband and be of great help. What assistance I give you now, she gave the same to her husband.' And though she said that last sentence with no forethought whatsoever, it caused shyness in her, and she hung her head.

But Rao responded without noticing it. 'It is not a question of me alone. Indian society is in a changeover phase now. Arranged marriages of yore were advantageous. In a society where families were profession-centric, a bride from a family that pursued the same profession came in handy. The days of the profession-centric family systems are past. Now professions are guided by an individual's aptitude. But the times wherein he can have a bride of his choice is not yet here. In this changeover phase, it is inevitable that many incompatible marriages shall result. Besides, a custom of forging a compatible marriage by way of independent thinking is yet to emerge and stabilize.'

Karuna asked, 'The concept of marriage is quite different now from how it was in ancient India, right?'

'In ancient times, there was the concept that marriage is for adhering to the *gṛhasthadharma* and for taking the lineage further. Though the former is extant to a large degree, the latter has lost most of its significance. The concept of "taking the lineage further" is losing its potential. I have a son, too, but I am not sure if he will uphold my lineage. So, I nurse an irresistible desire that the tome, the compilation of which I have taken up in all earnestness, should attain the form of my progeny by drawing on my willpower, intellect, blood and cells all my life, and live forever. To this offspring of mine, my lawfully wedded wife is unable to provide any sustenance and nutrition. Instead, you have worked for it with utmost application.'

Hearing the last words of Rao, Karuna's face once again flushed from bashfulness. As he hadn't intended to convey any suggestive meaning by such statement, Rao felt no hesitation. He continued, 'Given that you have honed your understanding of these matters in a way superior to that of mine, I firmly believe that you will choose a compatible partner if you decide to enter wedlock. For man or woman, family life is must. Else life will be insipid.' Karuna, who inadvertently almost mouthed the word 'yes,' soon became aware of its import in the circumstance, and checked herself.

By then it was past 6. Even if they started now, they would not be able to catch the 6:30-train. They now had to inevitably catch the 8 pm train. So, they continued to loll for half an hour more. They both delved to cogitating in their disparate domains. Rao had today, for the first time ever, given explicit expression to his loneliness in life. In his cogitation, he was honing his understanding of it. On her part, though she couldn't envision the advent of any man anytime in the horizon of her life, her hopeful mind aspired for one. By 7, the entire environ was enveloped in dusk. As it wasn't a weekend or a special day, Brindavan was not illuminated. 'We were oblivious to the descent of dusk! Get up, let's leave,' said Rao.

Karuna got up. Passing through the fruits garden and the bridge across a stream, they were to go past the restaurant to the railway station. Rao, who wore spectacles, could not see the path clearly. Noticing, Karuna lent a hand, 'It is strenuous for you to walk. Until we reach an illuminated zone, let me hold your hand.' Holding her by the hand, Rao could walk briskly. After about ten steps he said, 'In research, I am your guide. In this darkness you are my guide,' and laughed.

Karuna's mind was away into a very distant future. But still, she heard his words. Holding his hand more firmly, she led him away apace.

CHAPTER 8

1

Katyayani's college education progressed smoothly. She would have breakfast at 8:45 am daily, then pack some rice in curd or coulis, and pickle to go with it, and taking her books, would reach the railway station soon after in the company of Vasanti. She would board the ladies' car of the 9 am train and alight at Chamarajapura station. She had actually more company for, besides Vasanti, there were seven to eight girls commuting from Nanjangud; more than 30 boys would board other cars. The journey time was one hour, and the daily commuters would banter amongst themselves and revel in humour. There were gossips of a certain girl talking to a certain boy! A recently betrothed girl would be pestered much on the pretext of being congratulated. Being witness to all this, Nagalakshmi would permit herself a smile. That would expunge the monotony of daily commute. But nobody would humour her; her widowhood probably being the reason. Or the solemnity that motherhood gave to her face would have deterred them from taking liberties with her.

The theatre association would enact plays monthly in the open-air auditorium of the college; Katyayani would not stay back to watch them. Plays would open at 6 pm, and many girls would watch them and return by the 9 pm train. Katyayani too desired to watch, but thought the better of being delayed too late into the night. Besides, she found it impossible to defer seeing her kid any later than evening. Even when Vasanti—now more friendly and intimate than before—urged her to stay on, she wouldn't.

Many a day when there were no classroom sessions, Katyayani would go to Rao's house. Especially during her periods, she felt it convenient to go to Nagalakshmi's house than use the girls' lounge. The very reserved Katyayani who wore no vermilion was at home with Nagalakshmi's company vis-à-vis those teenage college girls who would babble with gay abandon. Nagalakshmi took a liking towards Katyayani as well, for she was neither haughty nor sulking, and in whose nature the countryside innocence lingered pristine. Besides, she yearned for chatting company. Many a day, she would prepare hot snacks for her. Usually, Katyayani's classroom sessions would be over by 3 pm, and then on till 5 she would have no work. Now and then Raja would be home. A chatterbox that he was, he would pull Katyayani into conversation. He was her teacher too. He was handling one paper in General English and one paper in Optional English for her class. All his pupils were mesmerized by the way he handled Macbeth for the General English class. Such was his reputation that students of Maharaja college would attend his sessions here. Being a core theatre person, he would be very expressive by instilling the roles unto himself. By the way he read out the play by modulating his voice so as to depict fear, wonder, valour, and such emotions of the characters—and by the way he would charge the imagination of the listeners so as to impart them an experience of having watched a real show—a torrent of awe would permeate the classroom.

Raja had developed a delitescent interest in Katyayani, who frequented his house. The resplendence of her maturity and modesty had engendered sympathy of sorts in him. One day he asked her, 'Do you read stories and novels in your spare time?'

'I used to. Now I hardly have spare time. Still, I read a little.'

'Who are your favourite novelists?'

'Sharat.'

'For what reason?'

Katyayani didn't know what precise reply to give. She said, 'It is interesting.'

'That isn't an answer to my question.'

She was very appreciative of Sharat's female characters. Parvati of *Devadas*, Kamala of *Sheshprashna*, and Rajalakshmi of *Srikant* had enthralled her mind. But she could not get to analyze why she appreciated those characters. 'I like his female characters,' is all she said.

'Sharat's female characters are very loving. The characters will be succulent with that trait natural in women. Is that the reason for your liking?'

She felt inhibited to answer this question. Her face blushed, and she turned aside to hide it from him. In another minute, she was taken aback when her face perspired slightly. She got up and went looking for Nagalakshmi.

Not even on one of her visits did Katyayani spot Rao in that house. She knew that he always stuck to his cabin in the library, and so, she subtly grasped that Nagalakshmi was virtually a loner. But they never broached that subject. One day, Katyayani volunteered to ask Nagalakshmi, 'It is boring to spend time at home. Get your brother-in-law married. You will have company.'

'As one gains on formal education, wisdom suffers. On the eve of leaving for England, he had said "I shall wed immediately on return; your choice of bride." Now he says he wants to remain single. "Can't a man live celibate?" he asks.'

Katyayani wondered why one who has a penchant for theatre, is a darling of his pupils, and has landed a fine career is disposed thus! All the same, she would leave it at that, thinking that it was none of her business.

Another day, Raja asked her, 'In all these days you haven't once watched any of my plays. May I ask why?'

'I desire to, but I have to be home on time. If I stay back to watch a play, it will be 10 pm by the time I return home.'

'There are many girls from Nanjangud who stay back to watch the plays. Your friend Vasanti even played a role in one of them.'

Nagalakshmi, who was thereabouts, intervened. 'Yes, I heard someone remark that an actor was from Nanjangud. What role was that?'

'The "Jeevu" role in *Guttersnipe Gasconade*.'

She said to Katyayani, 'Raja always takes me to the theatre. Why don't you join me? He directs them fine.'

'I will ask my in-laws.'

Srotri and Bhageerathamma were aware that once a month all the girls stay back to watch the plays and return at 10 in the night—except Katyayani, who would be home the usual time. They were appreciative of her for her realizing the solemnity of her circumstance. On returning home, she would change, wash her feet and start assisting her mother-in-law. 'You are just back from college. Leave it to me, girl,' Bhageerathamma would check her. At times, Srotri would apprise her of their agricultural lands, the income and expenditure therefrom, dealings with farmers, etc. 'I am getting old. You should know these matters, child,' he would say, and shared with her such statistics as survey number, extent, tax, etc. of the lands. Recently he had properly segregated all the land records of the family and kept them orderly in a wooden box; he had also devolved onto her the responsibility of retrieving any document required by him. He would go on to explain the reason he sought such a document, as also the transaction he had subjected it to. 'You are an educated one. You should be aware of all these matters. In case I breathe my last, who else will apprise Cheeni of all this?' he would clarify. Moved, she would say, 'Please do not say so, appa. Let no such thing happen.'

One day Vasanti came to her house and sought out Bhageerathamma. 'Today, a good play will be enacted…the English play *Macbeth*. We have to study it for our exams too. I invited your daughter-in-law, promising to keep her company on the return journey, but she refused. Please advise her.'

Though Bhageerathamma was not for it, Srotri said, 'Child, if it will serve for your exams, please stay back with her and watch it. Watching it once will aid retention better than reading it 10 times.'

That day, Katyayani watched a play at her college for the first time. Raja himself essayed the role of Macbeth and earned the appreciation of all. After the show, the principal of the college appeared on stage and praised Raja profusely, 'I wouldn't know that an Indian actor could so well essay a role created by Shakespeare.'

'How was the play?' Raja asked Katyayani the next day.

'Your acting was magnificent. You hadn't brought such luster to Macbeth in the classroom lectures.'

'Thanks for staying on yesterday to watch it. If the likes of you don't watch and appreciate, how can the likes of me who strive derive contentment?'

Though she felt glad that he gratified her with his words, she remained silent from inhibition. Nagalakshmi intervened, 'Not a single song or dance. Language alien to me. English play is insipid. I got bored.'

Raja laughed. Katyayani too.

2

Katyayani completed one year of her undergraduate course. She didn't even know how nine months had passed by. She had done well in her junior exams. Though she had thought of summer vacations a good riddance from daily commute, she felt bored when the vacations actually started. She would wake up early, bathe and then wash everyone's clothes; her child would still be asleep. For two hours, she would take to studying. Besides her husband's books, she would read those she borrowed from the library. She would peer into a novel and save herself from being bored during the train commute. She would resume reading it in the girls' lounge whenever she had spare time. She would sometimes go to Nagalakshmi's house too.

One week into the vacations, Vasanti visited Katyayani. There was a new gleam on her face. She was through with her final year exams. Katyayani asked, 'You are very gleeful. What news?'

'Nothing.'

'You can't fool me by saying so. Your face is beaming. Are you confident of a first class in the exams?'

'No buddy. Who wants a first class!'

Katyayani understood her priorities. 'What else then?' she asked.

She had, in fact, visited there to share some news. Coy, she said, 'Twenty days from now, you have to attend a banquet in our house.'

'Really! Congratulations. Where is the groom from?'

'Mysore. He is pursuing his MA at our college.'

'Without me getting wind of it, you have secretly fallen in love with him, right? Well, congratulations.'

Vasanti's face turned cerise from bashfulness. The boy she loved belonged to the same caste as hers; a distant relative, in fact. They would meet daily at college. Vasanti would never go to the girls lounge during leisure hours. She would go with her fiancé to roam the bund of Kukkarahalli tank. But she had not revealed anything to Katyayani. Other girls knew about it, but none had shared it with the solemn Katyayani.

After Vasanti exited, Katyayani was happy for her. She prayed to God that he gift her husband with a full life. *She will move to a life of happiness. She will spend her future happily. But what is my future? I will attend college for just one more year. After that, it will be the same old life. If I have to take to indoor life forever, why attend college? On completion of my BA, what heavens would it be that my husband merits? In what way would my BA be especially beneficial for running the economics of the household and farm holdings?* These thoughts bubbled up in Katyayani's mind. Of course, she had enrolled for the course to complete the unfinished academics of her husband. But, of late, that proposition was no more alluring. Still, she would attend college one more year.

Katyayani would reminisce about Nagalakshmi. Whenever she recalled the innocent and cordial nature of Nagalakshmi, a feeling of camaraderie would swell in her heart. During the entire year, Katyayani had not seen Dr Rao at their home. She was given to know that he was possessed by the scrivener devil. He was always immersed in scribing. Poor Nagalakshmi would be vexed! Nevertheless, she was a fortunate one. She could at least stay contented that her husband was researching at his desk in the university library not far from home. She wore flowers in her plait and vermilion on her forehead, besides a small saffron dot in between her brows, daily. That was no less a fortune!

Alongside memories of Nagalakshmi come memories of Raja Rao. What a talented person! Who can teach Shakespeare like he does? Every student of the college goes mad over his narration. He is accomplished in directing plays and donning the roles too. Many girls of the college find him attractive. Those assembled in the girls' lounge would shed inhibition and converse thus:

> 'How was Macbeth today?'
> 'Beautiful.'
> 'You shouldn't praise thus. You are no Lady Macbeth.'
> 'If I were Lady Macbeth, would you feel jealous?'
> 'Silly! Don't worry. We shall share.'

Some girls wouldn't hesitate to speak lightly of professors even. Maybe, they attended college just to while away time, Katyayani would surmise. Her musing would go on: *Still, Raja Rao is very accomplished, friendly and cheerful. How facilely he saw to it that I took to conversing with him, me that had turned mute! He will get me books from the library in his name. Despite being presentable, he had resolved to remain single! Why so? Any girl who weds him would live a contented life.*

In afternoons during the holidays, Katyayani would irrigate the flower and vegetable garden in the backyard. While irrigating the jasmine creeper that had entwined with the Indian coral tree, her husband would surface in her memory. It was while she irrigated this same tree that he had blandished her much. And though it was pleasurable to her, she would frown at him from the anxiety of being caught in the act, and she would move to another plant. She would wear so much jasmine that it would tug at her plait; her husband would only goad her to wear more and more of it. Even now, the jasmine creeper was yielding quite some quantum of flowers. Most of it now went into worship. After the worship, the mother-in-law wore just about a score flowers. Out of the remaining, some were used for evening worship, and the balance was given away to whichever woman asked for it.

She would, at times, ponder as to whether it would be right to use the flowers for wearing or for worship. She had no objections about using it for worship. But can the contentment derived from wearing it be decried? One day, she noticed that the Indian coral tree that the jasmine creeper hugged was parched from within; it was an old tree.

When she reported it to her father-in-law, he summoned a gardener and carefully got the tree cut. Separating the jasmine creepers carefully from its stem, the timber was disposed. A bamboo pole was erected in the place of the tree and the jasmine creeper was allowed to envelop it. Shortly thereafter, he got an Indian coral sapling planted there. He asked Katyayani to irrigate it regularly. Within a fortnight, it developed new sprouts. Srotri directed the jasmine creepers to the new Indian coral plant.

Katyayani was surprised when she noticed that the jasmine creeper bloomed as much now as before, despite of the substitute patron. For no reason at all, she had thought that the creeper would go the way of the erstwhile supporting tree.

3

It is only the likes of Dr Rao who work even during holidays. For Raja though, it was a taxing period. Commencing February up to a fortnight after reopening of the next academic year, his theatre association at the college would go dormant. And in that period, no classroom sessions were taken either. For a few days during the exams, there would be the invigilation work. Over the two months succeeding that, he would inevitably be idle. During the current vacation though, he experienced a vapidity that he could not truly comprehend. He started doing exercises daily. For two days he even went to the gymnasium of the college and did push-ups; day three saw the end of it though. He thought of taking tuitions in classical music. He intended to enhance the artistic worth of his plays with background music. He identified a teacher at a fee of Rs 15 per month. 'For your voice to become worthy of rendition, you have to practice intonation over three years. Why don't you take to instrumental?' said that musician. He also suggested that he take lessons in violin. That very day he bought a used violin for Rs 100, and got to know the *sa-pa-sa* sectors on the fingerboard. But even though he practiced for a few hours over the next 15 days, his fingers could not elicit the proper sounds. His interest waned. The music teacher continued to visit, and he was game for doing so as long as the fee flowed, irrespective of whether his pupil learned something or not.

Rao pondered as to why such boredom, which never bothered him all these years, assailed him now. Nothing flashes. Even chatting with his sister-in-law held no interest, neither taking Prthvi for a ride on his bicycle. He would alone drive his bicycle seven to eight miles along Hunsur road at dawn. But in this summer, the vegetation in surrounding lands had dried up, and they appeared like ashen fields. That would set him thinking: society, doctrines, stipulations, ethics, directives, etc. were devised by humankind, and these were nothing but scourges that parched the basic vigour of life. Emancipation was nothing but the annulment of these scourges and experiencing the core vivaciousness of life. Might these fields that have forfeited vegetation, green integument, and the chirping of sparrows and cuckoos as they fly though the branches of trees, and are laid-back, be called Nature? He decreed that these fields were not representative of vivaciousness. He abstained from riding on that road thenceforth.

That year, it showered a few times right at the onset of the rainy season. The soaring heat of summer suddenly dipped. The desiccated earth got moist and smiled some.

Grass sprouted in the ground behind the college and it became lively. One week later, he once again rode his bicycle on Hunsur road. What a change within 15 days of rains! Farmers took to tilling. The bunds of fields were a resplendent soft green. The trees on either sides of the road sparkled with freshness. Birds chirped away as they flew gaily. 'This is the basic feature of Nature, for herein is resplendence,' he reflected. As he rode further, the trees were more and more luxurious. Branches of certain trees had hung so low that he could reach up to them from his bicycle. The prop roots of the Ficus trees resembled the decorative hangings of a festival pandal.

As he rode further, he noticed that a few farmers had climbed the trees of the avenue and were engaged in cutting the branches. He felt affected. Alighting, he asked the contractor who was supervising the pruning, 'The trees have grown sumptuously. Why cut?' Sucking on his *beedi* and exhaling the thick smoke from his nostrils, the contractor said, 'These bastard trees have no qualms about growing sumptuously. The sagging branches scrape the tops of buses that ply the road. The government sub-overseer has ordered that they be pruned.'

The contractor's words pained Raja, but he was helpless. He reversed the direction of his ride. On the way back, he realized that he had bicycled 15 miles into the countryside.

All day long, the contractor's words bore into his mind. Those are the ways of the people. They scythe into the fine expressions of Nature, and impose their own regulations.

It would assail human life, too, by throwing the spanner into humanity. Civilization is a bundle of such scourges. And what a price civilization demands! The essence of life cannot be experienced without disentangling from such scourges. When he retired that night, his mind weighed with humankind's act of scything into Nature to accommodate themselves, and civilization's act of rending individuals' happiness to infuse its roots…and he wondered if all these could be personified as characters in a play. He hadn't yet perceived a storyline, clear-cut characters, and the preface-events-climax. The whole of Nature was the heroine of that play. The entire human community was the hero that was incursive of that heroine. That was an only scene and the only oppression that kept unfolding on the stage of his mind. It was late into the night when sleep came, before which even his brother had called it a day.

Nearer to dawn, he had a dream. Even therein was that same play, but it was rid of abstractness and had inducted one well defined role. A beautiful young woman of 22-23 years, with her heart-winning ways, wearing no ornament whatsoever…her body glowing from the health within, her pink feet flushing with blood as they took turns in assuming her weight as she treaded, long slender fingers slightly angled outwards at the tip as can be found only in paintings, jet black hair cascading down her back, a solemn face. Her every organ was an expression of the tenderly feminine, and she was seated naked on a boulder beneath a flower plant with her legs dangling. She was moonlight personified, and she gleamed with life from the beauty and harmony of her contours and the grace of her youth. There was no garb on her that would conceal the pristine beauty of nature. The coyness from nudity that is innate in women had not caused this divine feminine's commensurable body sections to cringe. There was a heap of rose flowers beside her. She was stringing a sumptuous garland using both her hands. Beyond the plant were some hundred people who, as one voice, were screaming, 'You are a widow. None of us will accept that garland.'

The dream ceased at that. On waking up, he resolved to pen a play with that as the topic. He felt that he had somewhere seen the exquisitely beautiful woman of his dreams, and his mind attempted to recall who. Her face was clear in his memory, but he could not place her. A clue showed up after two days. It turned out to be none other than his pupil Katyayani. How come! He was taken aback.

4

On the day when college reopened, Raja was seated on a chair in the front yard of his house at 10 in the morning and emending the play he had written. He had scripted it in English, and had determined to have it as the first play of the year. He had already revised it a few times. As he wanted to give it to a pupil of his today to type, he was glancing over it one last time when the outer door flung open and someone entered. He lifted his head to look; it was Katyayani! In her hand was something packed in a handkerchief. From the fragrance, he soon got to know it was jasmine. He got up and asked, 'Here, give it to me.'

Having come face to face with him immediately on opening the compound door, she had got fidgety, and impulsively handed him the flowers. Raja opened it and checked. A luxuriously tied jasmine string! He was excited himself. He began wondering why incidents tend to so coincide. 'Who is this for?' he asked.

'For Nagalakshmi-amma.'

Disappointed, he said, 'Please have a seat. Sister-in-law is visiting a neighbouring house. She will return in a few minutes.'

Katyayani helped herself to a nearby chair. Raja asked how she kept herself engaged in the vacations. While they exchanged pleasantries, Nagalakshmi entered. Katyayani got up and went indoors with her. Raja handed over the jasmine string to his sister-in-law. When Katyayani emerged from the kitchen half an hour later, Raja said, 'Look, I need some help from you.'

'From me!' asked Katyayani, surprised.

'Yes. I have penned a play.'

'Really! I thought you only directed them, and acted in them.'

'No. I have written a few. None of them has seen print. I just penned one more. You have to act in it.'

Katyayani was perplexed. She said, 'What say thou! I will virtually be dead.'

'I got to know that you had played a role when you studied for Inter.'

'Who told you?'

'Doesn't matter. You please consent to act in this.'

Katyayani got solemn. By then, Nagalakshmi arrived there. Katyayani said tentatively, 'The times are different between then and now. What would people think of it?'

'Nobody will say anything. Haven't many girls acted in the plays of our association? This is a play penned by me. I feel that you would aptly essay a role therein.'

Katyayani did not consent. She left for college. She consented to it after Raja urged her a few times. Once, on an earlier occasion in the past, she had experienced the pleasure of make-up and acting in a play. Even now, she was swayed by it. She got anxious that her in-laws might get to know that she acted in a play. It could not be through Vasanti, for she was not attending college this year. Married by now, she had moved to Mysore. No other girls would carry the news to her house.

'Sir, the play that you have penned is in English language. No, I cannot.'

'On the contrary, I feel that you can acquit yourself well. If it were in Canarese, I would have got any other girl enact it. Many a girl pesters me for a role too. A student of optional English, it is you that has to enact it.'

Handing her the typed manuscript, he said, 'Keep one thing in mind. This is a play; it is art. The tale does not diametrically relate to any real life individual. The roles herein are just suggestive symbols. The import of this play is such that the roles transcend the tale and go deeper. By just reading the dialogues, nothing is understood. I will train you in all the detail.'

Katyayani took the draft with her. When she returned the next day, her face was grim. But considering that he was her teacher, she said demurely, 'Sir, please get the role played by someone else.'

'You should think of this as art, a play.'

'Have your created that role after me?' Her voice was heavy.

'Never think so. This crystallized in my mind in a different way altogether. The play is just metaphoric of that imagination of mine.' He related to her about his dream and how he adapted it to the play. But he did not reveal that it was she that was in the dream, and that she was naked. In the play were lines that Katyayani had to deliver from behind a transparent screen, and other lines that she had to deliver under a dim light on the stage. It was a play of novel techniques, novel metaphors and novel messages.

Katyayani visited Nagalakshmi's house daily for rehearsal; Raja trained her there. Nagalakshmi, who knew no English, just sat and watched Raja's direction and Katyayani practice. Raja trained the three male roles in the association room in the college. The play was titled *The Primordial*, wherein nature was the heroine and souls were the heroes. A hero merely appears on the stage; no enactment by him. He just gets to deliver a few lines once. Out of the other two, one is Indra, who rules the world by authority; the other is the Divine Preceptor Brhaspati, who sanctifies such authority with a seal of *dharma*.

On 1 August at 6 in the evening, the show opened. As it was the first play of the year, the Vice Chancellor (VC) of the university was also present. If for the freshers it was a matter of curiosity, for the senior students it was the excitement to watch a play penned by their darling professor Raja. The open-air theatre was houseful.

Moving about in virginal green environs, Nature harvests flowers. She speaks naught, but a voiceover related the circumstances. She then took to stringing a big garland of flowers. That done, she appreciatively looked at the garland that she had just strung. Then a soul enters the stage. Attracted to the soul, she nears him with romantic speak. She is about to adorn his neck with that garland, and the soul has stretched his arm to hold her hand. Before they accomplish it, thunder strikes and darkness descends on the entire place.

Next scene is Indra's court. To one side stands Nature, tied up in chains. Indra is seated on the throne. The preceptor Brhaspati, who is seated on another seat, tells her, 'You are accused of violating *dharma*.'

'Devaguru, what is the *dharma* that I have violated?'

'Earlier, you were in conjugation with another man. Attaining his emancipation, he freed himself from you and passed on. Widowed, now you accost another man to adorn him with a garland. This is against *dharma*.'

'Devaguru, isn't it anti-dharmic to impose contrived *dharma* on Nature that is evergreen and ever-zestful? Brimming with zest is my intrinsic character. No *dharma* would, by imposition of widowhood, vitiate the vegetation that appeals to the mind, the eye-catching panorama, and my seamless expanse that provides sustenance to all souls. Devaguru, would you answer a question of mine?'

'What is it?

'Isn't the emancipation of soul through unification with Nature?'

'Yes.'

'If ye condemn me to widowhood, what would be the fate of the countless souls that seek emancipation? Now, isn't your *dharma*, of withholding their rightly deserved emancipation, contrived?'

Devaguru was silenced from the lack of an answer. Nature continues, '*Dharma*, ethics, polity, social norms and accusations by people, which artificially withhold my intrinsic characteristics, are all facets of falsehood. Nature is an eternal maiden. A *dharma* that attempts to suppress her beautiful constitution is self-destructive.'

It thunders again and darkness descends of the stage. When the lights come up dimly, Indra and Brhaspati repent their misdeeds, become lame and collapse. Light picks up and the stage is now bright. Once again, Nature appears with her garland. When she narrates about the eternality of her youth, the soul nears her. But this time Nature would not readily adorn him with the garland. The soul says, 'Nature, thou art not a widow. Thou art an eternally auspicious woman.' Nature now adorns him with the garland. The soul holds her hand. She casts an amnestying glance at Indra and Brhaspati who lay limp, and blesses them by gesturing her right palm. Cured of their ailment, they rise and prostrate in front of her. The light on the stage dims and the screen descends.

The audience clap thunderously.

Dashing to the greenroom, Raja firmly held both of Katyayani's hands and said, 'Magnificent. You have given appropriate expression to my creation.'

'It is all your guidance,' she paid back the compliment. She was oblivious of her hands continuing to be in his grasp for a lengthy minute.

By then a table and three chairs were laid on the stage. The VC and the principal came up on stage and sat on the chairs; Raja occupied the third. The secretary first garlanded the VC. Some students who had occupied the back seats yelled, 'Garland for the soul!' Of course, they were cheering their darling Raja Rao. The principal got up and said, 'Students, please calm down.'

When commotion subsided in the audience, the VC walked up to the mic and said, 'I was a zoology professor. I was not able to fully grasp the suggestion of the play. Mr Raja Rao has penned a fine play. I congratulate him on behalf of all of you. The actor who played the main role, Ms…Ms…,' he looked at Raja, and when told, he continued, 'Ms Katyayani, has given an excellent performance. The other three, too, have acquitted themselves fine. It was a fine production. I, a student of zoology, would grasp the ever contemporariness of Nature thus: The cells in a body keep dying. New cells keep growing. Even after a living being's death, the body cells may survive in the biome. We should understand the world as full of life thus.' He just said what he could think of at the moment and rested.

When the audience dispersed, it was still 8:30 pm. Raja asked Katyayani, 'You are not likely to have company now. I will accompany you to the railway station.'

Taking off her make-up, Katyayani dressed in her usual plain clothing and joined him. Enroute Raja said, 'VC referred to you thrice as 'Ms'. Did you notice?'

Katyayani kept silent. She was reflecting that she should not have played that part today. As long as she was on the stage, she had acted in the true spirit of an actor viz. forgetting her own self. But five minutes after it was over, she felt cringey. She was silent all the way to the railway station. Nearer to the station, she said, 'In the platform will be the girls and boys who are bound for Nanjangud. They may get ideas. You leave now, please.'

Raja said nothing. He simply returned.

CHAPTER 9

1

The penning of the first volume was done, and it was thoroughly revised thrice. It was thought to take up five years for compilation, but it was accomplished in just three. Until the advent of Karuna, Dr Rao had slogged it out alone. Since her arrival, work progressed apace. Karuna had scripted her thesis and had submitted it to the university, but she stayed on with a desire to type a fair copy of the first volume of her guru's compilation before returning to her country. She had accomplished the same by working day and night over six weeks. She had packed one copy and posted it to the publisher in England along with a letter by Rao.

On the eve of her return to her native place, Rao could not get sleep the entire night. For more than two years now, she had assisted his research. Analyzing his manuscript, she had brought to his notice errors therein. With an efficiency that even a paid secretary would not live up to, with a cordiality typical of a very intimate friend; and like a scholarly friend who would channel his/her intellectual support, she had submitted herself to the compilation of the volume. 'Will I successfully compile the next volumes alone?'

Rao cogitated within himself. Karuna is set to leave for her homeland by leaving him to fend for himself in the task of compiling a tome, which entailed taking apart a mountain and systematically piling up the debris so as to create a mansion of the same size. Considering that he attended to it himself before her advent, he would ask himself if he would have gone through it all by himself if she hadn't presented herself. Still, he could not rein in his restlessness.

He didn't lie down the entire night; sleep didn't come either. Exiting at 4 am, he went to her hostel. Nobody could be spotted thereabouts, but he noticed that there was light in her room. The attendant was asleep at the entrance of the peripheral compound that went around the front yard of the hostel. Waking him up, he asked the attendant to convey to Karunaratne madam that Dr Rao is here. Not fully awake, he said, 'There is no rules for the girls to exit at this hour.' He shook him out of his sleep fully and got him going. Karunaratne came with him. 'Come, let's stroll for a while,' said Rao.

'Let me lock the door of the room.'

Karuna returned after securing her door. They headed for Kukkarahalli tank together. Karuna initiated the conversation, 'What is this, at this hour?'

'I couldn't get sleep all night. Aren't you leaving for your country today!'

She didn't say anything. She just extended her hand and held his. She recalled his words from their earlier outing to Brindavan gardens. Walking silently, they arrived at the bund of the Kukkarahalli tank. Coming to a halt by an arbour, Karuna said, 'How far should we keep walking? Let's sit here.'

It was not yet dawn. Entire Mysore was calm. Even the tank before them was serenely planar, with no waves whatsoever. Neither could think of anything to speak about. After a while, Rao said, 'You were awake at that early hour!'

'I, too, couldn't get sleep all night,' she said, and firmly squeezed his hand that was in hers. It was her dense reticence that had barraged the sadness within her. But the import of the words she just uttered got dense from memories of her agony of the previous night, and a cry billowed from within her. Consoling her, Rao held her in an embrace. Karuna lowered her head onto his thighs.

Their acquaintance of three years had brought them intimately close. They had even become conscious of the reciprocal call of their inner minds. Their lives had chosen the same purpose and direction. They both had, at times, swayed from discussion about their study to exchange intimate feelings.

Fully grasping Karuna's mind, Rao asked, 'What will you do after going back home?'

'You know it!' she said, and after a moment's silence, she asked, 'But you should soon take to penning the second volume.'

'It can't progress without you.'

'Don't say so. You would have penned the first even if I hadn't joined you. I served you as a clerk would. Employ a typist.' She went silent for a while and then said, 'Even without me, your tome will see compilation. But my mind says that without you, even the little capability in me shall not find worthy expression. But I have no choice.'

By then, crows heralded dawn. Darkness began clearing up. 'Get up, let's go,' Karuna pulled him by his arm. By the time they reached the hostel it was 6 am. As she was about to enter the main gate of the hostel, Rao said, 'The train is at 7:30, if you have to pack, go on. I will wait for you here and escort you to the railway station.'

'I am done with packing. Be on the lookout for a tonga. It is better I start right away. Well-wishers may drop in at the eleventh hour.'

They reached the railway station by 6:30. The train had parked by then. They got a porter to haul the luggage into a second-class car and sat in it. There was no one else in their cabin. For a while, nobody spoke. She broke the impasse. 'The printing of the first volume is likely to commence in one and half months. Write to the publisher this very day, asking them to send the dummy to my address for proofing and indexing.'

They discussed some about the second volume too. By then, a few others had occupied their seats in the cabin, and these two took to chatting something generic. A little later the gong was heard, signaling departure of the train. Rao alighted and stationed himself on the platform by the window of the train. Karuna hurried after him and prostrated at his feet. The guard blew the whistle. Karuna re-boarded. The train began rolling. Holding Karuna's hand through the window grills, Rao paced alongside the moving the train. The train gained speed and their hands parted, inducing tears from Karuna's eyes.

2

Rao took to studying for the second volume. As usual, he would report at the library at 9 am and work till late in the evening. But now that he was at it alone, the earlier enthusiasm was absent. Looking for reference books, making systematic notes, etc., which Karuna attended to earlier, now became additional burden. And these preparatory works formed a good part of the whole exercise time-wise. One Honnaiah, who had pursued PhD under his guidance, taught in the same college now. Rao tried soliciting his assistance, but that man was interested neither in studies nor in research. Having landed a good career and newly married, he was inclined to always making merry with his wife. There was none who had the abilities of Karuna viz. scholasticism, grasp over English language, knowledge of Sanskrit and Prakrit, shorthand and typing, and enthusiasm in work. Even if there were one, why would they oblige Rao?

Still, Rao kept up with his research systematically. He received letters from Karuna intimating him that the London publisher was regularly sending to her prints of the first volume in parts. Eventually, Rao heard from the publisher that printing was done, and that he was to send the preface. He penned it, wherein he unequivocally expressed his sincere thanks to the patronage by His Highness, and also, the exemplary assistance accorded by Karuna to this volume.

The volume was released within a month. It was the first of the volumes for which Rao had channelled his flesh, blood and intellect, and it was the outcome of his innermost aspirations. The hard cover was of black colour, the title was *Cultural History of India: Volume 1*, and his name was displayed in golden letters below it. When he received his copy, he swelled with glee. He avowed in his mind to 'complete the remaining volumes before I pass on'. He sent Karuna a copy on the same day. He wrote to His Highness' secretary that he aspired to personally hand over a copy to Maharaja Krishnaraja Wadiyar. The secretary replied that the Maharaja was presently indisposed, and that he would revert without fail after he recovered. Fourth day thence, the newspapers carried news of his demise.

Rao's subconscious would stay reassured all the while that his task had the backing of a noble blessing hand. That authority was now no more though. He was put into consternation as to who to look up to if obstacles surfaced. He volunteered to speak at the condolence meeting that was held in the college. It was the first time that all the students of the college and the newly appointed lecturers saw him in person. Before he was done with recounting the virtues of the departed Lord, Dr Rao had wiped his tears twice.

After the publication of the first volume of his tome, Rao's renown gained on in literary circles in the university. Many a professor thought it worthwhile to meet with Dr Rao during leisure hours and discuss a point with him. They inculcated the gentility of enquiring about the progress of his second volume. About the same time, the history professor of the college retired, and Rao had to serve as the department head. Still, he hardly left his cabin in the library.

As the days passed, the need for Karuna became more and more acute for Dr Rao. No researcher would be able to take to the primary tasks of cogitating and discoursing, if he also had to attend to the umpteen peripheral tasks, and successfully see through an accomplished research. Though six months passed by, not even a little of the groundwork for the compilation of the second volume could be undertaken. Time was being used up just for referencing and notes-making. Besides, owing to the non-availability of a cohort who would lend a keen ear to his exposition on the topics and actively discuss his inferences, his situation became akin to a lone voyager in a desert.

What is the point in reminiscing her, when there wasn't the possibility of her returning here? Telling himself that he should take to working independently, he attempted at applying his mind to his task. But the need for Karuna was not just for running the errands of a clerk; it wasn't even just the need for an erudite companion. Matching the teeming potential of his life that he channelled into his tome was the drive and conviction of Karuna in channelling her heart and soul into it. He would feel that a progress propelled just by his own potential was insipid sans the pith of her complementary resoluteness.

By then, Karuna's dissertation was awarded by the university. She was not only awarded the PhD, but the examiners recommended that the thesis be published. He wrote to her. After intimating the good news, he wrote:

> In your last letter you have enquired about the progress of my work. I am 38 now. I already have problems with my sight in the murky darkness of the night. I have been reading incessantly from the age of 16. I hope God continues to bless me with eyesight till the completion of these volumes. Without you to assist me, all my time is consumed by referencing and other peripheral work. The first volume that was allocated five years could be completed in three years, thanks to your cooperation. Many an international scholarly journal has published rave reviews about it. My confidence in being able to attend to the remaining four volumes all by myself is dwindling. Until I live on, I will stretch myself to accomplish it. Rest is God's will. Please let me know what you are keeping yourself engaged in.

Karuna's reply came within a week.

> Though my PhD is a result of my work, the credit for it goes to you. It could merit such distinction owing to your midas touch. If I land an opportunity to visit there, I will first place that certificate at your feet before taking possession of it.
>
> I, too, read the reviews of the first volume. I felt pride. In the preface, you have praised my service excessively. My service

was for my own contentment. But it is the flame of your erudition that lights up every sentence of the book. Nobody can grasp this better than I do.

You have asked what I am engaged in. Nothing actually. My mother passed away two months back. The grief from bereavement persists. Bereft of a partner who can humour me by kindling my spirits, I am leading a life of quiescence on this island. At times, I fancy that if you were a Sinhala and my native place were your domicile, or I were a Mysorean and lived there, I would have worked incessantly for our book. I could not get myself to refer to it as 'your book' and hence I said 'our book'. It is truly a terrible experience for a soul that has seen light to revert to gloom.

Keep those letters coming.

3

When she took leave of her guru and left for her home, Karuna was no doubt enthusiastic about reunion with her mother, father and brother, but greater was the tribulation caused by separation from her guru forever. There was no alternative for her than returning to her country.

Back in her place, the arrears of confabulation with her family members engaged her for two days. Now, there were those two children of her brother. She could while away some more time playing with them. Then on, she could put up with it no more. Now that she had earned her PhD, her parents began compelling her to get married. She made it categorically clear that they are not to bring up that proposition again, for she did not wish to marry. Her mother would not even be placated by her declaration that she would discern a teaching career at a university.

Commencing the 15th day of her return, the dummies of the first volume started arriving. For about two months, she was busy with proofing, indexing, etc. She aspired for Rao to witness her work regularly and appreciate it. Fifteen days later, her mother passed away. In the grief of bereavement, her interest in studies waned. For about a month, she kept weeping from grief. Realizing that she could not rein in her grief if she did not take to studies, she procured history books from the library of the local college and took to reading them. That caused her mind to coast to Mysore! Her mind went into cogitation: *shall I write to him that, if not for anything else, I shall move to Mysore just to serve as his research assistant? Or, can't I land a teaching career in Mysore?* Unless she shed the lassitude that ailed her soul, and engaged in an avocation commensurate with her intrinsic constitution, she couldn't live in peace. While she continued to be assailed by such feelings, she received a letter from Rao.

> I am writing this to you after going through one hell of a mental turbulence. I believe that at least *you* will not regard the aptness, or otherwise, of this as would commoners. Our relationship has not remained one of teacher-pupil. We are two souls that are set out for a distinguished task.

> It would serve to say that we are two devotees who, by way of invoking a common Goddess, endeavour to submit our lives in her service. In this worship, there is the need to channel both our crusades. While one chants the mantras, the other enchants with the wherewithal. While one goes about the rituals, the other makes arrangements to provide flowers, sandal, camphor and other necessary paraphernalia. Through such concordant worship, our unified supplication may attain its objective unobstructed.
>
> There, don't let yourself suffer by suppressing the call of your soul. Here, let me not suffer from helplessness. Start for here the moment you see this letter. You may think up a pretext of some research to be done here. Do not seek your family members' support for your livelihood here. The publishers have remitted to me half the royalty of the first volume. It is the kind of money that would provide sustenance to you for about four years. If you are not game for this arrangement, let us wed. Out of this matrimony, let us beget—before I pass on—the progeny we aspire for viz. the volumes of the tome. Do not reply. Just start.

The last few lines caused profuse perspiration in her. Many a time the two had conversed intimately; more intimately than would a very loving married couple. On the eve of her departure from Mysore, he had held her in an embrace at the arbour on the bund of the Kukkarahalli tank. She had lain with her head on his thigh. On all these instances, the question of propriety had never arisen in her mind; neither had consciousness as to what the external world would make of it. In all those moments, what she had noticed was a scholar who took to wade lonesome in *Oceani Eruditionem*, and who sought her nurturing. Even now he was a loner. He was in need of her nurturing more than before. But the proposal to unify in the spirit of marriage engendered some doubts in her mind. He was a family man, with a wife and son. She wasn't unaware of his feelings towards his wife. Still, she thought, it wasn't right on her part to intrude into that woman's marriage. Never had she cogitated this issue from the ethics point of view; not even now. It was just a sociological question. It was a question just of the affability of a woman who served her man with all faith and devotion despite his mounting indifference towards her. When she considered if it was right for her to wed him by unseating that woman, she recalled that the bonding intimacy had been desiccate in that couple for quite some years now.

She also gave it a thought as to whether they could stay in a common house as rival wives. But Karuna was a modern woman; Cambridge educated. Her modernistic mind always abhorred bigamy. Just as it is unimaginable for a woman to lead a conjugal life with two men concurrently, there is no possibility of one man leading a conjugal life with two women concurrently. *Between me and his current wife, only one can be his mate. For sure, he does not have intimate relations with his current wife. Considering that the bond that links her to him is too weak already, would she be deprived of anything at all if I were to marry him?*

Now, that was a complex postulate, the satisfactory resolution of which was beyond her ability. The more she thought about it, the more her head reeled. Besides, neither her father nor her brother would concur with her desire to move out of her country and marry a man who already had a lawfully wedded wife, belonged to a different religion, and was resident of a foreign country. She was not inclined to proposition this to them either, and add to their agony from bereavement consequent to the death of her mother. She just said to her father: 'You are aware of my proclivity. I have to engage in serious study if I have to overcome the memory of mother's death. The professor has written to me, informing me of the possibility of a study scholarship. I am taking it up and going there.'

Her father did not immediately consent. Even her brother did not take a liking to it, but he was convinced of his sister's proclivity and conviction. Eventually, the brother consented, and the father followed suit. At the moment of departure, when she touched at the feet of her father, there were tears in her eyes. Moved, he blessed her, 'May you find peace of mind, child.' Her brother accompanied her to the railway station. With a heavy heart, he said, 'It is not late for you to enter wedlock. When you feel like it, don't hesitate to let me know. I will look for a suitable groom.'

She touched at his feet, and as she boarded the train, her mind silently averred, 'I'll probably not return to this land.'

CHAPTER 10

1

After she acted in a play, Katyayani's name became well-known in the entire college. Every visitor to the girls' lounge met up with her and introduced themselves. But Katyayani continued to be solemn as before, wherefore those girls could not get intimate with her. Barring Vasanti who was her companion last year, nobody ever came as close to her as to be called a friend. But she got acquainted with quite a few.

The play titled *The Primordial* was performed in August. It was the beginning of the academic year, and no one was interested in classroom sessions. It was over a period of one month that Katyayani had taken to memorizing her dialogues. After the show, she took to her mainstream studies. Her mind would, every now and then, hum the script of the play that was ingrained into her memory. When she took to reading the textbooks, pages would turn over, but she grasped none of it. On the stage of her mind, the acts of the play would roll out in detail.

Not able to concentrate on her studies, Katyayani would come down the stairs to the ground floor. Her father-in-law would be in the puja chamber, and the mantras being chanted by him would have the ring of the gong of a bell. With that in her ears, the dialogues of the play would fade in memory. Bhageerathamma would be engaged in cooking in the kitchen, chatting with Cheeni. If she spotted Katyayani, she would say, 'Leave the cooking to me. You got to prepare for your tests. Stick to your study.' Knowing well that there was no point in returning to her desk, she would head for the backyard garden.

One morning, Katyayani was in the backyard. The newly planted plantain shoots had grown fine. The resplendence of greenery shone forth in other plants as well. The backyard sward was charged with green and caused her mind to swell. What caught her attention especially was the jasmine creeper. The new Indian coral shoot's roots were well entrenched into the earth, and buds appeared. The youngish climbing fingers of the jasmine clung to the tender arms of the Indian coral. From the east, the Sun's rays beamed everywhere. In that full illumination, the jasmine was silently unto herself, embracing her patron firmly. Ebullience, bliss and grace throbbed from her very silence. She wondered what would be in the nerves of a jasmine. She gently felt a creeper. Not at all affected by pseudo-stigma typical of the outer world, it revelled in the bounty of life's typical core disposition. Flowers revealed their smiling faces from the nooks of the leaves. Despite harvesting the flowers daily, the plant yielded quite a lot of them.

The script of the play clearly resonated in her inner ears. *Devaguru, isn't it anti-dharmic to impose contrived dharma on Nature that is evergreen and ever-zestful? Brimming with zest is my intrinsic character. No dharma would, by imposition of widowhood, vitiate the vegetation that appeals to the mind, the eye-catching panorama, and my seamless expanse that provides sustenance to all souls.*

Until now, Katyayani had just grasped the lexical meaning of these words. Now as she stood before the jasmine creeper, she could experience the feel at their base. Her entire body once shuddered as the import of that feel sunk in her. She found herself appreciating Raja's creativity... *What an eternal truth that playwright has depicted!* Soon, his face appeared in her mind's eye. Recalling that he had held her hand in the greenroom immediately after the show, she felt mild goosebumps. She also recalled that the VC, who spoke later, addressed her by prefixing her name with a 'Ms'—a title for maidens. She was wholly assailed by an inexplicable feeling, and the shudder doubled. Unable to bear it, she slumped to the ground; she did not know how long she sat there.

She was in a semiconscious state of mind when she heard her mother-in-law call out to her, 'Why are you sitting here? It is time for lunch, come eat.'

She went in, but could not really eat much. As usual, she took her bag and lunchbox, went to the railway station and boarded the train. While the train chugged on, she could think of nothing other than the evergreen nature. The river that the train came up against, the lush vegetation on its banks and the fields that were swaying with the standing crops were all redolent of the ebullience of nature. The Chamundi hill yonder appeared like a wonder woman, wearing a green sari. A curling cloud that floated in the sky appealed to her as a lover boy bound towards that wonder woman.

Raja Rao, who lectured them on *Macbeth* last year, was to teach them English poetry this year. The first classroom session of English poetry was underway, and the poem taken up for study was John Keats' *The Eve of Saint Agnes*. Such was the involvement of Raja Rao in reciting and elucidating it that the hearts of those who were able to grasp it creatively were served to a riot of vibrant feelings. The entire classroom was in rapt attention, and pin drop silence prevailed. Katyayani reflected that the description therein was, in fact, an expression of the prime spirit of nature. That day, she could not make notes. Her gaze was fixed on Raja Rao, who was elucidating the poem with gusto. Not just she, the entire class was engrossed in him. On his part, though Raja Rao was eyeing the students by turns as was typical of lecturers, he would at intervals glance at Katyayani with marked attention. Today especially, he glanced in her direction more frequently than usual, and his sight would linger on her for a lengthy second. Unable to withstand that gaze, though she would lower her sight to the book on her desk, a mellifluous impulse would cause her neck to gently crane and steal a glance at him.

2

Raja and Nagalakshmi had grown up together. She was first a childhood friend to him, and later a sister-in-law. After he secured his MA and landed a career, many a solicitous matrimonial proposal came his way. Nagalakshmi nursed her own selfish thought that such wedding would provide her with a companion. But Raja had not conceded. He was intent on earning a scholarship to visit England. Confident of landing such opportunity eventually, he had put matrimony on the backburner. And when he eventually landed that opportunity, Nagalakshmi desired that he wed before leaving for England, but her husband—Raja's elder brother—had not concurred. While in England, for a while he even chose to decry the veracity of the institution of marriage. Returning to Mysore, ever since he began teaching at the college, many a father of brides sought him out. His brother was not for forcing a marriage on one who was disinclined. In fact, considering the solitariness of his own research pursuit, and his own loneliness despite being married, he had honoured his brother's decision to remain single. He had clearly stated that he would come around if and when his brother had a change of mind and decided on a bride. A few avant-garde girls who hung around the theatre association were on their toes to propose to him in matrimony; he knew of it too. But none of them could get him attracted towards them. He suavely saw to it that none of them brought it up before him.

By now, his mind was completely focused on Katyayani. The image of her face was imprinted on the screen of his eyes. Immersed in thoughts about her, he would not get proper sleep at nights. He lost his appetite. His interest in the plays of the theatre association was diminishing too. If she were a maiden, he would have laid bare his mind before her by now. But her situation unsettled him. When he got to know that she sort of evinced special interest in him, he felt a bit assured. He reflected that he should somehow break this impasse and arrive at one or other resolution.

One day, he accosted her in college and asked, 'Tomorrow you are attending college, right?'

Something was amiss, but only for a moment. She recalled, 'Isn't tomorrow a holiday?'

'Still, come. I've got to discuss an important matter with you. I will be in the theatre association room. We can discuss undisturbed.'

'May I know what the matter is?'

'It is not as trivial as to be broached here,' he said smiling, but firmly.

The next morning, he was in the theatre association room well before 10 am. His mind was fidgety, and an unknown anxiety rent his mind. He gave enough thought as to how he should broach the matter, and aptly at that, but he could think up nothing. As he decided to go about it on the spur, Katyayani appeared in the doorway. As usual, she carried the books and her lunch box. 'Come in,' he said, getting up. But she vacillated by the threshold for a while.

When he called her in again, she entered and sat on a chair. Without uttering even a single word, she sat silently, but as if she was in anticipation of a definite proposition. After a few tentative attempts, he went off at on tangent! 'What time does the train you commute in arrives here?'

'10 am.'

That was Act one. He thought up a script for the next. 'You have gone thin of late.'

She lifted her head and looked at him. He laughed at the irrelevance of his words. She laughed in endorsement of it. Then shedding vacillation, he said in all seriousness, 'Let us not beat around the bush. Do you know what I intend to tell you?'

'No.'

'Then you are lying. Yet, it is okay. You and I aren't teacher and pupil any more. Though we have not expressed it vocally, we both know about it, right?'

She chose to be silent. He continued, 'I had planned never to marry, but that decision now stands squashed.'

Katyayani perspired mildly on hearing that. Though it was not unexpected, her mind was swept away by excitement, awe and glee. A hidden feeling now came to the forefront. The peculiarity of the situation had not appeared to her in all its compelling clarity till now. Her child, her parents-in-law, and memories of her husband surfaced in her mind all at once. It was in this moment that she severely experienced the duality of her situation.

'Why are you silent?'

'Are you fully aware of my situation?'

'Fully. I know that you have a kid too. I have seen it all in England; widowed women with kids from an earlier marriage marrying again. Those kids live with their mother. Your first child is my child too. I will never neglect him.'

He had addressed the very issue of dilemma that she wanted to broach. But that was not the whole of her dilemma. She said, 'There are my mother-in-law and father-in-law. I can't help giving a thought as to the reverence to their lineage, the respect commanded by them in their domicile and such.'

'Katyayani, these are no novel issues, and neither is it you who is thinking it up for the first time.' He looked her in the face. Her sight held promise for him to take her into confidence. He continued, 'The question of family status is at the base of all adversities that show up in our lives. Is that not what I have depicted in my play, *The Primordial*?'

Katyayani remained silent. Taking it as her consent, he neared her, held her hands and said, 'What do you say? One should not perpetrate injustice on the basic disposition of one's mind. It would suffice for you to fully understand this.'

She did not withdraw her hands. Notwithstanding that, she remained silent, a tempest of a conjecture howling within her. Confounded by it, she could not think of anything to say. In a while, it subsided. He now squeezed her hands, 'Let me have your response.'

'I can't live without you,' she said.

Tranquil descended on both minds. As if the meeting of two tempests nullified each other, they felt contentment. They kept on conversing till 1 pm. Then Katyayani said that she wished to see Nagalakshmi. 'Don't share this with sister-in-law right away,' he said, locked the door of the room, and joined her on her way to his house.

All day, her mind was gleeful. All through the train journey, Nature seemed to beam in delight. The beauty of Nature, which hitherto was just an expression of exuberance sans actualization of comeliness, now acquired a novel meaning. The time for the insipid green to hold a promise of fructification was here.

But when she retired after supper that night, her mind made a U-turn. As she was to face exams this year, Katyayani had shifted to the upper floor to engage in reading until sleep came. Cheeni slept with his grandmother downstairs; Lakshmi too. All of sudden Katyayani recalled the make-up of her mind when she first resolved to resume her academics. She had convinced her mother- and father-in-law that she only aspired to accomplish the unfinished academics of her husband. When she started for college on the first day, she had prostrated at the feet of her in-laws; they had appreciated her intent and had blessed her in memory of their son. The nascence of an incident that was way apart from that resolve pricked her mind now. Her father-in-law had given her money enough for expenses such as fee, books, train fare, etc. Of late, he even let her handle the financials of the farm and the household. Four-year-old Cheeni was to start his kindergarten in the coming academic year. The one desire to remarry was pitted against all these, and she thought of it as unethical. She reflected that her decision of that day was crime against her father-in-law, mother-in-law, child and late husband.

Greatly disturbed, she decided that commencing tomorrow she would not meet with Raja Rao, and would not even go to see Nagalakshmi. At exactly midnight, she climbed down the stairs, went to the bathroom, washed her feet, went to the puja chamber and prostrated before God. As she climbed the stairs, Srotri—who was in the living room, reading something—asked her, 'Why child? Sleepless?'

'I had gone to prostrate before God.'

'Well then, go retire. One shouldn't skip sleep.'

She climbed up to her study.

Noticing her father-in-law's interest in study, she resolved within herself that after the exams, she would get tutored in the Bhagavadgīta and Upanishads by him and study them daily.

3

For one full week, she didn't see Raja; didn't even attend his classes. Fearing that he would send for her in the girls' lounge, she did not even go there. For one week, she experienced a peculiar torture. At times, an irresistible craving to just walk up to him and talk would spurt from within her mind. But she would rein it in with a resolve that was greater in potency. Now, she never gave a thought to the Nature around. The inert Nature had taken to bustling, and her mind became the rostrum for the turbulence. The mandates of the concepts of *dharma*, society and ethics proliferated deep unto her. To tag along the lead of inquisition as to whether these beliefs were default per custom or as to whether they were the very construct of the inner atman, and to thereafter arrive at the truth was beyond the capability of her intellect. Besides, her mental composure was unseated by those conflicting forces.

One entire night, she could not get sleep. Musings about *dharma* and *karma* rendered her mind vacuous. The exhorting of her innermost mind nullified everything else. She got up late night, posted herself by the window and looked out. In the environs that seemed to be sanctified from ablution by milky moonlight, the resplendent jasmine creeper clung to the new Indian coral plant. She watched it till 3 am. By then, her father-in-law was awake. Exiting the back door, he headed for the Gundala stream. Katyayani continued to be seated by the window. She even heard him return and go into the bathroom.

She spent the next two hours with much discomfort, and then went downstairs. On that sleepless night, she arrived at a decision. She bathed and wore a fresh sari. Taking a basket, she went to the backyard to pluck the royal jasmine flowers. She strung them into a long thin string. Rolling it in a plantain leaf, she tied it in her handkerchief. After lunch, when she left for college, Cheeni's words—'Amma, come back choon'—were not clearly audible to her. Though the train rolled at its usual speed, she cursed if for its sloth, alighted at Chamarajapura and went to college. It was still 10:15 am; Raja's session was at 10:30. Surmising that he would have arrived by now, she walked up to the lecturers' room and asked the sentry to call Raja Rao. Exiting, Raja was thrilled to see her. 'All these days…' She cut him out and said, 'Apply for leave of absence today. Let's lose ourselves for a while and chat up.'

'Wait for me behind the college. I will join you in two minutes,' he said and went in.

Shortly, he turned up there, pushing his bicycle. They both headed in the direction of Hunsur road. When they passed beneath the luxurious tree behind the Kukkarahalli tank, he asked, 'Why did you dodge me all these days?'

'Ask nothing now. Keep moving. I will share everything with you. I will not commit that mistake again.'

With green fields on either side, the road was bordered on both sides by huge trees. Despite trekking for about half an hour, they still came up against pedestrians. Then he said, 'Sit on the bicycle. We can go faster. A little farther, it will be desolate.'

'I am not used to it. If I fall!'

'As long as you are in my grip, there is no question of you falling,' he looked at her face and smiled. Though she vacillated that someone would watch, he held her hand, seated her on the bar and began pedalling. At once, Katyayani was given to experience several complex feelings. His arms made contact with both her shoulders as he held the handle. As he alternately bent forward in consonance with pedalling, he felt as if she leaned against his chest. A few passersby watched them curiously. 'How far shall we ride thus?' he asked her.

'Let us ride till we die.'

A mile later, they arrived by a village. Passing that, they came up against a thicket of ficus trees, and a small tank a little later. They rode about four to five miles further. Presently, they were by a stream and there wasn't a soul around. Alighting by the bridge, he pushed his bicycle through the copse. After two furlongs' trek, they arrived at the bank of the stream. They were now surrounded by small trees and the place was truly desolate. Laying the bicycle to the ground, Raja said, 'Let's sit.'

Katyayani sat on the grass. Sitting by her side, Raja asked, 'Now tell me why you dodged me all these days.'

Sighing deeply, she said, 'My mind was assailed by a torturous dichotomy. Last night, I shook free of it.'

He took hold of her hands and asked, 'Does some of the dichotomy persist?'

'When you take me under your protection, there will be none of it. Please hold me firmly forever so that it never comes back.'

His eyes sailed in the direction of the handkerchief in which she had packed something. 'What is that?' he asked, despite knowing what it was by its aroma.

'I brought it for you,' she said, opened it and held the string before his eyes. She extended her arm to garland him. The way she sat, the sari she wore, and the floral string in her hands were captured in a snap as if his eyes were camera.

'You shall surely garland me, but hold on for a moment,' he said and rooted his gaze in her.

Katyayani was a beautiful woman. Twenty-three years of age, she was very captivating. Her body was aglow with health. When she set foot, her feet would go cerise from the profusion of blood. Her complexion was the personification of moonlight. Her fingers were slender; their beauty being the type that was depicted in paintings. She wore no ornaments whatsoever. Her hair were long and lustrous black; at the tip, they were curly. Though solemn, her face was gentle. Feminine exuberance issued forth from her body parts, graceful all.

Amazed, he regarded her closely.

'What is this gaping?'

'Plain wonder! I had told you that I based *The Primordial* on a dream that I had. In that dream, you were in this same posture! I was witness to these same enticing arms, stature and quintessence. In your hands was such a garland, but that was of red roses. You had appeared before me completely nude. Now you are draped in this white sari.'

Katyayani hung her head in coyness. After half a minute she asked, 'Was I the inspiration for that play?'

'Now I know for sure that it was you.'

'Why didn't you tell me that it was me that appeared in your dream?'

'We weren't this intimate then.'

Raja still beheld her. She garlanded him and closed her eyes. He held her close by her shoulders so that she made contact with his thighs, and embraced her smugly. The trees around shone forth with the resplendence of glaucous greenery. The stream that drifted along was symbolic of ardent zest. The royal jasmine garland around his neck elated their hearts to unfathomable heights. He mildly trembled from the intimate feel of a young woman. À la Nature enthused by soul, the prime force of her quintessence frolicked, and aroused her from her lackadaisical state. Regarding her beauty with half drawn eyes, he said, 'Natura.'

'Is nature a widow?'

'It is anti-dharmic to impose contrived dharma on Nature that is evergreen and ever-zestful.'

The script of the play that had found way into her heart surfaced in memory. Swayed by the mood of those words, she said, 'Brimming with zest is my intrinsic character. What *dharma* may, by imposing widowhood, vitiate the vegetation that appeals to the mind, the eye-catching panorama and the stream coursing here?'

They both ceased conversing, and lost themselves in silence charged with exuberance. The afternoon sun was West-bound. Then, without removing the garland, he put it around her neck too. As they shared a single garland, he said, 'Has the duality deep within you ceased now?'

She was in a state of reticence that transcended words. He lifted her face by the chin and asked, 'Tell me, is your mind mollified now?'

Sighing placidly, she said in a tone of having summarized the meaning of her experience, 'I have thought it all out much.

The dichotomy was never my basic disposition. Even before marital communion had gone through its full complement, when a situation arises wherein such communion is handed a setback, wouldn't one be affected by dichotomy? Now that I have expressed it, you may think of me as a shameless one!'

'No. Go on.'

'There are myriad obstacles to women's entitlements. They are all artificially enunciated by the men. Many a time these obstacles don't have the strength to put up with the prime force of the female. They then go on to invade the male's mind and sow many a fear and phobia. Some facets of the female are stigmatized, and we are deprived of male companionship. Anyways, isn't the male weaker than us?'

'Does that apply to me too?'

'No. Hence we have come together. Pray, will you ever take refuge under artificial obstacles and be at loggerheads with me?'

'Being at loggerheads is not typical of me.'

It was a state of transcendence of time and space, and they both attained their purest states with no anxiety whatsoever. In that kingdom of green, there was no trace of regimentation that cried foul of their unison.

4

Katyayani got a good night's sleep that night. Her mind, which of late had become a battlefield, was now a beautiful coliseum. That day onwards, she would meet with Raja every day. One day, she announced special classes and left home early to catch the 7 am train. That was a goods train that had just two cars for passengers. There was no exclusive car for women. Some farmers boarded the car she did. The abounding greenery seemed to be even more resplendent that morning. The entire world appealed to Katyayani as if it were merrymaking from happiness. The density of passengers in the car did not irritate her. Even the smoke exhaled by passengers' beedis didn't bother her. His eyes on the fields outside the window, one farmer averred, 'Finger millet crop this season is bountiful.'

'The seedlings are luxuriant alright, but there is need for more rains. If the earth and sky don't come together often, crops will suffer. Seems like it will rain today; clouds are pervading,' responded an experienced elderly farmer next to him.

Katyayani's ears picked up the elderly man's words. She saw out the window. The crops were in their prime, and were thirsty for irrigation. The earth was parched and was looking up to the skies for rain showers. The entire environ seemed to be yearning for the sight of water for quite some time. The farmer was heard saying, 'Feeling sultry. Rains may pound.'

Katyayani did not alight at Chamarajapura. She went straight to the main station. There was a train at 8:30 am to Arasikere. Raja awaited her there with two tickets. Typical of long-distance travellers, he held a holdall and a leather bag. He was wearing a suit with a tie. They both boarded the shuttle train and alighted at Kannambadi. Her books found their way into his leather bag. They hired a coolie for carrying the bags and headed for the big hotel in Brindavan. Raja paid advance and checked in as Madrasis. They then followed the porter to a well-appointed room.

By the time they had their breakfast, it was 9:45 am. It was already too hot outside. Clouds had overcast in a section of the sky. Due to the atmospheric temperature, Raja and Katyayani found themselves sweltering. The fan spinning on the ceiling was of no consequence. The vast earth outside had also heated up, and impatiently awaited the downpour. Vegetation that had lent grace to the very earth on which it had grown was now on the verge of withering due to lack of nutrition from the roots. It is not in the nature of earth to indent for rains. By then, the entire sky was overcast with clouds. Gradually, the density of the clouds increased to such an extent that it engendered fear in the minds of onlookers that if such quantum of skies were to thaw at once and descend on earth, the resultant flood would wash away the entire green covering of the earth and expose her grotesque form. On their part, the clouds stayed from descending, and simply hovered in one place as if from hesitation or primness. It was September now; earth had received adequate rains this season. It had basked in succulence to its fullest satisfaction. No sooner was the rainy season past than it looked up to the skies for rains again. But the clouds that had gathered now were virgin formations that were gearing up to shower their first.

Though it didn't have the strength to bear its own weight, it didn't have the experience of having showered on earth any time before either. Confounded and confused, the clouds had become inactive from the anxiety of being unable to comprehend their own novel interim state.

The sweltering heat that seemed to desiccate the whole world caused Raja and Katyayani to gasp for breath. Rain was *needed* now. Else, this heat would not abate. Katyayani sat like a mute one; Raja looked out the window. The clouds still wavered from indecision; they seemed to get dense and lightning flashed. The clouds' own dazzle would have brought to its notice the beauty of Nature as well as its craving for water. The entire set of clouds seemed to plummet to the earth at once. All ambivalence being swept away by the raging potency of water, and decisiveness serving as the impetus, the clouds embraced the earth. Rain poured incessantly, and characteristic of it this time was the absence of the havoc of lightning, of the ravings of thunder and thunderbolt, and of the onslaught of storm that threatened to carry away the decisiveness of the clouds.

By the time the rain ceased, it was afternoon. By the time Raja and Katyayani helped themselves to a late lunch, the simmering heat dissipated to make way for coolness that enchanted the mind. A distant breeze brought with it the aroma of moist earth. Such was the tranquility of the environment that while they lunched, neither wanted to converse. The green cover of earth received a fresh lease of life. By the time they finished their lunch, clouds were recasting. But the clouds that converged now were not new ones. The earlier ones that remained after thawing were gathering and getting dense. Absent was the unbearable heat that preceded the showers. It started to drizzle in serenity. Her craving for pounding downpour satiated, the earth now welcomed the soft caress of the drizzle. Notwithstanding the dark grey that prevailed, the sky was faintly aglow.

It was no more raining when Raja and Katyayani left for the railway station at 4 pm. Carrying the holdall and the bag, the porter walked ahead. Earth's face shone from the refreshing succulence it had just received. Sunshine surfaced; clouds cleared. It was 5 pm by the time they arrived at Mysore station. Katyayani boarded the Nanjangud train that was about to leave. Raja took leave of her saying, 'See you in college tomorrow.' She nodded assent. No words formed.

CHAPTER 11

1

Rao was in his cabin, and was attending to his studies as usual. The cabin was now stocked with more books. He would borrow a book he needed, and that would be the end of it. Storing them in an organized way or returning them duly was not in his disposition. If he wanted to refer to a particular book urgently, he had no choice but to tediously search for it from among the heap.

It had been about a fortnight since he'd written to Karuna; there was no reply from her yet. He thought that she might not come at all. The more he thought about it, the more his mind got stuck on her. His longing for her was aggravating by the day, and he craved for her to just appear this very moment.

One day, he was reclined on the armchair in a state of emptiness. His aptitude for work had dissipated. Holding his spectacles in his left hand, he had his eyes glued to the spinning fan, and was in a cadaver state. The sound of the flap door opening behind him didn't even register in his conscious. It was when the caller neared him that he heard the sound of it in retrospect. He lifted his eyes. Karuna was here! The Karuna that used to work with him then was now before him in her usual white sari and white blouse. 'You came!' said Rao cheerfully, and got up. 'Yes, I have,' she said, pulled a chair and sat close to him.

For five minutes he did not know what to say. His mind was brimming with delight. He just extended an arm and held her hand. Speaking nothing, she firmly held his hand with both her hands too. 'Where is your luggage?' he eventually asked.

'I have deposited it in the railway station cloak room.'

'Let's go make staying arrangements for you in the ladies' hostel.'

'No, I won't stay at a hostel.'

'Of course,' he said, and went silent. For a while, he did not know what to think of. He just said, 'Come, let's first have lunch.'

They both went to the restaurant at the Hindu Hotel. It was still half past midday. Though he had lunched at home, he still ate with Karuna. Lunch done, they returned to the library. After the mandatory enquiries, he asked, 'What are you thinking?'

'Nothing exclusively mine. I only aspire to derive self-satisfaction by working with you. Everything else is up to you.'

'First, let us wed.'

Reining in her voice and biting her lips, Karuna said, 'What if we don't?'

'I, too, thought so. We are not entering wedlock for the purpose that the world is familiar with. How long can we carry on thus? We will be spending our entire lives together. How many days will you stay in a hostel? If you take to residing in a separate house, how will I visit there with no social arrangement whatsoever? How would it even be possible for you to work here all day with me? What would people think of us? Even the university would not hesitate to accuse us of immorality. We can stymie them all by sporting the social proviso called marriage.'

'Won't people cry foul of your act, considering that you already are married?'

'For all of four days. Even if people were to cry foul for those four days, they will dare not shove us into the gorge of immorality. We can take to our task with renewed commitment.'

Karuna's musings were almost on the same lines; she agreed. She wanted to ask him if he had discussed this with his wife, but thinking that it was exclusively up to him, she decided against bringing up an interim situation.

They went to the railway station, retrieved her luggage, went to the Hindu Hotel, rented a single room and dumped her luggage there. Rao paid the rent in advance, and informed the manager that a lone researcher was here to stay for one month. By the time they were back at the library, it was 5 pm.

Noticing the heaps of books, Karuna asked, 'What is this disarray? Well, I will arrange them now in my own order. I am here now to fetch you the required book and zoom in on the required section of any book whatsoever anyway.' She went into work mode right away.

'You are spent from the journey, please take rest,' said Rao, to which she said in letter and spirit, 'All these days, my health has suffered from not working. It is convalescence for me now on.' She got engrossed in her work. Rao found himself abandoned.

2

Though Rao resolved within himself not to keep his family in the dark about his decision, he vacillated every day over the next fortnight. He was torn apart this way and that when he gave a thought as to how to broach this, how to state this, and how to face the reactions of his family. He was not unknowledgeable of the devastation this would cause Nagalakshmi. He was also aware that it would be a grave punishment perpetrated on an innocent being. But what would lend ethical support to his decision was the rescuing of his tome from being shelved, which would invariably happen if he deviated from the chosen path. He truly did not wish to be excused from that incompatible marriage. His need for Karuna did not mean that Nagalakshmi was needless. He never ever thought of dislodging Nagalakshmi.

One day, as he sat in his study at home, Rao could not concentrate on his studies. He retired to his bedroom as early as 11 pm and shut the door. Nagalakshmi was asleep in the middle on the big bed, with Prthvi to one side. To the other side, Rao's space awaited him. He was there with a resolve to spill everything before her. She had slid into sleep. Sitting close to her, he nudged her shoulder, 'Nagu…' Having slid to sleep just then, she awoke. The bed lamp of the bedroom glowed dimly. Not fully awake, she asked, 'What time is it?'

'11.'

'Is it?' Closing her eyes again, she embraced her husband in her arms and said, 'Why, today seems to be my lucky day. You are early to bed.'

Rao did not know what to say next. Gently, he just said, 'Nagu.' Embracing her husband's emaciated body in both her arms, she cooed in his ears, 'Got fed up of reading? In many years you never did retire at this hour and utter my name. I can understand. Am I not your wife? Sleep.' Rao went silent, and took off his spectacles. She gazed at his eyes for a while, kissed his eyes on the spur and said, 'I will ask something of you. Will you comply?'

'What is it?'

'You are parched. It is as if you are suffering from some perennial fever. Owing to incessant reading, your eyes have lost their spark. What if you lose your sight by continuing to strain your eyes thus? Henceforth, wake up a bit early on Saturdays. Before you go to your library, I will give you an oil bath. And daily after supper, be seated idly in your chair while I massage your feet with castor oil.'

Rao went silent. His eyes closed, he reclined by resting his face on her shoulders. 'Slid into sleep?' she asked, but he did not reply. 'Sleep,' she said and began patting his back gently. Rao's mind felt like it was ablaze. His brain was unstable and his willpower thawed. In a little while, he sighed heavily.

'Why, sleep won't come?' She held his face in her hands and looked. His eyes were moist.

'What ails you? Can't you share it with me?' she humoured him. No response even to that. 'It's okay if you don't want to. You lost your parents early in your life, and you had no one tending well to you. You even excused yourself soon from my native place and relocated to Mysore to pursue academics. Children who lose their mothers should not live on. But I am here now for everything. What ails you? Why are you so melancholic?' she wiped his eyes with the *pallu* of her sari.

'No worries. I am feeling drowsy now. Sleep.' Rao put his head on the pillow. Nagalakshmi pulled over the shawl on his feet and went silent herself. The entire night, Rao did not sleep. Nagalakshmi slipped into sleep by about 2 am. She had held him in an embrace with her left arm, as would a mother her night-fearing child. Though he didn't get sleep, not wanting to wake her up, he reclined immobile. All night, his mind was in a state of turbulence. The question as to what her fault was in all this remained unanswered. But the only justification his mind afforded was that he was not abandoning her; he was only partnering another to accomplish his life's aspiration.

Next morning, he got up early at 5. Raja was used to bathing by then and go for a stroll. Today, he was headed for the bathroom when Rao intercepted him and said, 'Let me know when you leave for your morning walk today. I will join you.' He smiled and asked, 'What! You, too, are becoming health conscious?'

The brothers took to strolling on the Hunsur road. Rao broached the subject. 'I wanted to share something with you.'

Raja had sensed that something ailed his brother's mind. He even had a vague idea as to what it was. 'What is it?' he asked. Vacillating as to how to broach the subject, Rao turned silent without giving any reply. To save him from his impasse, Raja gave him a helping hand. 'I got to know that Karunaratne is here.'

'How do you know?'

'They were gossiping so in the library, that she has lodged herself in the Hindu Hotel.'

Though he was surprised that Raja knew of it, Rao began relating his mind. Recounting the obstacles that his research was saddled with, and the fact of his eyesight dwindling, he said, 'Without her, the penning of the book cannot be accomplished. If I shelve it, I can't live on. It would not be socially appropriate for her to simply work for me thus. Therefore, we have decided to go for a civil marriage.'

Raja did not say anything. He had, at times, speculated that this or something like this would happen. This was very much a possibility in the lives of great scholars, littérateurs, artists, scientists, etc. But the fact that it happened in his backyard caused him some embarrassment. 'Have you given a thought as to what it would do to Nagu?' he asked.

'I shared all this with you so as to get you to share it with her and placate her. By wedding Karuna, I am not abandoning Nagu.'

'Yet, would she accede? Which woman would concur to the proposal of instating a rival wife? Our uncle raised us; orphans. He gave Nagu in marriage to you. He has passed on since; even the aunt. What is Nagu's fault in you penning your work? In the matter of your marriage, wasn't your consent prime vis-à-vis hers? You accorded consent out of your own volition.'

Ruminating within himself, Rao said, 'This is not an issue that can be resolved through discussion and petitioning. You have seen the literary life at Oxford. I know you like Nagu very much. I, too, love her much. But if this book is not accomplished, I will surely perish. Can you help me in place of Karuna? I will not abandon this house. I will not even leave Nagu. I know that you can put it across to her well and placate her. For once, give it a thought from my angle.'

Raja tried perceiving it from his brother's angle. It was very clear to him without the need for much cogitation. He had very friendly feelings towards his sister-in-law. He had great respect for his brother's intellectual task. Whenever he was introduced as 'the brother of Dr Sadashiva Rao', his mind would swell. But how could he set this matter right? His brother had trod such distance in his chosen path from where he could not retreat. His mind would not acquiesce to regard him harshly. Nothing would be gained from it either. He resigned to the fact that there was nothing else to do other than to regard his sister-in-law with greater feelings of friendship and placate her.

3

Nagalakshmi ate nothing for three days when she got to know of it. Her eyelids would not flap even once during the nights. She knew that she could in no way contribute to the literary endeavour of her husband. All the same, she could not acquiesce to a development of this magnitude just for the sake of his research. Without letting it affect her much, she had put up with her husband's nonchalance towards her. But her husband getting himself a second wife was beyond the limits of her endurance. Considering that his sister-in-law's mind was greatly disturbed, Raja took leave of absence from college and confined himself indoors. Rao was in and out. After supper, he would go to his study. If sleep overcame, he would fully unfold the armchair and doze off, stretching himself in it.

On the night of the day when she heard it all from Raja, she had gone to her husband's study and asked, 'What undoing of mine has caused you to do this?' Rao chose to remain silent. 'Unless you speak, I won't leave this room,' she said, and sat her place. She said everything that could be mouthed within the limits of a chaste woman's modesty. He still chose to remain silent. All he eventually had said was that *Raja would tell her everything.*

On the third day of her fasting, Raja said, 'If you continue with this, how will I have food?'

'To fast is in my *karma*. You help yourself to your nourishment.'

'I won't eat if you don't. Get up.' She didn't yield to his compulsion. Noticing her brother-in-law standing by her in her agonizing state and placating her every which way, affection towards him brimmed in her heart. She asked him, 'Raja, amma passed away. Papa too. Now, he is out to perpetrate this on me. And you! Why should you be affected by my plight?'

'You are unable to understand his work fully. He is passionate about that tome. And without her, he cannot see it through successfully. If he has to shelve it, he will be afflicted by mental ailment. May we let that happen?'

'Why should he assume an extreme passion and desert me?'

'He has no thoughts of abandoning you. It is not a clandestine relationship. She will move here and join us. It is I that look after the pantry and overheads. You are the one that runs the kitchen and the rest of the household. Let there be one more member here. How does it matter?'

'If he needed the assistance of an intelligent person, can't he avail of your help, an able sibling? You are capable of helping him, I suppose.'

'No. It is because of the fact that it is beyond me that this has gone to such extent. Nagu, the more you are adamant now, the more the situation worsens. Just concede to the marriage. The situation is not such that she will take to harass you. She is not interested in doing anything other than reading and writing. You are already a mother to a son. I am on your side. It is impossible for anybody to look down upon you in this house. She, too, is not a mean woman. Brother won't neglect you either.'

Compared to the dark complexioned Karuna, Nagalakshmi thought that she was truly presentable. Her contours and facial features still held resplendence. The mature grace had only enhanced her prettiness. *His brain has gone berserk, and hence he is abandoning a wife like me and taking to a dark one. In four days, he will be back on track.* But this self-consolation did not mitigate her misery. She still did not consume food. Prthvi had gone to school. The sound of opening of the main door announced a caller. Raja walked up and looked. 'For three days, you were not to be seen in college.' It was Katyayani, and she said it in a gentle voice. Nagalakshmi had noticed that of late, she had assumed informality in speaking to Raja. But she had never given any serious thought to it. Katyayani came in, and wasn't really taken aback at the gloom on Nagalakshmi's face. She seemed to know it all. Still, not giving it out, she said, 'It is more than five days since I last saw you. You seem to be worrisome. Why, aren't you keeping well?'

Nagalakshmi continued to be mute. 'Here, take this,' Katyayani gave her the floral string that she had brought packed in the handkerchief.

Shoving it away with her right hand, 'Why do I need flowers from now on?' Nagalakshmi started weeping.

'Nagu, don't say so. How can you refuse flowers?' said Raja. Nagalakshmi just pulled the packet to her arms. For five minutes, nobody spoke. Katyayani saw Raja's face. He looked at her with gloom in his eyes. Then she asked Raja, 'I heard some news in college today. Is it true?'

'What is it?'

'False or true, I do not know. But seeing Nagalakshmi amma weep, I think of it as factual.'

'Tell me what.'

'Your brother and his research pupil Karunaratne tied the knot in a civil marriage.'

'Who said so?'

'Everybody in the ladies' room. It is said that the wedding took place in the sub registrar's office yesterday afternoon.'

Raja could not have known that it would happen thus without their knowledge. While Raja was thinking why his brother hastened without obtaining his wife's consent, 'Look,' said Katyayani and hurriedly neared Nagalakshmi. Hearing news of her husband's wedding, Nagalakshmi fainted and fell unconscious. Raja hurried to the kitchen and brought water. Taking the vessel from Raja's hands, Katyayani sprinkled some on Nagalakshmi's face and soaked a fistful on her head. Raja brought a fan and began blowing air. Nagalakshmi did not regain consciousness even after five minutes. Neither had she lost consciousness fully, nor was she fully conscious. She lay in a state of semi-consciousness. Asking Katyayani to keep fanning, Raja said, 'I will fetch a doctor,' and left on his bicycle.

Five minutes after he left, Nagalakshmi's consciousness returned. When Katyayani saw her attempt to get up, she checked her, 'No. don't get up. You may feel giddy again.' She brought a cushion that was on a chair in the living room and placed it under Nagalakshmi's head. Speaking nothing, Nagalakshmi just held Katyayani's hand and sat beside her.

The doctor arrived in 10 minutes. Noticing that his sister-in-law had regained consciousness, Raja let out a sigh of relief. 'What happened,' asked the doctor of Nagalakshmi, and she said, 'I don't know.' The doctor asked if he may give an injection. Raja was not for it, so the doctor just gave a tablet and left.

'Nagu, your head reeled because you have eaten nothing in three days. Now, eat something,' Raja neared her.

'I won't. You go have it,' Nagalakshmi said, and continued to lie down.

Katyayani got to know of the situation. She gestured to Raja with her sight. Raja exited. Katyayani spent all her stock of consolations, and convinced Nagalakshmi to have lunch. Nagalakshmi said, 'Call Raja.' Raja came in. Taking them both inside the kitchen, Katyayani served them both. But neither ate more than a morsel.

4

Post wedding, there was no change in Karuna's routine whatsoever. She never sought clarification from Rao as to how they were to carry on living thenceforth. She would present herself at the library at 9 in the morning. Slogging till 7 in the evening, she would take dictation in shorthand. Rao's typewriter was now with her in the hotel room. She would type the manuscript till midnight. He had not yet started penning his second volume. On her advent, he shared with her what books he had studied in her absence. She had noted down all that, and made detailed systematic notes.

When her husband came home, Nagalakshmi served him food. But she had completely stopped talking to him. Raja would keep his brother company at all such times. Prthvi never mingled with his dad freely ever. Rao stuck to his study room and checked himself from entering the bedroom where Nagalakshmi and Prthvi slept.

One day Rao asked Karuna, 'Now on, why stay in a hotel? I have discussed in my house. Join my family.'

She had given a thought to this already. She said, 'I will tell you something frankly. You shouldn't mistake me.'

'Tell me.'

'She being traditionally inclined, she may consent to it. But my upbringing is different. I do not take a liking to rival wives residing under the same roof. The additional financial burden from another household may not be much.'

'I don't have in mind the economics of it at all.'

'What else?'

'I have in mind peace of mind for all three of us.' Holding his hand, Karuna said, 'My refusal stems from that very point of view. It is impossible that we stay together and be peaceful at the same time. I will stay in a different house. I will cook my food. You continue to go there. Have your nourishment there. Retire there for the nights. I have no objection whatsoever. I am not jealous. Isn't it for a different purpose that we have come together?'

Rao gazed her in the face. Her eyes shone from willpower. 'There is really no need for any clarification in the matter.' He squeezed her hands.

Within a week, a comfortable house was available in Sarasvatipura. And as good luck would have it, a reliable housemaid was also available. Karuna did not ask Rao to stay with her; Rao continued to stay with Nagalakshmi initially. But there was no communication whatsoever between the couple. Raja had tried to get Nagalakshmi to resume communication with her husband but was unsuccessful. At night, she would retire in the kitchen; she would roll a bed there and sleep with Prthvi. It was so for a couple of months. One afternoon Rao hired a cart and took all his books to Karuna's house. Raja was not in then. With divine neglect and without uttering one single syllable, Nagalakshmi confined herself to the kitchen as if she were unconcerned with her husband's activities.

Noticing, Karuna felt obliged to ask, 'It helps your study better alright, but I shall not insist that you move here.'

'Cut it,' said Rao, as if he were not inclined to discuss that matter.

Next day Raja went looking for his brother in the library. Karuna understood that if Raja, who never visited there, was visiting today, it must be to discuss yesterday's development. She greeted him, and after about five minutes, excused herself.

Rao told Raja, 'In fact, I wanted to send word for you. How long may I put up with it without any communication whatsoever? Besides, if I stay at Karuna's, it will be more helpful for my research. Karuna has no objections to my staying there. Please send word for me when Nagu's mind is clear. I will then pay regular visits.'

'She is very saddened.'

'I can understand.'

'Don't you wait for her to acquiesce. Keep visiting. Everything will be okay over a few days.'

'Okay,' Rao consented. Then, thinking up something, he said, 'Look, I am now getting twice the salary you earn. I also earn royalty from the publisher. It is you that has cared for Nagu and Prthvi all through. Even if I resume visiting there, they shall continue to be your ward. Come here on salary day. I will give you some amount regularly.'

Raja felt downcast. He said, 'Don't ever think about it. Should you give me money to provide victuals to Nagu? Take it off your mind. If mother were alive, would she have drawn maintenance money from the elder son and ate at her younger son's? If I am pressed for money, I will ask you myself. You may have to go on excursions for research, or you may have to buy books and stationery.'

When Raja started to leave, Rao said, 'You keep visiting here.'

'Will do,' said Raja and left.

Over the next week, it was Karuna's cuisine. Rao did not like it. Besides, he thought that the time spent by her in cooking was eating into her more important work. They hired a cook.

CHAPTER 12

1

The navarātra holidays were past. As were the December holidays. Raja and Katyayani would meet every day in college. They would confine themselves to the theatre association room and chat. Intermittently, Katyayani would go to Raja's house. Of late, Nagalakshmi talked to nobody. Cooking, serving food to Raja and Prthvi, and lying down on a mat in the kitchen had become her routine. When Raja took time to keep her company for a while and coaxed her into conversation, she would speak bare minimum. Prthvi, who never was intimate with his father, sensed no change whatsoever. The only change he noticed was that his mother ceased to sleep on the cot in the room and slept on a bed on the kitchen floor. Aged five years now, he attended school in the company of the neighbour boy. Whenever his uncle went shopping, he would take his little nephew on his bicycle.

One day Raja asked Nagalakshmi, 'Nagu, shall I marry this year?'

Happy that the reluctant brother-in-law brought up the matter of his marriage on his own, she said, 'Ask that of me!'

'Know who the bride is?'

'Katyayani.'

'You know! How?' he asked amused.

'Women get to know it readily. The way you take her to your room for chatting the moment she comes here says it all.'

'You never gave out all these days that you were aware of this!'

'Why did you not confide in me that you intended to marry her?'

Abashed, Raja fell silent. Nagalakshmi continued, 'She, too, has a child. How will she abandon him and come over?'

'She will bring him too. Tell me, are you for this marriage?'

'Why ask my opinion? If you go against accepted practices and *dharma-karma*, would it augur well for all?

Very many times he had explained to Nagalakshmi his views about *dharma* and *karma*. He went about it once again now in detail. 'If I wed an incompatible one, and develop aversion towards her soon after, what purpose is served? I feel Katyayani is just right for me. You must accord your consent.'

Nagalakshmi recounted her life's events. Besides, of late, she had taken to look at life the dispassionate way. She said, 'Maybe you are right. Okay.'

That afternoon Katyayani visited, prostrated at Nagalakshmi's feet and said, 'You should accept me.'

'May you both prosper,' Nagalakshmi said in her mind.

Katyayani's exams were scheduled for the third week of March. One day at the end of February, Raja told her, 'Let us not delay any more. You discuss with your in-laws and obtain their permission. Let's consummate the wedding. Let you not anymore be *some student I meet at the college*.'

Katyayani, too, was eager to just be done with it. For three months now she had longed to share it all with her in-laws, obtain their permission, and move to the household of her chosen life partner. But how might she break it to them? She knew that her decision would be a rude shock to them. She was in no doubt that her chosen step would only wreck the eminence of that lineage, the respect that the household commanded, the social status and the values that ran through its successive generations. It was still her house. She had gained an auspicious entry into it five years ago by customarily nudging, with the toe of her left foot, the metal beaker that was placed on the sill of the front door of that house, so as to spill on the floor of the house the rice grains that it contained, signalling the prosperity that would swell and flow in that house thenceforth. Her name was ingrained into the genealogical tree of that house, never to be erased. Though she resolved to erase it, she was aware that it would leave a gaping hole, a blotch rather, on that clear expanse of sheet. After the death of their lone son, her mother- and father-in-law had pinned their hopes on her and the next generation, their grandson.

All these musings assailed her quite a few times, and the first time they bore into her was when she had spilled her mind before Raja. But her insatiate marriage had suppressed all such finer aspects. When the time to put it across to her in-laws came, she became nervous. Raja kept asking daily if she had discussed it at home. One day he got vexed: 'If you don't have the courage to take it further, why did you urge me this far?' The thought of just leaving her house along with her kid without informing anyone, going away to Mysore, and then writing to them about her decision occurred to her for once, but she refrained from resorting to that mean method. Though she would end up proving herself to be unworthy of the trust reposed in her by her father-in-law, her mind would not acquiesce to make it as contemptible as that.

Even the first week of March was past by now. There would be a fortnight of study vacations, which would be followed by exams, during which period she would not travel to Mysore. That day Raja told her very strictly, 'If you don't discuss this at home yourself, I will write to them, informing them of the same. You stay back from going to Nanjangud today.'

'Tonight I will surely discuss this with them. Tomorrow, I will come over even though no classroom sessions are scheduled. You make yourselves available here. I will apprise you of the developments.' Assuring him thus, she returned by the evening train. How much ever she gave a thought as to how to break the news, she could not come up with a satisfactory solution. As the train approached Nanjangud station, her heartbeat kept on increasing. She shuddered from an unknown fear. Her face and body perspired. Her gait lost balance, and she tottered her way to her house.

'Why, child, you are perspiring? Summer is approaching. It is getting very hot. Why can't the government hold the exams expediently and be done with it?' her father-in-law said.

Not responding, she headed straight to the study upstairs. Placing the books on the shelf, she came down, washed her feet and face, and changed. 'Amma, why cho late?' Cheeni came asking her, and she hugged him. She spoke to none until after supper. She confined herself to the study room and kept thinking. Deciding to discuss with her father-in-law without fail after supper, she gathered all she could of her willpower. After supper, her father-in-law continued to be seated in the living room. But she still did not garner enough courage to approach him. When she got up to scale down the stairs, her legs became so weak as to cause her to slump. She sat soon. Everybody was asleep downstairs. At 11 pm, she had an idea. She would write on a sheet of paper all that she wanted to tell her father-in-law, and hand it over to him personally when she left for college tomorrow morning. When she returned that evening, he would bring it up himself. Then it would be easy for her to take it up from there.

When she took hold of the paper and pen, she could not think of what to write. Still, she started writing in about five minutes. It was four hours later that she finished it and it ran through 16 pages. She wrote about society's contrived stipulations that suppressed the basic disposition of human beings. She analyzed in detail as to how traditional tenets proved to be obstacles to the felicity of men and women.

She even debated on the stipulations of *dharma*. And on the last page she wrote thus:

> I pray at your feet to regard this with sympathy characteristic of a humane being. Please regard this with the compassion a father shows towards his own daughter who has made such an appeal, inevitably heeding her heart. I have never belied your trust. I will embark on my new life only after seeking your permission and sacred blessings. As I was unable to convey all this verbally, I have put it in writing. When I return this evening, I request you to kindly bless me.

When she arranged the letters in chronological order and tried pinning them together, the pin contorted. She punched a hole, tied them with a thread, placed the set in an envelope, sealed it with gum and lied down. A sort of relief caused her to slide into sleep. When she awoke, it was 7:30. She hurriedly went through her morning rituals and breakfast. She packed her books and lunchbox. When she picked up the envelope, her hands trembled. Fortifying her mind, she climbed down the stairs. Her father-in-law had just finished his puja and was headed to the living room. As if possessed by some passion, she prostrated at his feet.

'What's special today, child? Aren't the exams 15 days away?' asked Srotri.

'Yes, but please see this letter,' she said, placing it in his hands, and walked away briskly. Confounded, he kept looking in her direction. Then, his attention drawn to the envelope in his hand, he cut it open.

After leaving her house, Katyayani was perturbed. Somehow, she got into the train. She spotted Raja in Chamarajapura station. He was perturbed too. Discussing the matter right away, they headed for his house. Reporting what she had done, she assured to update him tomorrow without fail. 'I shall not be in anticipation of your report, but I shall be in anticipation of you,' he said.

2

On her way back home that evening, Katyayani was tense from trepidation. She was anxiously cogitating in her mind as to what her father-in-law would ask of her and what reply she should give. An unknown fear engulfed her too. But it was a day that called for testing the tenacity of her willpower and endurance. Marshalling all her fortitude, she entered the house. Her father-in-law was seated in the living room and talking to a visiting farmer. She went straight upstairs. She could not garner courage enough to see her mother-in-law as she usually did on returning. She knew that her father-in-law never left his mind at the mercy of anger, whatever the situation. But her mother-in-law was not so. Though she was mild mannered, she would get incensed at times. Sparingly, she would get incensed at her husband too. By now she would have got to know. Aware that a protracted tirade was on the cards, she was gearing up for that. But the senior lady had not yet got to know that her daughter-in-law was home. She was in the kitchen, and chatting with Cheeni. Katyayani did not go downstairs.

When he was done with his evening puja, Srotri called out to her for supper. Gathering all her fortitude again, she climbed down. As usual, her father-in-law and Cheeni were seated; the mother-in-law was serving. Katyayani thought that she would broach the burning issue now. But everything was calm and quiet. Her father-in-law munched silently, his head hung. Her mother-in-law was pampering and cajoling Cheeni, who was spilling the food more than ingesting. After she had eaten, Katyayani went upstairs again. Her father-in-law observed her as she climbed up the stairs. Still, he said nothing. Katyayani could not bear that reticence; she had anticipated censure. And had equipped herself to counter it well. But this reticence—contemptuous reticence rather—was beyond her endurance. She fidgeted from impatience. Eventually, she garnered some courage and went downstairs. Srotri was seated in the living room. Though he held some manuscript in his hand, his sight was fixed on the ceiling, and he seemed to be lost in thought. She went up to him and asked, 'Appa, will you please come upstairs for a minute?'

'Oh, yes.'

She climbed up the stairs again. He appeared there in two minutes, headed for his study and said, 'Come in.' By the time she entered there, he was seated on the tiger hide mat by the window. She went up to him and stood leaning against a pillar. 'Come near. Sit here,' he said. She complied. Silence prevailed again.

Slicing the torturous silence, after about five minutes she said, 'Appa, did you read my letter?'

'I did.'

'You should accord permission, please.'

For a minute Srotri was silent. Then he said in his typical calm tone, 'There is no question of my permission here. You have the liberty to do as you like.'

Srotri's tone was not at all vituperative. He was very composed when he said it. Still, it pricked her.

'Why say so? You are the lord of the house, and I shall do nothing without your permission.'

'Do you still think of me as the lord of the house? As long as you think of yourselves as being a member of this family, it is but natural that till then I shall wield authority over you. The moment you resolve to choose a different living situation, my lordship over you becomes unfounded. Isn't it?'

Katyayani was in readiness to counter whatever tirade he would fling at her. She had rehearsed very many debate points to establish the propriety of her decision. All those seemed erased from her memory, and her head seemed like an empty pot. Still, she said, 'There is no recourse for women in this society if tragedy befalls her. A widower may remarry 10 times. From time immemorial, this world has never had the sympathy to understand the mind and the plight of women though. Besides…' Cutting her short, Srotri said, 'There is no need now for debating the conduct of society or of the world. This is an issue concerning only you. I haven't come in the way of your decision; I will not. You are free to heed your mind. But our intents and resolutions should be in consonance with our respective *dharma*, responsibilities and such, right?'

'Isn't it natural for one to have a life partner, especially at the appropriate phase?'

'What is natural need not be dharmic.' Even in that situation, he smiled and said, 'Conjugality is not the ultimate goal of life. The institution of marriage is for taking the lineage further through procreating. When the lineage is poised to flow on, it is not *dharma* to start another household for reason of obliteration of the previous household.'

She did not know what to say next. Srotri also fell silent. For 10 minutes, both sat silently. Then he said, 'Such issues cannot be taken to their logical end by debating. *Dharma* and *adharma* can be perceived properly only when one stands tall by transcending the minuteness of personal covetousness. You just said that a man might remarry 10 times. I have stated, too, that we need not debate about the ways of the world. The need for such a remarriage had arisen in my life some years back. But I persisted with my *dharma*, rather *dharma* showed me the proper way and saved me. *Dharma* lends a helping hand to those that submit themselves to it. Your husband would have told you this. You may even go downstairs and get to know of it from your mother-in-law, or Lakshmi. Well, it is getting late. Go sleep.'

Srotri got up. He walked up to the door, stopped and said, 'The freedom in this matter is yours. Yes, I am convinced that the contrived stipulations imposed on individuals by the society are not in the full spirit of *dharma*.'

He scaled down the stairs at his usual gentle pace, and went to the corner in the living room where he usually slept. Recalling that today she hadn't laid out the beds of her in-laws and Cheeni, she felt pricked in a corner of her mind. Getting up, she went to her bed and lay down. Her gumption drained. Her natural vivacity seemed to have petered out today. She lay cuddled in her bed as would a bird nestling after flying nonstop over gruelling distances.

Her husband, Nanjunda Srotri, would share with her the ways of his father. Long time back such a situation had arisen in Srinivasa Srotri's life. Treading the path of *dharma*, he had emerged victorious out of that quandary. Katyayani now recalled it in detail.

CHAPTER 13

1

When he lost his mother, Srinivasa Srotri was 15 years of age. An only son to his parents, he attended the Sanskrit school in Mysore. His mother was 50 when she died. The elderly father, who was 55 years old, recalled his son from Mysore. He never went back to school. It was just the two of them in the entire family. There was a hut in the backyard of that house, in which lived Macha—a loyal manservant who was entirely dependent on the Srotri family—along with his daughter Lakshmi. When Macha's wife passed away after giving birth to Lakshmi, he had not married again. For three years, he had left the child under the care of a relative in Kyatanahalli. After that he brought her back. The father-daughter duo ate in their master's house and worked full-time there.

After the death of his wife, the elderly Nanjunda Srotri took to the kitchen himself as there was no woman in the family. The lad Srinivasa assisted his father. Macha, too, took to cooking in his hut for them both. Now, Lakshmi was 10, about five years younger to Srinivasa. Nanjunda Srotri was fed up with daubing his arms and face with the soot of the firewood stoves. But Srinivasa's interest had not liberated itself from education. Though he was weaned away from Mysore, he still got himself tutored in Nyāya, Vaiśeṣika, Sāṅkhya, Yoga and other philosophical studies from Yankappa Shastri at his residence in the Narayana-Rao precinct. Srinivasa had memorized the Amarakośa when he was just six. While in Mysore he had studied *Ramayana* and *Mahabharata* in Sanskrit language. The medium of instruction in that school being Sanskrit, Srinivasa had soon realized the beauty of that language, and was urging himself to gain proficiency in it.

Srinivasa's father did not discourage his quest for knowledge, but he was not ready to spend money for his education. Whatever estate Srinivasa Srotri has now, was available to the family even then. A patch of the floor between the puja chamber and the kitchen was dug up, and an earthen pot full of silver coins—and gold and silver ornaments—was stored there. Nanjunda Srotri would spread his bed there and retire each night. Aware of the father's frugality, and the son's quest for knowledge, Yankappa Shastri imparted education to the lad without aspiring for remuneration. But the Shastri himself was unable to afford certain books; and to that extent, Srinivasa's study suffered.

To save himself from the chore of cooking, Nanjunda Srotri—on the very next day of his wife's first death anniversary—decided to get his son married. Everybody knew that Nanjunda Srotri was of the type who would even wash a corroded paisa and save it in the piggy bank in the puja chamber. Still, parents vied to give their daughters to this flourishing household. Besides, Srinivasa was a handsome man, wholly unlike his father who was dark, short and rancorous. He was of fair complexion, lanky, with sparkling eyes and a broad forehead. His ears were adorned with goodly ruby-embedded ear studs. Many a Nanjangud family desired to have him as their son-in-law; but not inclined to bring in a local bride, Nanjunda Srotri had decided on a bride from a distant Hassan village. The bride belonged to a respectable family. Besides, it was very rare that the horoscopes of the bride and the groom matched as favourably. It was the days of yore when it was not customary for the groom to have a look at the bride before the wedding. Though the bride's age was above optimum, Nanjunda Srotri readily accorded his consent, for he was urgently in need of a hand to relieve him from the kitchen chores. Though dark-complexioned, the 11-year-old Bhageerathamma was good-looking. The diminutive girl was, however, no match to her husband physically. At the wedding venue, someone remarked that it was a wedding between the white bull of the palace and a village calf, and many concurred. The bride's father gave one silver coin, two copper utensils for *sandhyāvandana*, a pair of dhoti, slippers and an umbrella to his son-in-law as dowry, and carried out an elaborate eight-day wedding.

It was not in Nanjunda Srotri's good fortune to benefit from his daughter-in-law's culinary skills for long. Six months after the wedding, he passed away from excessive vomiting and diarrhea. Some people went to the extent of surmising that the bride was born in a star that bode inauspicious to her father-in-law. Before he passed away, his father had, in confidence, told Srinivasa of the hidden treasure. After the funeral rites of his father were consummated over the fortnight, Srinivasa Srotri dug it out. The silver coins alone numbered 6,000. Gold and silver ornaments were so heavy that he could not lift them all in one go. He knew that most of the ornaments were pledged ones that were never redeemed by the borrowers. After the treasure was thus retrieved and lordship devolved on Srinivasa Srotri, the charter of the house underwent a sea of change. Happy at being capable of honourably acquitting himself of his monetary indebtedness to his guru, he gave 1,000 silver coins to his teacher Yankappa Shastri on the occasion of the wedding of the teacher's daughter. He collected the books recommended by his guru—whatever was available of them—and arranged them in the study on the upper floor of his house.

Lakshmi, the daughter of the manservant Macha, was already 12. Macha was tall and robust. He earlier worked in tea farms in the Nilgiris. A beautiful woman, who was a child-widow, fell in love with him. He eloped with her and landed in Nanjangud; Nanjunda Srotri had provided protection to them. He needed such an able-bodied and honest manservant to guard his treasure. Lakshmi inherited her fair complexion and cute smile from her mother, and lankiness from her father. People gossiped that Macha's wife was two years elder to him. But her beauty concealed her age. Four years into marriage, she got pregnant. She delivered Lakshmi and passed away. Though just 12, Lakshmi's beauty attracted everyone. She would address her childhood companion—Srinivasa Srotri—as Sheenappa. Having had her upbringing in that house, she took to speaking the Srotris' pure tongue. When he first saw his bride on his wedding day, the thought 'if Lakshmi were my bride!' flashed in Srinivasa's mind. But he almost immediately dismissed it as sinful thinking on his part.

Her beauty notwithstanding, Macha had no pecuniary capability whatsoever to conduct the wedding of his daughter. He did receive some offers, but the grooms' financial status were no better than his own. Srinivasa Srotri, the new lord of the Srotri family, told him, 'Look for a fine groom. I will give you a 1,000 rupees.' The new lord knew that the wealth accumulated in this house had drawn on the sweat of Macha. Making pertinent enquiries, he discerned a groom from Kodiyala, near Mandya. Lakshmi's wedding was conducted in a grand way.

One year thence, Bhageerathamma menarched, and was duly bequeathed to her husband. Srinivasa's household reacquired the resplendence of a presiding female. Even after the advent of his wife, Srinivasa Srotri did not discontinue his studies. He would often go to Mysore and buy books; he would get tutored from the scholars at the Sanskrit School those aspects which he could not grasp himself. On his part, Yankappa Shastri had wholeheartedly tutored Srinivasa Srotri in all the knowledge that he was privy to.

When the reigning Srotri was beginning to lead a happy new life, plague visited Nanjangud. Among the many that were affected was Macha. Somebody sent word for his daughter, but by the time she arrived, Macha had breathed his last. Lakshmi went to see her childhood companion Sheenappa the next day. Srinivasa Srotri consoled her much, and when she took leave, he gave her 100 rupees and said, 'Get the funeral rites of Macha performed in your village. You keep visiting here. You are the daughter of this house.' Lakshmi was dumbfounded at Sheenappa's magnanimity. She prostrated at his feet and left with her husband.

Srotri's learning saw no interval. His early conjugal days were thrilling too. Even after three years into their marriage, Bhageerathamma did not conceive. By then, Srotri had gained quite some knowledge in *dharmaśāstra*, Vedas, Upanishads and other philosophies. He would recite the *Ramayana* daily. The treatises he studied wielded a great influence on him. He would delve deep to understand, cogitate and memorize concepts that explained what the goal of human life was, what gṛhasthāśrama was, what the obligations of the *gṛhastha* were, etc. The fact that he hadn't sired three years into his marriage bothered him much. His belief was that the primary purpose of marriage was procreation to take forward the lineage.

One evening, Lakshmi visited. The moment she arrived, she prostrated at Srotri's feet, held his feet firmly and began crying. After consoling her much, he asked her what the matter was. She narrated. Her father had been fooled; her husband was a gambler. As he would always wear gold rings and chains, Macha had given him his daughter in marriage thinking he was a decent man. Though Lakshmi's husband had some lands, he had mortgaged them to secure loan for gambling. Twenty days ago, while gambling in Mandya, he had won all the monies of his opponents. The losers had murdered him a little past midnight and escaped. Three days ago, the police tracked them. Destitute Lakshmi went to her 'natal home', seeking refuge.

'Everything happens as per *karma*. Don't worry Lakshmi. Can't this house provide you staple food?' said her Sheenappa, consoled her and played host to her. Bhageerathamma, too, needed Lakshmi's assistance. Lakshmi had to pay a few visits to the Mysore court to attend the proceedings of the criminal case. Srotri had taken her there. The criminals were sentenced to life imprisonment.

Two more years passed. Bhageerathamma did not go the family way. Srotri was 24 now, and Bhageerathamma was 19. Srotri was now a worried man. He experienced the same agony that the childless kings in the epics, the *Ramayana* and the *Mahabharata* experienced. But he never once slandered his wife. Neither had he made known his sorrow to her. Bhageerathamma knew his mind nevertheless. Her barrenness was searing her. She had utmost love and faith in her husband, and had high regard for his gentle disposition. They avowed before myriad Gods. Srotri avowed to get the feet of the idol of Lord Nanjundeshvara gilded. One year thence, Bhageerathamma announced pregnancy.

Though her father visited to take her to her natal place as was the custom, Srinivasa Srotri opined that she better go through the labour in Nanjangud. Three months before the date of delivery, Bhageerathamma's mother came over to Nanjangud to attend to her daughter's pre-natal care. Bhageerathamma was doing well as she progressed towards the delivery day. But she did not deliver even after suffering three days of labour pain. The local Pundit checked her and said that she must be taken to Mysore. Srotri telephoned for a taxi, and expediently took her to the big hospital in Mysore. He was upset. He had carried with him enough silver coins in a pouch tied to his waist. He kept impatiently stomping in the front yard of the hospital. Lakshmi, who kept him company, was consoling him. After about four to five hours of hospitalization, the doctor sent word: 'We have to do surgery. She won't survive otherwise.'

Srotri signed every document as instructed. Outside the operation theatre, Lakshmi, Srotri and his mother-in-law waited anxiously. A few people from Nanjangud joined him. Srotri was reciting a verse in his mind while he simply waited:

He is a sage that stays composed in mind
Stays from getting agitated when grief assails
Covets not in times of prosperity
Is rid of desires, fear and anger at all times

After three hours, they were informed that the surgery was successful, a baby boy was born, and the woman was out of danger. Everyone sighed in relief. Srotri kept reciting that verse.

Bhageerathamma received treatment in the hospital for about a month. In the special ward, her mother and Lakshmi kept her company. Srotri would visit there every morning and stay till evening. On the day of discharge, the doctor exclusively called Srotri for counselling. 'The size of the fetus was bigger than what the womb could accommodate. You are a physically incompatible couple. The surgery saved her. If she gets pregnant again, she will face certain death. Henceforth, you should stay away from coition with her.'

The doctor would surely have despaired in putting it across to a man of such fine build and height, and whose face reflected his bouncing health. The same counsel was given to Bhageerathamma by a nurse.

Srinivasa Srotri christened his son after his father's name—Nanjunda Srotri. The baby resembled his father in every way. Bhageerathamma's mother stayed on to attend to her daughter's post-natal care till the kid completed eight months.

2

After being discharged from the hospital, the newborn and his mother had taken to a room on the ground floor. Srotri slept in the study upstairs. Srotri's mind was sedate all through his mother-in-law's sojourn. With her exit, as if patrol were called off, Srotri's mind coasted towards his conjugal partner.

Nobody would be in the house; Lakshmi would go herding the cattle all day long. His wife would be alone. Srotri was in his prime; a robust man of 26. But the doctor had cautioned him: ' You are a physically incompatible couple. The surgery saved her. If she gets pregnant again, she will face certain death. Henceforth, you should stay away from coition with her.'

The doctor's words always rung like a warning bell in Srotri's mind. He would, at times, glance at his wife who would be feeding the baby. The buxom baby would occupy all the space in her lap, and with a smiling face would draw on its nourishment. Vis-à-vis the well-grown baby, Bhageerathamma would seem like a teenage girl. Srotri would feel sympathy towards her. 'Come over,' she would ask him to sit by her side. But he would walk away and exit the house. A few months passed by thus. He could not rein in his amorous mind. Even when he attended to the worship, his mind would shed its typical calmness, and would waver like the flame of a torch in breeze. He would abandon the puja, thinking there was no point in going through it in such a state of mind.

Bhageerathamma was not ignorant of this. But she was helpless. The nurse's words had sown fear in her mind too. Though she was sure that her husband would not resort to force, she had noticed the natural turmoil of his mind. As if to make up for her inability to bestow conjugal pleasure on him, she took to serving him with more devotion and concern. A few more months passed. Srotri forsook his daily consumption of milk. He took to digging the vast backyard for raising a garden every morning. Owing to the laborious work and relenting on nourishment, he would slide into sleep instantly on retiring at night; undisturbed until daybreak. But in a few months, he was emaciated. His physical strength and the sparkle in his eyes had all but diminished. One day, Bhageerathamma took an exception to it. 'See what you have brought yourselves to by foregoing milk and ghee.' And when she served him an extra spoonful of ghee, he checked her, 'These should be foregone if one has to rein in his mind.'

Bhageerathamma greatly loved her husband. She prided in his striking physique. She could not stomach his dwindling from austerity. One day she thought of an idea. She had an unmarried younger sister. She was 12, and still single. If she brought her in as a rival wife, all problems would be solved. The new wife being her own sister and she being elder to her, her own rights would not be infringed upon. But she wondered if her parents would concur. In another month, Srotri became more emaciated. Bhageerathamma's resolve steeled. She wrote to her mother stating what the doctor had told her, what had become of her husband, and everything else, and sought her mother's counsel. Unlike Bhageerathamma, her sister was of attractive physique. Srotri's father-in-law visited within the week. The next day, he took his son-in-law out for a walk. Crossing the stream, they headed in the direction of Hejjige village and rested on the bund of a paddy field. The old man proposed, 'I know everything. It is all God's wish. You wed Kaveri; Bhagu is for it. Back home, everyone concurs. The sisters will be mutually sociable.'

Srotri was taken aback. 'Are you here for this?' he asked.

'Yes. Bhagu wrote to us. Oh dear, look at you! Knowing how you were, my belly curdles to see you emaciated. I can understand everything.' Srotri's father-in-law was a Casanova. He had three extramarital affairs in Hassan, and the son-in-law knew it.

The son-in-law went silent. Grasping it as his consent, the father-in-law got up and said, 'Horoscopes match. I have got them checked.'

That night, as usual, Srotri retired to his study. The treatises and monographs that he had studied till date surfaced in his memory. The *Ramayana* that he had taken to reciting daily appeared before his eyes. His mind underwent a great upheaval, and it troubled him till midnight. It calmed down at 2. After *sandhyāvandana* and puja next morning, and after his father-in-law had had his breakfast, Srotri took him out for a stroll. When they rested on the bund of the stream by the Dalavai bridge, which was desolate, Srotri said, 'I gave it a thought yesterday night. The very purpose of marriage is for adhering to *gṛhasthadharma* and for procreating. Now I have a son for taking my lineage further. For adhering to *gṛhasthadharma*, there is my wife. To marry a second time is *adharma*. I don't want it.'

The father-in-law was taken aback at his son-in-law's clarity of understanding. He was aware of all those ideals too.

He was educated in Sanskrit as well; had studied the *śāstras* to some extent. But to a greater extent, he had a propensity for material living, and was living it fully. He said, 'Yet, we may not ignore the *dharma* of youth. You should care for your health. For a good living, you need a good physique. If you go haggard thus, how shall you live life? What shall become of Bhagu's fate?'

The son-in-law did not cede to the debate of his father-in-law. They returned home. That night, Bhageerathamma joined her father in coaxing Srotri to accede to the ballgame of life. He still didn't accede. The father-in-law continued to stay there for two more days. He studied the situation of that household, observed Lakshmi, the resident maidservant, and eventually announced that he was leaving. He apprised his daughter confidentially of a solution he thought out, chanted a mantra to bless the couple that reverentially prostrated at his feet, received the wide-bordered dhoti that was given him customarily, placed a gold coin in his grandson's palm and left for his town.

3

The conflict between life's ideals that he believed in and the irrepressible force of human instincts waged an incessant war in Srotri's mind. During the days of self-study in the immediate past, he had got to know that there was no go for man other than to rid himself of the stranglehold of Nature. That knowledge was to evidence itself in the execution of his life's obligations now and conquer Nature's dominion. Towards this end, he urged himself to his limits. He spent most of his daytime in strenuous work. The remaining hours were to be spent in studying. Whenever his mind anchored at equilibrium, he would think of it to be his conquest, and he would rejoice. But his mind would fall prey to derangement within an hour or two. The faces of beautiful women that he had seen and heard about would parade before his eyes. He would feel that he conciliated with them. At times, the illusion would be so strong that he would feel a tender arm manifest around his shoulders. The more his conscience attempted to countermand such manifestations, the more his insatiate desires and masculine virility surged with Herculean potency by shredding the fragile strings of conscience. An hour or two later, post their deluge, when the river of his mind would return to flowing quietly, he would repent. His health received a further setback.

The solution that her father apprised her of was not to her liking, but Bhageerathamma feared that the situation might turn grave if her husband, who rejected the proposal for a second marriage, kept up with his recent ways and kept getting wasted by the day. Her father was a practical man; his suggestion was practical too. Bhageerathamma gave a thought to the orphaned Lakshmi's situation. *She had experienced marital bliss for four years. Would she not be yearning for physical pleasures? If she served my husband, no outsiders would get to know of it. There is only the need to see to it that she does not conceive. In case there is a slip up,* *it could be cleared by feeding tender bamboo shoots, plantain stem and raw papaya to her. In case there is need for medical treatment, there is a native healer in Hassan who is well known to her father...*Bhageerathamma's musings rolled on. Men supporting maidservants or other women was not unheard of. Her father, grandfather and uncle had affairs as much as they could sustain. Father was still having affairs; still, her mother was happy with her children at home.

Bhageerathamma and Lakshmi shared a bedroom. Overnight, if the baby woke up and cried, it was Lakshmi who tended to it. One night, Bhageerathamma asked her, 'He is wasting away. You know why?'

'How would I know, amma?'

'It's okay to tell me,' said Bhageerathamma and looked in her eyes.

'You told me about it yourself when we returned from Mysore. You also told me about your father's recent visit.'

'Oh, it had slipped from my mind.'

That exchange went no further. 'Hear,' Bhageerathamma pulled her back to conversation a little later.

'Tell me, amma.'

'I have given it enough thought. He should live on. You, too, want it, right?'

'What are you driving at, amma! If Sheenappa is dead, will I live on?'

'No outsider will get to know of it. You be of service to him. It is in my fate to be of no use despite being his wife.' Tears came to her eyes. She continued, 'One day, you were not home. The baby was asleep. One look at his face and I knew. "The doctor's words could be false. Just once, it will not be detrimental. Come on," I encouraged him. He said, "What would be the inducement for the doctor to lie? As bad luck would have it, even one episode may turn out to be detrimental. Despite the doctor's admonition, would I indulge in this to only see you dead?" he said, and went to the backyard.'

Lakshmi was surprised by Bhageerathamma's suggestion. She reflected as to what wife would volunteer to think up so. Lakshmi had known Sheenappa since her early years. She revered him for his noble character, and had developed devotion towards him. During her brief marital life, whenever her husband went to wager, Sheenappa would surface in her memory. She had, many a time, wished that her husband were like Sheenappa. After her husband's murder when she returned to Sheenappa, she felt dismal. But thanks to his friendly conduct and Bhageerathamma's simplicity, she had soon regained her equanimity. Cupid did unsettle her. Notwithstanding that her husband was a gambler and an alcoholic of sorts, she found it difficult to lead a life sans him. While she herded the cattle, many a cowboy would cast amorous glances at her, but her mind would steer clear of the inducements. But towards Sheenappa, at all times, her mind harboured a mellifluous feeling and a unique attraction. It was never merely amorous though.

She did not accede to Bhageerathamma's proposition. Bhageerathamma kept parroting it daily, and on the fifteenth day Lakshmi said, 'If he consents, well!' For a few days thence, Lakshmi could simply not look at Sheenappa's face. Until then, she would address him as she would a childhood friend. Sheenappa, too, was okay with it. But when, of late, Lakshmi took to addressing him deferentially, though he was confounded, he accorded it no special consideration. One night after supper, Bhageerathamma held Srotri's hands and said, 'I got something for you. You should accede.'

'What is it?'

'You should accord your consent and should not step back on it.'

'Is it a marriage proposal? You have gone mad. What about me worries you into doing all that?'

'No, not marriage,' she sat him beside her and placed before him her proposition. Rudely shocked, Srotri said, 'Who do you think Lakshmi is?'

'She has consented. She, too, wants it.'

A bewildered Srotri kept his gaze rooted in his wife's face. Bhageerathamma said, 'I cannot do you conjugal service. What is proposed is nothing novel. Even with my mother around, my dad has three mistresses. There are definite solutions in case of mishap. You should regain your flesh and blood. Is it not said that worry is man's mortality?' Srotri intently listened to his wife's words. 'Tonight, Lakshmi will retire upstairs. I have instructed her accordingly. You go there.'

Srotri spoke nothing. His mind succumbed to enamour. All through his post marital days, even in the light of his wife's ailment of late, he had not imagined Lakshmi as a bedmate. He was friendly to her and felt sympathy for her. Born in that house and having familiarized herself with the joys and sorrows of that household, she had started a family with help from that house, and had eventually returned empty-handed to that same house. Now, even she had conceded to Bhageerathamma's proposition. His own wife had made all arrangements to this end. There wasn't the need for him to convey even a monosyllabic consent. He just had to climb up the stairs, and awaiting him there was a joy that he never dreamt was in his destiny; an ultimate bliss that any man would desire to come his way on its own. Wasn't it sheer insanity to resist it?

4

Cool breeze wafted through the windows. At times it became a draught, but it was refreshing. Lakshmi was in the antechamber adjacent to Srotri's bedroom. He was seated on his bed, his mind disturbed. All the latent characteristics of nature attained their delirious potential and romped on the stage of his mind. His mind fancied Lakshmi in a way that it never had hitherto. Lakshmi was a woman born to the robust man Macha with a presentable woman of the Nilgiri habitat; her mother was a beautiful woman. At 23, Lakshmi was now full-grown and very captivating. She had blossomed fine, and the quality of her skin brought to mind the ripe oranges of Coorg. She was very apt for the height and robust physique of Srotri. Though she would cover herself fully with the *pallu* of her sari, her attractive contours did not escape attention. Now, she was lying down on her bed in the antechamber, in all probability waiting for Srotri. He could make merry with her with no anxiety as to the external world. His body trembled imperceptibly. His mind was swept away by amorous notions and his breathing became laboured.

Lakshmi lay there in the antechamber in sweet anticipation of the conjugal pleasure she had forgotten and forsaken over these four years of being widowed. *Sheenappa will come, and when he does, what shall I speak to him about? How to comport with him? He has been of a calm and composed nature ever since his childhood. As the friendly lord of the house, he has lent a hand for my well-being all through. Now, he is crestfallen from annulment of corporeal association with his wife. Henceforth, our relationship will proceed till we breathe our last.* Lakshmi was thinking along these lines, and was not affected by the question of sin in all this. She fancied their upcoming relationship as akin to marriage. The sound of restiveness was heard from Sheenappa's room. He would have got up from his bed. The sound of footsteps was heard. Her body trembled. She got up from her lying position and sat up, head hung.

Srotri got to his feet in his room. He paced two steps in the direction of the antechamber. He perspired despite the cool breeze. The dhoti he wore was wet from sweat in five minutes. The sweat beads on his chest and back flowed incessantly. He wiped the sweat off his face and body with the lapel of his dhoti, and posted himself by the window. It was dark outside, but the stars shone bright in the dark firmament. Never forfeiting their luster, they have been glistening from time immemorial. Srotri exited another door, went to the balcony and looked up to the sky. The Saptarṣi-maṇḍala viz., Ursa Major was shining distinctly; nearby Arundhati was shining as well. He looked to the North. The star Dhṛva glistened soft as ever from its eternal anchor. Mind attempted to measure the times of the seven sages, Arundhati and the North star. He let go of it thinking that it was a futile exercise. He held the belief that they were ones with no origin or terminus. Mind was becoming calmer and calmer. For about half an hour, he continued to stand in that balcony. Pain surfaced in his legs. He tread leisurely to his room and lay down on the bed.

In 10 minutes, his mind got agitated again. Lakshmi's form emerged. Fancying her in all her nudity, his mind indulged in coition with her variously. For about 10 minutes, his mind and discretion were not under the regulation of conscience. He perspired again. Getting up, he started pacing in the direction of the antechamber.

Blood coursed through rapidly in Lakshmi's veins from the intensity of anticipation. Sheenappa's frantic pacing in his room, his visit to the balcony, return from there and lying down on his bed, his getting up again and pacing about were all being registered in her conscious mind. She even wondered if Sheenappa was vacillating from coyness, wherefore should she volunteer to go there. All her organs were excited and cried to be palliated. For them to palliate on their own wasn't inherent in *constitutione corporis*. They could be palliated only by revisiting their latent intense ardour in the conjugal company of the male.

Bhageerathamma, who lay in her room downstairs with her baby, hadn't slept either. It had been about an hour and a half since her husband went upstairs. By now he would have copulated with Lakshmi. She could not withstand the pertinent details that surfaced in her mind. Her eyes brimmed up and she began sobbing. But careful that her weeping should not be heard upstairs, she thrust some of the *pallu* of her sari into her mouth. She, too, had bodily desires just as her husband did. The doctor had only barred her from conceiving again. Bodily desires had not ceased in her. A mother to a child that she was, she had somehow reined in such desires. Though she hadn't the youthful physique typical of her husband, bodily desires very much assailed her. This was the most sorrowful night of her life, but it was one that she herself had envisaged. Her husband's health and his diminishing physical strength surfaced in her memory. It was very much possible that he would have contracted mental illness soon. His refusal to get a second wife for himself engendered much love towards him in her. She recalled her father's subsidiary families; also her mother's frame of mind. She tried begetting peace of mind. Ever-gently, she placed her palm on the baby in her lap and kissed his head without causing it to wake up.

Srotri once again wiped the sweat from his face and

body. Holding a lapel of his dhoti against the breeze, he lit the lantern. Lakshmi, who was seated on her bed, came to know of the light that went up in Srotri's room. 'He will be here any moment, or he will summon me to his room,' she said to herself. Her heart began pounding. Blood rushed to her face and her complexion became more pink. Her eyes swam in delight.

For once, Srotri thought of summoning Lakshmi into his room. But his tongue was as immobile as if it were dead. Therefore, he paced a few steps himself in the direction of her bed. He was soon swept by a feeling of shame, and he could not look at himself. And so as to douse the shame which, being latent within him, was now crushing him, he blew out the flame of the lantern. Lakshmi got to know Sheenappa did so out of vacillation, wherefore she thought if it was imperative on her part to accost him. The sound of pacing was heard in that room. Intending to go sit by his feet, she got up. Pacing slowly, by the time she arrived at the door of his room, she had started breathing heavily from excitement. She was also assailed by an unknown fear. Unable to pace one more step, she slumped to the floor by the door.

By then, the wind had begun to blow intensely. A windowpane slammed twice. Wanting to shut the window, Srotri struck a match to light the lantern but the wind blew it away. In the interval, he sighted Lakshmi. He felt as if swayed by the surge of the entirety of man's amorousness. In that darkness, he strode towards Lakshmi, but soon slumped to the floor as if an unknown fear plucked at his innards. There remained no strength in his legs to walk any more. He sat so for more than half an hour. Lakshmi continued to squat by the door. Srotri got up slowly and went to the balcony through that other door.

For the next one hour, he kept gazing at the sky. By then, his mind assuaged. For once, he glanced at the antechamber. She was no more seated by the door of his room. Silently, he walked up to the door and shut the door to the antechamber. He then shut the window and the other door, lit the lantern, and walked up to the bookshelves. He retrieved a white hard-bound book, and squatted on the tiger hide mat. It was Sāṅkhyakārikā. He went directly to the section that delineated the nexus between nature and souls:

Raṅgasya darśayitvā nivartate nartakī yathā nṛtyāt|
Puruṣasya tathātmānaṁ vinivartate prakṛtiḥ||

Just as a danseuse excuses herself after performing for the audience, so does Nature excuse itself after making known its characteristics to the souls.

Srotri's mind was stuck in the question as to what the intent of Nature was; what its culmination was. Another verse went thus:

Prakṛteḥ sukumārataraṁ na kiñcidastīti me matirbhavati|
Yā dṛṣṭāsmīti punarna darśanamupaiti puruṣasya||

There is nothing as demure as Nature. Once a soul regards her, he is captivated; and captivation is bondage! So as to save the souls from being troubled, Nature then takes to stay clear of being beheld by them again. *It only means that Nature reigns over us only till we gain discretionary wisdom. When will I merit such wisdom?* Srotri thought thus, and knew very well that such wisdom is not just a factor of intelligence. He kept cogitating as to whether disentangling from the delusion of the web of enamour was indicative of wisdom, or would the very phosphorescence of knowledge thaw out bondage.

Vexed from the prolonged anticipation, Lakshmi went downstairs to use the washroom. When she scaled up the stairs, Bhageerathamma heard it. In a way typical of a female, she understood the need for a woman to use the bathroom. Once again, cry billowed in efforts to suppress it. She tried getting sleep but was unsuccessful.

Sick of waiting, Lakshmi lay down on her bed. She long knew of Sheenappa's character. She guessed that his mind would be assailed by thoughts of *dharma* and *karma*. But Lakshmi saw nothing unethical in the conjugation they were poised for. It was a result of mutual consent, it was proposed by the very Bhageerathamma herself, and given the doctor's prescription that the couple stay from conjugation, the arrangement was but worldly. Sheenappa's vacillation seemed peculiar. The agitation in Lakshmi's mind was abating. Excitement mellowed and trembling ceased. She closed her eyes. Still, a corner of her mind held hope. Her mind did not acquiesce to shred even that and slide into sleep.

Srotri kept reading till 2:30 am. Now, his mind was

tranquil. His body was under control. Sleep evaporated. He closed the book, left the lamp burning, climbed down the stairs gently and headed for the river. Kapila flowed serenely. For a while, he sat on the shore with his feet immersed in the water. Moonlight had lit up the sky. It was the tenth day of the second fortnight of the month, and the moon had the contours of a sliced gooseberry. He bathed in the river wearing the clothes he was, then squeeze-dried the clothes, wore the same and returned home. His wife was asleep by then. He went to the puja chamber and locked himself in. He applied *bhasma* on his forehead. After the regular *sandhyāvandana*, he began reciting 1008 Gāyatri-mantras unhurriedly. Then he chafed some sandal, exited, harvested some flowers from the backyard and returned to the puja chamber. Bhageerathamma who was awake unto the small hours, was in deep sleep. When Srotri concluded puja at 9 am, he prostrated before God for one last time when in his mind he recited the maxim *dharmo rakṣati rakṣitaḥ* (protected *dharma* protects).

5

By the time Srotri exited the puja chamber, the dhoti he wore was dry. Bhageerathamma had bathed, and was attending to her cooking. Hearing the puja chamber door open, she went there and asked her husband to hold on. Not knowing what that was all about, he complied. She walked up to him, prostrated at his feet and said, 'Lakshmi told me everything.

I did not know that you were disposed so.' Srotri was still in the afterglow of his morning worship. He said nothing. His mind was brimming with a sort of unfathomable beatitude that transcended expression. He walked away silently to the backyard, and took to clearing the beds of the plants and irrigating them.

At lunch, he said, 'I have resolved to consume nutritious food and still reign in bodily desires. I am confident that I will succeed in that. Commencing today, you serve me ghee and give me milk.' While he helped himself to rice in buttermilk, he asked his wife, 'How could you come to conceive of this idea?

'When he was here, my father advised me so. "You do not know the ways of the good health of the males. Do as I say" is what he said.'

Srotri smiled within himself, and said nothing. He started having nutritious food thence. He started doing yoga every morning like he did while pursuing academics in Mysore. He spent more and more time in his study, and his collection of books kept swelling steadily.

After Srotri, it was now Lakshmi's turn to go physically emaciated. After that night, she resumed sleeping in Bhageerathamma's room. But she gradually lost interest in nourishment. What peace of mind she attained over one year subsequent to her widowhood now seemed to evaporate. Wherever she stood, wherever she went, Sheenappa's face would come floating before her mind's eye. Mind would always immerse itself in imaginary physical pleasure. While she bathed, she would regard the proportionate contours of her own body and would be mesmerized. She would fret at Sheenappa's peculiar behaviour. She even stopped talking to him; she even evaded him. He noticed it, too, but never volunteered to start a conversation.

In one month, she got lean and became like a cow at monsoon time. Her cheekbones became prominent. Her lithe gait was no more, and her steps became heavy. There seemed to be no meaning in life, and gloom doused her mind. Her eyes sunk into their sockets and their lustre faded. Srotri could not get to know of these developments for she never appeared before him. Bhageerathamma noticed all this and asked, 'What has become of you Lakshmi? Has somebody poisoned you? Lakshmi gave no clear reply. Bhageerathamma could not gather that her mind had become a stage for a tremendous struggle.

One day, Lakshmi was down with fever. It continued through the night. Srotri got to know of it only when Bhageerathamma told him about it. He went in, checked her pulse, and looked in her face. He could grasp everything. One and half months ago, his face was this way too. He had noticed it in the mirror while applying the sandal paste and vermilion to his forehead. He said nothing in that moment. He fetched the pundit. Lakshmi's fever persisted for a fortnight. During those days, Srotri stuck to her bedside. At nights he would roll his bed thereabouts and sleep. He would, with great care, administer the medicines and diet as prescribed by the pundit. Those days, he could not stick to his *sandhyāvandana* and puja schedule. He would recite some mantras in his mind. Meanwhile, Bhageerathamma was having her monthly period, so Srotri had to attend to cooking too. Lakshmi's sari would gather dirt from the heat of the fever, and Srotri would himself remove it and dress her in a clean sari. In her unconscious state, Lakshmi would utter feebly at times, 'Sheenappa, if you abandon me, who else will lend me a helping hand? Haven't I the desire to lead a conjugal life? Why did you do so?'

Her fever subsided on the sixteenth day. On regaining consciousness, she saw Sheenappa beside her attending to her medical care. She got demure, but Sheenappa reassured her with his affable speak. One week thence, Lakshmi could sit up on her bed. Srotri told his wife, 'I now have to offer some consolation to Lakshmi. You stay away for a while.' He then went in and held Lakshmi's hands. Lakshmi hung her head in astonishment. Still holding her hands, Srotri said, 'Lakshmi, it is easy for man to bite the dust, but difficult to come around. Every man has to go through his *karma*. It is so with familial bliss too. *Dharma* has destined that I live life thus despite having a wife. That same *dharma* has destined you with widowhood. You are about 24 now, and I am 28. If we fall prey to pleasures that wouldn't last more than about two decades from now, we will be violating *dharma*. We should restrain ourselves even if we find it difficult to adhere to. You, too, know that if we violate *dharma*, the previous seven heads will fall into hell. Our forefathers better not suffer because of us, right?'

Lakshmi said nothing. She kept ruminating his words. Srotri continued, 'I will not abandon you any day. I hold your hand and assure you thus. Henceforth, you must bathe daily morning too. I will give you tīrtha after worship. Take it with all devotion. You shall get peace of mind. Henceforth, you harvest the flowers for my daily worship. Worship the cows every morning.'

In a few days, Lakshmi was up and about. She began conversing with Srotri as with a childhood friend—as she did before. One day, Srotri handed a document to Lakshmi and said, 'Lakshmi, nobody's life is eternal. As long as I live, I shall care for you. But if something should befall me, you should not be put to hardship. I have registered to your name two acres of land in the eastern corner of the Hejjige farm. Keep this document safely in your trunk. This record is available with the government office as well. In case this document is lost, there will still be the government record.'

Lakshmi's eyes got wet. 'Why all this, Sheenappa? One morsel of food per day, and filling my sight with you is more than enough for me.'

'What you say is right, but these are imperatives of a transactional world,' said Srotri.

CHAPTER 14

1

Doing the rounds, well past midnight, in Katyayani's mind was her husband's detailed account of the incident. It was not possible that all the details were related by him. Her mother-in-law Bhageerathamma had one day shared with her the same. As the very imaginative Katyayani recalled both the narratives, the bits and pieces gelled perfectly and appeared like a play before her eyes. Even now, her father-in-law and Lakshmi are mutually cordial. Lakshmi would not dine until Srotri is done with his food. She bathes daily, and until she partakes of the tīrtha given by Srotri, she doesn't drink or eat anything. She attends to cow worship daily. She has found her niche in this family. And in all important family matters, her opinion is valued.

Katyayani knows that she enjoys greater regard than Lakshmi does in this house. Of late, her father-in-law would put through financial transactions only after apprising her of them. Four years ago, he had informed her before gifting a 1,000 rupees to Dr Rao. He had placed an envelope containing the cash along with the usual betel leaves, arecanut and coconut on a tray, had his wife dribble a spoonful of propitious water on them, and given it to Dr Rao. She now thought if she was worthy of such authority bestowed on her by her father-in-law. It was 3 am when she gave in to sleep.

She got up at 8 and bathed. Today, she had to go to Mysore and share with Raja Rao the discussions she'd had at home. Go there and share what? Her father-in-law had stated that the freedom in the matter was completely hers. If she did not arrive at a decision and act accordingly, what would she take to Mysore to share with him? She was not able to arrive at any decision. She hurriedly bathed as she contemplated all this. She finished her breakfast in a hurry. She took hold of one notebook and the lunchbox that her mother-in-law gave, and arrived at the gates of the railway station out of sheer habit. Her mind teetered from non-specific and inconclusive thoughts. It was more than five months since she confided in Raja regarding her feelings. She had even conducted herself in the spirit of a wife. That experience had drawn her towards him categorically so as to not leave room for even a trace of adversity. Her mind was eager to arrive at a decision even as the train rolled on. The decision she had arrived at five months ago seemed to slacken yesterday night to her utter consternation; but it had not completely disintegrated. Maybe Raja was awaiting her at the railway station today. She was flustered as to what she'd tell him upon immediately after alighting from the train.

Even before the slow-chugging train reached Kadakola, she could see the Chamundi hill through the window of her car. It being summer, the scorched rocks had lent a bald look to the entire hill. The morning sun was behind the hill; its shadow could also be noticed. Soon, memories of her father-in-law came up. His physique, too, was as majestic as the hill. She thought of every simile to liken the two: his age of sixty, his height, robustness, the tread of his firm steps, the way he sat still with his eyes closed while performing worship. And in consonance with the steadfastness of the hill were his prowess at reining his mind, his temperance, and the way he addressed life's problems. When everybody was grieving after her husband had died, he who had lost his only son in his prime had swallowed the grief with the steadfastness of the hill, and appeared composed on the outside. He was a towering personality that merited to be looked up to! She was appreciative of all his traits.

While her musings rolled on thus, the train arrived at Chamarajapura station. Anxiously, she looked out the window. Raja was not to be seen. Alighting, she exited the station. The hill was still within view. Though it was 10 am and the atmospheric temperature kept increasing, the attraction of the hill did not dwindle. For no reason at all, she desired to scale the hill, and headed for it. She walked past Krishnamurthypura and through the betel fields of Chamundipura. The roads were dusty. A gust of wind deposited some of the dust on her face and body.

She had been to the hill twice before. Once in the company of her husband, she had scaled it on foot. So she knew the trek route. Ignoring the scorching sun, she walked on and crossed the Nilgiri road. As she headed for the foot of the hill, she noticed a bonfire to her left. She stopped to look. The blaze soared high. About five people surrounded it and looked intently into it. One of them had a long bamboo stick in his hand. Though she hadn't seen Mysore's graveyard, she had heard Mysoreans oft mouth the adage 'To carry the dead to the foot of the hill'. She understood that it was a pyre. If it were other times, she would have been frightened at the sight. Now, even that seemed attractive. In a little while, a crackle was heard from within the blazing pyre. The man with the bamboo stick nudged the cindered corpse into the centre of the pyre. The priest, who wore a dhoti for a headdress, was uttering the mantras. After the rites were consummated, every one of them left without looking back at the pyre.

The pyre still burned. Katyayani neared it and kept looking intently. The corpse had burned so much that it was not possible to be differentiated from the firewood. The blaze, smoke and crackle ceased, and the pyre was just aglow now. Her mind was pervaded with the thought that man's desires, wishes, wants, feelings, good wishes would all turn into ash in this fire. She let out a long sigh. By then, another corpse was being brought. Four people carried the bamboo frame on which the corpse was laid, and a man walked ahead with heavy steps, carrying a pot containing embers. Two young, sullen-looking youths brought up the behind. Beside them strode the priest with an unaffected mien on his face. He wore a red shawl and held a bunch of halfa-grass in one hand. Presently, they all neared her. The corpse was lowered thereabouts. The priest approached Katyayani and said, 'What has a woman got to do here? You should not be here alone. This is not a spot to be visited by you. Get going.' She left from there and soon arrived at the foot of the hill. She began scaling the stairs that spiralled up before her. But soon, she felt spent. Her breathing got laboured and she perspired, but she continued to walk. When she had covered half the distance, she was fully drained and her head seemed to reel. She sat on the balustrade. Beneath, she could see half of Mysore clustered around the hill. The city's gigantic mansions, the grand palace, etc. appeared small.

She identified her college that was beyond the shining tank, to the west. Soon came memories of Raja. He was waiting for her in college. She thought that by now he would be fidgeting from anxiety. Though the desire to scale down the hill, go to college and meet him surfaced in her mind and began steeling, she still continued uphill.

Uphill is always strenuous. Until now, there wasn't breeze enough to even move the leaves. But presently, cool air began coursing. She felt refreshed. Soon, the cool air became strong. Her mind strove to arrive at a decision. Mysore was to one side of the hill. Ten miles farther to the other side was Nanjangud. Wedged between these two, her mind lost direction. The wind was now a gale. In another five minutes, a whirlwind kicked up a lot of dust and did the rounds about her. Wildly spinning along with the dust were dry leaves, discarded broomsticks blown to smithereens, rags of cloth, bits of paper and sundry other waste materials.

So much was the quantum of brown dust kicked up, that it obscured the city of Mysore and the college that were visible a few minutes ago. A gust of wind coursed about her, akin to a stream coursing through rocky parts. Katyayani was afraid. She feared that it would carry her away and cast her some place. She sat by a boulder and hugged it firmly. She closed her eyes to check the dust from pricking them. The tempest ceased abruptly in a split second. When she opened her eyes, she was astounded at the sight of clouds that were forming in the sky. One big cloud gathered right above her head and obscured the sun. She got up and continued scaling the hill. The sultry weather caused from the proximate cloud caused her to sweat, making her inner garments sticky. She had never before experienced such stifling heat. The pyre she had witnessed an hour ago still glowed in her eyes. Her mind had gone to such depths as to render her incapable of any cogitation.

In 10 minutes, rain droplets descended. She lifted her head and looked up. Black clouds had formed overhead. It now started to pour torrentially as if through a sieve. She did not scurry to stand beneath a tree; she kept scaling the hill in the rain. When it rained more heavily, she submitted herself to the blitz and sat on the ground. It rained continuously for 15 minutes. Absent were the storm, the brown dust, and the bits and pieces of waste. It was calm everywhere. Mysore city appeared as new; in a new light. The matchbox-sized college, too, appeared in a novel shape. The clouds dispersed. The sun shone as before, but it was not scorching. A strange rain! It showed up accidentally out of season and vanished as accidentally.

Katyayani began scaling the hill. Her clothes were being caressed by the wind. She no more felt it difficult to scale. In fact, it was gleeful in a way. Her father-in-law surfaced in her memory. He would be experiencing such delight all his life; would have guided Lakshmi into experiencing similar delight. She reflected that the source of such happiness and calmness was in such scaling. In five minutes, she had arrived at the peak. She went into the temple, prostrated before the deity, exited and sat beneath a tree. At that altitude, her mind became cheerful. It was now like a stream that flowed calmly on an even bed of sand, unobstructed by boulders. In the calmness, she arrived at a decision.

She felt hungry. She drank water from a tap near the temple, returned to where she sat beneath the tree and helped herself to the lunch she had packed. She then washed the empty lunchbox, and began scaling down the hill. By then her clothes were also dry. The hard cover of the notebook was still moist though. While she climbed down, she did not feel tired. There were none of the kin that had brought the corpse to the graveyard. The rain had doused the pyres. The graveyard was tranquil. The atmosphere was free of dust. Though her legs ached, she walked the distance to her college, and reached there by 4. She was there to convey to Raja Rao her decision. The door to the theatre association was closed. As there was one more hour to catch the return train, she climbed up the steps and stood in the balcony to the fore. The hill sought her attention again. She kept looking at it. She did not know how long she stood so. When she glanced downward once, she saw Raja Rao with his bicycle. He was looking in her direction and his sight was stern. 'Come down,' he said.

Returning her gaze to the hill, she eyed it for two minutes silently, then turned to him and said, 'You come up.'

He who was torn asunder from waiting for her all day thought of it as a sign of indifference on her part. He boarded his bicycle in a fit of anger. Without the need for any effort on his part, it began rolling down the gradient.

Katyayani kept looking at the hill.

After returning home that evening and changing, she called her father-in-law upstairs. Srotri who was headed to the puja chamber for his evening prayers went upstairs. She prostrated by touching his feet and said, 'I had let my thoughts drift at some inappropriate moment. I have realized that they are misplaced. Pardon me.'

'Such unfounded thoughts spare none. No need to fret about it. You stick to your studies,' said Srotri calmly.

When he started to climb down, Katyayani once again called out to him and asked demurely, 'What I shared with you yesterday, and the contents of that letter, did you share with amma?'

'No, I haven't. Will never. That letter is on the shelf in the living room. You take it yourself and destroy it,' he said and climbed down the stairs.

2

Raja got incensed at Katyayani for having kept him guessing for long hours since 10 in the morning, and then disregarding him at 4 in the evening despite seeing him. He surmised that her in-laws wouldn't have accorded consent. He reflected that to seek the concurrence of in-laws to such a marriage was impracticable, considering that traditionally-minded parents themselves would not accord their consent. That their marriage was not possible unless Katyayani herself took a bold initiative to forsake her in-laws and move on. Why did she so disregard him yesterday? Did it mean to convey to him that he should forget her?

He waited for her the next day in college too. She did not turn up. The next few days, he awaited her at the railway station and returned disappointed. Though he thought of writing a letter to her, he thought the better of it. Her exams would start in 10 days. He tried to get solace by thinking that he would be able to meet her then, for she would surely come to take the exams. There was no way he could kill time at home. Nagalakshmi had now turned fully reticent. She would not talk to him freely like before. He tried speaking to her several times, but her mind was always lost in thought so as to not even mumble a reply. She had no interest other than preparing and serving food on time.

One day while she served food, Nagalakshmi said to Raja, 'An astrologer visited our neighbouring house today. He told me that it would augur well for my next birth if I took to rote-writing the name Rama. I have decided to write it one crore times before passing on. Get me notebook, inkstand and ink.'

That evening, he brought her a notebook and pen. She held the pen and said, 'I do not know how to use this. The steel of an inkstand is fine with me. Get me that.' He brought it the next day. She prepared ink by dissolving the ink powder in water. She kept them all—inkpot, notebook and steel in the altar of the puja chamber, applied vermilion and turmeric to them and prostrated. She then took the notebook, pressed it to both her eyes, exited and asked Raja, 'If I write a certain number of names each day, how many days will this book last? How many names will this book accommodate? If I have to accomplish one crore names, how many such books do I need to fill up? Calculate and tell me.'

Counting the number of lines in a page, Raja said, 'If you write 10 names in a line, this notebook will hold 40,000 names. You need 250 such books to write one crore names.'

'Okay then. As and when I complete one book, get me another. Will you get me ink powder too?'

'Of course, I will. If you just write names, what will you get?'

'Who will just write names? I will write with all my devotion.'

Raja smiled within himself at her naïveté, giving out nothing. Nagalakshmi began with her rote-writing. In every line of the notebook, she would write *Sri Rama Sri Rama*... 10 times. She would conclude each page by writing *Sri Rama Jai*

Rama Jai-jai Rama Seeta-Rama. The last she wrote anything formally was when she studied for her middle school. Later, when Raja was in England, she had written a few letters to him. Of late, she had lost touch. Therefore, her fingers would pain initially, and she could not write speedily. 'It is okay to write slowly. I only have to finish it before I die,' she said to herself, and went about it with that composure of mind. Her mind had been in a state of void in the leisure hours hitherto, but it now found something to fall back upon.

Raja eagerly awaited Katyayani on exam day. He was assigned invigilation duty for those days. He had to report half hour ahead of exam time. He had to then go to an assigned classroom and be there all through the duration of the exam, and a little after. Thus, he could not get to see her for the first six days. Fortunately, on the seventh day, he was assigned invigilation of a classroom where she had to write her exams. Entering the room, Katyayani was shocked to see Raja. She could not write well that day. Raja found a break to near her and whisper in her ears, 'See me after the exams.'

'Hmm,' she said helplessly.

They met up after the exams and exited. When they had neared a tree to the west side of the college, she said, 'Forget me.' Her voice was heavy.

'Why say so?'

'Don't ask anything. You fell in love with an ineligible one. Wed another girl and be happy. I feel like I am an old woman.' Her eyes welled up. 'Let us not debate anymore. There is no possibility of us meeting henceforth,' she said, and hurriedly walked away from there. Dumbfounded, Raja kept looking her way.

Next day, he especially requested the chief supervisor to allot him a different classroom. His brain had gone grungy. Katyayani, who had over the last six months lent accretion to the meaning of his life, now walked out on him by stating so, giving no room for him to respond anything. How could he forget her, her who had fully occupied his mind, heart and brain? Not possible in this lifetime. He was also unable to think up a way of earning her back. Tears welled up in his eyes. Unable to put up with his agony, he spilled it all before Nagalakshmi one day. She said, 'These matters are always thus. You, too, rote-write Rama's name. Agitation of the mind will assuage. Later, you shall wed another girl.'

'Nagu, you can never understand this,' he said and left her to her rote-writing.

He could not think of a plausible explanation as to why she should have got so close to him if eventually she would subject him to this. Her statement that she was an old woman—she who was all of 24 years of age and of attractive physique—had still not brought his intelligence to think up an explanation. What an imaginary falsity she delineated herself with! He was confounded again. His mind, though, was immersed in memory of the times he had spent in her company.

3

On the last day of the exams, Katyayani's mind desired to see Raja. But it was she who had distanced herself from him. Though she desired to visit his house and say a word of gratitude typical of a pupil to a teacher, she resisted it, boarded the Nanjangud train and went home. 'That was the last commute to Mysore. I am relieved of it tomorrow onwards,' she told her mother-in-law.

'Yes, kiddo. If you pass, his name will reign,' Bhageerathamma reminisced her son.

Now, Katyayani spent more time with her kid. Cheeni was now a five-year-old. After the summer vacations, he had to take to schooling. Sometime in March-April on an auspicious day, his *cūḍākarma* had to be performed traditionally, as part of which he should be made to lick honey smeared on a silver coin, and write *Sri Rama* with his index finger on rice grains spread in a tray. Bhageerathamma had plans to get traditional snack hampers done in quite some quantity for the guests for that ceremony. Srotri had full belief in this traditional rite. It should have been performed in his third year. A sort of apathy had checked him then. Though he was not for holding it in a grand manner, he did not want to come in the way of his family members' happiness.

Cheeni was a chatterbox. His grandparents were fed up of answering his unending questions about all and sundry—what is this? Why that? Where did this come from? Why is this here? Nowadays, he followed Lakshmi while she herded the cattle. Many a day, he got stubborn with his desire to sleep in her company.

The first few days after the exams, Katyayani felt bored. She thought that it would abate with the passage of time, and she would get accustomed to a different routine. She urged herself to involve more and more in household chores. She would look for some new work and attend to it. She even took to reciting the Bhagavadgīta in the afternoons. She would bathe in the morning well in time and be in attendance at her father-in-law's daily puja rites. Despite all these, her boredom did not abate even after a full month. Instead, restlessness of mind increased. She stayed away from the first-floor room and took to retiring in her mother-in-law's room. Cheeni slept with his grandmother as he had been doing all through. Katyayani would not get sleep at nights. She would always reminisce Raja. What would he be doing now? Would he be reminiscing me? Consequent to my telling him off, would he be incensed at me? Or had he resolved to wed another girl? She would find herself unable to bear that even in her imagination.

While her mind went haywire thus, she would take hold of the Bhagavadgīta and start reciting. She would read each verse deliberately and try to grasp its meaning. Whatever she read would be registered in her intellect, but her mind would completely miss it. The tenets of the Bhagavadgīta would prove a barrier, and her mind would endeavour to demolish that barrier and surge forward. It would devise a beautiful craft, and take her and Raja on a pleasure trip in it. As the days passed by, her life became more and more insipid. She saw no meaning in it. Food lost its taste. Her body that nursed desires began to wilt as would a tender creeper that came in contact with flames. The strength of her body dwindled. Conversely to the dwindling bodily strength, the strength of her desires became tremendous. In a tussle between contrived realization and pristine Nature, it was Nature that earned the upper hand, and her life was rife with darkness from disappointment. Wherever she stood or sat or went, Raja's face would appear before her eyes. Vivid in her memory would be their long walks, corporeal proximity, the trip to Brindavan, and the sweet nothings whispered into each other's ears. Memories of such experiences that were as cool as moonlight just a few days ago, now scorched her more severely than the graveyard pyre. One morning she could not eat even one morsel of food. The afternoon static did not cause her to slide into sleep. Though she shoved some food down her gullet at supper, she vomited it all while washing her hands. When she retired, she felt feverish. Soon, the fever set in. She kept tossing this way and that all night. She thought that she would not live for long. A few hours past midnight, a resolve rived from within her—she should take permission of her father-in-law and leave for Mysore first thing the next morning. But how to put it across to him? The very thought of presenting herself before him sent a fear down her spine. Not a fear that would befall one that saw a snake, but the sort of fear that a sinner would experience on thinking of God. Would it be right to leave without informing him? The impediment would surface, that it would tantamount to belie the faith that he had reposed in her if she walked out on him so. *But hasn't he entitled me discretion in matters of my life?* Though her mind sought refuge in his words '*You are free to do as you wish*', she would reflect if exercising discretion was an attribute of freedom.

The duel between propriety and impropriety went on incessantly in her mind. That night, she decided on the new course her life would take. Either she should tread that path, or she should die from emaciation here. She was not ready to just shed her life.

First thing the next morning, she told her mother-in-law, 'I had forgotten. A teacher of mine has invited me to her wedding dinner, which is today. I've got to visit Mysore.'

Her father-in-law was at his routine worship, so the mother-in-law consented.

When she wore a fresh sari and exited, Cheeni asked, 'Amma, where you going?' She gave a thought to her kid. Without ensuring her exit, how might she take along her kid? She neared him and kissed him on both his cheeks. 'Amma, take me too,' he said. 'You shall join me later,' she said, and went away hurriedly. While going past that block, she looked back to see her house for once. Her sight was a blur. She boarded the usual train. Until she reached Mysore, her heart was beating rapidly.

She went straight to Raja's house and knocked on the door. Prthvi opened it. 'Where is uncle,' she asked, and he pointed to his room. When she pushed the door and stepped in, she was aghast at what she saw. Raja had emaciated so much that he appeared like a skeleton. He'd even grown a beard. The clothes he wore were soiled. He eyed her suspiciously. Sealing the door, she walked up to him, placed her face on his chest and said, 'Now, you believe me. I will not return to that house. Commencing today, let us be man and wife to the society.'

Raja did not immediately believe Katyayani's words. He looked at her with bewilderment and wonder in his eyes. She said, 'Look at me. I have just rushed here, carrying nothing with me whatsoever. Let us go through a wedding ceremony as you wish. I am okay with civil marriage or at a temple with well-wishers as the witnesses. Or, if you say "no need for any such thing, you just live with me," I am game for that too. You are my man.' She embraced him with her arms. Raja now knew that her words held credence. He, too, embraced her. The agitation of both their hearts subsided. Her heartbeat returned to normalcy.

CHAPTER 15

1

When Katyayani did not return by the 6 pm train, everyone in the house was in anticipation of her returning by the 10 pm train. As it was summer vacations, she wouldn't have company, wherefore Srotri went to the railway station to escort her home. That train came and then moved on towards Chamarajanagar. His daughter-in-law was nowhere to be seen. For a while, Srotri sat on a bench meant for the passengers. His mind was contemplating as to why she hadn't returned. He had subtly noticed that over the past two weeks she was not her usual self. But he had thought the better of volunteering to question her about it, for it was a sensitive matter to pry into, given that she was a mother to a five-year-old kid, had taken to manage the finances of the household, had written her BA exams, and was aware of her responsibilities, *dharma* and *karma*. Though it crossed his mind that she would have returned to *him*, he convinced himself not to suspect anything in the absence of proof. He returned home and said, 'She hasn't returned by this train even. She said it was a wedding. They would have asked her to stay back. She may return tomorrow.'

That day, even Cheeni did not get sleep. Before he eventually slipped into sleep, he had twice asked, 'Why is amma still not back?' He slept only after his grandmother told him that she would return tomorrow. The night passed and the next day came. The morning train from Mysore arrived too, but not the daughter-in-law. Srotri, who was in the puja chamber, had forgotten everything and was all concentration in his worship. When he exited the puja chamber at about 9 and gave tīrtha to Bhageerathamma, Lakshmi and Cheeni, Bhageerathamma handed him an envelope. It had arrived by the morning post. He readily recognized that the address on it was in Katyayani's handwriting. His inner mind readily got to know fully what the content was. Abstaining from opening the envelope immediately, he purchased time to maintain his mental balance at even keel, went to the living room, rested some in a chair and opened it after five minutes. Four pages in the handwriting of his daughter-in-law; the matter was exactly what he thought it would be. Her state of mind when she sought his permission the last time, the reason for backtracking on her resolve, and the agony she experienced again. After explaining all these, she had written:

> Encouraged by your towering personality, I tried reining in my mind. I couldn't. Every individual is unique in their own way, and their strengths and limitations are their own. Before exiting from there, I desired to confide it all in you, but I could not garner the courage required to face you. Our wedding shall he held at a social event in a few days. To

> invite you to it would be impudence on my part. I prostrate at your feet and request you to bless me with peace and contentment in my chosen life. A motherless child, and one who didn't get the full complement of father's love, I was fortunate enough to benefit from parental love for six years in your house. Your blessings should infuse happiness into the life of this daughter of yours.

Srotri sat mute. Though he could not fully grasp the state of her mind, he did not get incensed at her. Before his mind's eye appeared the picture of an unfortunate soul who could not protect herself from the distraction of Nature. His mind filled with compassion. He recalled her conduct all through ever since she entered this house as its daughter-in-law. Not even on a single occasion had she conducted or spoken so as to cause discomfort to her in-laws. She had served them as she would her own parents. She had been a loving wife to her husband when he was alive. She had all the qualities that Srotri expected of a member of this family. In the end, she excused herself thus.

He thought about his ancestry. Adhering to the well-established *ārṣeya* tradition, it had never before witnessed such a situation. He was in possession of the record of the genealogical tree of his ancestry, in which were details of the last 12 generations. The roots of the generations prior to these 12 were deep beyond his grasp. He believed that those roots were very much vivacious and auspicious, and would egg him on endlessly deep if he went about seeking them.

Among the ones listed in the line of descent were those that had lived only half a life span, those that had married a second time though the first wife lived, and those that were widowed, but there were no cases that served as precedence for Katyayani's act. Every woman who had moved here from other pedigrees had stayed till they passed on. Just as it was impossible for a tributary of a river to earn back its individualism and move on to another river, so was it for a maiden who secured admission into one pedigree to shift loyalty subsequently. The novel conduct of Katyayani was an irrevocable blotch on the history of this ancestry. Would at least the sanctity of the other pedigree that she checked into remain intact? Another question popped up as if in answer to that question: do those that have admitted her into their lineage have any perception as to their ancestry?

The clock struck noon while he was still deep in his musings. Bhageerathamma came into the living room and said, 'Why simply sit? Come on, have your lunch. She hasn't yet returned. What letter is that?'

'Some matter,' he said and got up. Cheeni, too, lunched with his grandfather and kept up with his usual blabber. Srotri could not ingest the food. Try as he might, the ingested morsel did not go down his gullet. 'What is this? Why, are you not feeling well?' Bhageerathamma asked him. 'You lunch. I am not feeling like it,' he said, and went through the customary winding up rituals, his plate almost untouched. When Lakshmi and Bhageerathamma were through with their lunch, he summoned them into an inner room, explained to them about Katyayani, and read out her letter. Dumbfounded, Bhageerathamma asked, 'So, she had already discussed this with you?'

'Yes.'

'Why didn't you inform me of it?'

'She had checked me from revealing it. Besides, she had contained her mind on her own, and had atoned for thinking it up.'

'And now she needed no permission! Who is the guy that is wedding her?'

'Sadashiva Rao's brother Raja Rao.'

'It is!' Bhageerathamma's anger reached its peak. 'That man has benefited greatly from this house, and his brother does this?'

'How can he be blamed for his brother's act?'

'Would an elder brother be tongue-tied as not to discipline his younger sibling?'

'Rao might not know of this. He now lives separately with his second wife.' Srotri related the second marriage of Dr Rao as much as he knew of it.

'Who told you all this?'

'Katyayani herself.'

'She told you everything, but you didn't share any of it with us. That cunning sinner bimbo behaved as if she were a chaste one, and now has packed off by tarnishing the image of this house. It is better if she were dead...' Bhageerathamma went on deriding her daughter-in-law, the man who had come forward to wed this widow, and his brother Sadashiva Rao individually and collectively.

'You should not mouth such bad words. You forfeit the calmness that comes with age!' Srotri's placation had no influence on her whatsoever. 'Keep it down, my Lord. You are elderly, but wisdom has not yet dawned on you. When I objected to getting her enrolled for the college, you sided with her and jumped in jubilation the same way she did. She went to the college in her husband's name and has now chosen to tarnish his ancestry. We should have got her tonsured, restricted her to wearing red saris and confined her indoors. It was you that gave much leeway…"My daughter-in-law, my daughter-in-law" all the time, wasn't it? I would say she did you right. Tell me, will you at least now do as I say, or not? We got to salvage the family honour.'

'What is it? Tell me calmly.'

'Keep all that calmness to yourself. Just do as I say. She has written that her scandalous wedding is scheduled to be held three days from now. I will join you. Let us go and give that man a show down, whack her head fine and drag her back by her tresses.'

Srotri calmy considered her suggestions. Bhageerathamma asked, 'Why are you silent?'

'No use going to Mysore. She is not juvenile. And don't you think for once that she is any less perturbed by this. Anything achieved by coercion will not endure. One conducts oneself as per one's nature.'

'It is always your Vedanta! You are one saint. You stay home. I will take Lakshmi with me, and drag her back here.'

Lakshmi, who was till then cogitating on the developments calmly, said, 'What Sheenappa says is right. It can't be set right even if we force her into coming here. Her *karma*!'

'That's another of my counsellors!' said Bhageerathamma scornfully. Asking Lakshmi to console her, Srotri exited from there and went to his study upstairs. His mind was disturbed too.

2

Raja and Katyayani heralded their marriage by exchanging garlands in the convention hall of Sriprakash Boarding and Lodging. For a fee of 50 rupees, a priest put through a simple one-hour rite wherein Raja adorned Katyayani's neckline with the connubial string. After the august guests collectively blessed the newly-wed couple with consecrated grain, they met them individually, gave them gifts and congratulated them. All guests were Raja's friends. As it was summer vacations, and the wedding had to be held at a short notice of two days, many could not make it. Though Nagalakshmi did not want to go any place, she felt obliged to visit the hotel. There were no surrogate parents on the part of either the groom or the bride to perform their respective religious rites. Rao was visiting in Kolkata to take a study tour of the museum there and to help themselves to some rare books in the library of the university, and they were in the dark about these developments. Rao knew nothing about the Raja-Katyayani affair.

When the wedding rites were consummated, the three took leave of the guests for a while and went into the privacy of the rented room there. Katyayani prostrated at Nagalakshmi's feet and said, 'Sister, maybe you do not concur with what I have done. You are the lady of the house. Though no bride-accepting ritual was observed as part of the wedding rites, you have admitted me into your household. Please be my guardian.'

Nagalakshmi said in apathy, 'Being Raja's wife, you belong in our house. Even though I am a member of the household, I am preparing to stay detached. Henceforth, you take charge of everything.'

In the hall outside, the carpet was removed, the floor broomed and plantain leaves were laid out for supper. As desired by the guests, the newly-weds dined on a common ensemble of plantain leaves. The hotel's kitchen staff had prepared a variety of dishes—sweets, snacks, fruit salad, coulis, vegetables curry, curd curry, curd, etc. The supper progressed leisurely, and the guests permitted themselves to chatting this and that:

'Lucky, I would say, this Raja Rao. What if she is a widow, he has got himself a lovely damsel. If a woman were so lovely, even a four-time widow is marriageable.'

'You better not be a pioneer at that. Such a woman has the propensity to become a widow for the fifth time!'

'He seems to be romantic just like his elder brother. The trait runs in the family, I would say.'

'Well, well. Dr Rao is not to be seen.'

'The woman wearing the yellow sari, seated close to Raja Rao, is Dr Rao's first wife. Knowing that she would be here, those two would have stayed back.'

'No, no, you are mistaken. They have gone to Kolkata on a study tour. He doesn't have an inkling of this development. You should not refer to him as *romantic*. He is a great scholar, the type that loses oneself in research.'

'Man, the cuisine is fine. Instead of gratefully helping yourself to supper, you choose to pass loose comments on the ways of the host!' said a man who had played a role in one of Raja's plays.

Then on, everybody ate silently. By the end, when rice was served for curd, the Sanskrit professor rendered two verses tunefully. Someone else took cue and recited another verse. A student who had bagged a prize at the inter-collegiate singing competition the previous year, and who was pursuing his MA this year, sang a song. Everyone was following the rhythm by tapping on their left thighs with their left palms. By the time he finished it, supper was through. The guests once again shook hands with Raja Rao, and left one by one, collecting their gift hampers on the way out. Settling the hotel bill, Raja, Katyayani, Nagalakshmi and Prthvi returned home in a tonga.

For 15 days thence, the newly-weds were lost to the external world. Nagalakshmi, as usual, prepared food. As it was still vacations, Prthvi went to play with his friends in the neighbourhood. Raja and Katyayani kept to their bedroom. They wanted no loitering and they didn't want to watch plays. They were just content in telling each other how they would be agonized by even a minute's separation, that the experience of non-duality in their union was eternal. Raja delineated such eternality in the parlance of the everlasting, the truth, the incessant, etc. While he expounded on the unique beauty of the contours of her body and sung in praise of it, she would, on her part, expound on the finesse of the contours of his face. Days were nights and nights were days, and in the unison of Nature and soul, time seemed to have forgotten its routine.

As she had walked-in in just the clothes she wore and had brought nothing else along, Raja took her to a store and got her new designer saris. Katyayani would wear them, wear vermilion, and wear floral strings at the nape. When she looked at her image in the mirror, she would feel that her femininity had attained its fulfillment. Whenever Raja held her in his arms and praised her beauty, she would brim with a feeling of fulfillment. She would bow before her man and silently submit to him. Her happiness would swell from the feeling that her very existence was for his pleasure.

After some days, Katyayani took to assisting Nagalakshmi in the kitchen. Nagalakshmi neither refused her assistance nor worried if she didn't turn up. She would be unto herself. Work was no burden for her, and she would take to her rote-writing after she was done with her chores. She showed no interest in it even if Katyayani picked up a chat with her. Noticing that she had changed and taken to being more of a silent person, Katyayani would not pull her into conversation much. But she would assist her in cooking.

Prthvi was familiar with Katyayani. He even knew that she was now married to his uncle. His playmates had said, 'Your uncle has married a widow.' He even knew what that meant. Aged seven, he was of keen intellect. Raja asked him to address Katyayani as aunty. He complied. Even now, Raja carried him about lovingly. At times, he took him for a ride on his bicycle still. Katyayani would express love by pulling him up and passing her palm over his head. He was a bit hesitant in mixing freely with his new aunt. But he would not shy away from her so as not to let her think of him as being unfriendly. By and by, they got close. He began conversing freely with her. He would even get his homework checked by her.

Whenever she eyed Prthvi, Katyayani's mind would think of Cheeni. That was a baby born out of her flesh and blood. On the day when she walked out on that house, Cheeni had said, 'Amma, take me too'. She had told him that he shall join her later, and had walked away apace. Now, memories of her kid began haunting her. Initially it was Prthvi's sight that would bring Cheeni to her mind. By and by, Cheeni's face would vividly surface in her memory at all times, wherever she was and while attending to whatever work. She, therefore, decided that she would bring over her kid. At times her father- and mother-in-law would surface in memory too. If she brought the baby over, who would they look up to in the days to come? The memory of that aging couple would engender compassion in her mind. At times, a feeble voice from deep within her would aver that it was improper on her part to have abandoned them, but her mind would douse it. But she could never imagine living on without her kid.

One night, Katyayani shared with Raja the exhorting of her heart. 'What is your opinion about bringing over my child here?' she asked. He went silent. Noticing, she asked, 'Why silence?'

'Nothing at all,' he said. Recalling something he said, 'Hadn't I told you clearly once before? Bring him over. He is our child.'

She was extremely happy to hear that. She embraced him with both arms and said, 'You are a very good man. Will you join me in fetching him?'

'It would not be proper for me to go. You should do this yourself.'

'I find it impossible to go there and say "let me have my child" all by myself. With you alongside, I possibly can request them.'

He gave it a thought and said, 'You first write to them a letter explaining everything, request them to send Cheeni with you, and inform them of your proposed date and time of visit. When you go there on that date, there will be no need to make that inhibiting proposal verbally.'

Next day, she took to drafting the letter. But the matter seemed to elude her. Her fingers trembled as well. Still, she gathered all her courage, and wrote a five-page letter. Informing them of the consummation of her wedding, she told them that she would visit there to prostrate at their feet to seek their blessings. Then she went on to state that the mother-son relationship was basic to all relationships. Explaining the tremendous pull of the mother's womb, and her agony at not having the company of her baby, she had concluded it thus:

> It is not at all difficult for you to understand the agony of this mother-of-a-child. Fourth day from now, i.e. on the 20th, I will visit there by the noon train. Please send my child with me. Please convey my respects to my mother-in-law and Lakshmi.

She placed it in an envelope and gave it to Raja. He affixed the required postage stamps on it and posted it immediately.

3

When Katyayani started on the 20th after having lunch, the drizzle of the June had set in. It had rained fine in the Western Ghats, and all the rivers were flowing fairly full. Holding an umbrella, Raja walked her to the railway station and saw her off. Her mind was filled with an unknown fear. When the train was about to leave, he said, 'I will be here to pick you up at six.' She was going to Nanjangud one and half months after she had walked out on that house. This was probably her last trip there. It drizzled all through the journey. She could not spot where the sun was in the sky. It continued to rain when the train halted and resumed its journey in the intervening stations. When the train crossed Kambalimath and chugged along slowly on the bridge, she could fully see the river Kapila flowing half full. In the distance were the bathing decks, and yonder was the temple and the stretch of vegetation to its left, interspersed with big trees; familiar all. It came to her mind all of a sudden: it was in the same June a certain year, when it was drizzling so, that Kapila had swallowed her first husband. She also recalled the quantum of tears she had shed since. While her thoughts proceeded to think up all the agonies she underwent thence, the train arrived in Nanjangud.

When she alighted from the train, her heart began pounding. If anybody recognized her en route! By now the entire town would have got to know of the developments in her life. She resolutely exited the station and walked in the direction of her house, telling herself that she needn't fear anyone. By now, her in-laws would have received her letter and arrived at a decision. If in unison they refused to part with the child, what would she do? Mother-in-law would certainly be seething in rage. But father-in-law would acquiesce to supplication. *Anyway, I have written in that letter all I got to say. No need to speak afresh now.* She arrived at the door of the house, which was half open. She entered the living room and then on to the inner quarters, to one side of which was the kitchen, dining hall and puja chamber. She could not garner courage to go in. She sat on a chair in the living room. Recitation of mantras was heard from inside: '...to my father Nanjunda Sharma belonging in Kāṣyapa-gotra, as part of the annual death rites...'

She got wind of what was going on inside. She craned her neck to look at the main door. Though the front yard was broomed and cleaned, raṅgoli was not laid. That was a confirmation that annual death rites were underway. Whose? She soon recalled. It was in this month that her husband Nanjunda Srotri had passed away. And every year, it would drizzle on the day of his death anniversary. She began regretting as to what a day she had chosen to visit! Without giving it so much as a thought, she had volunteered to visit here on this unusual date. She thought of leaving and visiting some other day. She got up and walked up to the main door. There she came face to face with Lakshmi, who was entering the house. Katyayani hung her head, but Lakshmi spoke to her cordially. 'Did you just come? Are you leaving already? Oh come on, sit here.'

'No, Lakshmi. Today is his death anniversary.'

'Yes, Nanjunda's. Had you forgotten? Come sit. We got your letter.'

Realizing that there was no point in debating, Katyayani returned to the living room and sat. Lakshmi, too, sat in her company for a while. However, neither could think of anything to converse. Katyayani sat with her head hung. Lakshmi got up and went to the backyard through the door to the right. The mantras continued to coast from within and Katyayani could fathom the respective rites. Cheeni was not entitled to perform the rites of his late father, for he had not yet undergone *upanayana*, wherefore—as before—this year, too, it was Kuppaiah of the new colony that substituted for him in performing the rites. The local priest Subbaiah Shastri was reciting the mantras and directing the procedures. Katyayani could not get to know who *the two designates*—one representing the ancestors and the other representing the Gods—were, for their voices were feeble. In between, Cheeni was bringing up his usual queries, to which Srotri was giving succinct replies in hushed voice. In about 15 minutes, the pre-lunch rites concluded. Reciting the pertinent mantra, the priest instructed that food be served in the specified chronology. Finally, Kuppaiah told the two designates, 'I request you to please help yourself to this food that I have strove to put together, so that ye shall not be famished tonight.' The twain said, 'So be it.' Katyayani concentrated on the auditory leads. The ritual for commencement of lunch was heard, and Bhageerathamma was serving food.

For a while, silence prevailed. Then someone brought up a query: 'What is the difference between rites for ancestors and rites for Gods?'

Katyayani was surprised, for she got to know that it was her father Srikantaiah. Why was he visiting today? After the death of his son-in-law, for a few days he had taken her to his place, and that was all. He hadn't visited her since. He hadn't even written one single letter to her. Initially he had expressed much love towards her, but it had faded with the arrival of her stepmother. If he had visited now...would Srotri have sent word for the sake of his grandson?

Srotri's reply was heard. 'In rites for the Gods, the *yajñopavīta* should be worn on the left shoulder and should pass under the right arm. Circumambulation should be done clockwise. When water is proffered, we should say "svaahaa" and "vashat". In rites for the ancestors, the *yajñopavīta* should be worn on the right shoulder and should pass under the left arm. The rites should be performed by facing south. When water is proffered, we should say "svadhaa". The halfa used for the former should be cut grass, but for the latter it should be uprooted grass.'

The conversation went on thus, and topics pertinent to the occasion were discussed. Srikantaiah was a lawyer. He asked a legal question. 'What here is the meaning of the word *son*? Does it mean just the immediate next-generation or does it encompass subsequent generations also?'

Srotri answered, 'The clarification in this matter is in the section pertaining to estate-sharing: *putrapadaṁ prapautraparyantānāmēva pārvaṇavidhinā piṇḍadānopakārakatvasyāviśeṣāt.* The term *son* shall encompass the immediately succeeding three generations. Those three are entitled to perform the rites of their ancestors, and the ancestors shall be pleased to accept the symbolic victuals provided by them.' His words then moved from the death rites to estate-sharing methodologies of the yore. 'Though a son does not inherit any wealth from his father, he has to repay his father's debts with interest. The grandson shall repay the principal debt amount only. If the grandson were not deemed to be his grandfather's son, why should he repay the principal amount even?'

Katyayani pondered if they even knew that she was there. Lakshmi had exited through a different door. She remained assured that they were surely not discussing those points with a view to pour it into her ears. By then, Cheeni exited from within. It seemed like he, too, had participated in the death rites of his father. A five-year-old, he had on just a wet loin cloth at his waist. He, who came jumping, saw Katyayani in the living room. Though for a moment he was perplexed as if he sighted a stranger, he recognized her soon and asked, 'Amma, where had you gone all these days?' His voice seemed to reach every corner of the silent house. She beckoned him. He walked up to the door of the living room. 'Come to me Cheeni,' she said in a hushed voice. 'Amma, today is appa's death anniversary. Don't you know? I am not to touch anyone,' he said and ran away inside. Katyayani was saddened. However, he was back in five minutes. He went up to his mother, placed his elbows on her thighs and asked, 'All these days where had you been, amma?'

'I was in Mysore, child.'

'Now on, go nowhere,' he said, lifting his face and looking at hers. She held his face in her palms, and bent forward to hug him to his chest. 'I will return after the rites. It seems appa will bring consecrations. I will give them to you too,' he said, pulled himself from her and walked away. He stopped at the door and said, 'Why are you sitting here? Come on in.' He trotted away.

By then, the *two designates*' lunch was over. Mantra-tantras resumed. Half an hour later, the rites were consummated. For 10 minutes, Subbaiah Shastri went to the kitchen to talk to Bhageerathamma. Eventually, he said, 'We'll leave. You all eat lunch now,' and exited. He was escorted by one of the *two designates*, and on their way out they eyed Katyayani. Kuppaiah headed for the river, with the rice balls in a broad brass vessel, the symbolic victuals for the dead. On his way out his sight, too, swayed on Katyayani. Katyayani felt as if her belly were burning in kerosene fire. She just kept staring at a wall. When Kuppaiah returned after dissolving the rice balls in the river, his sight again slyly swayed on Katyayani. On earlier such occasions, this same Kuppaiah would hold his head hung before her; Katyayani did not take a liking to his glancing at her in such a way, but she was helpless.

Srotri came to her after a quarter hour and said, 'Food is served. Come lunch, child.' Though she was moved by his soothing words and the usual way he addressed her, she excused herself. 'My lunch is done. You please have it,' she said. But Srotri continued to stand his place by the sill. He said insistently, 'It is okay, come on. It is quite some hours since you had breakfast, no?' She made no more fuss. Getting up, she went in. Her father-in-law, her father and Cheeni sat in a line. A plantain leaf was laid separately for Katyayani. Kuppaiah sat before a leaf inside the kitchen. Nobody spoke while they ate. Bhageerathamma served in a spirit of silence that seemed to squeeze one by the neck. Pudding, donuts, fried delicacies and mango-banana pulp—the plantain leaves were fully appointed. Katyayani just ate two morsels of rice with plain curry. Nobody urged her. By the time the last item of the menu, viz. rice and curd came up, Cheeni had dozed off. Today being his father's death anniversary, he had fasted since morning, and it had taken its toll with just a few morsels of food hitting his parched belly. As per protocol, Srikantaiah was waiting for Srotri to finish his lunch. He got up hurriedly even as the latter went through the ritual to mark the same.

After her lunch, Katyayani returned to her chair in the living room. Nobody turned up there for about half an hour. Every moment was so heavy and seemed to squeeze her to death. Then Srotri came up and sat to the corner of the cot near her. Katyayani didn't know what to say. After five minutes Srotri said, 'We received your letter.'

Gathering some courage, Katyayani only said, 'I have conveyed everything in that letter.' Just then Bhageerathamma appeared by the door to participate in the debate. 'Why wouldn't you write all that? By your act you have brought disgrace to your natal house as well as this. Now you are here to purge this house of its lineage by taking away this child and goading him with blasphemy typical of you.' She said it all in one breath. Behind her came Srikantaiah, and sat to the other end of the cot where Srotri sat. He was a tall man, obese of late. He was shrewd in dealings, but he was orthodox. Bhageerathamma continued, 'Not content with your ignominious remarriage, you want to now take this child to show your newly-wed husband to him and tell him, "Cheeni, this is your father who has sired you!" Are you ashamed at all? Your father is here. Let's see if he will approve of your act. We shall take it up from there. Have we scolded you for anything? Have we deprived you of anything in this house? Report it all to your father now.'

Lawyer Srikantaiah took over in the manner of cross-examining a witness. He cleared his throat as if to convey to his daughter 'here, turn towards me and speak'. Pin drop silence prevailed. He cleared his throat again. His daughter said nothing. He could not get her to take the initiative though he coughed louder again. He began speaking in English. Though Bhageerathamma could not understand anything of it, she noticed the typical eloquence of a seasoned lawyer. Though he could not get every word of it, Srotri could grasp the essence of it. For half an hour he waxed eloquent about *dharmaśāstra*. Then he stated an aspect of law, 'Even in England, the right to custody of children vests in the family of the biological father. Even if the woman were to be widowed, the names of the children shall continue in the name of their biological father.' Then stating that she had brought disgrace even to her sacred natal lineage, he began deriding his daughter. 'You are a rascal, a disgrace to the family. Such an unworthy daughter had better not been born…' He would have gone on and on with his tirade. Sensing it, Srotri stood up, turned towards the lawyer, and said, 'What has happened has happened. No point in anyone deriding anyone else. We should not mouth foul words. You both leave. I will talk to her in confidence.'

Bhageerathamma had faith in the lawyer's oration. She paid no attention to her husband's words. 'You are a dunce, a *dharma* nerd. He is a lawyer. Let him speak. You keep quiet,' she said, and stood her place. By then Katyayani was seized by grief. Her father almost never visited his in-laws. *He never enquired after the health of his daughter. Now he comes here and scolds me as a police would a thief. If only my mother were alive! After my mother passed on, did he not wed again?* She reflected thus. That thought caused cry to billow from within her.

'You both go inside,' said Srotri again, especially to his wife. Bhageerathamma was not to be silenced. 'I won't go anywhere. He is not just your grandson. I am the one who delivered my son. Can you ever feel the pain of my womb? This is his child, and I am the one who has tended to him,' she began crying aloud.

'If an elder like you grieves, it will not augur well for anyone. Please control yourself,' said Srikantaiah, and neared her to console her. Srotri spoke in a tone of authority now. He said, 'Leave me to see through this,' caught them both by their arms, led them out of the living room and shut the door on them. Bhageerathamma kept weeping. Srotri locked the door from inside.

4

Katyayani was still sobbing. Pulling a chair close to her, Srotri sat and said, 'In these matters, there is no point in crying.

Please control yourself, child. There is no one here now to offend you. Speak to me.'

Katyayani lifted her head and looked at her father-in-law. His face was as calm as ever. In five minutes, her crying ceased. She then wiped her eyes with the *pallu* of her sari and said, 'You very well know how difficult it is for a mother to live without her son. I need say no more.'

'True,' Srotri nodded his head in comprehension.

'I know that it would cause anguish in you too. But how shall I live without Cheeni? Please send him with me.'

He was silent for about two minutes. He then said, 'Child, this is not just a question of the mind or heart. This should be perceived in a greater context. A mother loves her kid, alright. But, don't we do as much? You lost your husband, but you got yourself another. Will we get a substitute for our dead son?'

Katyayani could not think of any reply. She kept still. Srotri continued, 'The deceased son was ours. How will his son belong to you alone? In my view, children neither belong to the mother or the father exclusively. They are the assets of the lineage. Whoever tries to establish their individual right over them only ends up denying them to all concerned. A person shall wield authority over everything of a family as long as such person is part of that family. How can one who goes off at a tangent stake a claim to the core of a family?'

'I did not broach the subject of rights and justice. I just laid bare before you a mother's agony.'

'Outside of the genealogical tree, no sprout shall speak in praise of motherhood. Motherhood, fatherhood, kinship are all pivoted on lineage. If man and woman unite in the name of marriage for the sole purpose of furthering the cause of the lineage, where is the locus of motherhood outside of this purpose?'

Katyayani was drawn into the heat of the debate. She said, 'Yours and mine are different views of life. If you maintain that an individual is for the sake of lineage, I will rather accord importance to his individual life.'

For a while, Srotri went silent. Not wanting to continue with the line of debate, he said, 'A debate is not worthwhile when there is no consensus as to the premise. Let us not debate. Will you at least concede that as much as offspring are children to their parents, they are grandchildren to their grandparents too?'

Katyayani recalled an incident. When Cheeni was a six-month-old infant, she and her husband had engaged in a squabble in good faith. He had said, 'The child is mine,' to which she had said, 'No, it is mine.' Nanjunda had appealed to his father who passed by. The senior had said smilingly, 'Children belong neither to father nor mother. They belong to grandparents.' The young couple had heartily concurred with his words. Katyayani now sensed that his view was thus all through.

Srotri said, 'Let's say you will take the child with you now. Will you be able to tend to him so as to uphold the Srotri family name honourably? Should it not be cognizant of the gene that has given birth to it? Just as he has done today, will he discharge his cosmic debt by continuing to perform the death rites of his father and forefathers? Don't these seem absurd in the setting of your new family?

'I have no belief in all that.'

'You have no belief, that's okay. When this kid grows up, he shall inherit all the estate of the Srotri family. Would it be just on his part to receive the estate of a lineage whose faith, beliefs, practices and dharmic obligations he spurns? I am not speaking all economics. I am debating very seriously. What we derive from our parents is not just our body, but also their mental and cultural make-up. It would be shortsightedness to reckon just the physique to the exclusion of the rest.'

Katyayani went mum. She could think of nothing to counter him. Srotri continued, 'It is for reason of perpetuating the seed of one lineage that another lineage donates its habitat. The habitat attains its emancipation on receiving that seed and tending it into a plant. Once a mother always a mother. How may it be said that she can revert to her maiden state and attain new motherhood? For empiricism to revert to a previous phase in the process of evolution is against the very dictum of creation. It would be sinful to aspire for a phase that has forever elapsed in the path of evolution.'

Listening to his discourse, Katyayani's face became sullen. It even creased as if from torment. Noticing, Srotri said in a soft voice, 'Child, I am not saying all these to cause pain in you. Let's say my tongue has a mind of its own. As per the laws of the State, you may take your child with you. But *dharma* cannot be harvested from out of statute. And I will not concede for Srotri family's honour to tread the precincts of a court. If you are game, I want to tell you something in finality.'

'Please do.'

Now Srotri's voice became firm, but not coarse. 'The freedom of final decision is yours. I haven't the authority to physically hand over the child to you with my own hands. One branch of a lineage has no authority to sever and donate another branch of that same lineage. On my part or on the part of that old woman of the house, I will not beg of you to leave back the child here. I haven't even an iota of aspiration that he look after us in our old age. The kid is asleep on the upper floor. You go there by yourself. For a moment ruminate on my words calmly. If your innards tell you to take him, please take him away with you. I will see to it that neither she nor your father obstructs you.'

After having said this much in a firm voice, he exited, closed the door behind him, and went inside. Bhageerathamma, who was eagerly waiting outside, asked anxiously as to what transpired. 'Do not speak anything. Come,' he said, held her by her arm, and led her to the kitchen. Katyayani heard him lock the kitchen from within.

The abruptness of his words was not only unexpected to her, but she also felt that he had laden her with something heavy beyond her stamina, and instructed her to bear with it. Of course, she would conduct herself within the bounds of humility, but she had come here well-prepared to debate with her father-in-law. He had not given much leeway for debating. She was there just to make them hear the throb of a mother's womb and the exhorting of her heart. He heard it alright, but he had made her know the way in which he understood it! Having put across his opinion softly but succinctly, he had devolved the onus onto her, and had left her to fend for herself. He could have let loose his anger on her. Instead, he took along with him his aged irascible wife and locked her up in the kitchen, so that, as committed by him, there would be no obstruction if she chose to take away her child.

Katyayani gave a thought to it from the viewpoint of the weeping aged woman inside. Srotri said that she got herself a new husband in place of her deceased first husband, whereas Bhageerathamma has no substitute son to forget the grief of the death of her only son. Now, that son's place is occupied by this grandson. If she took him away, what hopes would be left for them? She gave it a thought from her father-in-law's viewpoint too. To him, even feelings such as love, enamour, interpersonal relationships, etc. existed only as can be delineated on the premise of traditional values. In his view, motherhood outside of lineage—past and future—was not symbolic of any tenacious value. But what self-respect! 'I will not concede for Srotri family's honour to tread the precincts of a court…On my part or on the part of that old woman of the house, I will not beg of you to leave back the child here. I haven't even an iota of aspiration that he look after us in our old age.' And that final word! 'If your innards tell you to take him, please take him away with you. I will see to it that neither she nor your father will obstruct you.' She reflected that by devolving all onus onto her, he had also subjected her to a stringent soul searching.

She was greatly afflicted. Leaving back the child would mean nipping her craving for it, which would be contentious with her very motherhood. An immense conflict between those thoughts and feelings rent her mind. But the motherhood would not be easily slighted. For a while, she sat silent. There wasn't enough strength in her legs to even get up. Neither had her mind the strength to arrive at a decision. She garnered all her strength and stood up. The other door was open. To that side were the steps that led to the upper floor. She silently walked in that direction. There was no sound whatsoever on the ground floor. The silence was typical of an abandoned house. She silently climbed up the stairs. There, where she had studied for two years and also retired at nights, Cheeni was asleep on the big tiger hide mat. His grandfather's blue shawl that served as a blanket had half uncovered him so as to reveal his belly and sides. Not yet initiated to the worries of life, Cheeni's gentle breathing caused his small chest to pulsate imperceptibly so. Katyayani sat by him and began intently observing his face. Her first husband surfaced in memory. The very same face and physical contours could be seen on Cheeni. The same posture of lying down, the same straight nose, broad forehead, and alluring face. His grandfather's genes were handed down to him through his father. Her mind cogitated as to whose child he was. She could not dismiss it as having no nexus whatsoever to the Srotri clan. She was a 'habitat' that moved over to this house, and a 'seed' of the Srotri clan had sprouted in her. *Now it is becoming a tree. It shall always exhibit the qualities of the seed. But what about the blood, tissues, milk that it has drawn from me? And what of the desires, cravings, love that I have showered on him? Haven't they any value? God, why subject me to this quandary? Should I have to put forth arguments to establish my authority over my child? Has the mother's innate right dwindled so as to be shored up by debating? What a situation did I slide into, which has caused the obliteration of the truth of my motherhood?* She felt as if someone plunged a multipronged dagger through her entrails and twirled it. She felt a cruel torment in her stomach and chest. She pressed her chest with her palm and sat down beside him. Cry billowed and the tears seemed to bring out the magma within her. She cried her heart's content. The sound of her cry would have been sensed by the kid, for the rhythm of its breathing varied for a moment as he turned on his other side. The movement caused the blanket to come off completely and exposed the kid naked except for the loincloth. The mother shut out the sound of her cry by covering her mouth. She looked at her child from head to toe. Her first husband Nanjunda Srotri surfaced in her memory again. She could not check her mind from coasting to the past. Her heart squealed once again. She bent over and gently kissed his head. On her face surfaced the onset of a firm decision. She kissed Cheeni's feet and got up. Once again, a deluge of a cry billowed from within. Before it could burst out, she thrust some of her *pallu* into her mouth and scaled down the stairs. There was no sign of life on the ground floor. The kitchen door remained closed. She had exited the house by the time the cry found its vent.

5

Outside, it was still drizzling. As the sky was completely covered by clouds, she could not know what time it was; it was getting dark though. Katyayani walked through the road that had been made sloppy by the wandering cattle. At the end of that road, as she turned towards the railway station, she came up against Lakshmi. Actually, Lakshmi had stationed herself in that corner when she spotted Katyayani approaching. 'Come with me,' she said and tugged at Katyayani's arm. Lakshmi carried an umbrella. She opened it and they both went to the railway station and sat on a bench there. Lakshmi knew everything. She had even guessed what Sheenappa would have told her. Seeing Katyayani alone, everything was clear to her. Katyayani asked her, 'When did my father come here?'

'Yesterday night.'

'Who invited him?'

'Bhagamma.'

'Is it? Not father-in-law?'

'When Bhagamma asked him to invite her father, Sheenappa had asked her not to invite him, saying that this was an internal matter of the house and was to be resolved by only us. Bhagamma wrote to your father without informing Sheenappa.'

Everything was clear to Katyayani. She sighed. Lakshmi asked her, 'Without sharing anything with us, why did you do so?' Katyayani only said, 'Of all the people, you should know why.' Lakshmi went into introspection for a while. After five minutes, she said, 'It is our *karma* that makes us act so.' Katyayani wanted to be one with silence. So she said, 'It is getting dark. You go home.' Lakshmi then passed a palm over her back and consoled her, 'Steel your mind. No point in worrying.' She opened her umbrella and left.

It was dark everywhere. The train had not yet arrived. Suddenly alerted, she went to the ticket counter to buy a ticket. She got to know that a goods train had derailed near Kadakola, wherefore all train services were suspended till tomorrow. The clock in the station displayed 7:15. How to reach Mysore now? She returned to the bench and sat. Though there were many acquaintances in that town, she was not inclined to go to anybody's house and ask to stay overnight. If she continued to sit there, somebody might recognize her. She could spend the night inside the station, but thinking it better to go spend time elsewhere and return late night when the town would be asleep, she exited. Her legs took her past Pindargeri to the bank of the river Kapila. She walked up to the Gauri deck and sat on a step. The river was overflowing. It was very dark, and a semblance of light beamed from a nearby lamppost. She was quite far away from it, wherefore she could not see anything clearly. As of now, she preferred darkness to light. It was drizzling still, but far and in between. Her sari was fully wet. She pulled the *pallu* over her head and continued to sit. Her mind began recollecting everything that had transpired that day.

When everything had once rolled before her mind's eye, she recalled the incident that had occurred five years ago. It was in this same month of Jun, this same lunar day, that her husband Nanjunda Srotri had drowned in this same Kapila. She had loved him more than she loved her own life; she had given him all her heart. Who can measure her sorrow of the day he left her alone and passed on? At that moment, she had felt the compulsion to die. She desired to similarly drown herself in this same river. Or, she had thought, if she had taken to Sati like they did in the olden days, she would have not have faced these agonies. Her father-in-law had sensed the intensity of her grief. He had, therefore, said the right thing at the right time: you have to live at least for the sake of this child.

That child shall now live even without me! After five long years, today, life had once again subjected Katyayani to such tribulations, and had separated her womb from her. She had fallen from grace even in the eyes of the people. Is it ever late? Why, she could walk into the river even now!

The desire to die kept swelling. But some silent force seemed to obstruct it. She gave a thought as to what the nature of that force was, which impeded her death, when life itself held no meaning! During these musings, she had twice walked up to the edge of the flow of the river. She had again climbed up two steps and sat. In that forlorn place, the river flowed past her with the susurration of milk overflowing from a vessel on a stove.

Suddenly a flash of light seemed to beam at her from above the stairs. To save herself from being recognized, she turned her back on it. She felt that the light pointedly converged on her. Who would it be? She gathered courage and turned to look. It was a human form treading slowly with faltering steps, and it was headed diametrically in her direction. The vague form came up to her and unmistakably held her hand! A moist hand it was, and the touch was incredibly frigid. From the grip she got to know that it was masculine. It sat beside her and hugged her close. Her wet sari was dripping. Her head seemed to reel, and she felt that she was sliding into unconsciousness. In that semi-conscious state, she eyed it, hugged it as would a sinking man a straw, began sobbing, and said, 'Oh you! Why come for me? I am a sinner.'

'Come, let's go,' it whispered in her ear.

'Yes. Take me away with you,' she mumbled as if in a dream, and lowered herself as if to immerse herself in the river. It pulled her back with tremendous force. Not just that, it even admonished her from anxiety. The loudness of the admonition brought her back to consciousness. 'What are you up to? If you had committed this, how would I live on? When I got news of the derailment of the goods train, I bicycled my way here.'

She got to know that it was Raja; not that other one! She began wailing as would a wounded animal. The drizzle beat on mercilessly. 'My God, you have taken pains to go in search of me here at this hour!' She buried her face in his chest as if to become one with him.

CHAPTER 16

1

Eight years into Rao's marriage with Karuna, two volumes of his tome had seen publication, and the typed manuscript of the third volume had reached the publishers in London. By now Rao was well regarded in literary circles. The All India History Council had elected him President of its upcoming annual conference. Two British universities and three American universities had invited him to be a visiting professor there. Owing to these foreign recognitions, Mysore University had promoted him to Professor. He now lived in a bungalow earmarked for professors. But his routine had not changed. He would work in his library from nine in the morning till eight late evening. If she had typing work to do, Karuna would stay back in the house. Else she would work alongside him in the library. Returning at eight, they would help themselves to supper prepared by the cook, and would go on a walk for about an hour. Even then their conversation would be centered on their chosen topic of research. Rao would share with her a new learning that resulted from his studies of the day. She would debate on the possibilities or otherwise of that statement. Rao would then shore it up with detailed explanation and establish its veracity. Many a day they would be so deeply involved in their discussions that they would eventually discover that they had walked as far as the district office grounds, or they were standing under a tree in the garden of the Court, and that the time was eleven! On returning home, they would record the outcomes of their discussions. Karuna's working hours had by now aligned with those of Rao. She too would work till it was past midnight and wake up at eight next morning.

The manuscript of the third volume had not seen print even two years after the publishers had received it. The War had caused shortage of paper everywhere in the world. Printing presses were brimming with war related printing. Though Rao's publishers were professional people who had their own press, they could not help in any way. Hence they wrote to Rao: 'We have received the manuscript of your third volume. But we are unable to print it till the war comes to an end. We are unable to procure any quantum of paper. Though we have our own press, we are restrained from using it for our own publications. We have stashed away all our stock of books in the cellar. Your manuscript too is thereat. This metropolis is affected by bombing. Nothing strange if your manuscript is destroyed. You would have a copy of it. If our London office perishes from bombing, we will surely publish your books from our branch offices in New York, Toronto or Sydney. Please do not let this development deter you from working on the fourth volume.'

India too felt the repercussion of war. At times Rao needed to personally go, with his wife, on study tours to Java, Borneo, Sumatra etc. Those being danger zones, he was unable to obtain permission to travel. He found it difficult to travel within India even. As the European countries were involved in the war, his letters to the scholars there remained undelivered. Even if they reached them, no replies would be received from them. A professor from Paris wrote a one-sentence letter to him: 'If it survives this war, then shall mankind's history survive. Else, nothing strange if history perishes.' Nevertheless, Rao kept up with his task.

Four years into her marriage, Karuna lost her father. The fact of his daughter marrying the Mysore professor despite the fact that his first wife lived had caused him much grief. But he had resigned to that development, for there was no use raking up something that was past. He eventually tried to get peace of mind by grasping that it was but natural considering his daughter's penchant for learning and the compatibility of a companion like Dr Rao in such pursuits. When she got news of it, Karuna visited her hometown and stayed with her brother for a week. She had neither the leisure nor the inclination to pay another visit any time later.

By now she had put together her own dialect of Canarese, shorn of much of the parts of speech, but quite enough to commune with the cook. Ragappa was madhva-brahmin by caste. Neither was cooking his profession nor was he trained in it. He was a simpleton that attended to petty errands for a few households. An orphan, he had married, but had lost his wife within six months. When he ended up in Rao's house, Ratne had taught him whatever culinary she knew of. Adhering religiously to those tuitions, he prepared and served them food that was unwavering in menu and taste—rice, curry, vegetable stew. Luckily for him, preparing curd from milk was no complex skill. Though a more capable cook could be availed of, they persisted with him. He was fifty, and had no other place to go. Purchasing groceries, vegetables, milk, toiletries would all be handled by him, and he never indulged in embezzlement from out the monies given to him for those effects. When they went out on study tours for a month or more, he would double up as a reliable watch and ward. More than his culinary skills, he was handy to them by virtue of his loyalty. Daily at 3 pm, he would take coffee and bread to the library for them.

2

Work for the fourth volume was progressing incessantly. Proposed to be depicted there was the cultural life of India during the entire Muslim rule commencing tenth century, and the corresponding struggles. Towards this they had undertaken research tour of the palaces of Jaipur and had studied the historical records available thereat. Rao was not yet confident of getting on with penning it. He aspired to gather some more information of the Vijayanagar era in a new light. He felt that it was very arduous to write about a period when India's culture underwent great turmoil.

By the end of February, Rao's health received a setback. He had by then worked incessantly over twelve years for his tome. On his own he hadn't rested even for a single day. His enthusiasm was tremendous alright, but his body hadn't the stamina to sustain the demands of such enthusiasm. He was just forty-seven, but he appeared as if he were sixty. Of late when they went on their usual walk after supper, he would get exhausted within five minutes. Seated on the armchair, when he took to reading an oversized book, his hands would give away from weakness even as he kept reading it. When he would take to dictating notes to Karuna, he would feel even the speak draining. Despite all this, he had to lecture to Honors and MA students five hours every week. He couldn't even ingest his normal amount of food.

Karuna summoned a doctor. The doctor took him to the hospital and did a detailed examination. He then said, 'No physical illness whatsoever. He is just strained from excess work. Just as body needs rest, the brain needs too. Give him this tonic. Stop all your work forthwith, and go someplace for two months. Better a hill station. Every morning and evening take to walking till you sweat. He would do well to stay from reading newspapers even. The mind needs complete rest. If you don't comply in letter and spirit, his condition might turn grave.'

Karuna readily concurred with the doctor. As there was quite some work to do, Dr Rao did not consent to take a break. But Karuna insisted till he consented. As suggested by the doctor they went to Nandi hill. It was the third week of March and vacation time for college. Though they asked Ragappa to join them, he stayed back saying that he would get bored there. They reserved a spacious room in the Cubbon House in advance. Raja was now not in Mysore. He had moved to Bangalore along with his family. Rao desired to visit his brother, but Karuna did not consent to it. So, they hired a taxi at Bangalore and headed straight to the peak of Nandi hill.

Not just Rao, Karuna too took a liking to the climate on the hill. They made it a habit to retire early at nights. Waking up at five in the morning they would go on a long walk after having coffee. At times they would do seven to eight rounds along the jogging track atop. At times they would trek downhill from the Gavi-Veerabhadraswamy temple towards the Nandi village. They would rest for a while under a pergola and climb back again. The upward trek would be very exhausting for Rao. Karuna would hold his hands and walk with him. They would return to their lodge by eight, and by the time they bathed, breakfast and milk would have arrived from the restaurant. Their evening walk would be usually one mile down the tar road. Some afternoons they would go sit under a tree in the garden and relish the cool shade. They would just spend their time watching the tourists milling about, and those enjoying their summer sojourn in the lodge just like them. Some afternoons when Rao would be asleep, Karuna alone would spend time under the shade of a tree outside their lodge. Until now her mind had fully committed itself to research. Now during this leisure, which was in fact a shadow of the break in Rao's dedicated life, she engaged in thoughts about her personal life. From where she sat, she could see quite some expanse of earth on all sides. In between were tanks that seemed like patches of silver sheets. Though the surrounding terrain was undulating, replete with knolls and valleys, it seemed to her that it was a monotonous stretch, and was an insipid expanse sans any splendor. An abominable silence reigned from the skies to the earth as if to constrict human living. The flare of the summer heat was strenuous to the eyes too.

On one such day, she reminisced her parents. Her mother aspired to see her married. She aspired that her daughter too beget children whom she could tend and play with. Her father wished for the same. Now they are both no more. Barring Dr Rao, which other soul was there that could be called kin who could establish their authority over her? Between her and her brother in Sinhala there wasn't even exchange of letters of late. She was removed from her Sinhala, and her life was planted in a foreign place. Her association with her husband was just of scholasticism, research and in the domain of intellect. It wasn't simply possible to conduct with him in a plane any inferior to these. Very many times Rao would speak to her in light vein; would speak cordially too. She got accustomed to such life, and was okay with it. All the same, she aspired for a soul with whom she could relate just emotionally, to the exclusion of those other aspects whatsoever.

She desired to become the mother of a flesh-and-blood child from their marriage. This was not the first time that she desired so. Very many times earlier she had fancied a small baby in her arms, and would lose herself in further thoughts. The incessant work had awarded her no time to immerse herself in such wishful thoughts. She would brush aside such thoughts as a *figment of imagination* and would apply herself to the tasks on hand. Their married life had gone on thus for ten years. Of course, they permitted themselves to conjugation, but exercised care so that she would not get pregnant.

Now, after the two-month long recuperative break, the desire to beget a child got irresistibly intense deep within her. Her mind would variously fancy that her baby came up to her crying the moment she went home in the evening, that she picked it up lovingly and breastfed it, that even in sleep it held her embraced, that it pined to call out to her, 'amma.' She would also think that her motherhood would mean that Rao's tome would suffer… 'Let's employ a nurse… When I attend to my typing work, the nurse will tend my baby… Each time I feed a new paper into the typewriter, I will turn to have a glimpse of my kid's cute smile and resume my work… Instead of Ragappa bringing coffee and bread at three, I will take a break, go home myself, hold my baby for a while, kiss it, and take the snacks to my husband… When we go walking late evening, let the baby be in my arms… If we rest some place on the way, let the baby sleep in my lap… Whom should my kid resemble? It should be a boy, he should imbibe his father's calm disposition, and like him he should become a great scholar. Just as we penned this cultural history of India, he should pen the cultural history of the entire world and should be reckoned second to none in the history of historians...'

She would think of her age. She was thirty-seven now. If she had borne a baby at the appropriate time, she would have now been a mother of a son or daughter of twenty. If it were a son, he would be pursuing higher education. It is not late even now, she thought; she must beget a child. She recalled a medical fact, that a woman getting pregnant late would get into labor difficulties, and it might prove fatal for the mother. Now thirty-seven, twice the optimal age for conceiving! If the labor proves fatal! That eventuality played before her eyes. *She is suffering from excess labor pain. The nurse nearby is comforting her. After two days of near fatal suffering, there are signs of delivery. While she held her fists tight, closed her eyes, and when it almost seemed that she passed on, the baby arrives! Her body would go limp, pulse would diminish, and then the heart would stop beating. She is dead. But the child? She prayed to God in her mind: God, it is okay if I die, let the baby live on, for it is evidence to my motherhood. Okay, the baby survived. Who will tend it unto the future?* That culminating thought caused her soaring imagination to lose its wings and fall to the ground. Death or motherhood? She preferred the latter. A life bereft of the joy of motherhood is more depressing than death. She thought of sharing this thought with her husband, but felt inhibited. She soon shored up her courage thinking that he would not think of such thought as queer. She was sure that he would never slight the basic disposition of womanhood, that too of his own wife.

One night when they retired, she asked her husband, 'What would a man think worthy of leaving behind after his death?'

Rao who was deep in some thought said, 'What brings up this thought in you?'

'Whatever it be, answer me.'

Rao drew upon his knowledge of history. 'Each individual is inclined in his own way. There are those that wish to set up a mighty dynasty before dying, those that are interested in constructing mighty temples, and those of the rare breed like the Buddha, who wish to give the world a new truth. The rest form the bigger chunk, and they are just concerned about themselves and their children.'

'Do you think of that last class as frivolous?'

'No, I never think of anybody as frivolous. Why?'

She gave no reply. She held his hand even as they slept and said after a while, 'Tell me, what the progeny of our marriage is? What is it that will remain after we have passed on?'

'Why ask so?' Rao continued, without getting wind of what was in her mind, 'Nobody that is interested in knowing in detail about the history of the world may ignore our work. Future Indian historians would not be able to gain any ground by circumventing our work. Even as of now it has gained appreciation by all scholars. Is there the need for anything else that we need to leave back to the world and its culture?'

Karuna fell silent. She very well knew about the success and the acclaim showered by the scholars to the volumes published by now. She was in no doubt that their tome would uphold their names for decades, even centuries, after they passed on. For once she felt pride in the fact that there could be no greater progeny than this scholastic work, which sought to delineate the cultural history of mankind from time immemorial till the present. Nonetheless, the irrepressible desire for motherhood that had consumed her over the past one week had made that achievement appear insipid vis-à-vis. How to break this to her husband? She gave it a thought and asked, 'Asleep?'

'No.'

She put on the bed light and sat facing him. 'Guess what I have on mind now?'

'How would I know?'

She brought her face above his and said, 'Look in my face and you will know.'

Rao looked intently in his wife's face. He could understand nothing.

'Yes…'

'You would be joking. I don't get a thing.'

'He that can delineate the course of history with all substantiation, and he that can grasp the core of a great culture and put it across clearly to others, cannot but grasp the one thing in his wife's mind!' She reached for the switch and put off the light.

Dumbfounded, Rao asked, 'Why don't you tell me what?'

'No woman would express it in words.'

Rao could still not get wind of it. She had never spoken in riddles till now. Neither had he faced a situation wherein he had to decipher one. From the faith in her voice, he could so much as understand that she wanted to convey something very dear to her. He held her face with both his hands, turned it his way, and asked, 'Tell me what.'

She placed her face on his chest, gave it a thought for two minutes, and said, 'Well…'

'Tell me.'

'How about we begetting a child?'

It was now clear to Rao. He cogitated on her words while he passed his left hand over her back. She asked, 'Why silence?'

'No,' he said lovingly, 'why didn't you come out with your desire all these days?'

'All these years we have slogged it out incessantly making it impossible for any such desire to rent our minds. Isn't it during such recuperative breaks that thoughts emerge from deep within us?'

'Haven't you any other desire?'

'None at all.'

Rao hugged her lovingly. She slept with her face on his chest. Her heart was filled with contentment. Her husband had accorded his consent to her wish. It was for the first time that she had expressed such a wish from their marriage. Until now she never had the opportunity to know if he was inclined favorably and would concur in this matter. Her hankering mind spread its wings to envision the future. A child lay smiling between them. Taking off his glasses, Rao would bring his face close to the child's and strike his fingers to humor it. All the tedium of the day long work at the library would dissipate by one smile of the kid.

Karuna's wish for a baby brought Prthvi to Rao's mind. He was cute when he was an infant. When he would be seated on the armchair and would be engaged in reading, Prthvi would approach him on all fours and tug at his leg. Though for a moment he would feel disturbed, the sighting of the kid's face would wipe out his displeasure, and he would put the book aside and pick up the baby. At other times he could not give much time to the baby. His mind would always be immersed in the tome he had taken to pen. Prthvi got more accustomed to his uncle than to his father. He would be fourteen now. Yes fourteen. Rao had not seen him in the past eight years. He would not recognize his father even if he met him now. Even if he recognized, would he near him? Anon Nagalakshmi surfaced in memory. Even after he moved out, he had visited there a few times. Though he had tried to commune with her, she had not responded any. Later he could not find time to visit. On the eve of all of them moving to Bangalore, Raja had visited him at the library just with his wife. Rao invited him to his house. Raja couldn't find time to. The household things were already dispatched in a lorry. They all had to leave by the evening train. They talked to Karuna for about ten minutes, prostrated at Rao's feet and left. Rao did not enquire about Nagalakshmi. Neither did the couple inform him. How would she be now? Should go once to see her. Now her anger would have subsided. Rao thought that she would be inclined to talk now if he took the initiative. That way he could revisit his son.

'What are you thinking about?' asked Karuna, who lay with her head placed on his shoulder.

'What were *you* thinking about?'

'I told you. Dreams about our kid.'

He hugged her with all the more ardor. Now his mind began thinking about her wish. She had expressed no such wish till date since their wedding. Prior to the wedding, they had mutually agreed upon unequivocally as to the purpose of their marriage. After they started living together, they had taken care so that she would not get pregnant. All through the eight years of their married life, she had worked day in and day out for his tome. After the death of her father, she had none she could fall back upon even in her native place. She has completely submitted herself to her mentor, and had channeled her entire flesh and blood to the task taken up by him. The desire for motherhood that remained suppressed till now has now surfaced irresistibly. It is but natural. A desire for a progeny from this marriage tentatively surfaced in him too. Besides the tome that would live on as proof of their union, he aspired that a living progeny complement it, lead a life in this world, and look up to its parents lovingly. He hugged her so as to press her face to his chest, 'Karuna.'

'Hmm.'

'What a fine woman you are.'

She did not speak any. She was immersed in a feeling of joy that transcended words.

3

The next morning, they got up a bit late and were very cheerful. After having coffee, they trekked down the hill from the Gavi-Veerabhadraswamy temple. They walked hand in hand, and chatted away intimately like never before. The rising sun was pleasantly warm. When they had scaled down half the way, Karuna said, 'Look, there are a few villages down there. We haven't once been there. Let's go visit one now.'

They trekked till the foot of the hill. They walked the streets of Sultanpalya they first came up against and then proceeded to Nandigrama. By then they were famished. They went to a restaurant, ate *idli* that was served in aluminum plates. They topped it up with coffee that the chef prepared with special care. They then visited the Bhoganandishvara temple, and by the time they returned to the foot of the hill, it was half past nine. They began the uphill trek slowly. The sun beat upon them fiercely from their left. By the time they scaled about a hundred feet, Rao was exhausted, and he rested for a while. When he got up to resume the trek, his wife held his right hand. '*Lead kindly hand in climbing steep hill,*' crooned Rao smiling and continued to climb. By the time they scaled half the way, he was exhausted again. He rested for a while. After resuming the climb, they had scaled about a hundred steps when Rao's head began to reel. 'I am slumping. Hold me,' he called out and sat down, placed his head on the upper stair and let loose his limbs. Confounded, Ratne took his head onto her thigh, and wiped the sweat from his face and neck. She unbuttoned his shirt and held her *pallu* to shield his face against the hot sun. Rao was not unconscious, but his heartbeat was very rapid. He was still panting. After five minutes he said, 'Don't get anxious. I felt some uneasiness, nothing else.'

The sunrays were getting warmer. Karuna carefully walked him to the shade of a shrub nearby. There wasn't a drop of drinking water nearby. Rao said, 'Let's rest for ten minutes and resume,' but she cut him out. 'Wait for me here. I will go to the village and bring a palanquin team along.' Rao tried checking her, but she scurried away downhill. She went to the restaurant they had just been to, and apprised them of the situation in whatever Canarese she knew. Sipping his coffee, an English school teacher was seated nearby. He intervened and facilitated. In fifteen minutes, a team of two arrived with a palanquin. When she consented to their charge of ten rupees, they followed her.

It was half past noon by the time they reached their lodge. After bath and lunch, Rao rested. He could not get his usual sleep. He rolled this way and that on his bed from fatigue. The exposure to heat had caused some headache. When afternoon was past and evening set in, his body temperature increased a bit. When Karuna felt his forehead and body and got anxious at the increase in temperature, Rao comforted her, 'No worry. This uphill trek is beyond my stamina. I am forty-seven now.'

Complacence was not typical of her. She sent for a doctor. The doctor dispensed some tablets. All through the night a moderately high temperature persisted. It was dawn by the time he got some sleep. Until then even Karuna was awake. After he slept, she too lied down on a bed and slipped to sleep. The headache persisted in Rao the next morning. Presently even his body ached. Fever had subsided.

They received post that afternoon. It was redirected from their Mysore address. From the color, it was clearly evident that it was from London. Karuna opened it and read their publisher's letter: 'Even two years into the war we were unable to resume the publication work. We were unable to procure the required quality and quantity of paper. Of late things have returned to normalcy and the company is functioning as before. By the Lord's grace our cellar is safe. In fifteen days, we will take up the printing of your third volume and will regularly send you the proofs. Hope there is much progress in the fourth volume. Regards.'

That was good news! Rao was gleeful as he went through his lunch. As his headache persisted, she gave him a tablet. A little later she exited the building and sat under the shade of a tree in the front yard. The terrain before her was bleakness personified. There were those small tanks and hillocks-range yonder. The burning sky above was bleak too. For a while her mind turned inwardly. It then gave a thought as to what she has to do now on. In three weeks, the proofs shall begin flowing in from London. Proofing would take away all her time. Then she would have to do the detailed indexing. Alongside, preparations have to get underway for the fourth volume. At least in the next one year the work of collating information should be gone through and scripting should commence. Five volumes might not suffice to hold the entire content as planned. The fifth volume is likely to end even before European history is fully covered. It now seems like eight more years are needed to go through it fully.

She now gave a thought to her husband's health. She was truly scared yesterday when he slumped down on the steps from that bout of dizziness. She very well knew what would become of the physical health of one who strained his intellect to its limits. Her stamina too had reduced over the years. But as she was born with an energetic physique, she was able to sustain such workload. But her husband's body had succumbed. She reflected if he had the strength to go through the remaining task.

Surfaced in her mind their discussion of the day before yesterday about she begetting a child. If she got pregnant now, work would not progress at the current pace till at least the labors. Even during the postnatal care, she would not be able to work any, for she should fully rest. Until the kid is one year old, it should be cared for well. If a matronly nurse were not available, it would be so much more difficult. Even if a nurse would be available, one should be watchful to make good her lapses. A feeble voice was heard from deep within her: 'If you take to motherhood, your contribution in this project will suffer, and he will die before accomplishment.' Though she could not think up any substantiation to take that inner voice for granted, her mind would not disregard the admonition. The thought of her husband's death caused her heart to wring and her face to go somber from grief. Her forehead creased and her eyebrows converged. She revisited her will-power. The very same will-power, which had earlier caused her to leave her hometown and her parents, and had enabled her to brace all blame that she would come up against in the path of teaming up with him in his mission in a faraway land, now showed her the way. She resolved that she would nullify the possibility of he facing death until he accomplished the mission for which she had married him. Still his physical condition caused apprehension in her. He was very scrawny and he weighed not more than a young lad. She thought of his emaciating physique and his decreasing eyesight. He got himself new spectacles once again recently. She would not beget a child, she decided, and all her love and affection would be channeled towards the completion of the tome. Even as the vigor of her resolve showed in her face, tears escaped from her eyes and her sight got hazy. She silently experienced the agony of a mother who has set out to exterminate her own fetus. Holding her face between her knees she began sobbing. Over the last two days, she was fancying herself in an expectant exhilarant situation. All the organs of her body had blossomed in that novel phase and had acquired a new luster. She had fancied a lively river flowing alongside their austere intellectual life. That imagination had acquired a clear form just in a matter of two days, and had rooted deeper than real life. And though the resolve steeled in her to revert to her initially assumed lifestyle at the cost of such a dream, she was pained as if her innards were wrung.

CHAPTER 17

1

The preceding eight years had brought about much change in Katyayani's life. There was no decrease in her husband's love and affection whatsoever. She was never at loggerheads with Nagalakshmi. Still, she was not as hitherto. After she moved over from Nanjangud, she had aspired to keep herself engaged. Raja suggested that she should pursue Honours, and post-graduation later. She felt inhibited to be once again found in the company of the same buddies and teachers in the college, but she still aspired to pursue academics. They eventually decided that she shall enroll for a correspondence course with the Banaras Hindu University, and Raja shall tutor her at home. Intelligent as she was, this posed no difficulty at all. In two years, she even got her MA degree.

When she went to Banaras to write her second-year exams, she was four months into pregnancy. As she had concentrated much on her studies, she had not given much attention to her foetus. A maid attended to all the chores of the house except cooking, which was attended to by Nagalakshmi. Katyayani would engage herself fully in studies.

It was when they were returning from Banaras after the exams that her attention was drawn to the baby in her belly. Raja was too eager about their first child. He always liked children. Prthvi was now a lad of eight and went to school. With him, Raja would no longer derive the delight of playing with a small kid. Besides, his heart would be brimming with the gleeful anticipation of the arrival of his own child. After returning from Banaras, he would kiss her belly and look at her face. Getting to know his mind, she would embrace him as if he were a baby. As instructed by the doctor, and also to be of assistance to Nagalakshmi, Katyayani would attend to some household chores. They would go on a walk every evening for more than two kilometres. Raja gave her fruits and nutritive tonics.

As the baby in her belly grew, Katyayani would reminisce Cheeni. Seven years of age now, he would be studying Kannada second standard. He would be tutored at home by his grandfather. By now he would be initiated to Sanskrit and would have memorized many a *śloka* and devotional song. She longed to see him once. But how? She would sigh and move on to think about something else. Her mind would course to the baby in her belly. She got curious whether it would be a boy or girl. Her mind wished for a baby girl, for she had already given birth to a boy. But she would wake up to a reality: 'That boy belongs in that lineage. I want a boy for this lineage too.'

One day the same topic came up before her husband. She asked, 'Do you desire for a baby boy or a baby girl?'

'Is it in your capability to conceive what I desire?'

'Enough of your chiding. Tell me.'

'If it is a girl, it shall move on to another family. Let this first child be a boy that will uphold this family name.'

'He who did not want to marry at all now thinks of perpetuating his pedigree. What a change!' she chided. 'You bring about that change,' he rooted his gaze in hers and smiled.

Katyayani was running six months now. A beautiful woman that she was, the life that was sprouting within her lent her a novel radiance. Whenever he sat face to face with her, he would recall their meeting on the bank of that stream by Hunsur highway. She now seemed exactly the maiden that had appeared in his dream once—beautiful of face, attractive of body. The vegetation around was similarly pregnant with lively green. There flowed a burbling stream. It was against this backdrop that he had looked at her then. Her body was aglow from health. When she set foot, her feet would go cerise from the profusion of blood. Her complexion was the personification of moonlight. Her fingers were slender, their beauty being the type that was depicted in paintings. She wore no ornaments whatsoever. Her hair were long and lustrous black; at the tip it was curly. Her face was majestic. Feminine exuberance issued forth from her body. Even now Raja discerned them all. Even now her body shone with the same lustre. The same feminine exuberance issued forth from her body. In addition to these was a novel radiance that was not seen then. It was the same beautiful green tree, but it was now resplendent with fruits.

'Why do you stare at me so?'

'The swell in the lustre of Nature is maddening,' he said softly, holding her face in his hands.

'It is all the result of proximity of a soul. The happy result of a soul enjoying Nature,' she smiled. Though she recalled the statement 'it is anti-dharmic to impose contrived *dharma* on Nature that is evergreen and ever zestful,' she didn't utter it. She looked at her own body. Lost in the beauty of her own body, she even forgot Raja for a moment.

Katyayani was in good health all through. It was still the sixth month. It was just after the summer vacations and Raja was away in his college. It was June, and it was drizzling as usual in the afternoon. Katyayani's mind would subconsciously go melancholic during this season. She vaguely recalled that it was at dusk two years ago that she had sat on the banks of the overflowing river, Kapila, that her mind had hankered to drown in it, and that Raja had appeared there from nowhere to save her. Cheeni surfaced in her memory. There was a sudden stab of pain in her stomach. In another half an hour, it became unbearable. She got anxious. It was the same pain that she had experienced seven years previously when she was about to deliver Cheeni. She went in and reported it to Nagalakshmi who was rote-writing Rama. Nagalakshmi felt her stomach to check. She couldn't gather anything. She called a neighbour. She opined that it would be better to shift her to a hospital immediately. Raja was promptly informed;

he came running. He hired a taxi and they all went to Cheluvamba hospital. After admitting Katyayani, the doctor examined her and said to Raja, 'No room for anxiety. Seems like she will abort. We will do our best.' Raja stayed outside. Nagalakshmi went in to join Katyayani.

Nagalakshmi was moved by the pregnant girl's agony. Katyayani was wriggling as would a frog on scorching earth, and Nagalakshmi placed her left hand on Katyayani's shoulder while she ran her right palm over her back. Intermittently she would massage behind her waist. Katyayani had not experienced such extreme pain when Cheeni was born. In a little while, she was bleeding. Two nurses took her to the labour ward. Nagalakshmi stayed outside. In the next one hour, she aborted, and the episode was over. Katyayani was unconscious, and the doctor gave her two injections. After she regained consciousness, she was brought to the ward on a stretcher. Nagalakshmi went outside and informed Raja, who then sought permission to see the doctor. Katyayani lay half-conscious on her bed. The vitality was missing from her face. As she had bled profusely, she was drained of energy and her resplendent face had wilted. Her fingers were sagged as if they had lost the power to grip. The couple forfeited the fruit of their joy. She now resembled a tree whose branches drooped, and had shed its ripe fruits due to some disease. Nagalakshmi consoled Raja, 'They said that there is no danger to her life. We should be happy that Rama spared her.' Then she said, 'You go home and get the thermos, two glasses, sugar, spoon and one towel. Also, a carpet and blanket for me. I will stay here till she is discharged. You get food from a restaurant for yourself and Prthvi.'

Four days thence, Katyayani could speak in a low voice. But the doctor said that it would be a fortnight before she could sit up. Since then, Nagalakshmi would go home in the morning, bathe, cook, have lunch, and return to hospital by noon. She would go back home only the next morning.

Eight days after the premature passing away of a baby that would have been his, Raja went to the university library to inform his brother of the same. 'Why didn't you keep me informed all these days?' Rao was angry. Immediately, he hired a tonga and went to the hospital along with Karuna. Raja bicycled his way behind the tonga. After 10 minutes of silence by the bedside, Rao consoled her. 'How are you my dear? Don't worry too much. These things are typical of life,' he said and exited. Karuna sat beside the bed on a stool and chatted with Katyayani. Beneath a tree outside the hospital, the elder brother was placating the younger. After Karuna came out, they hired a tonga. Rao said, 'Raja, come with me to my house. You shall go home from there.' Rao led him to his Sarasvatipura house where he then lived.

Exiting from his bedroom, he handed Raja a cheque and said, 'She is very weak. Take good care of her.' Raja saw that it was for 1,000 rupees. Staring at it he said, 'Why so much money?' Rao said, 'She needs greater care than that of a normal labour. She needs extra nourishment from tonics. I am getting good royalty from the publisher. Don't worry. Now, leave.' He saw him off.

2

Katyayani got pregnant again. Even this time she aborted, at third month. Though this caused great agony in the couple, she convalesced in about a year. Though she forfeited some of her erstwhile physical verdure, her build and charm remained. By then Raja was promoted to Assistant Professor and transferred to Bangalore. Though he was happy with the promotion, he felt gloom at distancing from the theatre association that he had floated and nurtured. Katyayani was eager to move to the new place. Nagalakshmi welcomed the change with the sense of uninterest that she espoused in everything else. Change in domicile meant nothing to her. Wherever she was, all she had to do was attend to the household chores, and take to rote-writing Rama in all her spare time. Barring these, she had no other work. Through two years of rote-writing Rama, her mind had begot equanimity. Her ire on her husband subsided, and she was willing to speak to him if he accosted her on his own. At home, Raja cared for her with the same love and affection as hitherto. Katyayani, too, regarded her as the mistress of the house. Not only did Raja and Katyayani shower love on Prthvi, they also accorded special attention to his education. Still, Nagalakshmi's mind would be amiss. 'This is no home of mine. My home is the one where he lives. It is okay even if she stays, I would rather cook for them both just like I do here,' she would think many a time. But she never told this to anyone at home. When the day for moving to Bangalore neared, she anticipated that he would visit to see her at least now. He hadn't. They left for Bangalore by a night train. Her rote-writing continued in Bangalore. In the last four years she had written twenty lakh Ramas. Fifty notebooks were full. Raja would buy more of new notebooks, new steel nib and ink powder for her. On filling up each book, at the end of it she would write:

> *He that bestows all goodness, is wind that blows away clouds of adversity*
> *And is a very compassionate one, I bow to that God Hanuman|*
> *He that takes away our misfortunes, bestows good fortune upon us*
> *I bow repeatedly to that God Rama, dear to everyone in the universe||*

She would then smear its corners with turmeric powder, tie it with a thread dyed auspiciously with turmeric, and place it on top of the existing stack kept secluded in the puja chamber. 'How much will it be if 50 books are full,' she would ask Katyayani.

'Twenty lakh.'

'How many more years for one crore?'

'You have completed twenty lakh in four years. At this rate, writing one crore will take up 16 more years.'

'Whatever, I must finish it before I die. Sri Ramachandra, please give me 16 more years of life,' she would bring her palms together and pray.

One day Katyayani asked her, 'What will you get from this rote-writing?'

'Sri Rama will at least bless well for my next birth.'

Katyayani gave a thought to the legend of Sri Rama. Though she appreciated his valour, sacrifice and such qualities, she did not take a liking to his act of abandoning his beloved wife Seeta by heeding the blabber of a launderer. She said, 'But I have to state this. Rama's act of sending a wife like Seeta to the forest in fear of public censure cannot be called righteous.'

'Nah, never say so. Atone for having said so. Who are we to criticize Sri Rama? He is God almighty. Doesn't he know everything?'

That entire day Nagalakshmi reminisced her husband. Though she was an abandoned one just like Seeta was, her husband had gone on to marry another woman and had distanced himself from his longtime wife. Rama hadn't done so. Her devotion towards Rama increased by leaps and bounds.

Prthvi was now a lad of 12. He had enrolled at the Malleswaram High School. He was good at studies. At times, Nagalakshmi would get irritated as to why her husband did not even aspire to see his son.

There was an opening for an English lecturer in the college in Bangalore where Raja taught. He asked Katyayani, 'Instead of idling at home, will you take it?' Though she was apprehensive at first, Raja's presence as an Assistant Professor in the same faculty in the same college fostered confidence in her. Raja made efforts to get her the job, and also wrote to his brother to see if he could intervene beneficially. By then, Rao was designated professor. Higher up authorities at the university would now regard his words with respect. Katyayani landed that job. In this new engagement of hers, she tried taking many an agonizing event of her past off her mind. She would commute to and fro along with her husband. Raja founded a theatre association in Bangalore too. It functioned well and his name became popular in the entire college. Now, Nagalakshmi had to shoulder more of the household chores. One day Katyayani said, 'Sister, the chores are too much to be handled by you alone. We both are earning now. Let's appoint a cook.' Nagalakshmi refused. 'Wasn't I handling everything before you came over here consequent to wedding Raja? Cooking is no draining chore. Moreover, I cannot eat a cook's food.'

Four years had passed since Katyayani had taken to the teaching career. She was well-accustomed to lecturing by now. And killing time was a non-issue in the college. Her time at home would be consumed by assisting Nagalakshmi in household chores, preparing for the next day's lectures, and helping Prthvi with his studies. She would go the market daily with her husband and buy vegetables, fruits and flowers.

But soon, she got vexed with life in general. She got to feel that she was a loner. At times, Cheeni surfaced in her memory and she longed to see him. She got curious to know if he reminisced her, and if he asked his grandfather to take him to her. He was 13 now. He would have grown tall. Father-in-law would have carried out his *upanayana* in his eighth year. By now he would have memorized quite many sections of the Vedas and the Upanishads. He would have been tutored in Sanskrit too. She thought that if she had taken her father-in-law's advice, she would have memorized the Bhagavadgīta and the Upanishads by now as well. But she was not inclined to learn them. His grandfather would have ingrained it into him right from his innocent days. Would he be going to high school now? She would think of him at least once a day. She would overcome some of her loneliness by imagining how he looked presently.

Soon there were signs of her being pregnant again. It was Raja who was happiest of them all. He was to become a father two years into his marriage. But that had not materialized, and his hopes were dashed. It was his bad luck that it had happened a second time. Now his wife was pregnant again. His happiness swelling, he held his wife's hands and said, 'Let's see a female doctor right away. This time, you should go for follow-ups weekly. You should take all the care in the world.'

The female doctor examined Katyayani. She asked her to take calcium. She prescribed some tablets and tonic as well, and instructed her to consume enough of milk and fruits. She asked to visit her for follow-ups weekly, and asked her to do blood and urine tests monthly. Katyayani religiously adhered to all the advice. She had completed her fourth month now. Except for the weakness and lethargy, she was healthy enough. Two more months into her pregnancy and

Katyayani's body gained on vitality. Her fullness was akin to that of a ready-to-harvest mango tree with red fruits. When she tread, her feet would become reddish from profusion of blood. The vivacity of the developing foetus was noticeable all over her. Raja kept gazing at her and felt that she was exactly thus during her last pregnancy. He took her to the full-length mirror and said, 'Look!'

She looked at herself in it. She felt delighted, but at the base of it was a streak of trepidation. But she could not regard the beauty of her advancing motherhood sloppily. She asked her husband, 'What are your feelers when you behold me?'

'I feel that Nature has attained her zenith as a result of association with a soul.'

'No, never say so.' She placed a hand over his mouth and continued, 'The last two failures have brought about a feeling of apprehension in me about the Nature-soul relationship.' Her voice trembled, and in her eyes was nervousness.

This time, they were truly not concerned as to the gender of the baby. They both concurred in praying that they be back home soon from hospital, blessed with easy labour and a healthy baby. She had applied for maternity leave. One day, Nagalakshmi said, 'You can't rest assured about peoples' glances. Now on, when you go out, wear an old sari. If you go well-dressed and all decked up, you will have to face the portent of their leer.' Katyayani complied without demur. Raja, too, held faith in it.

She had just completed the sixth month. Raja was in his classroom, delivering a lecture. The college attendant delivered a note to him. It was from Katyayani: 'I am in the teachers' room. My belly is paining much. I am anxious. Come immediately.' He abandoned the lecture and left immediately. He got anxious on seeing her face. A pupil of his drove his car to the college. He sent for him and went to Vanivilas hospital in that car. By the time they reached the hospital, she was experiencing hell. She seemed to bleed some too. Even before the doctor could examine her, Raja and Katyayani knew that that this time, too, it would abort. Raja remained at the hospital while his pupil fetched Nagalakshmi. By then, Katyayani was taken to the labour ward. The sighting of his sister-in-law brought tears to Raja's eyes. At heart, he was feminine. He loved children. His expectation had been foiled twice. This third time, too, it seemed like it would be the same fate. 'God, why do this to us?' he screamed within his heart.

After 2 pm, the maids of the hospital brought Katyayani on a stretcher and shifted her to a bed. The nurse said that nobody would be allowed near her till tomorrow morning. Katyayani could gain consciousness only after one full day. For her to recall what had transpired in that intervening time, it took all of half an hour. When she fully got to know the fact, her eyes welled up. Though she had no strength even to cry, sob she did. Nagalakshmi, who was at her bedside, held her head in both her hands. The sound of the cry caused the nurse to scurry. She warned Katyayani, 'If you cry, your condition will become serious.' She then turned to Nagalakshmi. 'If you are by her, she will recall all that and cry. You go outside.' Nagalakshmi tried pleading, but she sent her out mercilessly.

That evening Raja met the senior female doctor. The doctor recognized him and said, 'Good evening. My daughter is pupil to you both.'

'What is her name?'

'Sudha Rao. Last year, you even had her play the role of Ophelia. She is very appreciative of your wife too. I am very pained to know of her condition.'

She told briefly about Katyayani. 'This is happening to her for the third time. Let her be in the hospital for one month. Thereafter, she should rest at home for at least for six months. We will give the necessary medical certificate. She should apply for leave of absence.'

'I hope she is out of danger?' Raja asked anxiously.

'Thanks to you for bringing her here expediently. She is safe. But if she gets pregnant again, much is the probability of recurrence of complication. And if it does, the possibility of her surviving is not even one anna in a rupee.' Raja was crestfallen. The doctor continued, 'For one year, she should forego sexual intercourse. And she should never get pregnant. It is better you get yourself a contraceptive surgery.'

Raja returned home with a heavy heart. He knew that the university would not sanction her six months' leave of absence. Still, he obtained the certificate from the hospital, made out a letter on her behalf for leave, and left for Mysore. The reticent Nagalakshmi just said, 'Go through everything leisurely. Don't worry even if you have to stay there for a day or two. I will be in the hospital all the time. Our neighbour will be with Prthvi in our house during nights.'

He went straight to the university library. Rao was engaged in scripting. He, too, was saddened on hearing all that had happened. 'You go meet the VC first and give him the application form. I will talk to him later,' said Rao. Raja complied. Karuna took Raja home. Rao met with the VC later. Back home, he reported, 'They will sanction the leave applied for, but she will not be paid salary for that period. But they said they would not consider it as break in tenure.' After supper, Rao said, 'You leave by the shuttle train. Without you, they may be put into difficulties,' and handed him a cheque for 1,500 rupees. 'Why again?' Raja protested and refused to take it. But Rao urged him to take it. 'No salary for her for six months. Now she needs all the more care. Keep it. I have enough money on me. If you want more, don't hesitate to ask me. Don't worry.'

3

One month had passed since Katyayani was discharged from hospital, but she still stuck to her bed. She had to be regularly administered medicines, tonic and fruit juices. A female doctor made home visits once in three days. Now, she was no more the person that she was before. Her ever-charming face was now like a dehydrated mango. Her beautiful fingers were now like twigs. The ring would not stay in place now. The lustre in her eyes waned and disappointment was writ large on her face. She suffered hair fall, and only a fistful of it remained now. Nobody could fancy that such a healthy body would ever resign to the bed in a cadaver state. Except for his college hours, Raja would always be by her side. Now, he had withdrawn from his theatre entirely. When he was away, Nagalakshmi would confine herself to Katyayani's bedside, and talk to her whatever little she could think of. Of late, Nagalakshmi worshipped Rama every Saturday and read Rama's story fully. Some of those Saturdays, as per Katyayani's wish, Nagalakshmi would read Rama's story seated on a wooden seat by her bed. Katyayani listened to it intently. For a while, she too immersed herself in a feeling of devotion.

When she lay alone or when sleep eluded her during nights, she would go deep into thought. Her mind would think up reasons for her recurring ill fate. This third time, Raja had taken all the care that was humanly possible. An accomplished female doctor's counsel was sought regularly. When Cheeni was born, there was no such medical facility. When she was into her fifth month, Bhageerathamma had wet-ground some home herbs that she knew of, filtered them, and had administered it to Katyayani. She augmented her daily diet with quite some ghee and milk. There was no tonic then. Yet, that labour was facile and Cheeni was born healthy. Why did these three conceptions go this way? What the senior doctor had advised him, Raja had shared with her a few days back. *If I get pregnant, the probability of such complication is much; I might not survive it. What is the meaning of all this? What cause?* After she analyzed the causes she knew of, her mind would delve into analysis of sins and virtues. She vividly remembered what Srotri had told her when she had gone there to ask for her kid: it is for reason of perpetuating the seed of one lineage that another lineage donates its habitat. The habitat attains its emancipation on receiving that seed and tending it into a sprout. She had tended to a seed of the Srotri pedigree in her womb and had been instrumental in causing that lineage to branch out. Was that the culmination of the purposefulness of her womanhood? Didn't she have the capability of being the progenitor of another lineage?

But she hadn't wed Raja with an intent to be the progenitor of a new lineage! He, too, hadn't then desired for her to be the mother of his progeny in his lineage. They had passionately fallen in love with each other. Their love had rooted so strong as to make it impossible for them to live without each other. She was going mad, and he had gone mad. They had paired up in submission to the call of life, a la Nature and soul. Wasn't their aspiration for the next phase natural? His desire to sire was intense. She, too, aspired for motherhood in the same measure. She would successfully conceive. But the recurrent tragedy! *What is the cause? Has my womb forfeited its ethical and spiritual capability of being a mother to a new pedigree?* She didn't have faith in the concept 'mother of pedigree'; she just thought in terms of 'mother of a newborn'. Still, she would recall Srotri's words 'there was nothing like motherhood and fatherhood outside of lineage'.

Soon, another statement of his would surface in her memory and stab her like a dagger: it is sinful to aspire to revert to an experience that has elapsed in the process of evolution. She had experienced bliss in the company of her first husband as a maiden and wife. She had graduated to motherhood. She fell in love with another man as would a maiden, and had wed him. She would take to cogitating if it meant that once a mother was always a mother, and that she ceased to be a wife. 'God, are we assailed by real sin or just an assumption of sin?' she would sigh in desperation.

One day, she asked Nagalakshmi, 'Sister, what does sin mean? Please tell me.'

'What do I know of it? You are the learned one. You tell me.'

'I asked you because I do not know what it is. Tell me what you know.'

Without contemplating, but with conviction and confidence, Nagalakshmi said, 'To trouble others is sin. To aspire for something we are not entitled to is sin. Isn't it?'

'Is there no other sin other than these two in this world?'

'What more do I know?' Nagalakshmi went silent.

Whom have I troubled? Katyayani went into rumination mode. The aged couple Srotri and Bhageerathamma surfaced in memory. Would they be agonized by the loss of their daughter-in-law in their old age? But Srotri had made it very clear: on my part or on the part of that old woman of the house, I will not beg of you to leave back the child here. I haven't even an iota of aspiration that he look after us in our old age.

If they nursed such disinterest in the kid, would they lament at the loss of their daughter-in-law? It was probably my duty to serve them! Nagalakshmi's statement came back to her mind, this time sharp: to aspire for something we are not entitled to is sin. *Is it unbecoming of me to aspire for progeny again? God, what an incomprehensible labyrinth of knots have you tied my life with? And towards what end?* she would silently beseech.

In two months, she could just about get up on her feet and walk in the house. Evening, she would go walking for about a furlong outside. Prthvi had written his final year high school exams. When she felt like it, she would tutor him at home. As she braced thus, her health picked up. In another month, she had to return to her teaching work. Her body was gaining on stamina. Though she would feel tired when she walked about, the erstwhile appealing contours of her body were unmistakably evident. Though the vim of health was absent, her soft complexion lent a certain aura to her. Though there was no more profusion of blood in her feet when she walked, their softness was attractive nevertheless.

One day, when they were alone, Raja asked her, 'Of late, you are gaining stamina, right?' Noticing the way he said it, and grasping the allusion thereat, she put her arms around his neck and said, 'Were you disheartened all these days?

'Nah.'

'I can understand it. Don't lie.' Fixating her gaze in his, she said, 'You had to suffer all this for marrying me.' For a while nobody spoke. Eventually she asked, 'Did the doctor truly say so?'

'What?'

'That you get yourself a contraceptive surgery?'

'Yes. Why ask?'

'Instead of you, why don't I undergo it?'

'Not much difference there.' His voice had sunk to its depths.

The next day, she went with him to the hospital. Hearing her out, the female doctor said, 'In my opinion, it is better that your husband undergo it. Over the last five months you haven't fully recovered from the onslaught of illness. To regain the stamina required to undergo a surgery, you need to convalesce for two or three years more.'

When she shared this with her husband on exiting from the doctor's clinic, Raja said nothing. What caused disillusionment in him was not just the impossibility of conjugation with her sans a contraceptive surgery. It was rather his fate of resigning to childlessness. Ten years earlier if anybody were to apprise him of a couple brooding from childlessness, he would have laughed it off. He had then considered it to be excessive sentimentality. But he liked children very much. He would gaily play with Prthvi. His thoughts were that one needn't derive such happiness from one's children alone; any child would serve. So why had his mind shrunk when he got to know that his wife cannot bear his own offspring anymore? His ignorance was beyond his own comprehension. At times, he would have liked to have sex with his wife, but he would abstain from fear of the consequence.

Katyayani could well grasp her husband's predicament. But what could she do? One day, she said, 'The doctor's words need not prevail always. You don't worry.' He parried her saying, 'I know too well to impair your well-being.' For once Katyayani got anxious, and doubtful too…*If ever he thought of wedding another woman to beget progeny!* She would think if a woman could successfully persist just with her matrimonial authority to the exclusion of maternal authority. Disappointment set in. One day, she gave a thought as to what would befall her if it really transpired so. Presently, she only cried.

Raja slept with Prthvi in the living room. The lad who was preparing for his exams slogged it out till 11 pm, and would babble algebra formulae in his sleep. Once Raja placed his palm on his cheek and said, 'Sleep kid.' The lad stopped babbling; his sleep was not disturbed. Raja moved closer to him, and hugged him by his right arm. The lad continued to sleep fine. The entire night Raja held him so. All night, he was lost in thought. *Though a nephew, Prthvi is more intimate with me than with his father. No more possibility of me siring! Can't I practice celibacy now on? Am 37 now. I am past my prime and will soon be past my middle age. How many more years should I yearn for marital pleasures? When there is no possibility of procreation, of what allure is synthetic corporeal conjugation leveraged through surgery? No need for any surgery. I will take to a life of celibacy. Will retire here with*

Prthvi daily. Resolving thus, he shared it with Katyayani. She resigned to silence.

But in two days, his resolve slackened. He lost confidence in the matter of reining in his natural urges. Reflecting that celibacy was beyond him, he arrived at his final decision. Next day, he went to the female doctor to obtain medical certificate for his wife. He then went to see the surgeon in the male ward. The surgery was not at all painful; but still, his eyes welled up. When the root prospect of his very existence was deposed, no intellectual elucidation had the wherewithal to rid him of his mental agony.

When Raja returned from the hospital, the couple simply hugged each other and were one with silence. Tears flowed from Katyayani's eyes. He didn't have the ability to placate her. He was so deep in despair that even tears wouldn't come to his eyes.

CHAPTER 18

1

The same eight years had caused Srotri's mind to retreat more than ever before. Nearing 70 now, he wasn't interested in family matters. It had started long back when he got his son married, and he had initiated him to all family matters. After the untimely death of that son, he had to revert to all that again. Two years thence, he had initiated his daughter-in-law into household matters and was in anticipation of her taking over fully in a matter of a few years. He was failed again when his daughter-in-law walked out on the house, and he had to once again revert to the worldly matters. Though he was aware that his next renunciation was delayed until his grandson grew up, was initiated to household matters and got married, at least in his mind he would be detached from everything. He inculcated disinterestedness and selflessness in everything. A few times he even desired to take to asceticism. After having lived these many years and having cogently discharged his obligations all through, the aspiration to spend the rest of his life by meditating upon God by ridding himself of bondage to one's household and kin grew stronger and stronger. Of late, he had taken to reading many treatises that delineated the ways of recluses. He had taken to recount the goals and motives of a recluse as delineated in Sanyāsopaniṣat, Vaikhānasasūtra, Dharmasindhu, Jīvanmuktiviveka and such treatises.

He knew that it was impropriety viz. *adharma* to abandon his family and take to sanyāsa in the current situation. Neither was he unaware that entitlement to it entailed provision of economic stability to the dependents prior to getting initiated formally to such renunciation, and that the permission of kin and wife—if alive—should be sought for such transition. The grandson, the torchbearer of this family name, was 13 now. Him assuming such responsibility was at least eight years away. It was also unreasonable to expect a sixty-year-old wife to accord such permission in the current situation. He would, therefore, repeatedly resign to the present. Though his mind aspired for renunciation, it would not go mad for it. He knew that the desire for renunciation was like any other desire, and hankering after a desire would only cause imbalance of mind, which was dire. Renunciation was synonymous with detachedness and equanimity. He was mindful of reining in the desire for renunciation, for he reflected that the distortion of the mind brought about by hankering for it was in fact a disqualification to assume the ascetic way of life.

From the very academic year that his daughter-in-law abandoned her house, he'd got Cheeni enrolled in the Government Primary School, and soon after performed his *cūḍākarma*. Bhageerathamma aspired to hold that ceremony in a grand manner. But she was let down by her daughter-in-law's conduct. They still performed it formally over one full day. They scheduled his *upanayana* for his eighth year of age. Bhageerathamma partook in that ceremony enthusiastically. Srotri was not at all interested in the grandiosity, but he did not come in the way of her wish. He only aspired that the lad merit entitlement to recite the Gāyatri-mantra, perform *sandhyāvandana* thrice a day, and take to studying the Vedas. On the auspicious day, Srotri himself seated his grandson on his thighs, and in the privacy of the canopy of a dhoti, he indoctrinated the lad by softly pronouncing the Gāyatri-mantra in his ears. Bhageerathamma was the first to serve the customary dole into his silver bowl. His forehead adorned with sandal paste, and the halfa-grass girdle tied to his waist, Cheeni wore a turmeric-pigmented dhoti and formally stated his extraction as he went about receiving doles from his grandmother and other women: *I, Sri Srinivasa Srotri, belonging in the Kāṣyapa-gotra of the ancestral triad Kāṣyapa-Āvatsāra-Naidhṛva, adhering to the Āṣvalāyana tenets, and pursuer of Rigveda, prostrate before thee.* Watching this, Srotri felt pride at the statement of his extraction viz. ancestry, lineage, tenets, Vedas, etc. The practice of honouring the pedigree by christening a newborn after his grandfather filled him with a sense of self-esteem.

Commencing the very next day, he took to training the lad in regular *sandhyāvandana* and *homa*. As he was already initiated to Sanskrit studies, he could pronounce the mantras clearly. Every evening he would make him recite

Veda-mantras so that he would commit them to memory, and he would explain their meaning as well. Even at that old age, Srotri hadn't lost even a single tooth. The Veda-mantras issued forth from his mouth very clearly. Cheeni was a studious one; he excelled even in his school.

Of late, Bhageerathamma had not been keeping well. Her physical stamina had dwindled. The exit of her daughter-in-law had dashed all her hopes. She now slept on the living room ground floor. To her bedside would sleep Cheeni, and beside him, Lakshmi. On a cot ahead, slept Srotri. Bhageerathamma would reminisce her daughter-in-law. In this old age of hers, her daughter-in-law should have assumed much of her domestic burden. She should have tutored Cheeni who took to English studies. She should have managed the household's income and expenses. She would get incensed and wish that God shouldn't bless her daughter-in-law with emancipation in life as punishment for having abandoned all these responsibilities. She would discuss the same with Lakshmi. But her husband who slept nearby would intervene: 'Is the lad asleep?'

'Yes. Why ask?'

'What has happened has happened. How many times have I to ask you never to revisit it? Why do we have to debate God's act of bestowing benefaction or distress onto others? If you keep discussing thus, what feelers will it send to the lad about his mother? You should not rake up pointless debates.'

Bhageerathamma would go mum. Sheenappa's words would go well with Lakshmi. Though Bhageerathamma would know that her husband's words were right, she would still discuss those matters privately with Lakshmi whenever her mind was unbearably disturbed. Lakshmi could very well understand her sorrow. Neither contesting nor participating proactively in the debate, she would just mumble understanding. Such occasional catharsis for about half an hour would relieve Bhageerathamma of her pent up woes. She would then stay sedate for about a week.

2

Five years after Cheeni's *upanayana*, he graduated from middle school. He was good at studies. Well before leaving for school, he would wear the exclusive laundered dhoti, and bring two pots of drinking water every day from the river. His grandmother was now not as healthy as she used to be. In stark contrast to her, his grandfather was hale and healthy even for his age. Even at 70, his eyesight was fine. He could read without glasses. His limbs were steady and he would walk about firmly. Not even a single tooth was missing.

Even though he was now 13, Cheeni slept with his grandmother. Barring his school hours and tuition time with his grandfather, he would spend all his spare time with his grandmother. Friendship, intimacy and such feelings typical of his age were all with his grandmother. The grandmother would relate to him all matters about the town that would humour such a lad. He would ask, 'Granny, why does Vasanti of Sripadarao house always bring me biscuits?' Though the reason would surface in the elderly woman's mind, she would just say, 'You have been her darling for long.' At times he would ask, 'They say that silver coins are interred in the puja chamber of the Chakrapanis. Is it true, granny?' 'They say that there are seven vats of gold coins interred in the Parashurama temple premises, and that a seven-hooded snake keeps vigil over it. Isn't it, granny?' 'Last week when I had been to Hejjige, they gave me a fistful of butter and half a cube of jaggery to eat. Do those people eat that much butter daily, granny?' The grandmother would not only give satisfactory answers to all those questions, she would also share with him many a curious matter.

Cheeni knew of his father's death, for he performed his death rights annually. His grandfather, too, performed his (the senior Srotri's) father's death rites annually; mother's too. But Cheeni would perform only his father's rites. Where was his mother? One day when he enquired his grandmother, she had said that she had gone away to her natal house. 'Why?' Cheeni had asked. 'Oh, never ask, kid,' she had said sullenly. Though he could clearly recall a woman whom he addressed 'mother' before he was tonsured, he had not shown undue interest in it. But one day when he had picked up a brawl with a buddy in school, he had derided him, 'You are one whose mom has eloped with a man.' On coming back home, Cheeni asked his grandmother, 'Naani of the precinct told me that my mom had eloped with a man. Is it true, granny?' His grandmother had chastised him, 'Should you mouth the same if some brat said so? You shouldn't say so.' Not only did he ask anybody about it thence, he let it slip from his memory thinking that if his loving granny had to chastise him so, it was improper to even think about it.

The middle school graduation exam was just over. The teacher averred that Cheeni would pass with first class. After the vacations, he had to enroll for high school. He was delighted that he would become a *highschool* student. About the same time, his granny became bedridden. Of late, she would get ill every other month. Srotri would attend to the cooking. Usually, she would recover in a matter of days. But this time, she did not recover even after many days of administering the usual home-made decoction. When the pundit was sent for, they were told that the pundit was away and that he would not be returning in a month's time. The elderly woman's fever increased. All her body organs ached. Srotri prepared and administered some medicine that he knew of. She was pretty conscious though. Initially, he had diagnosed it as typhoid, but he was not so sure now. The next day onwards, she even vomited the milk that was ingested. 'Pundit is not available. I will fetch the government doctor,' said Srotri. 'I have managed all these years. I don't know what that English medicine is made from. I'll have none of it,' protested Bhageerathamma. And she saw to it that Srotri didn't exit the house all day.

But that night, she slipped into unconsciousness. Srotri panicked. Lakshmi hurriedly fetched the government doctor. 'You delayed much,' said the doctor, gave her an injection, and asked someone to be sent to the hospital to collect medicines. Cheeni went with the doctor and brought the medicines. But when a spoon of liquid medicine was pressed against her lips, she did not open her mouth. Noticing her resistance to hospital medicine even in her unconscious state, Srotri checked himself. Three more days passed. All were awake one entire night. 'You sleep kid,' said Srotri and Lakshmi, but Cheeni didn't. His face was sullen. Apprehension was writ large on Lakshmi's face. Srotri was mentally getting ready for a next phase in his life. His 50 years' family life rolled past in his memory: marriage, the agony of childlessness, the eventual birth of Nanjunda, the life of celibacy that he resigned to by steadfastly steering clear of conjugation with Lakshmi as propositioned by his own wife, Nanjunda's death, the exit of his daughter-in-law, and Bhageerathamma taking to tend Cheeni with great love and affection thereafter. Bhageerathamma was a good-natured woman. Never did she cast aspersions on anyone. She helped others to whatever extent possible. But she was not one who had conquered anger fully. But then, not everyone is perfect, Srotri told himself. Until she was bedridden, she attended to her husband's needs with all devotion. She had cooperated with full application in Srotri's dharmic activities. Srotri was appreciative of her commitment in discharging a devoted wife's obligations.

At about midnight, Bhageerathamma mumbled something in her unconscious state, 'What would befall the kid…If she were here…If Cheeni were married by now…' Cheeni heard his grandmother's mumbling and was scared, but he was not able to gather the full import of her words. Lakshmi once looked in the direction of Srotri. He returned the gaze mutely. He understood that the patient's inner mind was aware of her imminent meeting with death.

The doctor visited the next day again, and gave her an injection. By then her breathing was erratic. 'How is she now?' Srotri asked. 'I have done my best,' was all the doctor said.

The doctor's efforts were not fruitful. Bhageerathamma passed away at 5 the next morning. A little prior to that, from her erratic breathing, Srotri had got to know that she would not endure much. He did not send word for the neighbours. That night, Cheeni had slid into sleep. Srotri went to the puja chamber, opened a sealed container of the water of the river Ganga, pried her lips open and poured a spoonful of it into her mouth. Ganga was ingested by her body. Half an hour later, she breathed her last. Doubly ensuring her demise, when Srotri withdrew his fingers from beneath her nostrils, Lakshmi began crying her heart out. For 45 years, Bhageerathamma had provided victuals to her, had confided her joys and sorrows in her as if she were her best friend. She had recommended that the widowed Lakshmi have a conjugal relationship with her husband Srotri. Later, when Srotri had gifted her two acres of land in Hejjige, Bhageerathamma had happily consented. Now, she had concluded her life. Lakshmi's responsibilities in the Srotri family shall only increase now. She was sobbing profusely. Noticing that, Srotri said, 'What is this, Lakshmi? All these days you have partaken of the tīrtha, you have worshipped the cow. Do you forget that man should pass on sooner or later?' But even before he could finish his words, Lakshmi's grief abounded. 'No one is spared of grief. We all have to put up with it,' she said intermittently even as she cried aloud. That woke Cheeni up abruptly. When he saw his grandfather's face, he understood everything. 'Granny!' he started crying aloud, placing his head on his grandmother's chest. His granny said nothing. Lakshmi hugged him.

Srotri took the news to his neighbours at dawn. Some of them objected: 'You are an exalted one. We dare not find fault with you. But why didn't you inform us earlier? Are we lost to you? Couldn't you have called us in yesterday night?' They all made a beeline to his house. In 10 minutes, the customary embers were laid at the fore of the house, which conveyed the news to passersby and confirmed the news to visitors. Women and children visited in hordes to have one final glimpse of the elderly Srotri woman. But there was no delay in cremation. The body was taken away at 8. While inserting a few grains of rice into his grandmother's mouth as was the custom, Cheeni's head reeled and he fell unconscious. All the people that had assembled there wept at the plight of the kid. Once again, Lakshmi neared him and picked him up.

Commencing on the seventh day of death, Bhageerathamma's death rites were carried out as per tradition, as part of which enough donations were given.

The Srotri family routine was different now. Though Srotri would wake up at his usual hour, he would not attend to puja with the details he earlier did. Winding it up soon, he would depute himself in the kitchen by 6 am. Cheeni, too, would wake up early, and by the time he would bathe and do *sandhyāvandana*, his grandfather would hand him his glass of milk. A highschool student now, he would take to studies in the morning. He would have his breakfast at 9:30 am. After his exit, Srotri would serve Lakshmi her breakfast, and would have his soon after. Lakshmi would then attend to cleaning the vessels. They engaged the services of a servant to herd the cattle, attend to brooming, and other such works. In the evening, Cheeni would receive tuitions in Vedas as usual. Though Srotri would ask his grandson to go play on Sundays, he would return soon to assist his grandfather.

At times, Cheeni would reminisce his grandmother. On returning from school, he would dash to the kitchen to meet with his grandmother. The unmanned kitchen would bring him to the present, and he would exit disappointed. At times, he would stay in the kitchen for a while and cry to his heart's content. He would then beget some solace. One night, he babbled 'granny, granny' in his sleep and began crying. Srotri told Lakshmi to henceforth lay Cheeni's bed beside hers; hitherto, he slept beside his grandfather. Though he developed fondness for Lakshmi, memories of his grandmother troubled him nonetheless. The smile that always lingered on his face was never to be seen again; in its place was a weary solemnity. Ensuring that he was asleep, Srotri would converse some with Lakshmi. Usually, it would be something about Bhageerathamma. Then it would turn to Cheeni and his future. It seemed that they had arrived at an unexpressed consensus not to discuss about the eloped daughter-in-law of the house. 'Cheeni is now 14. In another four or five years, let's bring in a bride. Everything will be okay then,' said Lakshmi. 'Is that early age okay for marriage in modern times?' Srotri would ask. Lakshmi said, 'Why not? How old were you when you got married? Times may change, but our lad will adhere to our instructions.' 'Rightly so,' Srotri would concur.

CHAPTER 19

1

Katyayani endeavoured to rein in her mind so that it did not get agitated. She adopted a strategy of never being alone even for a single minute without reason. She would go on a walk daily with her husband. They watched movies much more than they did before. She began taking greater interest in household chores. She got herself trained in preparing traditional snacks from Nagalakshmi, and would prepare them intermittently. Every Saturday she would join Nagalakshmi in her worship of Lord Rama. Try as she might to forget the three foetuses that she'd aborted, they would surface in memory. The recalling of the impairment of her ability to procreate anymore would shatter her mind. And each time this happened, Cheeni would surface in her mind. What class would he be in this year? His intellectual faculties mature by now, would he think about his mother? If he enquired about his mother, there would be nothing strange if his grandmother said, 'Your mother is a vile woman. She eloped with some man.' *If he meets up with me any time in the future, will he recognize me? He last saw me when he was five. He has no dearth of love from his grandparents. Why would he recognize me? If I were introduced to him, how would his conduct be? What if he regarded me as being unworthy of the love and devotion a mother deserved!* These thoughts would rend her heart. She would unsuccessfully attempt to forget about the matter altogether.

Of late, she took to loving Prthvi more and more. He was in intermediate first year now. When she would go out for a walk with her husband, she would buy clothes for Prthvi, and a bat and a ball for playing. She would see to it that he went well-dressed to college. She would tutor him. Prthvi, too, would conduct himself with love and affection towards his aunt, but it was more a feeling of reverence, at the root of which were trepidation and diffidence. At times, Katyayani would apply castor oil on him and bathe him. He would be cowering as he sat in the bathroom. While she scrubbed his back, he would move as farther away from her as possible, but she would pull him close and give him a fine scrubbing.

After he underwent contraceptive surgery, Raja's love entirely converged on Prthvi. He even handed over the keys to the safe, where he kept money, to him. He would have lunch and supper with him always. Instead of calling him by his name as he did hitherto, he started calling him 'kid'. Katyayani could get wind of her husband's feelings. She was not at all jealous. She even tried to sync with him in this. She was anyway grieving at the fate of her husband whose natural desires remained unfulfilled.

Though she resumed her normal teaching work, and though she helped herself to regular walks, she was not as capable as before physically. Her complexion used to be pinkish, but it had become pale ever since her final abortion. The resplendence and gaiety typical of physical well-being was absent. She would take the tonics prescribed by the doctor just for Raja's sake. The doctor would often tell them that a change of place for a month or two would be helpful. They decided to go someplace in the ensuing summer vacations. They first thought of Nandi, but then they decided that it would be taxing to spend two full months in that one small place. For that same reason, they let go of Kemmannugundi even. A pupil of Raja was from Udakamandalam. He offered to get them a full house for two months on rent if the entire family wanted to sojourn. On returning home for the vacations, he wrote to Raja to inform him of a development:

> No need to hire a house even. The family of a relative of mine has relocated to a foreign country for one year. I have the key to their house. There is no need to carry vessels. Milk and other dairy products are all available nearby. You please let me know the date on which you will be arriving. I will meet you at the railway station.

Nagalakshmi asked them to go on, and that she would not be joining them. But they were persistent. 'Why should you be alone for two months? Let's take the kid too. If he gets to see places around, he will be agile. You, too, come with us. You shall see Nilgiris,' Raja insisted. Nagalakshmi and Katyayani prepared and stocked enough of curry powder, chutneys, etc.

Raja wrote back to his pupil, informing him of their travel date. All the clothes were stacked into one trunk, and two beds were packed. They were fully prepared for the night journey. A watchman was also appointed. That evening, a messenger from the college came to see Raja, but he was not home. He handed over a telegram to Katyayani and said, 'This was received yesterday. It just said "Raja" instead of "Raja Rao", so nobody knew who it was for. Just now the accountant said that it could be for Raja Rao and asked me to deliver it accordingly.' The telegram was unsealed. Katyayani read it. The address was not clear, but it read 'Your brother and sister-in-law are seriously bedridden. There's nobody to take care of them. All of you start immediately—regards, Ragappa.' The messenger left. While Katyayani was deep in thought about the fate of Rao and Karuna, Raja entered. Raja knew that Ragappa was the cook working at his brother's house.

'Instead of Nilgiri, let us all go to Mysore by the night train,' said Raja, and Katyayani readily agreed. Nagalakshmi said, 'You two go.'

'The telegram says that they are in serious condition. And it is dated yesterday. What would have happened meanwhile is anybody's guess. You should not be adamant, Nagu. After he is no more, will he be available even if you want to serve him?' said Raja. She acquiesced in a matter of moments. She wiped tears even as she said, 'Yes, I will join you.'

'The night train will reach only tomorrow morning. Hire a taxi. It is okay if it costs a bit more. We can reach there by 9 tonight,' suggested Katyayani. Raja thought it right.

The luggage they packed for Udakamandalam went with them to Mysore. While the taxi sped to its destination, Nagalakshmi, who was seated in the hind seat, was deep in thought. Her mind was a melee of peculiar thoughts. It had been more than 10 years since her husband wed an educated woman and separated himself from her. In the early days of that marriage, he had paid occasional visits to this house and attempted talking to her. She had angrily turned away. Eventually, he had stopped visiting. All these rolled on in her mind. She had initially thought that he had married again for no fault of hers. Whenever each of the volumes were published, he would send a copy of it to Raja, who had neatly placed on the shelf in his room three such volumes. They were black and hardbound, and the title and her husband's name were printed in golden letters on them. He would invariably show them to all the guests and say with pride, 'He is my brother.' When she heard it, Nagalakshmi would also pride in the fact that the author was her husband. At times, Raja would relate to her the invaluable assistance provided by his new wife. Though she heard it, she ignored it. She tried to forget everything in rote-writing Rama. After a certain phase, she had acquiesced to go live with her husband if he asked her to. He never once came to invite her; not even to see her once. Raja would intermittently visit Mysore. She was given to know that his new wife looked after him well. *So why did he fall ill now? If I were to be there, I would have cared for him well. Would have given him an oil bath once a week. I would be content with that. What if something befell them by the time we reach there?* Nagalakshmi's heart trembled with these thoughts. 'Rama, Janakirama, please see to it that nothing befalls him,' she prayed in her mind.

Prthvi very well remembered having seen his father. His hair had greyed, and he wore red rimmed spectacles. It was said that he abandoned his mother and married another woman for the sake of writing a book, and that she was his protégé. But why should he have left mother? His mind recalled the lecturers in his college and began likening them to his father. He had heard his uncle say to his friends that his brother was a great scholar, and there wasn't an equal in the entire university. Why did such a scholar marry two women? Nevertheless, uncle had great respect for his brother, wherefore he must be a virtuous man. *Why didn't he send word for us before his health worsened? What if something grave had happened by the time we reach there?* He could not brace himself against these thoughts. He silently and sullenly kept watching the speedy car slice the darkness as it rolled on.

When the taxi arrived at Rao's residence at quarter past nine, it was locked. Alighting, Raja was about to enquire with a neighbour when Ragappa appeared from nowhere, recognized Raja, neared him and said, 'Come in sir, come in. I am just returning from the hospital. Both of them are in the hospital. Both are unconscious. I am anxious.'

He unlocked the door to the house and placed the luggage inside. Even as she entered the house, an alien feeling invaded Nagalakshmi's mind. It was a bungalow she hadn't known. On entering, she saw furniture that was strange to her. The doors to all the rooms were open. There were books everywhere. To one side were manuscripts, to another was a table with a typewriter on it. On another table were the three volumes of his tome, which were the only things familiar to her. On no wall of the house was a picture of God or man. No trace of raṅgoli in the front yard. No sign of mango leaf festoon on any doorframe.

Ragappa was replying to Raja's question. 'He is in *pecial* ward. She is in ladies' *pecial* ward. They will permit us to visit if we go even now. The doctor used to pay home visits. Seeing the situation here, he himself suggested that they get admitted in the hospital. I went and informed the *propesur* living next door. They called the hospital and arranged everything. They then took them in their car to the hospital. I stayed there all day long. The neighbour *propesur* visited the hospital today too.'

They had not dismissed the taxi yet. They all left for the hospital in it along with Ragappa. Raja carried with him two carpets and two blankets. By the time they went to the hospital, the doctor had done the rounds, and just the nurse was present in the special wards. The nurse told Raja that nobody would be admitted without the permission of the doctor. Raja met the duty doctor and introduced himself. 'Both the patients are unconscious. You have to just retire there. Please come with me,' he led them to the ward. In the mens' ward, Dr Rao lay on a bed. The bedding was white, and he had covered himself with a red shawl. In a bedside cabinet were medicines, fruits, etc. A case-history sheet of the patient was affixed on the cabinet. Beneath the cot to one corner was a urine bottle. There was only one patient per ward; there was a chair by the door of the ward for the nurse. Rao's face was covered with a beard. As he was not wearing spectacles, the closed eyelids were whitish and very scary. Even in his unconscious state, his breathing was steady. Leaving Nagalakshmi and Prthvi there, Raja left with Katyayani for the ladies' ward.

Nagalakshmi was aghast at the sight of her husband's condition. After Raja exited from there, a wail erupted from within her. She could not contain it; she wept volubly. The nurse neared her and said, 'You shouldn't cry. You should contain yourself. A little while ago the senior doctor had visited and given him an injection. He might regain consciousness by tomorrow. When Nagalakshmi contained herself, she asked, 'What are you to him?'

'He is my husband.'

'The one in the ladies' ward, isn't she his wife too?'

'Yes.'

'Are you staying at his brother's house? That man who was here, is he your brother-in-law? Are you all staying in Bangalore? The professor who got them admitted was here this evening. He was apprising the senior doctor, "His brother's family is in Bangalore. We have sent a telegram. They are not yet here. They will be here soon."'

The nurse was talking to Nagalakshmi in a hushed voice. Prthvi stood a mute witness.

When Raja and Katyayani went in, Karuna had just regained consciousness. But she could not recognize them. Signalling them to not talk to the patient, the doctor said, 'Flu had spread hereabouts; it still persists. These two were affected. Their family doctor has treated them successfully. This condition calls for complete and protracted convalescence. These two ignored such instruction and took to their research work. Three days later, the fever relapsed. On his regular visit, the family doctor discovered them half unconscious. If the neighbouring professor hadn't brought them here, it would have been grave. Now they are out of danger. Your brother just has to come out of his unconscious state.' Karuna, who was in a grave situation, seemed to be recovering now. The singe of the fever had extirpated the sparkle of her eyes.

Giving one carpet and one blanket to Katyayani, Raja asked her to retire in that ward and went over to his brother's ward. He gave the other carpet and blanket to Nagalakshmi, and asked her to retire in her husband's ward. It was past supper time. Ragappa asked if he may go home and prepare some rice. Nagalakshmi wanted none of it; Raja left for Rao's house with Prthvi and Ragappa.

2

Just as the nurse had said, Rao came out of his unconsciousness at dawn. But he could recognize people and communicate with them only three days later. The doctor had strictly imposed on the family members that no one shall talk to the patients much. Nagalakshmi and Katyayani would go to the house every morning for bath and lunch. Ragappa would bring their supper to the hospital. Prthvi was shuttling between the hospital and the house. Raja was taking care of the patients' needs in both the wards.

One day, after he regained full consciousness, Rao could recognize the people before him. But he didn't have the strength to speak. He rolled his eyes and saw that Nagalakshmi was seated on the floor by the facing wall. He could not believe it, but he surmised what could have happened during the period of his unconsciousness. Nagalakshmi got to know that Rao saw her. There was no one else in the ward. The nurse, too, had instructed to call her if necessary, and had gone to chat with a fellow nurse in the neighbouring ward. Nagalakshmi could not think of anything to speak. Though she felt that she should get up and go near him, she still sat there with her head hung. Try as he might, Rao found it difficult to open his mouth and garner the strength required to activate his vocal cords. Nagalakshmi's mind was rent by a medley of feelings of bashfulness, nervousness, sympathy, love and puny revenge. While one of them pulled her in one direction, another pulled her with matching force in the opposite direction. She was actually rendered torpid by the influence of such conflicting forces. Half an hour after submitting herself to the influences of the mind, a voice from deep within her transcended all those influences and caused her head to lift emphatically. But by then the patient had closed his eyes. He was slipping into sleep.

Nagalakshmi got up, walked up to the bed and stood by him. She gently placed a hand on his shoulder, bent over and looked at his face for about five minutes. His drowsiness had not worn yet. In between, there was a perceptible change in the rhythm of his breath, and it seemed that he would wake from sleep. She expediently withdrew her hand, hurried back and sat in her place, head hung. That day and the next, she would steal glances at him. If he was eyeing her, she would put her head down again.

The next night, she was asleep in the ward as usual. The ward was lit by a faint lamp. The nurse on duty was sitting outside the door in a big chair, and had dozed off. Nagalakshmi did not get sleep, and she would sit up very frequently. Once when she saw in the direction of her husband, she noticed that he was gazing at her intently. She put her head down again. She heard him call out feebly, 'Na… gu…' Though her mind was not sure if it was true or just an illusion, her heart swelled in glee. She still held her head hung, owing to bashfulness and nervousness. In another five minutes, the same feeble voice was heard, 'Na…gu…' All the complex feelings that assailed her till now thawed out. Subconsciously, she walked up to his bed and stood by him. Rao slowly moved his hand. Her right hand eagerly grasped his. Rao's eyes welled up. She sobbed uncontrollably. He hadn't enough strength to placate her. She contained herself, and two minutes later she bent over and covered his face with her chest. Then she held his hand and sat by him on the bed. Nobody spoke. One didn't have the physical strength to speak, and an emotion that transcended words had forfeited the other's drive to speak. She continued to sit there till the nurse came at 3 am to administer medicine to him, but the patient was asleep.

Though he could gain strength enough to speak in four days, the doctor restricted him from speaking as such. He had cautioned Nagalakshmi not to speak to him either. Now, Nagalakshmi took to serving the patient. She would receive the medicines from the nurse and administer them herself. She would remove his clothes that were soiled from sweat, and would clothe him in fresh ones. She would give him the urine bottle, clear it, clean it and keep it in its place. She would prepare fruit juice, mix glucose in it and make him sip it. In between, when nobody would be there, she would hold his hand and sit on the edge of the bed silently. When Rao tried to tell her something, she would check him by placing a palm on his mouth. 'The doctor has instructed strictly. Don't speak. It may affect you adversely.' When the doctor came to see him, he would report to him about Karuna's condition. 'She is recovering faster than you. Don't you worry.' Rao would be relieved.

One day Rao held Nagalakshmi's hands and said in a choking voice, 'You came here for my sake!'

'For your sake? Have I ever quarreled with you? Just because our fates did us in, does our relationship become false?' Her voice was succulent with sorrow.

After five minutes' silence, Rao said in a feeble voice, 'Raja's wife is a fine woman. She has looked after you and Prthvi well, right?'

'Yes.'

That was one day's quota of conversation. Two days later, when Prthvi appeared in that ward, his parents were engaged in conversation. Entering, he held his head hung from vacillation. 'Come here, kid,' Rao called out to him. When he complied, Rao held his son's hand and asked, 'What standard are you in now?'

'Finished junior inter.'

'You have grown tall now. Do you remember me well?'

'Yes.'

He stayed there for five minutes and exited.

Another day, Rao held Nagalakshmi's hand and said, 'Nagu, by marrying me, you only submitted yourself to suffering.'

'Nothing of it,' she said.

'I can understand,' he added.

'Why then did you leave me?' she asked, but he didn't answer her. She continued, 'I am not actually suffering. Raja looks after me with greater love and affection than before. Katyayani, too, conducts herself like my younger sister. But will that be the same as living with you? Whatever you do to me, how else may I derive the peace of mind that I get from preparing and serving food to you and looking after you?'

Rao lay silently. She continued further. 'You wed her. Let's say that was willed by Providence. Even now, I will not object to her living with us. But who knows how to look after your health like I do? Your eyeballs are now swollen. Even if I were to search for it, I cannot collect one fistful of blood and one fistful of flesh from your body. Your chest has caved in. Though Ragappa serves you with all devotion, he is not good at cooking. Aren't we eating his food for 15 days now? If he had cooked well, at least you would have eaten well and been strong and healthy. I would even give you an oil bath weekly.' Her face displayed the innocent scorn of a caring person.

Rao began recollecting all that Nagalakshmi would do for his well-being while he was living with her. She would compellingly daub him with castor oil and bathe him with warm water weekly. After supper, while he sat on the armchair and took to reading, she would sit by his feet on the floor, and massage his feet with castor oil. She would prepare varieties of curry, coulis, papad, etc. each day, and fill his plate again and again. His health had never deteriorated as it had now.

'I still got a proposal for you. Will you heed it?'

'Tell me.'

'I will stay with you. Let her too. After these many years, whatever way you two want to comport yourselves doesn't mean much to me. Raja tells me that she will assist you in her own way. Let Ragappa attend to the outside chores. I will cook for all and give you a weekly oil bath. Will you consent to this?' By the time she finished saying this, tears gushed forth from her eyes. That proposition meant bartering away her priceless self-esteem for a novel personality trait, wherefore it had shaken up her innards.

Nagalakshmi's words thawed Rao's mind. He cursed himself for having abandoned her all these years. He recalled his early life ever since he moved to his uncle's house on being orphaned. *What a confidence this Nagalakshmi's, a girl of 13, to wed me, move to Mysore and start a family of her own! What a spirit of going about the household chores without so much as blighting her ubiquitous smile! What thoughtfulness of hers to run the household on a shoestring budget that my meager salary permitted, so as to leave back money for me to buy books!* He felt that he had misplaced some valuable object of his life 10 years ago so as to never be retrieved. But that very object had gone in search of him, and had found him now. His heart swelled, he held her hand and said, 'Just do so. Forget whatever misdeed of mine. You and Prthvi move here.'

She pressed his hands compassionately and said, 'Let Prthvi be there. If we take him away from them, Raja and Katyayani will feel sad. I will tell you about it later.'

3

Katyayani was seated on a chair by the wall when Karuna came out of her slumber. Karuna could not recognize who it was. She eyed her, wondering who could be visiting her. 'Recognize me?' Katyayani volunteered. Karuna said, 'I think I have seen you earlier.'

'Katyayani.'

'Oh.' The recognition brought a flash of smile to Karuna's face, 'I recall now. It was five years ago that we met, on the eve of you relocating to Bangalore. When did you come?'

Exhaustion took over her and she closed her eyes. It was an hour before she opened her eyes again. 'Where is he? How is he?' she asked.

'We have all come from Bangalore. Your brother-in-law, my sister, are all here. Sister is with him.'

'Hmm,' once again Karuna's eyelids drew up.

The following day she had strength enough to speak. When at 9 in the morning Raja came there to relieve Katyayani, she spoke to him. 'Thank God you came. Who else would care for us? How did you get to know?'

'Ragappa sent us a telegram.'

Raja kept conversing with Karuna till Katyayani returned at noon after her bath and lunch. Karuna asked, 'You have emaciated since I last saw you. It is the same with Katyayani, but I can understand her situation. I think something ails you.'

'Nothing at all,' said Raja, dodging that topic.

After Raja's exit, Karuna slept for two hours. On waking up, she drank half a glass of the glucose mixed fruit juice that Katyayani gave her. She then said, 'Will you please raise the pillow? I want to lie with my shoulders raised for a while.' Katyayani lifted her head a bit, inserted another pillow, and pulled the lower one below her shoulder. Karuna wriggled herself to a comfortable position and said, 'You are all serving us at this hour of distress. I do not know what to say about your virtuosity.'

'We are not serving strangers. Virtuosity some! Isn't a brother-in-law's wife a sister?'

Karuna felt glad. She felt contentment that she had *relatives* in this country. She remained immersed in this contentment for two minutes and then said, 'When you were acutely ill then, Raja was here to submit your leave application to the university. Then I should have come over and served you. But I was then attending to the typing of the fourth volume. The publishers had announced the date of release of the volume. Besides, I subsequently thought the better of coming over there.' Katyayani said nothing. Karuna continued, 'Raja told me everything. Very unfortunate. He said that every care was exercised. There will be many such instances that are beyond our control. You should get over it all. You, too, have emaciated much.'

Prthvi entered the ward. In his hands were a pack of sweet lemons and two injection vials. He handed them over to Katyayani and said, 'Aunty, I could get the injection vials that the doctor prescribed. The tablets are not available in any store. One store has assured that it would be available tomorrow. Convey this to the doctor.'

After reporting thus, he was about to leave when Karuna called out to him, 'Lad, come over here.' He stood his place. Katyayani said, 'He is the one son to us all, Prthvi.' Though Prthvi had visited that ward a few times, never before had he found his father's second wife awake. He would look in her face when she was asleep. A queer feeling would cross his mind. He would quietly exit from there on the pretext of some errand. Now she was talking to him on her own. He vacillated. He stood still and looked towards the wall. 'Come near me,' said Karuna. He still stood his place. Katyayani got up from her chair, neared him, held him by his arm and said in Canarese, 'Go over. Why hesitate?'

Karuna could almost grasp it, but she could not converse with him in Canarese. Prthvi went over and stood beside her bed, his sight still fixed on the wall. Karuna looked intently in his face. She thought that his face was like his mother's, but body contours, eyes and nose were like his father's. The lad was healthy. He wore a shirt—which was more expensive than what his uncle wore—woollen trousers, tan shoes and a watch on his left wrist. Noticing that he was looked after well, she asked him, 'What is your name?'

'Prthvi.'

'Prthvi...beautiful name. Whenever that term surfaces in the history of India, I feel very pleased. What is the full name—Prthviraj or Prthvikumar or Prthvipati?'

'Prthviraj.'

'Good one. Will you tell me who chose that name for you?'

'I was told it is my uncle.'

Katyayani intervened, 'I was told that his uncle chose Prthviraj, the name of a role from the famous play. His father endorsed it, for he is a shining hero in the firmament of Indian history.'

Karuna said, 'A name that both liked,' tugged at his arm and made him sit by her on the bed. He hesitantly sat to the edge of the cot. 'Which class do you study in?'

'I just completed intermediate first year.'

She fell silent as she had nothing more to ask of him. As she lay, her left hand was in his right hand. Her silence was actually because she was lost in thought. Her mind coasted back to their stay at Nandi hill. She was oblivious of both Katyayani who sat on a chair nearby and Prthvi who sat beside her on the cot, hand in hand. The obliviousness caused by the reminiscing of the Nandi episode manifested so intensely that she slid into sleep. Prthvi continued to be seated for a while. The situation was bearing down upon him, thanks to his vacillation. He got up slowly and retrieved his hand. Karuna continued to sleep as if she was oblivious of it. He stepped out of the ward with gentle steps. She continued to sleep for another half hour.

After two days, she asked Katyayani, 'When Raja visited here during your illness, he had shared with his brother that it would be perilous for you to become pregnant again. Is it true?'

'Yes.'

Karuna said nothing immediately. She now knew why Katyayani had emaciated. She thought of her own state too. Though she could have borne a child, she had, out of her own volition, forgone that desire so as to work towards a goal. Though Katyayani had no such compulsions, her body constitution had made motherhood impossible. She got to know why Raja, too, had forfeited his earlier physical vigour. She now said, 'Motherhood is the basic proclivity of every woman. If that cannot be realized for some reason, you would do well to take up some mission and derive contentment. You both resolve to write a book and take to working on it with commitment.'

'Writing cannot be everyone's cuppa. Neither of us has the level of studiousness that you both have. Our interests are different; consequently, our lifestyles are different too.'

Till date Katyayani had not said anything about Nagalakshmi, for she thought it would only cause perturbation in Karuna. Raja didn't have to think about it even, for he hardly lingered in the ward. On her part, Karuna did not broach the subject. As she gained energy to speak without exhaustion, Karuna shared with Katyayani only matters pertaining to their task viz., the tome they were working on, Rao's methodologies in compiling the volumes, the basic objective of their writing, and the progress as of now. Only once did she tell her about her parents and brother. She never once asked about Katyayani's life prior to her marriage with Raja. Karuna knew that she had a son from an earlier marriage. But neither of them brought it up.

4

Rao and Karuna were discharged from the hospital, and were back home now. Rao was still weak, but Karuna had recovered well. When they were ill, copies of the fourth volume had been delivered. Seated in an armchair, Rao shuffled through the pages. He was neither intently engrossed nor did he have any particular interest in going through it. He had only engaged himself in it casually due to paucity of activity. The citation of the third volume was in the name of His Highness, and that of the fourth volume was in the name of Srinivasa Srotri of Nanjangud. The outline of the fifth volume was clear in his mind, but quite a lot of information needed to be collated for that.

All those who had come from Bangalore stayed on. The erstwhile cook now took to outside chores. Nagalakshmi's food was relished by all. After convalescence, Rao helped himself to sumptuous food. They would all have lunch and supper together. Nagalakshmi would serve food to them all. But Karuna and Nagalakshmi never conversed. While Nagalakshmi confined herself to the kitchen, Karuna never entered the kitchen. She would confine herself to the big study room to the fore. Raja and Katyayani would go there to chat some with her occasionally. At all other times, she would take to revising the typed matter. At times Rao would go there too. The two would discuss matters relating to the fifth volume. On returning from library each day, Rao and Nagalakshmi did not help themselves to private conversation whatsoever. Nagalakshmi was ready to talk with him if he came in the kitchen. With improvement in his health, the call of the fifth volume drew his preferential attention. After a long gap, Prthvi revisited all the sightseeing places of the historic city of Mysore: Mysore Palace, Brindavan,

Chamundi hill, Srirangapattana, etc. Towards this, Raja had stuffed his pocket with money.

Raja informed his brother that he would return to Bangalore in three to four days. Now that Nagalakshmi and Karuna were mutually acquainted, he desired that Rao would instruct him to leave Nagalakshmi behind. It was very saddening for him to let go of his sister-in-law. Her presence in the family boosted his mental strength. Ever since his intellectual capabilities gained on, he was never away from her, except for the two years he was overseas. That she would honour such proposition and stay in Mysore, he very much doubted. Nevertheless, he wished that she be by her husband. But it was impossible for him to let go of Prthvi. One day when he expressed all this before Katyayani, she opined, 'As far as my understanding goes, he will neither make that proposition, nor will sister consent.'

The discussions that he had with his wife in the hospital ward was fresh in Rao's memory. One evening he took Karuna along for a walk. It was two months since they had last gone on a walk. They were still discussing about Raja and Katyayani when they arrived at the playground behind the college. As it was vacations, it was forlorn. After they both sat under a tree, Rao said, 'I brought you here to discuss an important matter.'

'What is it?' she asked in a tone that partly held eagerness and partly anxiousness.

'When they leave, let us retain Nagalakshmi here.' Karuna said nothing. She solemnly held her face hung.

Observing her intently so as to discern what feeling could be in her mind, Rao said, 'She served me all through my ill health. She will not be disgruntled at you whatsoever. Instead of Ragappa's insipid cooking, she will cook tasty food for us all. Entrusting our welfare into her hands, we shall take to our research without any worries. Besides, to abandon her as hitherto would be an ethical lapse on my part. Give it a thought.'

Karuna was drawn into thought. She had desired a diametrically different type of matrimonial relationship vis-à-vis what Nagalakshmi looked up to. She was endowed with it even. She nursed no jealousy towards Nagalakshmi whatsoever. She was rather compassionate that for no fault of hers she was separated from her husband, a groom whom she had wed even before she was intellectually mature. She had no objection whatsoever to whatever facilitation Rao wanted to do to Nagalakshmi. But she was averse to rival wives staying under one roof with the common husband. During her study of Indian history, she had familiarized herself with the bigamy, trigamy and polygamy prevalent in society. For various reasons, not just kings, but commoners too took to more than one marriage. Notwithstanding that the rival wives were cooperative, they were not without basic human nature. She reflected that they suffered from jealousy, hatred, and other such intemperate feelings. She had seen the ways of European marriages. When one spouse discovered that the other was incompatible, they would obtain divorce, look for a compatible partner, and remarry. If Dr Rao were

British, he'd have to mandatorily divorce his first wife before marrying Karuna. There, it is not just a State regulation. It is rather the mindset of the society. When Rao wed Karuna, the statute against bigamy was not yet promulgated.

'Why silent? Speak out,' said Rao.

Karuna, who was deep in contemplation until then, said, 'I have never asked you to ignore her. Even now, you move to a different house with her. Or else, you both stay here, and arrange for my stay in a smaller house. It would suffice for us to keep up with the task we set out to engage in. I will bear with it even if you live separately.'

'Will you able to live by just working with me for that task, but without my companionship?'

'Yes, I can,' she said, but her voice trembled. With trembling hands, she held his. There were tears in her eyes.

'Why are you so obstinate?' asked Rao.

'Not obstinacy. It is just my basic disposition. My mind shall never acquiesce to bigamy. We have avowed to carry on an entirely different mission. And I am content that such mission is being accomplished. That is my life's felicity. In our marriage hitherto, we have had the benefit of both intellectual union and the emotional union. I will never intervene in her life. You start another household. You be there too, come to me too. I shall not nurse any jealousy.'

Rao knew Karuna's nature well. Her willpower was strong. He knew that he could not unsettle her decision. 'Let's go,' he said and got up. It was dark by the time they returned home. There wasn't enough light in the playground.

Karuna led him by his hand. On the way home, she asked, 'What decision have you arrived at?'

'I am still thinking,' he answered.

Rao thought about it all night. He was not for two homes. Even if he housed Nagalakshmi separately, he had to stay overnight with Karuna for the compilation. He had to spend the entire daytime in the library. It was not at all okay with him to visit Nagalakshmi just for lunch and supper, and leave her unto herself at all other times. 'What a situation!' he thought. Though he was displeased by Karuna's nature, he was well aware of her upbringing and her erudition. He repeatedly sighed from disappointment that his life was torn asunder by such duality.

Plans were laid for Raja's return in three days. Nagalakshmi was in eager anticipation that her husband would discuss the matter with her soon. She even reflected as to how she would live without the company of Raja, Katyayani and Prthvi; these two nerds would be engrossed in reading and writing. Eventually, she convinced herself that she would simply take to rote-writing Rama's name as before, and just serve them in whatever way. But the matter was not broached till the eve of their return. Her pride came in the way of her propositioning it to her husband again. Eventually, she called Raja in and asked, 'Did your brother say anything?'

'About what?'

'Nothing at all,' she went silent. Even though Raja prodded her, she said nothing. That night, she did not get any sleep. She would intermittently weep. She tried consoling herself that if she could live by herself over the last 10 or 11 years, why should she get timorous now. But try as she might, she could not rein in her grief. With no sleep, she got up earlier than usual, bathed, prepared breakfast and asked Katyayani to serve it to everyone. They were to leave by the morning train. A taxi stood by the gate of the house. Raja moved the luggage to the boot. Raja, Katyayani and Prthvi first neared the taxi. Prthvi went in and called his mother. When Nagalakshmi exited, Rao was by the gate of the front yard garden. She prostrated at his feet. Without uttering any word, she went and sat in the taxi. Neither Rao nor Karuna seemed to join them to see them off at the railway station. When the taxi was gunned, Rao turned away and wiped his eyes. When the taxi left and by the time it cleared the block, Nagalakshmi was sobbing. Katyayani said, 'Sister, console yourself. We accomplished what we came for.'

'He forgot what he promised me,' said Nagalakshmi, resting her head on Katyayani's shoulders.

'What is it?' Raja asked from the front seat.

'Didn't I hint it yesterday? I will relate it during the train journey.'

CHAPTER 20

1

Rao was content that four volumes of his ambitious tome could be completed by his 49th year. One more volume, and his project would be done. But the information he collated for the fifth volume seemed to divvy up and cluster around three to four independent topics. The information collated for the fourth volume was copious enough for two volumes. The publishers had desired to include all of it in the fourth volume by precluding some portions here and there. Intending to publish the precluded portions as a separate title, Rao had conceded to their demand. Owing to this, the fourth volume was bigger than the previous three. The citation was in the name of Srinivasa Srotri. Though he had not seen Srotri in 10 years, he had forgotten neither his help nor his scholastic support. He did not know any other way of expressing it other than the said citation. He resolved to meet Srinivasa Srotri personally and give him a full set of the volumes in expression of gratitude. Besides, he had to discuss a point of *dharmaśāstra* with Srotri. A scholar from Germany had questioned the historical veracity of some of the issues discussed in the third volume.

All the same, Rao reflected if Srotri's mind would eschew him, now that his brother had married his daughter-in-law. Though he thought that the Srotri he knew of would not rent his mind with intemperate feelings, he was not sure how one would react in such sensitive matters. He had no inkling of their wedding or the interactions between them prior to that. At the time of their wedding, he was in Kolkata with Karuna on a work tour. It was only after he returned that he got to know of it all, when his brother and sister-in-law visited him and prostrated at his feet. *Had I known it earlier, would I have checked my brother?* He questioned himself. He was sure that he would certainly have apprised Raja of the repercussions it would have on the family of the elderly Srotri couple but, he thought, what would eventually transpire was left to the persons concerned.

Karuna suggested that instead of gate-crashing, it would be better to write to Srotri first, and then determine the course of action, based on the tenor of his reply. She, too, was eager to meet Srotri. He wrote to Srotri that they planned to visit for a four-day stay. He received a reply as early as the third day after posting the letter. Expressing his eagerness to host them, Srotri wrote, 'I am old already. What more good fortune may I wish for than hosting scholars like you for a few days? Please visit.'

The letter caused exhilaration in Rao. To him, that response portrayed the culture of India—Srotri seemed like an incarnation of the same. One evening, they left by the 4 pm train, taking with them the four volumes and a holdall.

Alighting at Nanjangud, they engaged a porter to carry the holdall and the books, and arrived at Srotri's door. After they tapped the door twice, a 15-year-old lad opened the door. They could easily gather that he was Srotri's grandson, and Katyayani's son from her earlier marriage.

He asked them to be seated in the living room and went inside. In two minutes, Srotri appeared there and brought his palms together in greeting them. Now he was bald, and a white beard covered his cheeks. As ever, he wore a white dhoti with red border, and covered his torso with a shawl. Though his teeth were intact, there were wrinkles on his forehead and worry was writ large on his face. He hunched slightly while he walked. Rao and Karuna both got up and prostrated at his feet. 'Cheeni,' Srotri called out to his grandson. When he appeared, Srotri said, 'Child, take this holdall and bag to the room on the upper floor.' When the guests had freshened up, Srotri himself gave them milk.

When they retired to the upper floor, Rao took out the four volumes from the bag, placed them before Srotri, and said, 'The fruit of your blessings. There is one more to go.' Srotri picked up each volume one by one and looked at them. He could just about read the title, authors' names, publishing company, etc. in English. In the title page of every book, Rao had written:

> To the venerable Sri Srinivasa Srotri
>
> Devoutly, Sadashiva Rao

Srotri was taken aback when he turned the second page of the fourth volume. Though a few words were not familiar in the boldface citation, he could gather that it meant 'This volume is a tribute to Sri Srinivasa Srotri of Nanjangud.' Pointing, he said, 'This was totally uncalled for.'

'Why not? You tended to my understanding by your knowledge. You boosted my resolve to keep up my research with your blessings. You have lent financial support for this compilation. If you say it is uncalled for, who else was entitled for my tribute?'

'Why citation? And who are the entitled?' he said circumspectly, 'It was God that urged you to take up this task. The same God encouraged 10 others to facilitate that mammoth task. I was fortunate to be among the select few. I got to know that, when he was alive, His Highness supported this project. It is *dharma* on the part of the likes of me to consecrate this worship-of-letters with a flower each. So, where is the warrant for thanking me or for gratifying an act of *dharma* of an individualist?'

Rao said nothing. He kept mum. For the next 10 more minutes Srotri kept on turning the pages of the volume. He observed the pictures on the pages. Then he turned to Karuna and said, 'Can you properly understand our conversation?'

Rao got to know that Srotri knew about Karuna. He answered, 'Only some. She can decipher more from the tone and tempo of the speak. She can just about communicate with a housemaid.' After five minutes of chatting, Srotri said, 'Rest for a while. I will catch you a little later,' and went downstairs. Knowing well that it was puja time for Srotri, Rao took to apprising Karuna, in English, of their conversation till then. They then took to browsing the printed books and manuscripts in Srotri's study.

At 8 pm, Srotri came upstairs and invited them for supper. At the usual place Rao ate on earlier visits, three plantain leaves were laid. 'You too eat, child,' said Srotri, and Cheeni complied. 'What about you?' asked Rao, to which Srotri said, 'I will serve you first.' 'And your wife?' Rao asked, without giving it any thought. Rao obviously still did not know. Srotri said, 'I will tell you later,' and Rao instantly knew what the matter was. It was 15 years ago that a similar conversation had taken place between them at a similar hour. Only, that time it was his son, Nanjunda. Srotri always refrained from sharing inauspicious news while eating; then and now. Rao felt inhibitive that an elderly man of 70 should cook and serve food to them. But he said nothing. Just as Bhageerathamma did earlier, Srotri also kept up lively conversation with the guests so that they felt no inhibition whatsoever in having their belly full. The food was both warm and tasty.

One hour after supper, Srotri appeared in the living room. By then, Cheeni had placed the betel box before the guests. Rao asked Srotri, 'Won't you have betel?' Srotri said, 'It's been quite some time since I quit it. Besides, I am not a full time gṛhastha now.'

'When was this? What happened?'

'Two years ago. Geriatrics; she was 60. "Live to be a hundred" nowadays exists only in the benediction mantras,' he said and smiled.

Rao felt bad. If it were any other widowed man, he would have offered a word of solace. Only he who enjoyed parity in age, knowledge and maturity of mind with the elderly person who sat before him could offer a word of solace. And, Rao thought, there was none such. But he still said, 'You shouldn't mistake me. I want to ask you something.'

'Never hesitate. Ask.'

'We will be staying here for three or four days. I can't put up with the thought of you cooking for us. Instead, it us who should cook for you. She is born into a different creed. She will cook for the two of us in another room. Please provide us with a stove, some vessels, rice and pulses. That should be enough.'

'Do I have to cook for you two separately? I will add some more rice to the vessel in which I cook for us three. I will similarly add an additional fistful of dal and a glass of water to the vessel in which I prepare curry. That is all the extra pains I take to cook. What excess strain does it cause this old man? Never hesitate again.'

After chatting thus for a while, they zeroed in on philosophy and history. The three kept up their discussion till midnight. Then Srotri led them upstairs. Their beds were laid by then. 'Now rest. Let's discuss more tomorrow,' he said and went downstairs.

Rao and Karuna stayed there for four days. Karuna developed respect and devotion for Srotri. She knew about maturity that came with age. She had noticed maturity in her father in his old age, just as she had in a few elderly professors in Europe. But she got to know that Srotri's was a unique personality. She had read Indian Purāṇas and epics. She had clear knowledge of characters such as Bhishma, Vasishta, Yudhishtira and Rama. She was so very conversant with the nature of these characters that she could speculate without erring in any detail as to how they would behave if they were placed in a hypothetical situation. Now, as she got acquainted with Srotri, all those characters surfaced in her memory. She knew that his daughter-in-law had walked out on this family and wed Rao's brother. She also knew that Katyayani got to know Raja through his brother Rao. Still, Srotri didn't nurse any ill will towards Rao. Even though he was past 70, his face was graceful. Decorum and culture were prominent in every word and deed of his. He would wake up daily at 3 am, bathe in the river, and begin his daily worship. That done, he would give the guests their morning coffee at 7. Though nobody in this house was habituated to coffee, he prepared it for the guests. Lunch was duly served at 10. After lunch, he and Rao held discussions until 3 pm. He would then go downstairs, and in half an hour bring them their coffee and snacks. He, however, didn't munch on anything. They'd revert to discussions till 6 pm. He'd then go downstairs to make arrangements for supper. After eating, they would resume their discussions until midnight. Not even for a minute would there be any sign of tedium on his face; not even lethargy.

During discussions, he'd cite from memory many a Sanskrit *śloka*. Karuna was surprised to discover that even she could grasp it by the way he aspirated certain syllables and clarified the meaning of certain words by delving into their etymology. Though he would put across explicative narrations in Canarese, the copiousness of Sanskrit words in his speak and the Sanskrit *śloka*s that were cited intermittently therein came in handy for her to almost fully grasp his narrative. Wherever he was in doubt, he would refer to a book from his collection and read out from it. His study was brimming with books on *dharma*, *śāstra*, Purāṇas, philosophy, literature, etc. At times, he would even take to conversing in Sanskrit. Karuna was surprised at his scholasticism. During the reprieve when Srotri went downstairs, Rao would relate it all in English to Karuna. She would make notes in shorthand. Rao explained in Canarese the doubts expressed by the scholar from Germany with regards to the historical veracity of some of the issues discussed in the third volume. Srotri gave satisfactory clarifications to them all; he even cited the authentic treatises from his collection. Rao made a comprehensive note of it all, for he wanted to, on the pretext of clarifying the doubts of that German scholar, pen an extensive and publishable essay.

Right from the day Rao set foot in that house, a thought kept bothering him in a corner of his mind. He felt that though the demise of his wife from old age was default in the flow of life, he would do well to live in comfort that the presence of his daughter-in-law would bring about. That Srotri never thought of anything to be strenuous was typical of his fortitude. Nevertheless, if his daughter-in-law were to be here, he would live peacefully; it would be supportive for the lad too. Rao had observed Cheeni closely. A lad of 15, he was tall and broad-faced like his grandfather, and had his sparkling eyes. He had grown able-bodied too. But he was too solemn for his age. He had seen Srotri talk to his grandson in light vein, but the family situation and his grandfather's life had brought about such solemnity in him. He probably would not have been so if his mother were here.

Raja was not acquainted with this family. Katyayani visiting my house and developing affinity towards Raja occurred through me. And it has culminated in this! I had no inkling whatsoever of the genesis and development of this matter. I was deep into my research. My life took a different turn, and I separated myself from my family. I was not in town when they wed. If I were, I would have discussed it with both of them. Whatever, I must for once submit my apologies to Srotri. Rao kept contemplating.

After supper on the eve of their return to Mysore, Rao asked Karuna to stay upstairs, and then he went downstairs and said to Srotri, 'There is no topic for discussion today. Let's stroll by the river, if you are not strained already.'

'No strain at all,' said Srotri, wearing his shawl, and they both started. Noticing that Rao alone was, he asked, 'Your wife is not joining us?'

'No. She is browsing a book,' Rao said, as they both stepped out. They passed by the front of the temple and reached the steps of the Manikarnika deck.

It was past the flooding months of June-July, and the river was flowing serenely. It would be the eighth or ninth day of the first fortnight of the lunar month. The moon in the sky was shining brightly. Both the shores of the river regarded, in solemn silence, the flow of the river that the milky moonlight showcased. Rao and Srotri sat on a step close to the shore. While both kept looking intently at the waters, Rao's lips parted as if he were about to say something, but words did not form. Srotri asked, 'What? Tell me.'

'Maybe, this doesn't hold much significance to you. But I wanted to share with you an old matter.'

'Go on.'

'I don't have to over-emphasize the need for the presence of your daughter-in-law in your house now. My brother is good natured alright. He knew nothing about your family. I was in the dark about his wedding and the preceding affairs. I would have intervened had I known! I ask for forgiveness from you on his behalf.'

'Why do you have to say this? What wrong is perpetrated on whom so as to call for forgiveness?'

'It is typical of you to view everything virtuously. But it would have augured well to your family if your daughter-in-law were here.'

'If everything were to happen as desired by us, why would we call this a *world*?' Srotri continued in his usual calm tenor, 'It would have been fine if my wife had lived on. It would have been all the more fine if my son had lived on. It would have been still better if my parents had lived on. But every one of them will be with us only as long as our cosmic obligation lasts. The moment that is used up, they depart. The departure may be by death or by forsaking even as we live. We have to admit to it, not lament.'

'Haven't you ever nursed any contempt or censure towards your daughter-in-law?

'Why?' He smiled and continued in the same calm tone, 'When my son had discharged the stock of his obligations towards me as assigned by Providence, he distanced himself from me by drowning in the river. For the same reason my wife distanced herself on the pretext of ailment. How may I nurse contempt or censure towards them? The way I regard life, it holds out no difference between those two distancing themselves at death and my daughter-in-law distancing while living. She fulfilled her quota of obligation towards me, and left. What is her fault in it?'

'At least for the kid's sake…'

Srotri cut him out, 'Yes, it is natural that we are pained at his orphanhood. But was it not agonizing for her to abandon a child that was born of her womb? She has experienced greater agony. A natural force that outdid such agony has drawn her. Don't we regard Nature as *maya*? Life in this world is in consonance with Nature's traits and ways. Is it a simple task to exist here but be rid of natural traits? It is not strange that she succumbed to it. Should we censure her for this reason?'

Rao very well knew of this philosophical viewpoint. That an individual, an elderly one, subscribed to such an exalted living even in the face of adversities increased his respect for Srotri many times over. 'Do you ever reminisce your daughter-in-law?' he asked.

'What is achieved by ruminating about life's losses? Always lamenting the death of my son and wife will only diminish my morale. Is the amount of work I have to discharge as of now meager? I have to see to it that my grandson is well-educated. I am already 72. After he settles in life, I have to look to the path of renunciation of worldly affairs. True, at times when I am distracted, all that floats up in my mind. To the maximum possible extent, I try not to cogitate about the past though.'

He was silent after that. For some unknown reason, Rao's mind took flight to his past. *Srotri has never taken to duality in his life, wherefore he is able to always look forward on his path. But the duality I have to put up with in my life often causes my mind to retreat to past memories and rends me. Is there a solution for this?*

Thinking that Srotri might come up with a solution for his quandary, Rao resumed the discussion. He asked, 'Are you aware of my second marriage, the situation then, the cause and all?'

'Yes, I know.'

'Without Karuna I was unable to go through my task effectively. I very much needed her to help me with the penning of the volumes. But my first wife is sinless.

Given these circumstances, do you think that my act was wrong?'

'How can I say that your act was wrong?'

'I am very well aware that you are not judgmental about the conduct of others. That was not what I asked. I want to know what you would have done in my place.'

'It is irrelevant to aver what I would have done if I had been in your place. My son once related to me what you had lectured in the history class: a beggar tells an emperor, "If I were an emperor, I would not have caused bloodshed," to which the emperor said, "If I were a beggar, the thought of war would not have occurred to my mind at all."'

He went silent for a minute, recollected his thoughts, and said, 'You maintain that this marriage was for facilitating the compilation of the volumes, which is a product of erudition. Erudition, too, is a state of Nature. Succumbing to a quest for erudition and resorting to a marriage of convenience for the sake of such a desire is also an attraction of Nature. Some take to bigamy for the sake of corporeal pleasure. Though the former attraction is superior to the latter, there is hardly any difference in principle. True quest for knowledge transcends the intellect. It needs no brace whatsoever. The call of a stalwart soul will suffice.'

Rao was quick to express a doubt. 'What value does a marriage, which is a hindrance in the path of the goal one has passionately taken to, hold? And how may a marriage, which is resorted to for achievement of such a life goal, be said to be a product of Nature's influence?'

'Your words are valid from a certain standpoint. The objective of marriage seems to be undergoing a change with the changing social milieu. The pros and cons of it are irrelevant here. Irrespective of whether we were serious or otherwise of our marital avowal, how may we belittle the marriage by ignoring the fact of faultlessness of the spouse?' Srotri recalled an event of his married life and continued, 'I admit to have got such a thought myself. I would always take to studying Sanskrit treatises. I would delve into Vedanta, *tarka* and *mīmāṃsa*, and would regard life accordingly. My wife is utterly Sanskrit-illiterate. She could not write a four-line letter even in the Canarese she spoke. Still, she served her husband well. She gave him a son for taking the lineage further. She would collect flowers, chafe sandal paste, and arrange other paraphernalia for his daily worship. There was absolutely no parity between us in the domain of intelligence. But she was an ideal wife.'

Rao sat silently. Placidity prevailed all around. Srotri knew that his words pained Rao. He said, 'Just as it would be irrelevant as to what I would have done in your place, the converse would be equally irrelevant. It all depends on each individual's perception of life. In any chosen path, one invariably runs into duality. If he chose to retreat from the chosen path, he may run into a different duality. Your achievement till date is significant. You should endeavour to consummate it. I can very well understand your need for that second marriage. But why did you keep the first wife at bay?'

'The second wife abhors bigamy. She didn't take a liking to rival wives living under one roof.'

'This, too, is a facet of modernity. Let's say that it isn't entirely wrong. But wasn't it for the sake of achieving a certain goal that she consented to marry an already married man? According complete priority to her goal, she could have reined in her internal conflicts and acceded to living with a rival wife. Be it an individual's life or social milieu, every system will accord unique opportunities. But in extraordinary situations, such systems should not be accorded undue importance. If the basic purpose of life is clear in mind, it should not be difficult to align the collaterals accordingly.'

Rao was deeply introspecting. He said nothing. They both sat silently for a while. Then Srotri said, 'It is time to retire. Shall we go?' Rao got up. When they were home it was 11, and Karuna was chatting with Cheeni in the living room. Seeing them, Cheeni went inside. 'A very intelligent boy,' Karuna reported to Rao.

They were to leave by the morning train the next day, and when they took leave of Srotri, Rao prostrated at Srotri's feet, but Srotri stepped back and checked him, 'You should not do this. Reserve it for the Gods.' Karuna bowed her head and brought her palms together. 'Please keep coming. I am an old man, so I can't move about much,' said Srotri, folding his hands to bid farewell to his guests.

2

When Rao and Karuna were back home in Mysore, it was 10:15 am. Seated on a chair and tying his shoes in the drawing was Raja! Surprised, Rao asked, 'Oh, when did you come?'

'Three days ago. Katyayani is here too. We have been transferred here.'

'Since when?' Rao sat on another chair. Karuna entered with the porter who carried the holdall and the bag, and led him straight in.

'We were issued transfer orders the day before yesterday, i.e. Monday, with instructions to report here in four days. I had written to you, informing of the date of our travel. But that letter was received by us when we came here! By then you had already left for Nanjangud, I was told.'

'Yes.'

'Are they all doing fine?' When he asked it, Raja's face was melancholic. But Rao didn't notice it.

'Srotri's wife passed away. Two years back.'

By then Katyayani and Karuna appeared there conversing. Katyayani was dressed to leave for college. She had in hand two textbooks and a notebook. After greeting her brother-in-law reverentially, she left for the college with Raja.

Nagalakshmi and Prthvi had stayed back in Bangalore. They would move to Mysore when Raja rented a house. Nagalakshmi was not eager about moving to Mysore.

Katyayani, too, did not like this town. But she could do nothing about the transfer orders.

There was no such rule that transfer of husband and wife be concurrent. As he was the brother of Dr Rao, the university had accommodated her even. Raja was posted to Maharaja College, and Katyayani was posted to the First Grade College next door.

Knowing that Karuna and Rao had visited Nanjangud, Katyayani got curious to know about the developments there from Karuna. Of late, Raja had become curious to know about the same as well. Katyayani's interest was not just curiosity. It was rather to know about the family that she was previously in, and about the kid she had given birth to. After her third abortion, she irresistibly longed to know about Cheeni. She would fancy in her mind as to how he looked in his adolescence now. Her longing would assume various forms as to whether he would reminisce his mother, and how his conduct was with his grandmother and grandfather, and desired to know about her mother- and father-in-law. They are old now, she would think, and that it would be helpful for them if she were with them. At times, she would reflect that if she had assumed the management of the household, her father-in-law could have unhurriedly attended to his *sandhyāvandana* and puja routines.

That afternoon she returned home from college at 3. By then Raja, too, had returned, but had gone looking for a house for renting. He had informed Karuna that he would be delayed till nightfall. Rao was away in his library. Karuna had stayed back thinking that Katyayani would feel bored from lack of company, and had taken to typing the notes dictated by Rao at Nanjangud. After Katyayani had her snacks and tea, they exchanged cordialities. Then Katyayani asked, 'You visited Nanjangud. Tell me about it.'

'All are fine.'

'Not just that much. You know very well why I am especially interested to know of the developments there. You do not know much Canarese. Still, please tell me all that you got to know. Don't leave out anything.'

'I felt that they were fine people. That elderly man wielded a great influence on my mind.'

'How are the rest? My mother-in-law, my son, Lakshmi?'

'Your mother-in-law passed away two years ago.'

'Is it?' Katyayani was not only shocked from bereavement, her subconscious felt the uprooting of a support that provided comfort to her. She asked, 'Who looks after the family now? Who looks after my son?'

'Everything is attended to by that elderly man. He wakes up at 3 in the morning, bathes in the river, and concludes his puja by 6. The lad is studying for his SSLC this year. On waking up in the morning, bathing and doing *sandhyāvandana*, he takes to studying. By then his grandfather cooks and serves his lunch. After he returns from school in the evening, his grandfather imparts him lessons in the Vedas. Then the old man takes to preparing supper.'

'How is he? Does he remember his mother? Is he very much worried, bereaved by his grandmother's death?'

'Yesterday night Rao and Srotri had gone out for a walk. I then talked to the lad for over two hours. Though he could understand the English I spoke, he hasn't enough grasp over that language so as to speak fluently in it. He was replying in Sanskrit. By now he has learnt the Vedas fine. He recites the Bhagavadgīta from memory. He can read the *Ramayana* and the *Mahabharata* himself and grasps the meaning of the verses without erring. I feel that he is an intelligent one. He is his grandfather personified. The same tall physique, broad chest and shoulders, broad face, sparkling eyes, studs in both ears.'

'Does he remember his mother? Did you ask that of him?' She packed all her curiosity in that question. Karuna could not think up an answer. She felt embarrassed and seemed to be thinking as to how to convey it. Katyayani said, 'Don't hesitate to say whatever the fact is. Promise me that you will hold back nothing. Just share with me what you have been witness to.'

'I did ask him, "Where is your mother? Do you remember having seen her?" From his face I could gather that he didn't like being asked that. I do not know if he knew that I was related to his mother. I then changed the topic and asked about his grandmother. I think he was greatly attached to his grandmother. Though he spoke in great restraint, I could unmistakably gather that much from his countenance and from the timbre of his voice. He related in detail about his grandmother—the cause of her death, the duration of her terminal ailment, where and how the death rites were undertaken, etc. Towards his grandfather, he has deep devotion and affection.'

'Is he joyous like adolescents, or does he seem to be troubled by worries always?'

'I think that he was a joyous lad till his grandmother was alive. He is very cordial with Lakshmi, the other elderly woman in that house. He rolls out his bed by hers while retiring daily. Seems like she, too, adores the lad. Now though, his face is too solemn for his age. But I cannot say if such solemnity is a result of his fine progress in studies or worry about the family situation.'

Karuna then spoke about Srotri. 'I had an idea of the existence of such individuals. That was because of my study of epics such as the *Ramayana* and the *Mahabharata*. I was fortunate to see, just 15 miles from here, a living individual who matched that imagination of mine. His knowledge is colossal, his balance of mind baffling. His face bears the resplendence of single-mindedness. And it is not just a maturity that elderly age merits. His eyes sparkle with a faith that issues from an inner conscience. Yet, I get to feel that in a corner of that gentle personality, there is an unfathomable austerity. I felt that resoluteness and purposefulness propel his life.'

Katyayani continued to be silent long after Karuna had finished reporting all that she had witnessed. Her face reflected the deep contemplation that went on in her mind. An inscrutable pain seemed to be a part of it. Realizing that such feeling was but natural, Karuna said, 'I have related to you my understanding. My knowledge of Canarese is very poor. My understanding may be incorrect. You should not be unduly disturbed by it. All these are but natural in life.'

Katyayani kept mum. Karuna went in to see what Ragappa was preparing for supper. Katyayani's mind was filled with images of Cheeni and Srotri. She extrapolated her last available mental image of Cheeni's face to imagine how his appearance would be now. With the details shared by Karuna fresh in her mind, the picture of Cheeni became clearer in her mind.

'He had deep love towards his grandmother. He has explained in full detail about her death. But when he was asked about his mother, he was evasive'. These words of Karuna resonated in Katyayani's mind. *Doesn't he know anything about me at all? But Karuna said that she felt that he knew about his mother. If so, what a belittling feeling would he nurse about me? Would someone at home have told him that his mother was a vile one, and that she eloped with some man?* She thought all this, and firmly believed that Srotri would not have spoken in such tenor. Her musings went on. *Before her death, would mother-in-law have told him so? She being short tempered, nothing unusual if she'd have told him so. He is a sensitive boy. He will grasp it all even if he were not told. It is but natural that he regards me with derision. Instead of walking out on them, if I were dead, he would not hold me in censure. He would reminisce me with the same devotion that he reminisced his father and grandmother; probably with greater love. There can be no creature viler in this world than a mother that is held in censure by her own son. Why didn't I get all these thoughts then? After marriage if I had taken him with me, I would not be facing such situation today. He would have loved and respected me. He would have held even his stepfather in reverence. I erred in leaving him back despite my father-in-law saying 'if your innards tell you to take him, please take him away with you.' I went upstairs to pick him up, but decided against it. What was the force that checked me? What feelings assailed me that caused me to act so? At that hour my mind led me to that path. Now that same mind is caught up in a different whirlpool! What is the root of this duality?* She kept on ruminating. No clarification emerged.

CHAPTER 21

1

Raja managed to rent a house in 15 days, and the couple moved there. In another week, Raja went to Bangalore, transported all the household items in a lorry, and brought Nagalakshmi and Prthvi to Mysore. The house in Lakshmipura was spacious and surrounded by garden all round.

After they moved out, Rao and Karuna felt boredom. Raja and Katyayani had kept them company at lunch; after supper they would all chat for a while...Katyayani would instruct Ragappa and get a variety of food prepared. Rao's bungalow had now regained its old ways—the monotone of research, notes, necks craning into library shelves, and Ragappa's inexorable food. The work of collating information for the fifth volume was underway. Amidst the unilinear work of compilation of the tome, Rao's mind had taken to contemplating about a development that bifurcated his life of late.

He would often recall Srotri's words...'Intelligence, too, is a state of Nature. Succumbing to a quest for erudition and resorting to a marriage of convenience for the sake of such a desire is also an attraction of Nature. Some take to bigamy for the sake of corporeal pleasure. Though the former attraction is superior to the latter, there is hardly any difference in-principle.' He ruminated on the situation that brought about his marriage with Karuna. Without her, the volumes would not be complied as expediently. If only he could've got an assistant who would assist him like she did! But no such person was available. Who would take it up as one's own passion and bestow their life for it? Avid in his memory would be one aspect, which he continued to experience: whenever Karuna praised his achievement, his mind would swell. Her words would be more inspiring than the accolades showered by renowned scholars the world over. Whenever she said 'this is our work', his heart would swell with bliss. When, during their walk after supper, he spoke eloquently on a certain topic, and Karuna gently squeezed his hand; and when, after returning home, she made notes of his statements, his mind many times silently predicated that she was the 'true wife in my life'. Eventually, his mind began questioning if he would feel similarly if his assistant were a male instead; whether, besides the assistance, wasn't his mind bound to hers in the above said way.

Alongside came memories of the ways of Srotri's marital life. 'He always took to studying Sanskrit treatises. He had studied Vedanta, *tarka*, *mīmāṃsa*, *dharmaśāstra*, etc. in-depth. His wife was not even half as educated as Nagu. Still, he didn't feel the need for another female companion like I did. That was because he did not take to pen a tome like

I did. What if Srotri were to be in my shoes? Though the comparison was uncalled for, it was obvious that he would have handled it all by himself. He would have at best hired a typist. He surely would have attended to all the other works himself. He would never tread the path I have.'

Rao, of late, called upon the memories of Nagalakshmi. She now lived just about half a mile away from his bungalow. How eager she was to live with her husband and serve him with devotion and commitment! Transcending all the injustice that she had suffered, she herself had proposed to return to live with him. She had come forward on her own to cook for him and her rival wife, and to take good care of his health. Rao recalled her homemaker's attributes ab initio. She saw to it that her husband always ate well. Even though he abhorred it, she would massage his head and body with castor oil and give him a steam bath. Though she was not academically educated, her personality traits were strong. In household matters, everyone necessarily adhered to what she ordained. There was no need for her to establish her authority, for nobody who came under her influence could stay from appreciating her earnestness. She had earned such merit by way of love, trust and service. Whoever she interacted with, an element of motherhood would be ever-active in her. It was this zest that had lent strength to her personality.

Rao lamented a scenario wherein he would end up keeping her at bay forever. When he was ill, he had asked her to stay on here. And he had noticed that she was happy at the proposition. As long as he was in the hospital, he had communed with her intimately. In her every act, albeit small, she would bestow her heart and soul on him. On returning home from the hospital, he was completely consumed by his academic activities; he did not speak to her much. He would reason that Karuna's presence brought about such vacillation. Eventually, Karuna rejected Rao's proposal for the three to live under one roof. When they all left for Bangalore, he had noticed Nagu's face when she prostrated at his feet. It was saturate with perturbance, and had wilted. Her eyes were drained of lustre from disappointment. She still prostrated at his feet and had walked away without causing any embarrassment to him. That incident had rent his heart.

What is the way out of this duality? Of these two forces, which shall I opt for at the price of abandoning the other? Studies and penning that tome is the breath of my life. Nagu's memory is a fire that burns my innards. And this fire is raging all the more from the air of that breath. How may I survive such onslaught? Shall I abandon my passionate task and Karuna, and just go over to Nagu? Or, as Karuna proposed, shall I lodge her in another house, or leave her here and move to Nagu's place? He had thought on these lines many times. But it was necessary for him to be with Karuna almost the whole of each day so as to complete his tome. When, for the umpteenth time, he thought of abandoning his research, Srotri's words would surface in his memory: in any chosen path, one invariably runs into duality. If he chose to retreat from the chosen path, he may run into a different duality. Rao was in no doubt about the veracity of that oracle. He very well knew that he would not be one with peace if he abandoned writing his tome, or even if he relented on the pace of its progress. When he considered the state of his bodily health, his mind would get eager to see through his task at the earliest. A voice from deep within told him that he would not live on much. He worked with an urgency to finish the last volume before he was no more.

His mental agony increased, and his bodily health decreased by the day.

2

He wasn't putting up with any disease, but his physical strength was waning and his propensity to engage in research was reducing. He was losing interest in food even. As he found it difficult to digest his lunch, he took to consuming bread and milk. Many a time, what he read would not register in his mind. His mind would reminisce Nagalakshmi and go numb. At times, both Nagalakshmi and Karuna would surface in memory and shred the canvas of his mind.

Noticing his physical deterioration, Karuna took him to a doctor. After detailed examination, the doctor said, 'No medical condition whatsoever. Seems like heartbeat is slightly uneven, but no danger there. Many a healthy man's heart will be so too. Take rest, and take a holiday. I will prescribe tonic and some tablets.'

Rao did not concede to going on a holiday. He stated that they better go through the last volume expediently, and not waste time in holidaying or resting. His innards told him that he would not live on much. His resolve to complete the fifth volume as soon as possible got stronger. But his physical strength would not cooperate with it. Karuna was distressed by the deterioration in his physical stamina. She got irritated, 'Why not listen to the doctor? Why are you adamant?' For two days she, too, skipped lunch. Noticing the gloom on his face, she tried comprehending what ailed him. One night, they went for a walk after supper. They ended up at the very spot where, on an earlier occasion, he had proposed to her that they retain Nagalakshmi here. It was just a chance happening that they arrived at that very spot. The discussion of that day readily surfaced in Karuna's memory. It then occurred to her that Rao had taken that matter seriously, and was suffering silently over it. The spot caused memories of Nagalakshmi surface in Rao's mind too. Karuna asked, 'You are troubled by some worry, and that is causing deterioration of your health. Can't you share it with me?'

'What worry? Nothing at all.'

'I get a hint. Come on then.'

Slowly craning his neck, Rao looked Karuna in the face. In the faint light of the distant lamppost, he could gather that her face was solemn. He said, 'If you know of it, why ask me? If you know the situation, the solution is within you too. Nothing is in my hands.'

Karuna went silent. Her mind became numb. It could not sustain even thinking process. Rao opened up. 'When I was ill, she visited and served me fine. It is not a service rendered as just a duty. It is a worship that a Hindu wife does with the devotion that comes from her culture. I repent for neglecting her. "What has happened has happened. Please let me at least now have the good fortune of serving you," she had said to me in the hospital. She was ready to cook for us both. She has gone one step ahead of thinking of herself as just a wife. I feel that she is attaining the state of being a mother to us. When I proposed that she live with us, you refused. Do I need a more disconcerting worry?'

After saying this, he went mum. Karuna, too, sat silently. Rao chose to breach the placidity. 'On the eve of leaving from Nanjangud, hadn't I gone with Srotri for a walk? We discussed this same issue on the bank of that river. I spilled before him my mind's agony. He said, "Abhorring the practice of bigamy is a facet of modernity. Let's say that it isn't entirely wrong. It was for the sake of achieving a certain goal that she consented to marry an already married man. According complete priority to her goal, she could have reined in her internal conflicts and acceded to living with a rival wife. Be it an individual's life or social milieu, every system will accord unique opportunities. But in extraordinary situations, such systems should not be accorded undue importance. If the basic purpose of life is clear in mind, it should not be difficult to align the collaterals accordingly."'

Rao asked again, 'Tell me now. Is the basic purpose of your life clear in your mind?'

Karuna did not speak. They both were silent again. After half an hour, Rao got up and said, 'Get up, let's go.' In the twilight, Karuna led him by his hand. That night, as usual, Rao walked up to his study room. Karuna had some typing work to do. She was attending to it in the other room. But her mind was in no mood to concentrate on her work. She had committed eight mistakes in typing half a page. She retrieved her fingers from the keyboard and sat quietly. Her mind was cogitating Rao's words. *Is the basic purpose of my life clear in my mind?*—she kept asking herself. Her attention was drawn to the deteriorating health of her husband. She had also noticed that the work of the fifth volume was not progressing apace. Her mind was reflecting on the nature and virtues of Nagalakshmi. As far as she knew, Nagalakshmi was not a vile woman. She had noticed her ways over one full month when she was here. Her face was dense from sorrow. She had confined herself to the kitchen as would a cook, but in the very house she was to rule as its queen, she being traditionally wedded to the man of the house. What was her undoing? She recalled Rao's words, 'She is attaining the state of being a mother to us'. She truly felt that Nagalakshmi had, in fact, graduated to a phase higher than her own in the evolvement of womanhood. Along came memories of Prthvi.

The matter rolled on in her mind in great turmoil. Greater was the turmoil of the feelings associated with that matter. One week later, in a state of happiness of attaining a higher state, but with a feeling of turmoil whose import she could not herself grasp, she said to Rao, 'Go bring her here. Let us three live here together.'

Rao could not believe her words at first. He looked intently at her face. The calm and earnest look in her eyes reassured Rao that she was speaking the truth.

3

When a promising desire was foiled, Nagalakshmi's mind became perturbed. If Rao's response in the hospital was negative, her wish would not have received impetus. But he had responded to her emotionally. Before bringing up that proposition, she was impeded by pride. But she had surrendered her pride at the altar of her mind's yearning to care for his good health, for the sake of serving him, and had propositioned him for her stay. It wasn't a palatable prospect for Nagalakshmi to live with a rival wife who had arrived 12 years after she was wedded to Rao. According priority to serve her husband, she had ignored it. She was doubly disappointed when Rao failed to bring it up after returning from the hospital. Until the eve of their departure from Mysore, she was in anticipation of him bringing up the matter of retaining her. She had desired that at least he would ask Raja to 'leave back Nagalakshmi here'. Nothing materialized, and she had to depart, weeping.

For some days after returning to Bangalore, she was sick of life. She would wonder if her life was such a trifling!

For quite some days, she did not partake of food regularly. On getting to know of it all, Raja and Katyayani felt bad. Raja inferred that it was rather his brother's clever new wife's doing, not his brother's. But he was helpless. He took to caring for his sister-in-law more than he did hitherto. Knowing Nagalakshmi too well, Katyayani's mind softened too. When she noticed that Nagalakshmi disregarded timely nourishment, she said, 'Sister, how many books of Rama name are done?'

'I have not counted.'

'You don't seem to have rote-written anything since returning from Mysore. Why?'

'What God will help in what way? Let go,' Nagalakshmi exhibited ennui.

'Sister, we should not disregard God for our ill fate of previous lives. Do I have to tell you this? We are now eating the fruits of our deeds of a bygone life. If we are negligent in praying to God, how can we expect good for our next life? Your rote-writing Rama will augur well for your brother-in-law. Now on, you relent on your household chores and take to writing. I will ask Prthvi to bring dye powder and fill the inkpot. How many books remain to be written?'

Nagalakshmi felt that it was incorrect on her part to have discontinued rote-writing Rama all these days. She prayed to Rama to forgive her mistake. When she lit the stove for preparing snacks for the afternoon, she also took to cooking some dal for supper. Taking over the cooking, Katyayani said, 'You go rote-write Rama.' In a few days, Nagalakshmi's mind stabilized. 'Whoever may ditch me, my Rama never does,' her mind consoled her. 'I am already 40. What more do I need? It is enough if good happens to Raja, Prthvi and Katyayani. Let those two in Mysore prosper too,' she prayed. She would try to forget the Mysore episode to the maximum extent possible. Unknown to her, a sort of harsh feeling developed in her towards her husband.

When Raja and Katyayani were transferred to Mysore, Nagalakshmi was in no mood to move with them. Katyayani, too, was not for moving to Mysore. Though they were apprehensive about Bangalore earlier, Raja and Prthvi soon got acclimatized to the city. But they all had to inevitably move to Mysore. Prthvi enrolled in a college here. Over the first few days, Nagalakshmi's mind was in disarray. The images of the hospital and the bungalow would surface in her memory and disturb the equilibrium of her mind. She impelled her mind to calm down, and she took to rote-writing Rama. By now, she had written in excess of 45 lakh, and a total of 110 notebooks were full. Resolving to go through it apace, and to accomplish the one crore target before she passed on, she gave it more and more time. The Saturday puja was undertaken in greater detail.

One afternoon, she was seated in the verandah and engrossed in writing. There was no one else in the house. Everyone had gone to their respective colleges. Somebody opened the compound door and entered. She looked up. And couldn't believe her eyes. Rao was approaching. By the time she got to know what was happening, he had entered the house. Nagalakshmi was confounded. She collected the book she was writing in, the inkpot and the inkstand, and went inside. Rao sat on a chair in the verandah. Her mind was in a state of injury from past memories. After sitting quietly for 10 minutes, Rao called out, 'Nagu.' She did not respond. He called out again. Still no response from inside. He again said, 'Can't you hear me. I am here to take you.'

Even now, she didn't speak. When Rao repeated it, she replied from within, 'I am fine by myself. Nobody need take me with them.'

'Nagu, do not say so in anger. After you left for Bangalore, I lamented much. Now she has consented.'

'I need not go there in honour of anybody's concurrence. I will go nowhere.' Not only was her voice was trembling, it was unintendedly voluble.

'Don't say so, Nagu. Give it a thought. I am here…' Her voice from within cut him off. 'It doesn't matter who comes. I have thought it out fully.'

Rao was silent for five minutes. She didn't emerge from within the house. Neither did she say anything. Finally, Rao said, 'I am leaving. But give it a thought. I will apprise Raja too. If you so desire, I will send her to invite you.'

'Raja knows everything. Not just his, I will not cede to anybody's request. If you report this to him, you will lose your honour. No one need come here to invite me. I can earn my sustenance by being a housemaid. That way, I can live a life of honour. You leave,' her words rolled out incessantly from within. For another minute, Rao stay put. Then he exited the house. When she heard the compound door shut, Nagalakshmi began sobbing.

Half an hour later, Katyayani returned from college. Noticing Nagalakshmi, she asked, 'Sister, were you crying?' Nagalakshmi said nothing. Katyayani could do nothing more than offering a word of general consolation.

When Rao returned from his brother's house, Karuna asked, 'What did she say?'

'She vehemently refused to come over. I hadn't anticipated that response.'

'Shall I go and invite her?'

'Don't. No use.' He fell silent.

For a week, Rao's mind was in an agitated state. Until then he had nursed the feeling that he wielded the husband's authority over Nagalakshmi. Now, that stood refuted. His mind was in a state of having lost something precious. He was overcome with the feeling that he had become an orphan again, just as he was at an orphanage prior to his marriage. He hadn't ever experienced such helplessness, such impotency till date. His mind averred that all the erudition, achievements and fame that he had achieved in his life were failures.

But he did not allow those feelings to rent his mind. The fifth volume took up all his attention. His inner voice kept iterating that he would not live much more. Garnering all his energy to channel it to the final volume, one day he said to Karuna, 'From now on we have to work at a greater pace and conclude this. On you rests greater work than hitherto.'

She applied herself to the task.

CHAPTER 22

1

Katyayani did not cease cogitating about the force that split her life in two and destined her for a life of eternal duality. It wasn't merely a conflict of unrelated philosophical tenets. Rather, it was a duality that rent her life by scything through the heart, emotions and state of mind. The stance that seemed apt when she abandoned Nanjangud now began to seem inapt. When she recalled the sacrifice made by her husband, she would console herself that she had not eloped with an ineligible man. But when she got to know from Karuna about her mother-in-law's demise and the current situation of that household, her mind became uncontrollably deranged. On the one side, memories of her child would bother her and she would long to see Cheeni, and on the other, Srotri's face would appear before her eyes. Having lost his wife, he leads a duty-bound life even at this age of his for the sake of his grandson! 'Resoluteness and purposefulness propel his life', she would recall Karuna's words about Srotri. She very well knew of the immensity of his resoluteness and the depth of his faith in life. *He lived his life by subscribing to the guiding canon that if we submit ourselves unreservedly to dharma, that same dharma would lend us a helping hand. His conscientiousness is an expression of such submission. There is no latitude for dual manifestation, dual perception, and dual objective in his life. He effectively wards off all influences that do not subscribe to his life's goal, and perseveres to his unitary drive. That is the secret of his peace of mind.* Her thoughts rolled on thus.

In a particular phase of her life, she had believed that it was *anti-dharmic to impose contrived dharma on Nature that is evergreen and ever-zestful.* Her mind was then coerced into thinking so by the basic evil forces of Nature. She did not know then that mind, too, was an aspect of Nature. Of late, she was given to thinking that she would have done better to align her deeds with *dharma* that was in transcension of the mind's ways. She would reminisce Srotri's words 'it was for reason of perpetuating the seed of one lineage that another lineage donates its habitat. The habitat attains its emancipation on receiving that seed and tending it into a plant.' She would repine that owing to her shift in loyalty to another lineage, she had failed in discharging her obligations to the Srotri family. She got to feel that she would not have been assailed by such duality if she had taken to serve her elderly mother-in-law and father-in-law, and tended to her offspring.

College reopened after the summer vacation. As admissions were yet underway, classes were not being held regularly. The drizzle of June had set in. Holding an open umbrella, Katyayani headed to college. The theatre association that had been dormant while Raja was away now regained its activity on his return to Mysore. Nowadays, he would go in early, on his bicycle, for the practice sessions of the opening play of the academic year. The drizzle always reminded Katyayani of Nanjangud. Kapila would now be in full flow. It was in the same season 16 years ago that her first husband Nanjunda Srotri had drowned in it. She permitted herself the wishful thinking that if he were alive she would not have been assailed by duality in life. Whenever her first husband came to her mind, memories of Cheeni would invariably disturb her. Once she thought of going to Nanjangud, see Cheeni, prostrate at father-in-law's feet and ask him to bless her with peace of mind. She was apprehensive of the same, too, but she was sure that his response would never be acrid. She was sure that if she prostrated at his feet with repentance, he would bless by passing his palm over her head. She could get to see Cheeni too. She thought she would get peace of mind if she visited there intermittently. These thoughts prevailed over a few days, but she could not garner the courage to visit. It was now time for the classroom sessions to go full swing. Looking forward to her mind being assuaged by engaging in the curriculum, she took to preparing for an upcoming session and left for college. There was news of the death of an ex-faculty member, and in his memorium, the college announced holiday for that day. She got to know of this after reaching the college. The students were leaving; there was no one in the teachers' room either. The drizzle outside was increasing. She sat there for a while. Her mind yearned to visit Nanjangud today. It was so much agitated that if she didn't make it today, she thought that she would surely go mad. Without contemplating much, she placed the books in her cupboard in that room and exited. The drizzle had not relented. Opening the umbrella, she headed straight to the Chamarajapura railway station. There was a posse of students that was bound for Nanjangud. In another half an hour, a train rolled by. She got into the ladies' car.

While the train rolled on, her student-days surfaced in memory. She had commuted in this very train for over two years when she herself was a student. It was then that her life had aspired for a different resort. After the train crossed south Mysore station, the Chamundi hill was visible. Beneath the sky that was pervaded by the clouds, the hill appeared denser, and as if it were stateliness personified. She recalled the day she had been there alone. She reflected that she would not have been overcome by her current predicament if she had stuck to her resolve of that day at the top of the hill. The sighting of the hill brought back memories of Srotri. The train halted in Kadakola, and after resuming its journey, it was soon rolling on the bridge over the Kapila. She helped herself to a full sight of the river; it was flowing with its usual elegance. The mangroves on either side were the same. The temples and the bathing decks yonder stood testimony to their historical era. In four minutes, the train rolled into Nanjangud station and halted. Katyayani alighted, but her heart began thumping. She stood her place on the platform until all those students and others who had embarked exited the station. She was apprehensive of exiting the station and going into town. While she stood so for 15 minutes in a state of indecision, the ticket examiner neared her and said, 'Let me see your ticket. Where are you bound to?' She gave him the ticket that was in her hand and exited the station. Apprehensive of being recognized, she walked on with her head hung, but regarding the houses on either side through the corners of her eyes. At that hour, there was no one on that entire road. She went ahead and arrived at the door of the house that had once been hers.

Though the door was shut, it wasn't locked. She recalled that during monsoon season, the main door of this big house was always kept shut. From the wet footprints on the steps, she could gather that someone who wore shoes had just entered the house. Alongside those marks was a line of drops of water that had trickled as if from an umbrella. She wanted to push the door open and go inside. But she felt trepidation, and smoke seemed to billow from within her lungs. Her entire body trembled. Such was the severity of the shudder that it was clearly perceptible to her own eyes; her torso, arms, legs and the umbrella she held were trembling! Even in the rain and the chill, she was sweating. She was seized by an unknown fear. She attempted to find the cause of her condition, but her brain went numb. She tried lifting her hand to knock the door but there was no strength in the arm. By then, she could hear voices from within the house. She got to know that the door would open any moment, somebody would exit and spot her. She froze with fear. Without being conscious of it, she was moving away from the door. Her feet took to the street. Forgetting to open the umbrella against the rain, she walked on. She came to the present only when she reached the railway station.

A goods train stood at the station. She asked a nearby porter as to when the next train to Mysore was. He extended his arm and said, 'There is a passenger car attached to this train. Board it.'

She bought a ticket and boarded the passenger car that was to the rear of the train. Barring a few villagers, there weren't many passengers. Her body continued to tremble even after the train had crossed the bridge.

2

It was drizzling the next day even. As she had not slept overnight, Katyayani felt sluggish. She had to handle a classroom session for junior intermediate class on the first floor at 10:30. When she entered the classroom, the students got up silently. For them, it was the first ever classroom session here. Katyayani sat in her chair and called out attendance. It was a class of 120. She called out just the first 50 names, and marked present for the rest without even looking at the names. Chamundi hill was visible through the window. Just as she had noticed yesterday during her onward train journey, its peak was covered in clouds now too. And as yesterday, it was stateliness personified. The mist of the clouds had made the green trees appear black, and that colour had lent firmness to the stateliness. Leaving the attendance register on the table, she kept looking at the hill. She seemed to be removed from the present. The students who had remained silent for five minutes started speaking among themselves in hushed tones. In another two minutes, the murmur became clearly audible. Retrieving her sight from the hill, she admonished them, 'Maintain silence.'

The students fell silent. She opened the text of her topic of the day and was about to begin her lecture when a boy appeared in the doorway and asked, 'May I come in?'

'Come in,' she said and looked in the direction of the door. Her face became solemn and she kept looking at the approaching lad. Broad face, wide eyes, straight nose, tall and sturdy, hair cropped. There was the traditional daub of grains in the middle on his forehead. He had worn trousers, shirt and shoes. In his hand was a wet umbrella. His gait gave away that he was not used to walking with such clothes on. Physique, bearing, facial features all resembled Srotri's. Her first husband, too, was thus on their wedding day.

The lad walked alongside a wall and sat at an empty desk. Her eyes were fixated on him. By then, the hushed talking recommenced in the classroom. She opened her book and resumed lecturing. She had hardly gone through two sentences when the lad who had just entered was told something by a student seated beside him. Accordingly, the lad got up and asked, 'Madam, my attendance.'

Her attention returned to him. Looking at him, she opened the attendance register and asked, 'Your name please?'

'N. Srinivasa Srotri.'

Katyayani's hand began to tremble imperceptibly, and sweat beads formed on her forehead. Unable to continue to stand, she sat on the chair. She had marked present for everyone. She gained control over her voice that had sunk, and picked up the book to continue to lecture. But she forgot what to say; her head was a ball of nullity. She thought it better to abstain from lecturing instead of telling something irrelevant. She closed her book, asked the students to silently file out, and even before the students of the first desk could clear out, she scuttled and posted herself at the door. That was the only door to that room and the students passed by one behind the other. She stood her place in full confidence that Cheeni who was seated in the last bench would near her and would talk to her himself, for he would definitely know who she was and would have got to know that she had recognized him. There really existed no premise for such confidence; her mind didn't browse for the premise even. Three-fourths of the students had cleared out. Cheeni was engaged in a chat with a student. *He would turn up any moment. He would definitely talk to me. The same face. He was so even when he was small.* He appeared by the door, but when he spotted the teacher by the door, he got demure, stopped chatting with the other lad, hung his head, held his books against his chest and went past the doorway. He did not speak to her. Disappointment rent her entrails.

She trotted to the teachers' lounge. She scribbled a note that she would not be handling the other session scheduled for that afternoon, asked the attendant to pin it to the notice board, and left for her house. Though she was awfully pained that he did not recognize his mother, by evening she contained herself. *I got to know who he is. But how would he know who I am? Karuna has told me that he knew of his mother, but how could he know precisely that I was his mother? Today was the first day at college for him. Would he even know my name? If he got to know my name, he will eventually realize.* She thus kept consoling herself. That class was not in her next day's timetable; it was on the day after that, at the same time.

By the time she appeared in that class on that day with the textbook and attendance register in hand, all students were in. As soon as she neared her table, she looked at the last desk. There was Cheeni. He, too, looked at her. She thought he recognized her. She was hopeful again that after the session he would walk up to her and speak to him. When she called out attendance, she did not miss his name. When he stood up and said, 'Present madam,' she looked at him. She then opened her book and started lecturing. In between, she looked at him intently. But he was engrossed in his book, and making notes of the meaning of new words. She just about kept lecturing, and the students listened silently. The bell rang. She closed the book, scurried and posted herself outside the door. As there was another period for the students, nobody exited—including Cheeni. She stood her place for five minutes thinking that he would come out at least to speak to her. But when she saw the teacher of the next period approaching, she left.

She was now in doubt if he knew her at all. Students would be eager to know their teachers' names on the very first day at school. He very well knows my name, she thought, but wouldn't he know of his mother's name and occupation? If he had grown up just with his grandfather, he would not know, but she reasoned that before her death his grandmother would have told him everything. He would have got to know some of it from Lakshmi. So, she thought, did he disown acquaintances with her? She felt as if her belly were pierced by a trident. Telling herself that she should not lament without knowing the truth, she spent two more days. That day she was to lecture his class at 3 pm. She went through the lecture. As usual, she walked up to the door and waited. As usual, he brought up the end. Though he knew that she waited by the door, he fumbled with the umbrella in his hand and was sneaking out. She then called out to him, 'Srinivasa Srotri.'

He turned and came to a stop. The other students moved on. His companion paced a few yards and waited for him. Noticing him, Katyayani said, 'He will join you later. You go on.' He eyed Cheeni for a lengthy second and left.

Srinivasa Srotri hung his head and stood his place. She asked, 'Where do you come from?'

'Nanjangud, madam.'

'Do you commute daily?'

'Yes.'

'By train?'

'Yes.'

He held his head hung all through. She neared him and asked, 'Come, let's go to my house today.'

He didn't answer. 'Come child, let's go.' When she prompted him again, he said, 'I will be delayed for my train.'

'The train is at 5:30. It is just 4 now.'

For a minute, he was speechless. Then he said, 'No madam. I will be delayed,' and without waiting for her response, fidgety, he walked away. Katyayani was now sure that he knew who she was. Though she was irate at his haughty conduct of resigning her invitation and walking away, she thought it incorrect to analyze his conduct typically as a teacher would. Rather than she analyzing his conduct, she thought that he had analyzed her earlier conduct, and by his present conduct he could be obliquely conveying his assessment of her. Her mind got muddled. She felt that her own soul detested her as if she were a vile creature. Holding on to the textbook and the attendance register in her hand, she slowly climbed down the stairs and went to the teachers' lounge. She placed the attendance register in the cupboard, took her umbrella and went home.

That entire day, she experienced searing agony. She knew at heart that he had recognized that she was his mother. If he had gone along with her when invited, and had directly asked her why she did so, she would have answered him. She could have put up with some ignominy, explained him the situation of yore, and asked apology of him. If he had derided her on her face, she could still have put up with it. But he was dodging her as if he never wanted to be acquainted to her, and as if their relationship were ignominious. She wondered if it was revenge or a premeditated punishment. Until Raja returned late evening, her mind was a medley of disturbing thoughts. Presently, her head got heated up and ached. Raja noticed it at supper. After eating, Prthvi went to the pharmacist and brought a tablet for her headache. When they retired, Raja soon slipped into sleep. Katyayani kept tossing this way and that. Cheeni's face seemed to incessantly damn her. By midnight, she felt drowsy. And she had dreams even in that semi-sleep state. The picture of Cheeni fidgeting and walking away saying 'No madam, I will be delayed' without waiting for her response passed before her mind's eye repeatedly. Sleep ended. She was sweating, and her body seemed heavy. She could not think of a way to evade such thoughts. She turned towards Raja and embraced him with her right arm. She felt a semblance of protection. She hugged him more firmly and pulled him towards her. He woke up. He placed a hand on her forehead. 'You are running fever. You are sweating,' he said and sat up. Tears came to her eyes. She placed her head on his thigh, and sobbed and cried. He was put to consternation. He asked her what this was about. She did not tell him even though he asked her repeatedly.

3

Katyayani was down with fever for about a week. After reporting back for work, she would deliver her lectures in a low voice, seated on the chair. Srinivasa Srotri attended the classes. He would sit at the same desk. Her resolve to rein in her mind would fail and she would look at him frequently. He would look into his book while listening to her lecture. In between, he would note down the meaning of difficult words. Noticing it, she tried convincing herself that he did not know who she was. She resolved to summon him someday and introduce herself.

One day his class was scheduled for the usual 10:30. At 10:35, she called the attendant and said, 'There is a Srinivasa Srotri in junior inter science D section. Inform him of my summons and bring him here. Also inform the class that I would not be taking the class today.'

In five minutes, the attendant returned with Srinivasa Srotri in tow. There was a watch on his left wrist. He held his books in his left hand and an umbrella in his right. The moment he entered, she got up and said, 'Today, you won't get late for the train. Come child, let's go to my house. When I invite you, you should not give a brash reply.'

The lad gave no answer. He just stood there, looking at the table. Without giving him any leeway, she took hold of his hand and said, 'Come on. Let's go.' He followed her. That day, there was no drizzle. She walked ahead; he was following her. After crossing the college mound and going past the

Ramaswamy Square, she turned to him and said, 'Walk alongside me. Why are you dragging behind me?' She slowed down to match his pace. Today, he wore slippers instead of shoes. When he lifted his foot, she could notice the abrasion caused by the new shoes. She couldn't think of anything to speak during their walk. He, too, kept walking dutifully.

Nagalakshmi was alone at home, and was engaged in her rote-writing in the kitchen. The other two had gone to college. As Nagalakshmi was used to visits by Katyayani's or Raja's pupils, she kept up with her work of writing without even lifting her head once. Katyayani mixed curd in rice, and took it to her bedroom along with a glass of milk and water. Placing it on the table there, she asked him to come over. He removed his slippers at the main door, entered the room, and sat in a chair shown by her. His face was red with hesitation and perplexity. Though he hung his head in a state of uncertainty, he was deep in thought.

'Take this,' she said, closed the door of the room, and sat beside him.

'No madam, I have had lunch.'

'This is not full lunch. Just a little. Have it. When a guru gives, you should not refuse.'

Without touching the plate he said, 'This is much for me.'

'Eat whatever you want and leave back the rest. Now, eat.'

He took the plate, set aside the spoon that was in it, and started eating with his hands.

'Did you say Nanjangud?' she asked.

'Yes.'

'What is your father's name?'

'Sri Nanjunda Srotri.'

'Your father and mother are both alive?'

'No.'

'Both?'

'Yes.' He held his head hung all through. He really didn't want the food. Noticing, Katyayani said, 'If you don't feel like it, leave it and wash your hands in the plate.' He placed the plate on the floor, took the glass containing water, walked up to the window, extended both his arms through the window grill, and washed his hands. When he returned to his chair, she said, 'Who is taking care of you?'

'My grandfather.'

'What is his name?'

'Sri Srinivasa Srotri.'

'Your grandfather would be finding it strenuous to tend to you?' she asked. He gave no reply. Not knowing what to ask next, she went silent for five minutes. Then she asked, 'A relative of mine is quite familiar with Nanjangud. She said that your father drowned in a flood, and that your mother is alive.'

He spoke nothing. He kept looking the floor. 'Isn't it?' she asked. 'I do not know,' he said. She asked again, 'Do you remember having seen your mother?'

'No.'

'I have heard that she is alive. Nobody in your house discusses about her?'

'No.'

She was tongue-tied. 'Don't you desire to see your mother?' she asked.

He remained silent. He kept looking the floor as if he were a stone statue. She asked again, 'Child, don't you desire to see your mother? Answer me.'

He still did not speak. When she asked it yet again, he said slowly but with a tremble in his voice, 'No.'

Katyayani felt as if a boulder was dragged over her chest. His reply caused all her desire to evaporate, and she went numb. Her head seemed to reel and she closed her eyes and leaned back in the chair she sat. Seated unconsciously thus for five minutes, she then sat erect and eyed him. He was staring at the floor. In eyes, nose, face, bearing and physique he resembled his grandfather. The pronounced lower lip and firm sight were representative of his grandfather's resoluteness. He had replied in the negative to all her questions, and had indicated that he was not interested in discussing the matter. Her innards felt that he surely knew of her identity. Still she asked him thus: 'You mother stays nearby. She is a good friend of mine. She pines to see you. Shall I summon her?'

He didn't speak. 'Child, give me a reply,' she asked again. He continued to be silent.

'You are silent, why?' Wait, let me send for her.'

'Don't, madam.'

Stupefaction struck her again. She partly closed her eyes and leaned back in her chair. 'I will get delayed, madam,' he said and got up. She slowly opened her eyes and looked. He walked up to the door, opened it and exited. She kept looking at him. Stupefied that she was, she lacked the physical strength to get up and check him. Her tongue lacked the strength to say, 'Stop. Don't go.' She heard him wear his slippers and leave. She turned towards the window and looked. She saw him walk away, his head hung as if it were more gravitous than his body. From within her issued forth a torturous cry that was more rapid than the flood of Kapila. 'Cheeni, you are my son, born in my womb. You shouldn't kill me so,' she screamed in her mind, got up from the chair, and lay on the floor. So as not to draw Nagalakshmi's attention, she arrested the sound of her cry by shoving her *pallu* into her mouth.

She cogitated even as she lay on the floor. *What a cruel dejection towards me! Seated before his mother, he listened to her words that held emotion enough to thaw anyone's heart. For everything that he was asked, he gave indifferent and disinterested answers. If it were anyone else, he would have at least shed a tear; would have neared her, his own mother. He sat like a stone statue. Eventually, he excused himself saying, 'I will be delayed, madam,' and exited as if he knew nothing. Is this his innate austerity, or is it equanimity derived at an early age from his exemplar grandfather?* She recalled Srotri. He would remain calm even in situations that would, in most others, cause heartbreak. Though there wasn't calmness in the face of Cheeni that sat before her, she had noticed that he had the resoluteness and the gumption to put up with heartrending incidents.

She continued to lie on the floor, deep in thought, till Raja was home. 'Why are you lying down here? Seems like you have cried much. Why?' he asked, noticing her face.

'Nothing,' she said and got up.

'Won't you share with me? What is it that is ailing you?'

'Nothing. Something of the past.'

He understood it that the triple abortion still troubled her. The surfacing of those incidents in memory caused grief in him too. 'What use recalling all that?' he consoled her. That night she had an attack of fever again. Raja got her medical treatment, stuck to her bedside, and kept an eye on her. Nagalakshmi consoled her in her own way. The fever abated on the third day. Though she went to college in a tonga on the fourth day, she could not lecture. She resumed her lectures in a couple of days. When she headed for Cheeni's classroom, she experienced extreme defeat. She went into his classroom with a resolve not to look at him. But the mother in her superseded such imposition. Unrestrainedly she looked at the last desk. He was not there. She let her eyes roam over the entire classroom. He was nowhere. While calling attendance, she expressly called out his name. There was no answer. She got anxious again. Her pulse aggravated. Two weeks passed thus. He never turned up. One day, she enquired in the administrative office of the college. The clerk verified the admission records of students and said, 'N. Srinivasa Srotri has taken a Transfer Certificate and left. It is already four days. He has remitted the full fee for this term and has obtained the TC.'

She understood it as his final rejection of her. She gave a thought as to which college he would have transferred to. It was not difficult to find out. But what use searching for an iron that would not bend? She resigned to the fact that by now he had laid bare his mind unambiguously. She dispensed with the thought of searching for him, but she didn't have the strength to put up with his conduct.

4

Cheeni wasn't ignorant about his mother. Some of his classmates had told him about it all when he was in middle school. They, in turn, had gathered such information from the conversation of their parents. When his grandmother was alive, Cheeni had asked her about it one day. Though she did not tell it in all detail, she just about adumbrated and categorically said, 'We should not be discussing about this, child. Your grandfather doesn't take a liking to it. One's sins and virtues are one's own.' Bhageerathamma knew from rumours that presently she was a lecturer at a college in Bangalore, and she had shared that fact with her grandson. He even knew her new husband's name. That matter never even received a mention in that house after his grandmother's death. His grandfather never said anything about it. Knowing that his grandfather didn't like it being discussed, he did not ask him even. Lakshmi was in perfect concordance with Srotri's opinion and conducted herself accordingly. The three in that house remained unconcerned with that issue, and stayed from mutually discussing it. The lad's traditional education was directly under the tutelage of his grandfather. He taught the Vedas and Upanishads to him, and explained their meaning. He discoursed on *dharma*, *karma*, obligations, the purpose of life, etc. Though he could not fully grasp all that was told, he had developed a feeling of devotion towards his grandfather, which bordered on fear. Deep-seated in his heart were his grandfather's duty-consciousness even at his age, the veneration shown to him by people, he cooking food for him daily like a woman of the house, etc. Lakshmi gave him a weekly oil bath. After the bath she would adorn his forehead with the ash from the kiln in the bathroom, and would say, 'Child, first bow to Agni, then prostrate at your grandfather's feet.' He would ask, 'To you?' to which she would say, 'It would suffice to prostrate before Sheenappa. It is as good as prostrating before all the Gods. There is no need to prostrate before me.' The lad stood mesmerized by his grandfather's personality.

He had gone to college on the first day on time. When an 'off day' was announced he had returned to Nanjangud on a midday train with the other students. His classmate at college was Chakrapani from his high school days. He was the son of Venkata Rao, a lawyer residing in Srikanteshvara layout. He was in the same section as Cheeni's. The next day, Chakrapani had commuted by the early morning train. He had occupied a seat on the last desk and had reserved a seat for Cheeni who would come by the 10 am train. When Cheeni entered Katyayani's class and occupied his seat beside Chakrapani, he was surprised that it was 'a *madam's* class'. For a while, he gazed at the lecturer thinking how a female teacher's lecture would be. Then on, he concentrated on the lesson. After that class, all students had to go to the laboratory. They all went. But nothing was imparted there that day. When all the students exited the lab, Chakrapani asked Cheeni, 'Do you know the name of the English madam?'

'No. What is it?'

'Mrs Katyayani Raja Rao.'

'Which means she is married?'

'Yes. Her husband is an Assistant Professor at Maharaja College.'

Cheeni could readily grasp who she was. Still, he asked Chakrapani, 'Has she been here all through?'

'No. They both were in Central College, Bangalore. Last year they were transferred here. Her husband Raja Rao is well-known for his plays. I came early today and went to my aunt's house here. Her daughter is pursuing her BA in Maharaja College. She told me everything.'

'What does "everything" mean?'

'Hers is a widow marriage.' Chakrapani stopped at that as if he had bit his tongue. Cheeni's face turned melancholic. Chakrapani had fully got to know who their new *madam* was. He had not related it all to Cheeni, for he thought that it would greatly pain him. He only wanted to apprise his friend of an important matter.

For a few days, Cheeni was subconsciously attracted towards the new teacher who was, in fact, his mother. In the classroom, he used to glance at her when she was not looking. When he received her first invitation to visit her house, he felt animated. He had given some reply that came to his mind and had dodged her. He got curious to go the college next door and have a look at her husband. One day, he went and enquired with a student, 'English Raja Rao, where is his session now?'

'In the senior BA hall.'

'Where is it?'

'I am headed there.'

Cheeni went there and occupied a seat. Raja Rao entered. Cheeni ogled him. He was handling Bernard Shaw's play *Saint Joan*. Though he could not grasp it fully, he was charmed by his gestural ways and the fluency of English oration. On getting to know that the new madam was his mother, he had accepted the fact albeit undeniably, but no feeling of intimacy oozed in him towards Raja Rao. A vague disdain showed up instead. He recalled his father; he had never seen his father. There wasn't even a photo of him in the house. He got fidgety. The lecture was in progress. He wanted to leave then and there, but apprehensive of reprimand, he stayed on the full hour.

His mind was assailed by a medley of peculiar feelings. At times, he desired to meet his mother and talk to her. His mind contemplated as to why she had gone away with a new husband. He got to know that she was a pupil of his. He recalled his grandmother saying that he enacted plays well. She and the accomplished thespian would have got friendly. She and he…He felt aversion to think any further. He thought why his mother did so. Once, he even thought of asking her straight to her face, 'Why did you do so?' But he soon warded it off thinking that she'd have reprimand him. *If she had not eloped to marry again, it would have been helpful for grandfather in his old age. She went away disregarding that! And how could she abandon her child?* All these questions troubled him. For a few days, his diet and sleep suffered. He once thought of sharing with his grandfather the thoughts that troubled him. But he nipped that thought in the bud knowing well that his grandfather would not take a liking to it, that it would make him woeful too. He told himself to remain calm by bottling up all worries like his grandfather did. At his regular *sandhyāvandana*, he started reciting additional 108 Gāyatri-mantras.

He would always recall his grandfather's oracle: 'Child, one's *dharma* and *karma* are one's own. We should not be judgmental about others' conduct.' He tried not to recall his mother's conduct. His willpower was remarkable, which was a direct result of being every which way his grandfather's protégé. He was repeatedly confronted with the imagination that she would one day summon him and aver that she was his mother. What to do then? He would think if he should admit: 'Yes, I am your son.' If he did so, their relationship would receive impetus. *By and by I will start adoring her, and eventually I may desire to live with her. What then would be grandfather's fate?* The disgusting thought of abandoning his grandfather just as his mother had done began smouldering him. *Or may I be a son on both sides?* Cheeni had studied quite many śāstras. He was, to a certain extent, cognizant of his self, his lineage, the *dharma* and *karma* that flowed in the lineage, etc. These were reinforced in him every day when he pronounced his extraction as part of the *sandhyāvandana*. He would recall his grandfather's words that not only shall every man uphold the significance and eminence of his lineage, he rather shall conduct himself so as to augment and invigorate the same. He had read in the Purāṇas as to how the kings of the *Sūryavaṃśa* and *Candravaṃśa* had lived up to the honour of their lineage. Having born into *Kāṣyapa* lineage, and being a scion of the Srotri family, how could he conduct himself as a son of another family? The edification he received was such that he would regard any elderly person with veneration as a son would. But he would think, what an irony it would be to establish a relationship with a woman who had abandoned her pedigree and moved on to another one, and eventually begin paying regular visits to her house.

He kept thinking as to what he should say and do if, one or the other day, she summoned him and revealed her identity. He would not cause pain to his mother's mind by giving an arrogant reply. His grandfather had often told him that one should not talk brashly with anyone so as to cause pain to their mind. He resolved that he shall put it all in the backburner and distance himself from this new relationship. Though he had conducted himself thus on his visit to Katyayani's house, he had cried when he exited from there. He had stood beneath a roadside tree and cried much.

Wiping his eyes with a handkerchief, he had gone to the playground behind the college and sat under a tree there.

He visited college daily. He would always think what he'd do if she summoned him again, if she wept before him, and if he felt like crying before her. He got to know from the college notice board that she was on leave of absence for four days. What will he do when she'd return after four days? He desired to see her again. At times, his feelings would swell so as to go to her and say, 'I am your son. My name is Cheeni.' But behind would surface his grandfather's admonition: 'Association with any object will only engender desire for it. Once desire gets intense, it is not easy to disassociate from it. Therefore, one should eschew association with the unpleasant.' He thought that he should stop seeing her, that he should quit this college, and that his mind would regain its tranquility in a few days thereafter.

One night he asked his grandfather, 'The quality of education in the government college that I study is not up to the mark. I made enquiries and discovered that it is advisable to study in Sharadavilas College. May I obtain Transfer Certificate (TC) and join that college?'

At first his grandfather did not accede to his thinking. He asked, 'Is it possible to get admissions to the new college now?'

The next day he went to Sharadavilas College, enquired and reported to his grandfather. 'They said that I would be enrolled. They asked me to get the TC. Unless I pay the fee for the full term, the government college will not give me

TC. I will have to pay the fee afresh for the new college. I need 60 rupees. I must enroll myself in the new college.'

'Money is in the box. Take it. Tell me what I have to write in the letter to the new college. A college that imparts good education is what is required,' said his grandfather.

In three days, Cheeni enrolled himself in the new college. Still, for quite some days, his mind would not be contained.

5

The despondency caused malady in Katyayani. Though she suffered from no fever or migraine and was not bedridden, she emaciated gradually. Her body that was healthy was now like the venational remains of a moth-eaten leaf. Raja took her to a doctor. She could not be diagnosed with any cognizable disease. The doctor prescribed some tonic and asked her to consume fruits and eggs. Expensive fruits found their way to her house. The quantum of milk purchased increased. But her deterioration continued unabated. Now she communicated less even with her husband. After returning from college, she took to solitary confinement in her room. Her mind would become a void; she would just keep staring at the opposite wall, or fix her sight on a tree outside the window. She would always contemplate what the worth of her life was. If a tree were to be disregarded by its own organ viz. a branch, what was the point in its exuberant growth? She would sigh in despondency intermittently at such thoughts. She would think of paying another visit to

Nanjangud. But that thought would bring about a shudder in her already frail body, and she would feel torn asunder. Of late, she had started babbling inconsistently in her sleep; at times, she would state something coherent. Raja would nudge her and say, 'You are babbling in your sleep. A bad dream?' She would wake up a little but simply slide into sleep again. One night, in her sleep she uttered in English, 'What is the basic axiom that evaluates *dharma* and *karma*?' Raja, who was awake, replied in English: 'The basic axiom of *dharma* is the 'well-being of every living being.'

Still in her trance, she took the conversation further. 'Just well-being is not *dharma*. What sort of well-being? Bodily well-being? Mental well-being? Intellectual well-being? The well-being derived from adhering to a dharmic way of life? The concept of well-being that is not delineated from these standpoints does not merit to be the core of *dharma*.'

When Raja began responding to it, she stopped babbling and slid into sleep. When he reported it to her the next morning, she would not believe it. This happened on many nights. When Raja suggested that they see a psychiatrist, she silenced him saying, 'There is no need for anyone to peek into my mind. The maxim "Know Thyself" will serve.'

One night, Raja was suddenly awakened. He saw that Katyayani wasn't beside him. He sat up and looked. The door to the room was open. He exited the room. The main door was open too. When he walked up to the street and looked, he saw a female figure slowly walking in the direction of Chamundipura. Recognizing it as Katyayani, he went for her. He soon overtook her and asked, 'Where are you going?' Her eyes were open, but the look on her face was as if she were asleep. She didn't seem to recognize the person facing her. She said as if in a trance, 'To the Chamundi hill.'

'Why are you going there?'

'Why? How can one live without scaling high? In my dreams, I was always descending. Now I am awake. I am out to ascend.'

'Come with me now. We shall go there in the morning together.'

'What a wise man you are!' she said, patting his shoulder appreciatively. He held her hand and led her home. He shut the main door, took her to the bedroom, sat her on the cot, and closed the bedroom door securely. In another minute, she closed her eyes and was fast asleep. For five minutes, he sat confounded. Then he nudged her gently and asked, 'Are you asleep?'

'No. I will always be in a wakeful state,' she said, but the regular rhythm of her respiration and the look on her face clearly indicated that she was asleep.

'Do you know who you are speaking to now?'

'Yes.'

'Who am I?'

'Soul.'

'And you?'

'Nature.'

His heart took a beating. Sweat beads formed on his forehead. He wanted to uncover what was deep in her mind. He asked, 'Isn't nature evergreen?'

'Neither evergreen nor ever zestful. She that hath defied the path of *dharma* doesn't merit living.'

For the next 10 minutes he was drawn into contemplation. Then he said, 'Nature, what benefit is it that I may bestow upon thee?'

Katyayani spoke nothing. She was fast asleep by then. She was not to be awakened even though he jostled her. Now Raja lost sleep. He didn't bat an eyelid the entire night. He got up from the bed, sunk himself into the armchair by the window and went into meditation. At some point, he had fancied man's life as being in a state rid of all bondage. He had given a thought to the hindrances caused by *dharma* and traditional practices to man's joyous and free life. He had fancied an ideal social set up on these lines. By nature, he was a good man. He never regarded anybody in bad light. To the extent possible he would help people. But his perception of life was a bit removed. He had encouraged Katyayani to subscribe to that view of his, and had eventually won her over. He spent the entire night cogitating on the despairing question as to what harborage their marriage was seeking now. When Katyayani awoke at 5 in the morning, she walked up to him and asked, 'Why are your eyes red? Did you sleep at all? Why are you sitting here?'

'Don't you remember anything at all?'

She couldn't get the head or tail of it. 'What are you driving at?'

He pulled her beside him and related everything in detail. There were tears in her eyes. 'Come here,' she led him to the cot, sat on it, pulled his head over her thigh and said, 'How much agony you suffer because of me! I don't know a thing of it. Now you sleep. I will stroke you to sleep.'

He closed his burning eyes. While she patted him as she would a baby, there were tears in her eyes. They ended up on his cheek.

'Why do you cry?' he said, eyes closed.

'To atone for having caused pain to you unknowingly. Don't talk. Just sleep.' She bent over and hid him in her bosom.

6

Raja was very perturbed by Katyayani's deteriorating health. He did not know how to get her to cope with whatever she was going through. The more her mind got turbulent, more was the love she sought from him. If he engaged himself in some chore, she would construe his transitory distancing from her as abatement of his love for her. If for some reason he got annoyed at her, she would fear that he would abandon her too. One day on their bed she held his feet and said, 'If you distance yourself from me, how will I put up with it? Don't you have any mercy towards me?'

'What wrong did I do you? You have hoarded some unfounded fears in your mind.' Consoling her, he said, 'I do not nurse any ill feeling towards you. I only strive to see to it that you regain fullness of health in body and mind, but you are going scrawny. Won't you not calm down your mind at least for my sake?'

'Can't you understand the amount of efforts I put towards that? You are destined to suffer because of me! You are a virtuous man. I did not give enough joy to you.' She hugged him and wept again.

He got to know the mental ailment that she suffered from. If even one of the three pregnancies had survived, there would have been something to fall back upon. He understood that she assumed the termination of them all to be an effect of her sins. He recalled that she had once babbled in her sleep that it was a sin for a habitat of the seed of one lineage to donate the same habitat to the seed of another lineage, and that the three foetuses had aborted as an effect of that sin. He could fully understand it, that the weighing of sins and virtues in her conscience was the cause of her decadence. The more helplessness he witnessed in her, the more he loved her. He spent a good amount of his time with her.

One night, he went to his brother's bungalow. Of late, Rao's health had deteriorated too. He was resting in an armchair in the verandah. Karuna was inside, peering into a book. After enquiring after their health, Raja reported to Rao about Katyayani's condition. He, too, was curious to know about the Srotri of Nanjangud. He had abstained from asking it of Katyayani, for it would hurt her. For the first time he enquired about it with his brother. Relating everything he knew, Rao said, 'When we had been there last year, we also felt that it would have been better for their daughter-in-law to be there.'

Raja went into deep thought. After a while, he asked, 'Even now, if Katyayani went there and asked pardon of them, that elderly man would feel contentment and Katyayani's mind would calm down too, right?'

'I talked to him about it. He doesn't even reminisce about all that. He will not retain in mind those matters that have lost contact with him. He leads a life of complete detachment. If seeing him and asking pardon of him will calm her mind, so be it.'

When Raja discussed this with her, she was aghast. A certain force within her caused her heart to wobble. She asked in apprehension, 'Why did you discuss this matter with brother-in-law? I can never go there. Instead of falling unconscious before him, I will rather collapse and die here.'

Raja was helpless. He said, 'Why don't you take to doing Rama puja like Nagu does? You may get peace of mind.'

'I have tried even that. For the likes of me, even Rama does not acquiesce.'

Raja was getting afflicted more and more by the day. Soon, he became an introvert. On the pretext of theatre work, he would leave early daily, drive to the outskirts of the city in one or other direction, and sit beneath a tree. The earlier vigour of cycling had abated in him. It was December winter vacations then. One day, he bicycled along Hunsur road. He was losing memories of that route. When he had driven some eight miles, he came up against the stream on whose banks he and Katyayani had spent time all those years ago. Towing the bicycle, he went to the same spot. He was amazed. The villagers had fully chopped the vegetation thereabouts. They had built a barrage across the stream, and had channelled the water to their fields. Nature had lost her freedom and had turned subservient to man's ventures. Raja strode up the barrage and looked. The pooled water surface was still like a mirror. He bent over and looked at his image. He was aghast. He appeared like an old man. His face had become gaunt. He was graying at the temples. The wrinkles on his forehead appeared clearly. He recalled that he was all of 40 years of age.

CHAPTER 23

1

They both worked vigorously for the fifth volume. To be discussed in this volume was the cultural transformation happening in India since the advent of the British till date. The content was too much. They had to depict the nexus between the colonization of this part of the world by the British, and the despondency that this nation's cultural life became saddled with. They had planned to conclude the volume by discussing the proposition 'Will the ancient Indian culture continue to be vibrant?' in the last two chapters. So that Rao was not subject to much strain, Karuna was handling most of the preparatory work. Rao just dictated the basic premise of the topics and his viewpoints thereat. Karuna would then look for source material that argued for and against such viewpoints, and bring them to his notice. She would keenly watch his health and invariably take him for a late evening walk. She would check him from working late into the night, and would see to it that he got enough sleep during nights.

One night at about 11, Rao was seated at his desk and preparing some notes. Karuna was seated on an armchair behind him and reading a book, with a pencil in hand. Rao, who was writing something, suddenly felt giddy. Though he blinked his eyelids a few times, he could not see the pen in his hands. By the time he removed his spectacles with his left hand, he was half unconscious. He didn't even have enough strength to move this side or that. But he was conscious enough to say what he was undergoing. In a low voice, he called out, 'Karuna.' Karuna, who was right behind, lifted her head. At that moment, a mortal pain surfaced in the left side of his chest. His breath seemed to be seized; it became difficult for him to breathe, and his chest tensed up. He closed his eyes and bit his teeth to bear the pain. He wanted to lift his left arm, but found it impossible to. By the time he lifted his right arm and placed it on his chest, Karuna neared him and pressed his head against her chest. For a minute mortal torture seized his face. The torture seemed to abate slowly, and he placed his head on her shoulders.

Karuna was shocked. It took all of two minutes for her to gather that it was a heart attack. She gathered some strength, placed her fingers beneath his nostrils and checked. He was breathing normally. She called out for Ragappa over and over. Ragappa, who had retired in an inner room, came running, dragging his blanket along. 'Go bring the neighbour professor. Run! Death has come to him,' she said in her clumsy Canarese. Ragappa ran. In two minutes, the neighbouring professor came running. After keenly noticing Rao's face, he said, 'The attack is past now. There is no danger to life. You please continue to hold him so,' he said to Karuna, and turned to Ragappa. 'You place a cot by this chair and put a bed on it. Look, when you bring the cot here, there should be no sound. Let me give you a hand.' They went to Rao's bedroom, together brought out a cot, and placed it by Rao's chair. After placing the pillow, he gently moved Rao onto the cot with Karuna's help and said, 'I am familiar with such cases. There shouldn't be much light here. You put off the light and be seated by his side. I will drive my car and bring the heart specialist, Dr Ananda Rao.'

The professor left. In two minutes, Karuna heard his car gun and clear out. Karuna put off the light in the room. Ragappa stood nearby. She neared the cot and continued to stand. She felt languid. She knew that Rao's health was deteriorating. She even knew that he had taken to worry too much about his first wife. So as to bring an end to his agony, she was even ready to go bring her. But Rao had checked her saying that the effort would go waste. Though Rao was not keeping well, not even in the remotest of her dreams did she think that his health would deteriorate this soon. Rao's body was faintly visible in the light of the adjoining room. She held her fingers beneath his nostrils. Breath was slow. Recalling the neighbour's words that the attack was past, and that there was no danger to his life, she sighed in relief for once. Still, she was filled with a sort of void. She could faintly see the picture of the tragedy. She recalled that for those who submitted their lifetime for the passionate pursuit of erudition, art, research and the like, the type of end was generally thus.

She heard the arrival of a car. By the time she went out, the professor entered with the doctor in tow. After examining the patient, the doctor exited the room and said, 'I will give two tablets. Dissolve it in water and have him sip it. I will come tomorrow and examine again. After one week we shall take him to the hospital and do some tests. You give him milk and fruit juice. No danger to life. Don't worry. I may be delayed tomorrow morning. Keep the curtains closed. There should be no strong breeze.'

When the doctor gave the tablets and exited, Karuna accompanied him and the professor to the door. The professor asked her, 'After dropping the doctor, may I bring your brother-in-law Raja Rao?'

'Please do. Rao's first wife too.'

The professor thought about it for a minute and said, 'I think it may not be good for her to visit. The patient should not be subject to upsurge of feelings. He turned to the doctor and said, 'I told you, there is some issue with his first wife. Would it be okay for us to bring her here?'

'Don't,' said the doctor.

After the doctor's exit, Karuna soaked the tablet in a few drops of water and had Rao lick it. He was very much conscious. 'Will you take some milk or fruit juice?' she asked. He waved his head sideways. Karuna sat in a chair beside the cot. Though the doctor's words had given her a semblance of relief, her mind was not eased of its gloom. She knew that though Rao would get through this, he would not be able to work as hitherto. And there was always the danger of a relapse, which would be invariably fatal. Her mind was filled with void so much so that she could not think of the future. She simply sat leaning in her chair. Ragappa was sitting against a wall in the living room. He was confounded.

By then, the wife of the neighbouring professor, his two daughters and elder son visited. Other than the two occasions on which she had spoken to them, Karuna wasn't much familiar with them. Her total involvement in work had not warranted socializing with the neighbourhood families. Checking themselves from speaking aloud, they waited by the main door. Ragappa informed Karuna of their visit. She exited and received them. The professor's wife spoke English well. Both her daughters were college students. The son was to write his exams for the final year of his undergraduate medical course. 'How is he?' the lady asked.

'Doctor said that the attack is past. He said that there was no danger to life. Your husband opined the same.'

'Don't you worry. There are many who have survived heart attack and returned to their normal life. It is enough for them to take to a lifestyle as instructed by the doctor. Rao's excessive work would have caused this,' said her son. By then the car was heard again. Raja alighted hurriedly. Anxiety was writ large on his face. Nearing Karuna, he asked, 'How is he?'

'I have just given him the tablets,' she said. The professor removed his footwear and went in. Raja had come barefoot. By then, Rao was snoozy. He exited and said, 'He has dozed off. Don't wake him up. See that no sound disturbs him.' He turned to his wife and said, 'He may need fruit juice. If there are any fruits in the house, bring them.' 'I have a stock of fruits,' said Karuna, but he waved her off. 'Let them be. Let her bring some more. Give him sweet lemon juice. He has had his supper. Don't force him to drink anything during the night. I have some glucose. Add two spoons of it to the juice.'

The neighbours brought the fruits and glucose, once again consoled her, and left. 'Don't worry at all. Raja Rao is here. I will visit at dawn,' said the professor, and joined his family back to his house. Inside, Rao was asleep. Deputing Ragappa to the bedside, Raja took Karuna to the kitchen and said gently, 'Tell me in detail what happened to brother.'

Karuna related everything and asked, 'What did you tell your family? Does Nagalakshmi know of it?'

'No. The professor took me outside, apprised me of the situation, and asked me not to reveal it to the others. I told them I was going to Mandya on some work and would be back soon.'

'Will you inform them of the developments tomorrow?'

'If she comes over, it will augur well for patient care.'

'Don't. You probably do not know something,' she said, and related the incident of Rao's earlier visit to his house to invite Nagalakshmi.

'Why didn't you or brother inform me of this?' he asked.

'Your brother checked me saying that it was of no use, for Nagalakshmi had assumed a terse stand in this regard.'

'Let's not inform her as of now. I will send for Katyayani tomorrow, and she will stay here for a few days. I can give some excuse to Nagalakshmi. I, too, will mostly be here. It is enough for me to go home by day's end.'

They entered the room where Rao lay. They sat on armchairs on either side of the cot, and were silent. Though they asked Ragappa to retire, he didn't.

The doctor visited the next morning, examined Rao and said, 'There is no need to take him to the hospital for tests. Let one week pass. Then let him get admitted at the hospital for a while. He should rest for two months after discharge from the hospital. See to it that he is not subject to any emotional stress. Let there not be frequent visitors. If you follow all these and give him medicines as directed by me, he may be up and about in about three months. I will pay a visit in four days.' Raja accompanied him to the car.

At 10 in the morning Raja reached home, took Katyayani to the bedroom and apprised her of everything. She was sad for her brother-in-law's ill health. He went to Nagalakshmi and said, 'Nagu, Karuna is not keeping well. Shall we send Katyayani over for a few days?' She just grunted consent. Since then, barring the two hours at college, Katyayani would be by Karuna. Drained of energy, Katyayani could not attend to any work, but her very presence was reassuring for Karuna.

Next week when Rao was shifted to the hospital, Karuna stayed there as the caretaker and Katyayani returned home.

2

Rao was in the hospital for one month. After he had strictly rested for two more months at home, the doctor permitted him to go outdoors. The university had granted him medical leave for the period. He went on walks twice a day. In the morning, he would go on a slow walk behind the Kukkarahalli tank. The doctor had instructed that he should avoid uneven terrain. He stopped going to the library during afternoons. He would just go to the college, give a few lectures to the MA students and return. Karuna attended to the library work regularly. After the two months' period, the doctor visited, examined him thoroughly, and said, 'Your heart is still fragile. You should completely abstain from rigorous reading, writing, compiling that book and everything else. It is okay for you to go to college and leisurely lecture for one hour per day. You should come to me for monthly check-ups and religiously take the medicines I prescribe. You should not go near heavy traffic zones. If you adhere to these, you may live 10 years more. If you ignore these, I can give no assurance. Anything may happen any time.'

The doctor's warning sent a chill down Karuna's spine. She contained Rao from reading or writing even one line. She was conversant with the outline of the fifth volume. She had herself taken to collating the necessary information. She had planned to completely work on it herself, draft it and finalize it, read it out to Rao, take notes, and hone it based on his inputs. Rao conceded to her affectionate orders lovingly. Karuna now set to think about her future. Her father and mother had died long back. The communication with her brother had ceased quite some time back. There was no bitterness between them, but it was impossible for her to systematically write anything other than the tomes. Until now she had not given a thought as to her life post his death. She loathed lamenting at the condition of her husband just for the sake of livelihood. Even now she had no anxieties as to the economics of living after his death. But what would she be left with after his death? Children? Kinfolk? The future seemed meaningless and cruel. With a resolve to conserve her husband's health, she began tending to him with utmost care and attention.

Initially, Rao adhered to the doctor's advice. But gradually boredom set in. Resting his body was within his volition. But it was impossible for him to send his mind into hibernation. He would recall Srotri's oracle: intelligence, too, is a state of Nature. Rao's musings went on. *If industriousness were a basic trait of Nature, how would intelligence go into hibernation? If the intellect were to achieve a state rid of activity, man would then become a liberated soul.* Many a time, he would meditate on liberation of the soul. He knew how this postulate was discussed in Indian philosophy. He was now contemplating it out of personal interest. *To a liberated soul, there was nothing to be earned through the acrobatics of intelligence. Given that a liberated soul is verily the personification of knowledge, the basic trait of Atman, of what use would the acrobatics of intelligence be to such a soul? Would I merit liberation in this sense?...* he would muse thus. The perseverance, the Aṣṭāṅgayoga, etc. required for meriting it would cross his mind. He would resign to the fact that the path assumed by him was a different one, and emancipation through those traditional means was not possible by him at his present age and situation. At times when he would look himself in the mirror, he would think, 'I am 53. I have become almost bald except for a few strands. It I continue on the path I have tread till now, I will at least accomplish my mission. If instead I take to a different goal before reaching the one already assumed, I will achieve neither. What remains is to finish my tome, nothing else.'

In violation of her instructions, he would peruse the material collated by Karuna. What information they had collated till that first instance of heart attack, he had cogitated them fine. At times, he would wonder if, instead of him, she could complete this volume on her own. He doubted it. He wasn't in doubt either of her intellectual capability or her mastery over the subject. But he would reflect, a treatise was the personification of the inner prowess of the thinker. The fingers that penned the first four volumes should pen the fifth even. Notwithstanding the quantum of efforts that would be put in by Karuna, the fifth would not be the similitude of the intrinsic essence of the earlier four if she penned it all by herself. Therefore, he decided in his mind that write it he should. At his next medical follow-up, he broached the subject with his doctor. By then the doctor had got to know fully about Rao's erudition, and he regarded him in high esteem. After hearing out Rao, he said, 'Of course, I can understand your mind. No expert can aver any cause-and-effect with certainty. But if you relieve yourself of all work, it is possible that you will live on 10 years more. The volume you referred to is in excess of six hundred pages, right?'

'Yes.'

'When you are drawn into writing, can you impose a restriction on yourself as to the number of pages you would pen in a day?'

'Not possible. Usually when I take to penning a certain topic, it will fully suck me into it within a week's time. Then on, I am not at liberty. It will pull along the pen at its own tempo. And till the scripting is complete, I will not feel any fatigue. But many a time, unable to cope with the pace of the brain, the body becomes tired. Yet, I will not feel that fatigue of the body till my writing is done.'

Regarding him appreciatively, the doctor shook his head. 'What do you suggest I do?' he asked.

'Without taking to writing, I cannot live. This stagnation of intellectual activity is worthless. The fact of "a certain writer called Sadashiva Rao, a cardiac patient, lived on these many years in the dread of death" is irrelevant to the world of scholasticism. Having been appreciative of four volumes of my work, that realm is rather in eager anticipation of the fifth in the series. If I do not pen it, my life is not worth even an atom. If I die on accomplishing it, I will have earned my life's goal. I will start penning it. In about four months, the first draft will be done. It is okay even if I die then, for my wife can emend it thence. Once I begin with it, can you see to it that I live on till it is finished?'

It was not just his tongue that was uttering those words. The desires and ambitions of his entire personality had converged onto his proposition. The doctor was deep in thought. A fleeting smile played on his lips. Rao missed it. The doctor knew of many a scholar who had sacrificed their lives for the sake of research. He reflected that if nobody had sacrificed themselves for the sake of erudition, civilization of humankind would have been at a low. He thought that if he could be cheered up by the reassuring words of a cardiologist, why should he prove a hindrance in the emergence of a great treatise? He held Rao's hands and said, 'Don't worry at all. I will stake all my knowledge to care for you. I will assure you that nothing shall ail you meanwhile.'

Contentment pervaded Rao's mind. He had no words to thank the doctor enough. The doctor himself drove him to his bungalow. That night, when he shared his resolve with Karuna, and the doctor's assurance, she was traumatized. Her eyes welled up in two minutes. Noticing, Rao asked, 'How can you cry like other ordinary women?'

'Am I not a human being? You have obligations to discharge towards the world of scholasticism, but none towards your lawfully wedded wife. You are not even related to her in any way, right?'

Rao held his head hung without answering her. Karuna's question strummed a sensitive spot in him. For the first time he reflected as to what he had given to this woman, one who had abandoned her people and was slogging it out in complete commitment to him, to *his* project. She hadn't expected anything from him. He thought that all that he could give her was to hold onto his life some more. The question 'what would happen to Karuna if I was dead?' arose in his mind, and he was grieved by it. He thought about it one full night and the next day, he said, 'I won't write. You start writing expeditiously. I will read it and emend it.'

Karuna's heart swelled from glee. She took his hands and squeezed them lovingly. She started writing within the week, and in 10 days she had written 50 pages. As it would be strenuous to read the handwriting, she typed it, and giving it to him, said, 'Don't read in one stretch. Read slowly, about four pages per day, and apprise me.' Rao read some. He was appreciative of her style of English and the richness of the content. Her commitment to the scripting was clearly evident. He knew of these traits of hers. Yet, the intrinsic essence of the previous four volumes was missing in this. She concurred with him.

Rao's life rolled on as usual. He would go on walks. He would eat ample fruits. But his inability to work towards his goal became unbearable to him. He, who led a life of incessant activity, felt that death was superior to such languorous life. In two weeks, this boredom reflected on his face and on his health. Karuna could readily sense it. One day, he told her, 'Karuna, you did not marry me for the sake of this languorous, lifeless body of mine. You resolve to see through the purpose for which you had wed me. Don't think the way an ordinary woman does, as to what would befall her if her husband were dead. You are not just one in a group.'

Karuna's face became solemn. In five minutes, her eyes glistened. She was deep in thought the whole night. By dawn, she seemed to have arrived at a decision. Now, Rao had taken to walking early morning. By the time he returned, she cleaned the inkstand that had not been used for the last six months, and filled ink in it. She arranged the papers and other things on his desk. On returning, Rao went through his bath and breakfast. She then led him by his hand to his study and said, 'All these days, I was deep in ignorance. You take to your writing. But do it within limits, without exerting yourself. Wherever possible, dictate, so that I can take it down in shorthand. I will always be seated behind you in this very room, and will attend to my work.'

Rao looked at her in the face. Her eyes were shining with love and effulgence.

CHAPTER 24

1

After he started attending college, Cheeni's pursuit of Sanskrit, the Vedas and the Upanishads received a setback. He would be away from 8:45 in the morning till 6:30 in the evening. On returning home, he would change and do *sandhyāvandana*, whereafter his grandfather would tutor him in Veda-mantras for two hours so that he would memorize them. On holidays, these tuitions would be held even during the afternoons. As he was commuting by train daily, his grandfather fed him more milk and ghee than before. When he volunteered to help him in cooking, Srotri would send him away, 'Child, go take to your studies.' One year passed, and he graduated from junior to senior intermediate.

At the beginning of winter, precisely on the fourteenth day of the second fortnight of the lunar month of Kartika, Srotri was to perform the annual death rites of his father. As he was, by and by, feeling it difficult to attend to cooking, besides attending to the rites on empty stomach, he would summon Kuppaiah for cooking. Kuppaiah would present himself on the eve, clean the kitchen, store water separately for the next day, and prepare curry powder and other ready-to-use meals. The priest was the usual Subbaiah Shastri. Srotri would attend to the annual death rites of his parents in all devotion and humility. He held both in equal esteem—worshipping God and performing annual rites of his ancestors. His firm belief was that there was no salvation for the lineage unless the ancestors were content. For the *two designates* that had to be part of the death rites, he would select righteous persons who performed *sandhyāvandana* daily, which entailed the chanting of Gāyatri-mantras and leading a virtuous life. They should also be able-bodied and short of old age—especially with their teeth intact—so that they were capable of consuming sumptuous food to the satisfaction of the performer; Srotri here. They should have the ability and the strength of voice to very clearly recite Veda-mantras. Srotri gave liberal donations to the priests who administered such annual death rites. He would give them a copper spoon and vessels suitable for religious rites, and also a pair of new dhotis. He would top it up with two silver coins, and prostrate at their feet in devotion. As mandatory, he would fast from the previous night. The next morning, he would recite a 1008 Gāyatri-mantras.

Kuppaiah had left after his duties of the eve. As the kitchen was sanctified and earmarked for the next day's cooking, Srotri cooked food for Lakshmi and Cheeni on a charcoal stove in another room. He had sent word for the main priest and the two designates, one representing the deceased ancestors and another representing the Gods, for the next day. At about 3 in the afternoon, he was searching for some book in his study. A doubt about a certain aspect of the death rites had surfaced in his mind. He faintly remembered that it was explained in the *Gobhila-smṛti*. Try as he might, he could not recall the pertinent verses. He did not have a printed copy of that treatise. He recalled that he had written it in a notebook that he'd himself prepared by stitching a set of white pages. He opened the box containing handwritten books and began checking. Besides such notes, there were old letters, and sundry notes made on loose sheets of paper. Even after an hour's search, he could not find that book. He was about to shut the box when his sight fell on a curious-looking sheet of paper. The paper and the cursive handwriting were both unfamiliar to him. The script had opened with the word 'Salutations.' He tried to recollect if anyone had written to him thus any time before. As he read on, not only was he surprised, he was seized by a peculiar predicament:

> 'Kittappa's salutations to the fatherly Nanjunda. All are well. I thought of writing this to you after a gap of 15 years. I have to make it out with great grief. You have defrauded many others, but you are a vile creature that betrayed your own younger brother. To take out your hatred on your brother, you two should not have stooped to this level just to deny his share of the estate which you have embezzled. We have all got to know the story of the legends-raconteur Shyamadas. Your act has caused the past seven generations of ancestors of the revered Srotri lineage to rot in hell. Neither I nor my

> children would have aspired for your assets; we wouldn't have regretted even if it were gnawed away by dogs and wolves. God will watch your sins and virtues. No more. Salutations, Kittappa, Edatore camp.'

Srotri had heard the name Kittappa in his younger days. He was his uncle, his father's younger brother to be precise. From the heated exchanges in the joint family, he had got to know that the brothers hated each other. But what was his parents' act that had caused the past seven generations of ancestors of the revered Srotri lineage to rot in hell? What sin was it that they had committed for reason of apportionment of assets between the brothers? Who is this Shyamadas? As he had to perform his father's death anniversary the next day, Srotri was given to think about his godly ancestors. He felt bad to read about his ancestors destined to rot in hell. He wanted to probe into the matter. But who would have information about this? He was 73 now. The letter bore neither the date nor the name of the year, wherefore its period was anybody's guess. Who would be aware of the incidents of yore? Instantly, Lakshmi came to his mind. She was born in this very house. Women would have gathered information from neighbouring women, many of which would not be known by the men. Inferring that if at all something could be gathered, it was through her, he climbed down the stairs. Lakshmi was seated in the living room, and peeling and chopping vegetables for tomorrow. Nearing her, Srotri asked, 'Have you heard the name Shyamadas?'

Lakshmi could not understand a thing. Gathering the expression on her face, Srotri said, 'Could be something from before my birth, but concerning our family.'

'Yes, I have heard of him,' said Lakshmi, and almost bit her tongue instantly.

Srotri read out the letter to her and asked, 'What matter is it that entailed our forefathers to rot in hell? What is the story of the legends-raconteur Shyamadas? Tell me.'

'I don't know anything of that, Sheenappa. I only know that he used to visit this town for legends-raconteuring.'

Srotri went up the stairs again. It was not in his nature to suspect anyone. But the intrigue of the day bordered on suspicion. He recalled that Lakshmi had almost bit her tongue after saying 'Yes, I have heard of him.' He came down the stairs again, stood before Lakshmi, and said, 'Lakshmi, hold my hand.'

She could not get it. 'Why?' she asked.

'Do as I say,' he said, himself took hold of her right hand and said, 'You are speaking on oath. Perjury shall cause you to rot in hell after death. Tell me the truth. Don't you know anything about that letter?'

Lakshmi hung her head. When Srotri repeated the question, she said in a tone saturate with pain, 'Why put me in a fix, Sheenappa?' But Srotri would not relent. Eventually, she said, 'I will tell you at night when Cheeni is asleep.'

After supper when Cheeni was asleep, he asked her. 'Not here. Let's go upstairs,' she said, led him to his study, closed the doors, and asked, 'For what purpose do you want to know? Why are you adamant?'

'Nothing of adamancy. I am just curious. Give it to me even if it is very bad news. I have the strength to put up with it. Swear on the faith you repose in me. You should not hold back anything.'

'Okay, sit down. What is there that is paramount for me than you?' she said, and sat on the carpet. Srotri was seated on the tiger hide mat opposite her. He who was always composed was now eager. While she recalled that episode, Lakshmi's eyes seemed to take in the sights from a past life.

2

Nanjunda Srotri, who was greedy by nature, was already the lord of the house by the time his father passed on. When at 28 he inherited the entire authority of his family, his only sibling, Kittappa, was 24. Vis-à-vis the elder who was greedy, the younger was generous. The elder was very calculative and businesslike, but the younger was emotionally sensitive. The younger had greater belief in God, *dharma*, etc. than the elder. Vis-à-vis the diminutive elder, Kittappa Srotri was well-built. And strangely, the wives were compatible with their respective husbands in character. If the brothers were not compatible, would the sisters-in-law be? One year into their marriage, Kittappa's wife became pregnant and begot a baby boy. Even unto her 24th year of age, Acchamma's womb did not sprout. Once when there was a tussle between the ladies of the house, Kittappa's wife told off her sister-in-law, 'God gives progeny according to the sins and virtues of people.'

Each year when they had to perform the annual death rites of their father together, the brothers invariably quarrelled. If the younger said that silver coins had to be given to the priests as remuneration, the elder would hold his fists tight, saying, 'You shall give them that when you start earning. As long as I live, I shall not give more than a quarter.' The tussle between them would take nasty turns at times, and they would go to the extent of using expletives against each other. Once it graduated from tongue to hands, and the younger Kittappa had struck his elder brother fine. Acchamma, too, joined in the fight. Seeing that her husband had to contend with two, Kittappa's wife joined on his side. Though Kittappa's mind continued to be rebellious for a month or so, Nanjunda Srotri relented on his anger and spoke cordially to his brother the very next day. Kittappa was not to be assuaged. 'You cold-warmonger, you are a shameless one,' he had said.

In one year's time, the tussle reached unbearable proportions, and it was decided they shall part. To decide upon the modalities of partition of the ancestral estate, a committee of four local arbiters and the fathers-in-law of both the brothers was formed. While relating the family affairs to the committee, Nanjunda Srotri tendered a document evidencing a loan of 20,000 rupees that was raised by mortgaging lands. The mortgage was in favour of a brother of his father-in-law. Kittappa raised a hue and cry that it was a fake transaction. He even went to court. But Nanjunda Srotri tendered to the court some documents which were signed by Kittappa Srotri even! Without disclosing the details of the documents, he had earlier deceitfully obtained his brother's signature feigning good faith. Net of all these, Kittappa got his share of two acres of wet land, which he sold, and left the town with his family of three children. He started a new life as a priest in a temple in the village Edatore. But his anger towards his brother still simmered.

Nanjunda Srotri was habituated to relieving himself thrice in the night. One night when he was relieving himself beside a Chaste plant by the shore of the Gundala stream behind his house, somebody struck him on the back. Before he could scream, another stuffed his mouth with cloth. The person who had struck him removed Nanjunda Srotri's dhoti and cinched his legs and hands with it. That was the only cloth he had worn, and he was now naked. The two pulled out a few linear branches of the chaste plant and lashed him. One of them withdrew, but the other stood before Nanjunda Srotri and said, 'Now eat the fruits of your misdeeds,' and ran away. Though he could recognize it as Kittappa's voice, Nanjunda Srotri could do nothing. His mouth was gagged and his limbs were tied up.

Acchamma, who was asleep at home then, knew nothing of it. When she woke up in the morning, she thought that her husband would have gone to the fields, and she took to her chores. At 7 am, a woman who had gone to bring water from the stream was greatly embarrassed to see a naked Nanjunda Srotri, his hands and legs tied up. She made a beeline to his house and reported it to Acchamma. When the neighbourhood men untied that Duryodhana, they smiled among themselves that the perpetrator was no archangel, but Kittappa. Nanjunda Srotri applied the sap of rose leaves to his skin for five days. Though he sued his brother, the case was dismissed for lack of evidence.

Within days of partition, Nanjunda Srotri's income began to grow by leaps and bounds. He bought lands near Devarasanahalli. He earned interest by lending against pledge of silver and gold. In a majority of the loans, the compound interest would soon add up to more than the worth of the pledged jewels, and he would impound them. In about 10 years, he had amassed enough of liquid cash even. He demolished the small house, and built a two-storied building in its place. Enough of gold and silver pooled. Golden ornaments covered Acchamma from her head to wrists and neck to chest. But as days passed by, the couple ailed from a disconcerting worry. Who would inherit all the assets? Who would all this go to? He would not think of donation and *dharma* even in his dreams. The thought that his estate would pass on to his brother and his children, if he passed on without progeny, burned his mind like fire. The burning memory of Kittappa's act of assaulting him and leaving him to be seen naked by all had remained warm from the air of hatred that kept the flame alive. But he was presently 38; and Acchamma, 34. He, who had never done acts of *dharma* and donation, prayed to Lord Manjunatha of Dharmasthala, and made a commitment. He avowed that if he were blessed with a baby, he would donate the baby's weight of silver to the temple when the baby would turn five. And in commitment to that vow, he tied a silver coin in a piece of cloth and placed it by the idols in the puja chamber. He began reciting the *Lalitāsahasranāma*, and took to giving the customary hamper of betel leaves and areca to a Brahmin daily, with all of one and half paise in it. Somebody said that he would beget children if he installed an idol of the serpent God. He did even that at a cost of 15 rupees with the help of two Brahmins. Nothing resulted.

He then befriended a man named Shyamadas. He was a tall man with longish arms, broad face, straight nose, and a pleasant voice. He was a legends-raconteur who went from town to town giving performances. He had his family in Kollegala. His rendition would be embellished by songs, and by his flawless pronunciation of Sanskrit *ślokas*. Noticing his knowledge of Sanskrit, Nanjunda Srotri invited him to his house and asked him what he could do for his childlessness. He suggested that the couple undertake a pilgrimage to Tirupati. They complied, but nothing resulted. Once Srotri went to Mysore and got himself thoroughly examined by a doctor. Steeling himself, when he asked the doctor the results of the tests, he got to know that his body constitution lacked the propensity for procreating. He resigned to the fact that no God would be of any help. He thought of adopting an heir, and made enquires with his neighbours. Nobody consented to giving their children to that house. By then, some news reached his ears. His brother in Edatore was heard averring, 'He is childless, and when he dies, all his estate shall be inherited by my children.' The news caused anger in Nanjunda Srotri from head to toe. 'It is okay even if my ancestors have to rot in hell. I will see to it that this rogue's children don't get even a pin from my estate,' he had snorted. His inability to procreate, the disappointment from childlessness and hatred for his brother burned him concurrently. But according to law, all his estate would go to his nephews. It was at this juncture that the idea of roping in Shyamadas struck him. Though it was revolting, he was determined to act, for his brother's declaration kept echoing in his ears.

At first, Acchamma would not consent. She was 40 then; and though she was greedy, selfish, scheming, fraudulent and variously vile, she was devoted to her husband. She loved her husband, but when she was childless even after two years into marriage, she burned from a desire to beget a child ever since. Her husband's plans engendered dejection in her. All the same, she could not tolerate it that their assets would accrue to her sister-in-law's children. Her desire for motherhood stood kindled again. Shyamadas was her age or a few years less, and he would visit Nanjangud twice a year. Though he would give performances in the villages around Nanjangud, he would headquarter at the Srotris'. On his upcoming visits, Nanjunda Srotri would be away at one or other of his farms. One month thence, a certain morning

Acchamma started vomiting. Now, Srotri began worrying about what would happen if Shyamadas himself gave publicity to that fact! One day he locked him up in a room, thrashed him fine and said, 'The reason I let you stay in my house and fed you during your intermittent stay here was my understanding that you were a virtuous one. But you have committed this crime! If I ever get to see you in Nanjangud or hereabouts, I will kill you. By the time I am back this evening you should have exited Nanjangud.' He then left for his fields. Seeing the sullen Shyamadas, Acchamma gave him a bag containing 500 silver coins and said, 'You do not know his nature. Never show your face hereabouts. He will definitely get you murdered.'

The chap was not unduly grieved. He kept off Nanjangud and its environs.

In the ninth month, Acchamma gave birth to a buxom baby boy with a broad face and a wide forehead. In a grand christening ceremony, Nanjunda Srotri named him 'Srinivasa Srotri' after his father. Some people drew some inferences, but none voiced anything. Almost everyone in that town and thereabouts had to take their gold and silver to him one or the other day for a loan.

Srinivasa Srotri was a very intelligent boy, and Nanjunda Srotri performed his *upanayana* in his eighth year, and sowed his lineage unto him by whispering his extraction into the boy's ears: I, Sri Srinivasa Srotri, belonging in the Kāṣyapa-*gotra* of the ancestral triad Kāṣyapa-Āvatsāra-Naidhṛva, adhering to the Āṣvalāyana tenets, and pursuer of Rigveda...'

3

In about half an hour's duration, Lakshmi related all that she knew. Srotri's mind cringed.

'Is this all true, Lakshmi?' he asked.

'Have I been witness to it? Am I not five years younger to you? I recall that as a young girl I'd overheard my father sharing this with someone.'

Srotri fell silent. His mind recalled Nanjunda Srotri and his mother who had given birth to him. Nanjunda Srotri was a diminutive man, dark of complexion, of bulbous nose, and his head seemed as if a pumpkin were placed on a potbelly. His mother, too, was not a beautiful woman. She was as tall as her husband, but she was not stout like him. Though round, her face was small. Srotri's attention was drawn towards his own physique. Even in his 74th year of age, he was tall, of good physique, his eyes were prominent on that broad face, his nose was straight, and his forehead was wide. He was instantly disgusted by his physique. Though he was never narcissistic, he was content with the health of his body. He had believed that health was one of the fortunes of a man. But as of now, his healthy body did not seem any prosperous.

'Get up, let's retire. We have to fast till tomorrow afternoon until the rites are fully carried out. There will be much work too,' he said to Lakshmi, and she got up. Srotri climbed down and lay on the cot that was across from where Cheeni slept. His mind was greatly disturbed. He very well knew of his parents' greedy life. He knew of his father's usury.

When Srotri became the lord of the house on his father's death, he not only did away with money lending, he had donated three fourths of the accumulated coins and jewellery to the deserving. But his mind never got judgmental about his parents' ways of living. He, who firmly believed that none had the authority to assess the sins and virtues of others, had never thought of weighing the sins and virtues of his own parents. He had thought of such endeavour as a manner of haughtiness. But today, the faith of his very mainstay was axed. He held his lineage in great respect. His belief was that it was everyone's primary obligation to uphold and invigorate the eminence of one's lineage. He had unwaveringly believed that marriage, *gṛhasthadharma* and such others were the systems that endeavoured to further the sacred objectives of the lineage; he had subscribed to it all in his thoughts and acts. The very foundation of a pedigree that went by the name Srotri, which in turn accredited itself to the Kāṣyapa lineage, seemed to cave in right before his eyes.

If he were a progeny of another lineage, and were given in adoption to the Srotri lineage, he would not have felt so disgusted. If Nanjunda Srotri had even bought a child from its penniless parents for the price of three measures of finger millet and raised it as his, Srotri's belief would not slump. He very well knew that adoption was enshrined in the traditional practices so as to benefit childless couples with a next generation. But Nanjunda Srotri's act was neither from mindfulness of his lineage nor from a desire that his next of kin perform his death rites after he passed on. His illegitimate act was redolent of greed, of hatred that sought to withhold his embezzled earnings from being shared with his brother. *I am a progeny born by such indulgence, born to serve as the pivot to make possible the perpetuation of hatred. What lineage do I belong in? What is the sanctity of my birth?* The old man thought all this. Instead of rejecting his parents, Srotri took to ridiculing his own birth. Sleep eluded him that night.

Lakshmi, who lay next to Cheeni, could not get sleep either. She had anticipated that this disclosure would be a great blow to Sheenappa's mind. All these years her mind had bottled up a question: in spite of being born to such parents and having grown up in such house, how did Sheenappa blossom into a virtuous *dharmarāya*? She never found an answer to it; she had never even given any hint of the incident to anyone all these years. And there were probably none other in this town who knew of it. None had the courage to let loose their tongue in this matter. Sheenappa was a sage of a man. Who thereabouts would dare speak lightly of him? Musing thus, Lakshmi had learned the lesson of life, that one was virtuous or lowly depending on his qualities and deeds. Her perception that Sheenappa was a godly man was the guiding light in her life. If he had not asked her to swear in his name, she would not have revealed it.

Noticing that Srotri was rolling over in his bed, she said, 'Don't take it too much to your heart. We all believe that we are all born to parents. Who knows the truth? I have concluded long back that all this is falsehood. It is in accordance with our sins and virtues that God hands us deliverance. From the moment I saw you, you have been a *dharmarāya* of a man till date. Whenever Yama comes and weighs, he has to assign you heaven only.'

Srotri said nothing. Her words kept filling his ears, but his mind was in such a disturbed state that nothing she said registered. He sensed that the support that had held him had given away, and he was falling into an abyss. He perceived himself as a small branch of a massive tree that emanated from the depths of the earth and reached up to the sky. Somebody had axed that branch, and it was falling from the sky. That grand tree stood motionless in divine indifference, rather with cruel placidity, as if it bore no relationship with that twig. *I am an orphan adrift, a baby born in an inauspicious way for an inauspicious purpose. God, for what sin of what previous life have you given me such a birth!*

His parents surfaced in memory. They had looked after him well. Barring his greediness, his father had tended to him well. Nearer his death, he had showed him where he had hidden the gold and silver coins. His mother doted on him all through her life. She derived happiness from evincing utmost interest in his victuals, dress, ornaments, etc. Even long after his parents passed on, Srotri would reminisce them. Each time he performed their annual death rites, their love for him would surface in his memory. The sacred sprout called 'son' had now become unfounded. What a paradox, he thought, and rolled over.

The epic, *Mahabharata*, surfaced in his memory. In that era, a family man who was incapable of procreating would, after following a certain ritual, let another man to be with his wife for the sole purpose of furthering his pedigree. But that other man should be a noble soul with a sage's outlook of life. Such a donor would be one who had conquered mundane corporeal pleasure, and would donate semen to the wife of that family man in the spirit of endowment. It was designated as one among the *yajñas*; it was called *niyoga*. This practice has ceased in the present era viz. Kaliyuga. The characteristics of this era are different; the practices are different. Greed for riches should not serve as the driving force to resort to *niyoga* for begetting progeny. *But what have my mother and Nanjunda Srotri done?* Srotri sighed heavily in the darkness.

Hearing the sigh, Lakshmi consoled him again. 'Sheenappa, all these days you have put up with many a trying time and have stood firm. Having thus forged into gold, why should you sigh in disappointment now? I have never known you sigh so. Just sleep. We should not worry for the acts of others. We have to look to Cheeni's future. Now get some sleep. There is lot of work to do tomorrow.'

He became especially conscious of the fact that the next day he was to perform the annual death rites of this father, Nanjunda Srotri, as his son. Soon, he sensed that it was a paradox. *I had, all these years—with all devotion and commitment—performed the annual death rites of a person of whose flesh and blood I was not born; a person of whose pedigree I was not appended in the dharmic process. He was rather a person who encouraged his wife's womb to receive me illegitimately with just ill-placed hatred serving as the impetus. But I had believed him to be my father. Now that the truth is out and the very rationale of belief stands obliterated, what is the point in playing a worthless drama? What a paradox of dharma!* Srotri knew of death rites being performed by others as an affectionate obligation. When one passed on without progeny, his friends could perform his death rites. But this was not even such an instance. He called out to Lakshmi. She was still awake. 'Sleep won't come?' she asked. Srotri said, 'After getting to know the truth, I feel that there is no point in performing tomorrow's rites. I will go to the houses of the two designates and check them from visiting tomorrow, telling them that I have called it off.'

'But having performed it all these years…' Srotri checked her midway and said, 'Unaware of the truth, a lineage may flow on any number of years just on belief. But just on that count it shall not merit sanctity. Now I am a different person: Just Srinivasa, not Srinivasa Srotri.'

Lakshmi went mum. Srotri continued to think. After half an hour, Lakshmi said, 'You would always say, "We should not act in haste. The stipulations of *dharma* are very subtle. We shall not be able to grasp it unless we deeply contemplate it." Now, you are acting in haste. Let tomorrow's work go on as scheduled. Who is there that is more knowledgeable than you? You shall think upon it leisurely.'

Srotri fell silent.

Neither of them slept that night. Though awake, wholly unlike himself, the disillusioned Srotri stayed in his bed till 6 in the morning. Lakshmi and Cheeni got up as usual and took to their chores. That day, Cheeni wasn't going to attend college. Kuppaiah arrived at 8. He drew water from the well in the backyard and emptied the pitcher over his head. He then cleaned the vegetables that Lakshmi had chopped yesterday and took them to the kitchen. Cheeni wore a wet dhoti in a traditional way and went into the kitchen to assist Kuppaiah. Kuppaiah readily took to cooking. All deep-fries would be fried in pure ghee. Srotri had not had his bath yet. He sat in the cattle shed in the backyard, and was massaging the dewlap of a cow. Even the cattle were living beings. Do they have any idea as to their lineage? They haven't an obligation of performing death rites of their deceased parents. When there is no social system that defines the ways of husband and wife, where is the locus for defining the obligation towards deceased parents? Impertinent atypical matters crossed his mind and lingered about like crass clouds. By noon, Subbaiah Shastri arrived. Soon thereafter arrived the two designates with necessary paraphernalia and dressed traditionally for the occasion. One of them, a school teacher named Anantaram, noticed that Srotri had not yet bathed. He asked in surprise, 'What is this? Why, are you not keeping well? Eyes are reddish… '

Srotri said nothing. He just headed to the bathroom.

A little later, the rites began. Srotri was thoroughly conversant with the meaning of all the mantras, but could not follow what the priest rendered today. He was so disoriented that instead of wearing the *pavitra* on the ring finger, he wore it on the middle finger! He seemed to forget the gestures of the various phases of the rites, wherefore Shastri had to instruct him each time. Thinking that Srotri was not keeping well, Shastri went about the rites leisurely. The procedure of ablution of feet of the other two was also done, and Srotri sprinkled a few drops of the sanctified water on his head. Those two started on their lunch. Cheeni was serving the dishes. Shastri, who was temporarily relieved of his procedures, now asked Srotri, 'Why, are you not keeping well?' He had to ask it a second time. Srotri said, 'Nothing. The usual.' Gathering that Srotri was indisposed to converse, Shastri kept quiet. Lunch progressed, and Cheeni was serving food methodically. Srotri's mind wandered in unknown directions. Eventually, he heard Shastri announce the completion of the lunch-break, and the rites to be performed thence. Srotri complied.

After customarily placing a few halfa-grass with their tips facing south and sprinkling water over them, Shastri instructed Srotri to take hold of one of the three rice balls placed in a vessel there. When Srotri complied, Shastri pronounced a mantra which said 'this is my father Nanjundadeva-Sharma....' and asked Srotri to place it on the halfa-grass that was spread there. When he heard that, Srotri's head reeled. He tried to contain himself but couldn't. He passed out and slumped onto the floor. The rice ball in his hand that was representative of his father rolled on the floor and breached.

Anantaram anxiously stepped up to Srotri, sat by him, and took his head on his thigh. The other Brahmin sprinkled water on Srotri's head. Shastri called out to Cheeni who was in the kitchen. 'Cheeni, your grandfather is unconscious. Get me a fan, quick.' Cheeni brought one. After quite some water was patted on his head and after vigourous fanning, Srotri came to. He tried getting up but couldn't. Making a pillow of a dhoti and placing it beneath Srotri's head, Shastri relieved Anantaram. He then said to Kuppaiah, 'Kuppaiah, come on. You wear a *pavitra* and let's go through the remaining rites.' Kuppaiah changed and substituted for Srotri. Srotri closed his eyes and slept. Cheeni sat by his side, fanning him. Shastri had another rice ball rolled and continued with the rites by repeating the mantra. He did the same with the remaining two rice balls that were representative of Srotri's grandfather and great grandfather.

After the consummation of the rites, the priests were rewarded with the usual dhotis, copper utensils and silver coins. By then, Srotri was fully awake and was able to speak. Shastri was reflecting that the breaching of the rice ball was the harbinger of some evil that might befall the Srotri family.

4

One day, Srotri told Cheeni, 'Cheeni, apply for two days' leave. We have to go to Edatore.'

'Why, grandfather?'

'I will relate it en route.'

Leaving Lakshmi back home, they both travelled to Mysore by train. After they were seated in a shuttle train bound to Edatore, Srotri began relating to Cheeni: 'There was a brother of my father called Kittappa. I have not seen him. My father deceitfully denied him his rightful share of the ancestral estate. Now I desire to share half of my estate with his descendants. It is righteous even. Will you concur?'

'Why ask me? Do as you think it fit, grandpa.'

'Still, when I have to part my estate with them, you have to sign the documents. I shall not live much more, but you are the future owner of it all, and your hearty consent is needed.'

'As you have stated,' Cheeni said with confidence, 'if what is to be given to them is righteous, I will consent wholeheartedly. Your words are always dharmic.'

Srotri was happy. They arrived at the Edatore railway station at 2 pm, hired a tonga to go to that newly-built town, and went to the house of an acquaintance. He then went about enquiring about the descendants of a certain Kittappa Srotri who 75 years ago was a person of 40 years of age. He got to know that there was no Srotri family in that town; in fact, there was no family in that town that migrated from Nanjangud. No grandfather of a priest at any temple was a Kittappa. He eventually met an elderly man of 85. He cordially greeted the guests from Nanjangud and said, 'When I was about 20, there was a man called Kittappa in this town; yes, he belonged in Nanjangud. He had three sons. He was about 40 or 45 then. A very short-tempered man, he was priest at a temple in a nearby village. Once there was a tussle between him and the temple trustee. He severely assaulted the trustee. The fault was the trustee's, but he was a rich man. He saw to it that Kittappa left the town. Nobody knows where he went with his family thereafter.'

Disappointed at the failure of his efforts, Srotri returned to Nanjangud. On getting the report, Lakshmi said, 'You cannot track his descendants. Just let go of that worry.'

Days rolled on. Cheeni attended college regularly. Of late, Srotri had lost interest in imparting Veda tuitions to him. Even if he took to tutoring him, his mind would drift, and the session would wind up at that. Srotri would go back to those thoughts: *this house, the lands, and money, none of them are mine. If I can track Kittappa Strotri's descendants, I would be happily relieved by the dharmic act of bequeathing everything to them.* But where to look for them?' Many a day he would not eat properly. *The food that is served on the plantain leaf is not grown on property belonging to me. Neither was it heartily donated to me by someone. Should I even consume it?* These thoughts would cause him to check himself from eating any further.

Legend-raconteurs, Brahmins on pilgrimage, seekers of contribution for weddings and *upanayana*s, beggars, etc. kept visiting Nanjangud. These people visited Srotri's house without fail. And Srotri never sent them back without donating adequately as part of the traditional gift hamper of betel, areca and coconut. Of late, Srotri would enquire of them, 'While you were travelling, have you come across a family named Srotri anywhere?' The answer would mostly be in the negative. 'In case you do come across one such, please drop me a letter.' He would give his address and add, 'Just Srotri is not enough. There should have been a person named Kittappa among their forefathers. And such Kittappa should have migrated from Nanjangud. After ensuring all this, please write to me. This old man will be greatly benefited.'

He even got an advertorial published in a newspaper, urging any Srotri who was originally from Nanjangud to please get in touch with him, for there was some estate to be shared with them. There was no response even to this.

Of late, Srotri started recalling Katyayani. Rejecting the restraints of widowhood, she discerned a new husband for herself in the peak of her youth and walked out on this house. She bore a child to one lineage, and married a man of another lineage. In his mind, he would weigh the conduct of Katyayani against that of his mother, and his namesake father Nanjunda Srotri. There was no evil intent in Katyayani's act. There was no such impurity as resorting to illegitimate means for the sake of fanning one's hatred or for committing fraud. She was swayed by modern thoughts. Her only drawback was her inability to contain the urges of her youth. To overcome it, she resorted to legitimate remarriage. In a way, her conduct was appreciable. When he recalled his parents' conduct, the disdain would cause his entire body to singe. For a few hours thence, his mind would be filled with anger and rejection. Then he would contain himself and regret having let his mind be susceptible to anger. *Why should I forfeit the peace of mind that I have cultivated all these years? Why let such feelings as indignation and indolence rent my mind? If I were destined to be born thus, whose fault may it be? Do I have the right to get angry with my parents and weigh their rights and wrongs? God, give me back my mind that never engaged in weighing the sins and virtues of others.* He closed his eyes and prayed silently.

CHAPTER 25

1

After five months of incessant scripting, Rao was done with the fifth volume, and he sighed in relief. When he wrote the last sentence, it was 10 pm on a certain night. Seated on a chair behind him, Karuna was reading a heretofore section of the manuscript. Placing his pen down, he called out, 'Karuna…' She got up and neared him. He grasped her hand and said emotionally, 'It is done.' Her heart swelled. Gently pressing his hands, she moved closer, pressed his head against her bosom, and said, 'Your life's mission stands accomplished. The Lord has bestowed his blessings. Now on, you must strictly adhere to the doctor's advice. You should not attend to any more work.'

That day onwards, Rao derived a certain contentment in life, which was not describable in words. Owing to his incessant work, commitment, and penance, and as a mark of Karuna's hearty devotion, his tome stood accomplished. He reflected thus: *each individual has to achieve fulfillment in life in his own way. In my own way, I have scaled one step in the path of fulfillment. The incidental information collated for this tome is copious enough to go into a few minor titles, and into a dozen articles. But I don't have the strength to attend to it. Let Karuna do it by herself. If I live on, I shall edit it.* Now, he took to regular walking. At times, he exhorted Karuna to join him on the morning walk, 'You shall attend to your work later. Come join me.' Karuna had a load of work on hand. She had to pay visits to the library to recheck the glossary, the style of scripting had to be emended here and there, she had to rectify the mix up in chronology of the narratives, and then she had to type it all and send it to the publisher. Rao aspired to bestow a citation in the last volume to his wife Karuna. But she didn't concur. She said that no father would officially give credits for bearing a child to its mother.

Karuna would always be engaged in her work. After his one-hour visit to the college, Rao would get some sleep. At times, he would see the neighbour professor to kill time. 'So, the legend survives it all!' the professor would chide Dr Rao. At times, he would invite his pupils from college, give fruits and coffee to them, and speak to them jovially. His mind was now weightless like a lingering thin cloud buoying in zephyr after shedding most of its mass in the form of rain. One day, Nagalakshmi surfaced in his memory. He reflected that she would not know of his heart attack, for if she did, she would have come running, swallowing all her pride. To conceal his ill health from her was a manner of perpetrating injustice on her. Though he recalled that she had responded to him sternly when he had gone to her place to invite her to move to his house, his recovery from the ailment and the consummation of his tomes had brought about a distinct feeling in him towards her. *How much more will I live? Should bring her here and live in her company till then,* he thought. When he shared with Karuna his desire to invite Nagalakshmi, she said, 'What if she retorted like she did earlier? The doctor has warned that you must not be subjected excruciating feelings.'

'I am confident that no such thing will happen now.'

'May I join you?'

'Don't. I will go alone. Raja will be there anyways.'

He diverted his morning walk in the direction of Lakshmipura. Raja was at home. It was he who received him at the door and took him in. Katyayani brought him a glass of milk. Her gaunt and blanch body reminded one of a white cockroach. The sum total of the blood that flowed through her veins appeared to be no more than a spoonful. Rao, who knew the reasons therefor, did not pry. He said to Raja, 'The penning of the tome is done. If she is now game, I want to take her with me.' Raja went inside. By then, Katyayani had brought Prthvi there. He prostrated at his father's feet. Rao blessed him by touching his head with his palm and asked, 'Which class now?'

'This year, I will enroll for B.Sc.'

'Keep visiting that house. Come in the evenings. We'll go walking.'

'Okay.'

When Raja went in and apprised Nagu, she categorically said, 'I won't go to anybody's house.' Raja slowly broke the news of his brother's ill health to her. Telling her that he had taken to writing the final volume despite the doctor's proscription, he said, 'It was probably on account of you that he had his first heart attack. His condition is still fragile. If you are adamant even now, anything can happen any time. Are you ready to take responsibility for that?'

In two minutes, Nagalakshmi thawed out. 'Why let your mind think bad stuff? Cooking will be done in an hour. Ask him to stay on. Let us all have breakfast, and then I will go. Here, Katyayani's health is no good. What will you people do?'

'Don't worry about us at all. We will manage. I will assist her in the cooking. Prthvi will be here; I'll summon Ragappa here as well. He can attend to the outside chores, which leaves Katyayani to just cook some rice and curry.'

Raja exited and gave the good news to his brother, 'So, stay on for lunch.' Rao took to conversation with his brother. By 9:30, Rao had had his bath there, and was about to eat when Karuna appeared there. She was panting when she encountered Raja first. 'His condition is very fragile. I got anxious because of his delay in returning. So I came.'

'Please come in. You have lunch too, then all three of you can leave together.'

Karuna entered. She washed her feet and hands, and before starting her lunch, she went into the kitchen and prostrated at Nagalakshmi's feet. Confounded, Nagalakshmi did not know what to say. She just stood. But her heart brimmed up. She had them all seated and took to serving food. By the time she was done with her lunch, Raja hired a tonga. While leaving, Rao said to Katyayani, 'Let there be no two establishments. All of you move there. It is better for me now to have the benefit of the company of you all.'

While they travelled in the tonga, all three minds were brimming with unknown glee. Karuna experienced a certain exalted feeling. Rao was relieved of the nagging duality, and he sort of attained an equilibrium state. Nagalakshmi simply kept thinking about her Rama, 'Thou shall never abandon anyone that trusts thee. Sri Rama Jai Rama Jai Rama,' she kept reciting.

The moment Nagalakshmi stepped in, the bungalow acquired a new charm. She went into the kitchen and inspected Ragappa's pantry. She opened the curry powder container and sniffed. That very afternoon, she drove Ragappa to the store to buy spices. She selected aliquots of them, fried them, and pounded them into a flavoursome curry powder. She sent him again to the market that evening to buy lemons, raw ginger, flowers, fruits, betel leaves, vegetables, arecanut and fresh lime. Prthvi visited there that evening, and she had him bring her the portrait of her God Rama, the Rama name rote book, inkstand, and steel from Raja's house. She cooked supper and served to her husband and Karuna. Ragappa would not acquiesce to have his supper before Nagalakshmi had had hers. Karuna would converse with Nagalakshmi in whatever Canarese she knew. When once she addressed Nagalakshmi 'sister', Rao taught her that the Canarese for sister was *akka*.

2

Nagalakshmi got up at 4 the next morning and started the fire in the bathroom kiln. She gave milk to Karuna and Rao, who had woken up at 5. Rao took his walking stick and went on his morning walk. Entering the kitchen, Karuna asked, 'Akka, shall I help you with the cooking?' 'No need,' Nagalakshmi said, 'You take to your reading and writing. You do what you are adept at. I will do what I am adept at.' Karuna smiled softly. She was enthused that she had gained a certain good fortune that she was deprived of till now. She left in merriment and took to verifying the manuscript in the study. When Rao returned from his walk at 8:30 am, Nagalakshmi led him by his hand to the bathroom, and bathed him with warm water by scrubbing him fine. 'What is this? Am I a baby?' he asked. 'What else are you, if you didn't know how to care for your health?' Her faked anger sent a torrent of zing through Rao's mind. Before serving them lunch, she led them to the puja chamber, 'First, prostrate before Rama. Then eat.' Rao complied. Pointing to her husband, Karuna said, 'He is the Rama of our house. Isn't it?' Rao remarked, 'But this Rama has two wives!' Both wives laughed heartily. The food tasted fine. Such flavour was witnessed earlier in this bungalow when Nagalakshmi had stayed for a while. Rao was recalling it. Curry, coulis, raita, vegetable stew—Rao was at a loss from the profusion. Each one was tasty and not to be forsaken. Karuna was taken back at the deliciousness of the food. She ate much more than the quantity she usually ate. Rao too.

After eating, Karuna collected her manuscripts and left for the library. While Nagalakshmi ate in the kitchen, Rao appeared there and served food to her. 'Nagu, the travails of those bygone days! Henceforth, you should let me serve your food.' He served more despite her protests. 'How is Katyayani? If she consents, let us all live together. This is quite a big bungalow. We have to pay a high rent anyway. Why pay double rent? She is not keeping well. Without you, Raja will feel estranged. Prthvi will get to enjoy the company of many here as well.'

After her turn, Ragappa started his. He said to Nagalakshmi, 'Mother, now you please leave it to me here on. I feel ashamed of idling while you slog it out. One will need Goddess Saraswati's blessings to be adept at cooking like you.' Nagalakshmi appointed a tray of betel, areca and lime, and exited. In their room, Rao was seated on the cot. Entering, Nagalakshmi shut the door, sat on a chair by the cot and said, 'Shall I garnish a leaf for you?'

'Don't. Doctor has barred it.'

She, too, did not partake of it. She was now 44, and most of her hair had gone grey. The neatly combed hair was lustrous. On her bun was the fresh chrysanthemum flower that had just arrived from the market. On her wide forehead was a prominent vermilion, and a speck of saffron beneath it. That auspicious face still had the same innocent beauty of yore. As before, her wrists were fully adorned with bangles. The amber of her cheeks, palms and feet evidenced the turmeric she regularly applied on them. Rao ogled her for two minutes. Then he said, 'Nagu, I had distanced myself from you all these days. If I were with you, I would have been very strong.' Nagalakshmi hung her head. Her eyes welled up. Noticing, Rao said, 'Come here,' and tugged her by her arm. After she was seated beside him on the cot, he held her hand and said, 'Don't cry. Now on, I will never leave you.'

'You are tired. Rest,' she said, and made him lie down with his head on her thigh. His legs stretched, as Rao lay on the bed with his head on Nagalakshmi's thigh, he was swayed by a feeling of delight that he had never before experienced. She held his face and asked, 'Why didn't you send for me when you were ill? When you had earlier come to invite me, I was angry with you. But am I a sinner that would abhor serving you when you are ill?'

'Don't say so Nagu. You are truly a virtuous one. It is rather me who is the sinner, who abandoned you.' She was moved. She placed a palm on his mouth and said, 'Not a word! You shouldn't say so.' Taking her hand off his mouth, he said, 'I am not weighing the sins and virtues. You know very well that I did not wed Karuna out of any lowly desire. Without her my tome would not be finished even 10 years from now. We three could have stayed together thus since then. But she of the modern outlook did not acquiesce. If I were not with her all the while, there would have been no progress in my tome. Fortunately, we are all together now, and that is heartening.'

Rao's glee was only mounting. The burst of happiness was truly the transcending of duality, and meriting peace.

He announced in an animated voice, 'I have penned the glorious cultural history of this great nation. This culture has given sublime philosophy, art, and *dharma* to the world. I have endeavoured to delineate the elemental essence of great souls that have contributed to this teeming milieu. This is not just an effort. This work has given me contentment. In the pursuit of a mammoth task, a few mistakes were but natural. Nagu, is it that our distancing and the agony you suffered were necessary for achieving this? Maybe that is how God willed it. With the consummation of it all, the time has now come for us to reunite, and for me to rest in peace with my head placed on your thigh. Nagu, do you know how happy I am now? Bend over and place your face on my chest. Hug me. Are you not happy?' He hugged her waist with both his arms. She hugged his face to her chest. 'Nagu, this happiness, this happiness...' Rao found it difficult to speak, 'is too much for me to bear,' he said with great difficulty. He was short of breath and was perspiring severely. An unbearable pain issued on the left side of his chest. He didn't know what to say next. Slowly, he brought his palms to his chest. Nagalakshmi was confounded. She took his face off her chest and slowly lowered him into her lap. For half a minute there was mortal agony on his face. Not knowing what to do, she called out, 'Ragappa!' By the time Ragappa came, the agony in Rao's face seemed to abate. His eyes pulled up. His limbs slumped. Ragappa touched Rao's hand and held his fingers beneath Rao's nostrils. Though he got to know it all, he said, 'I will get the propesur,' and ran out. Nagalakshmi got suspicious. She started crying loudly. From her eyes, which a second earlier shone from glee, tears of grief dribbled profusely.

The professor was not at home. His wife came running. By the time she came, Nagalakshmi knew it all. That lady held her hand. Nagalakshmi's cry reached a crescendo. In five minutes, Karuna came running in the company of Ragappa. When she saw the sight in the room, the words 'he suffered this heart attack as he gave vent to his emotions in your company' came to her tongue. But she said nothing. She fell on the body of Rao, who was her companion till date.

3

The news spread like wildfire. The faculty of the college and the students milled about his bungalow. The principal announced holiday for college. A condolence meeting was held at the college the next day, wherein on a table were placed the published works of Dr Rao, and on a chair nearby was placed a garlanded photo of Dr Rao. The Vice Chancellor, who spoke on the occasion, magnanimously said, 'It is such scholars and their writings that lend prestige to a university, not its administrators.' Three professors spoke and unanimously concurred that Dr Rao was a guru to the likes of them, and his mission for the pursuit of knowledge should always be held in reverence. One of them could not hold back tears.

Sealing the bungalow, Raja went home, taking Nagalakshmi and Karuna along that evening. As per the custom, Prthvi had to perform the rites, but he had not yet undergone *upanayana*. The responsibility devolved onto Raja. The rites began on the seventh day.

Nagalakshmi's pent up disappointment of many years had seemed to dissipate one morning when she had gone to her husband's place in a tonga along with him. Same time the next morning, he had breathed his last with his head on her thigh. 'Probably *karma* from my previous birth. His ill fate is due to my accumulated sins,' she lamented. All these days her husband was alive and she had only to live separately. Now he is no more. She felt that widowhood was crueler than estrangement. No amount of efforts by Raja, Katyayani and Prthvi could contain her tears. Though he didn't have a close bond with his father, Prthvi cried too. Katyayani held her brother-in-law in high reverence. She was devoted to his scholastic ways. She, too, cried through two days. She was consoling Karuna too. His brother's demise was a shock to Raja. He took to performing his death rites in the role of his son.

As per the customs, Nagalakshmi was not a widow till the tenth day of her husband's death. The female cook, who was engaged temporarily, would put the usual big vermilion on Nagalakshmi's forehead and adorn her locks with flowers daily. As the tenth day neared, Nagalakshmi wept incessantly from the grief that the auspicious vermilion and flowers would be forfeited from her thenceforth. She that looked in the mirror only once a day when she combed her hair, now repeatedly looked at her reflection that was adorned with turmeric and vermilion. Grief would billow from within, and unable to control herself, she would writhe on the floor. On the eve of the tenth day, she had a nasty argument with Raja.

'Raja, when the main breath has ceased, what of this rotten body? Tomorrow, I will shed my hairs and these auspicious saris. Get a red sari for me.'

'Don't act like one from a bygone era. Let the rites of today be undertaken. Let your hair be. You wear white saris.'

'Wearing a white sari, should I go work in some office? None of that.' She was adamant. Katyayani joined them and Nagalakshmi beseeched to her, 'At least you convince him. I will go austere.'

Katyayani felt as if her entrails were squeezed. She could not fancy her elderly sister Nagalakshmi, the lovely woman who was with her all through, in a red sari and with a tonsured head. Her memory drifted back to her widowhood. Twenty years ago, when her first husband passed away, over the next 10 days she had retained her auspicious attire and accessories too. On the tenth day when she took off the flowers from her plait, the connubial string from her neck, the glass bangles from her wrists, and the vermilion from her forehead and worn a white sari, she had become unconscious. Though her mother-in-law Bhageerathamma suggested that she get tonsured and wear a red sari, Srotri had convinced her against it so to save his young daughter-in-law from any more agony. But then came a day when her life changed. She took to wearing flowers, vermilion and bangles again. She even rejoiced at her renewed fortune. But now her thinking was entirely different. She thought about it for two full minutes and said to Raja, 'What sister says is right. You simply heed her.'

'Still, I can't bear to see Nagu in a red sari,' said Raja, sobbing.

'One should contain one's sorrows. In this matter, sister's understanding is more mature than yours. She is ready to symbolically take to her new situation. You cannot nullify the actuality of the situation. Why are you resisting its symbolism? In this matter, the inner voice of the woman is wiser than the logical debate of a man.'

Raja was silenced. Not wanting to weep while she was being rid of her auspicious embellishments, she resolutely held her teeth clenched. After those rites were done with, she sat by the door in the backyard. When she spilled a pitcher of cold water over her head and entered the house, her head reeled and she fell unconscious. Katyayani needed all of 15 minutes to resuscitate her. When all the rites were through, she sat before her Rama picture and said, 'Sri Rama, I held trust in you. You did this to me. Still, I will worship you. Please let him be my husband in my next life too. Then, don't forget to deny me widowhood.' From that very day, she stepped up the daily allocation of time for rote-writing Rama.

All household responsibilities devolved onto Katyayani. Her physical condition could not bear with such slogging. Soon, she had an attack of fever. There was none other than Nagalakshmi to care for her.

4

Reflecting that it would be incorrect to leave immediately after the cremation, Karuna stayed on till the thirteenth day. Since she wed Rao, she had taken to wearing the vermilion too. She always wore white saris. On the tenth day, of her own volition, she wiped away the vermilion from her forehead.

On the fourteenth morning, she said to Raja, 'I will make a move now.'

Raja was taken aback. 'Why should you stay in that bungalow alone? Besides, as per the rules, the university will take the possession back. Let's bring over those books and other things to here. You take to a room and go through your work. You, too, are sister-in-law to me.'

'You are very magnanimous. But I will attend to the pending work from that house. I can beget peace of mind only there.' She would not heed anybody's persuasion.

'Have no worries. I will send you money monthly for your effects,' said Raja.

'I have money on me. When that first heart attack happened, he got the bank account converted to a joint account by adding my name. There is much credit in it, plus recently the publishers sent some money too. Don't you worry. Ragappa will be there anyway. Don't forget to pay regular visits.' She informed Nagalakshmi, took leave formally of Katyayani, and when she boarded the tonga in the company of Ragappa, there were tears in her eyes.

That same evening, the Vice Chancellor of the university visited her with the neighbouring professor. After recalling the virtues of the deceased Dr Rao, the VC said, 'Why don't you stay with Raja Rao?'

'He, too, asked me to. But my mind desired to stay on here.'

'Do as your mind says. I got to know that the newspapers of Europe and America have published obituary of Dr Rao. I saw it broadcast on BBC as well. Many professors from the West have written to the college address in praise of Dr Rao's scholasticism, and have asked us to convey their condolences to the family. The university's esteem has received great impetus by the likes of Dr Rao. What is the progress on the fifth volume?'

'I will send it to the publishers in three to four months.'

'That is fine. Who else can attend to it? You stay on in this bungalow as long as you wish. I will see to it that you shall not pay any rent. I will also arrange for an honorarium of 2,000 rupees to be paid to you for editing the fifth volume and getting it ready for publication. You don't have to seek any help from anyone else.'

'I am very grateful to you. I will need this house. But I won't need the money. I have enough on me.'

She received a letter from the publisher the next day. She replied to them that Rao had completely penned it before he died, and that she would ready it for publication in three to four months. She wasted no time in taking to her task. For about a month, she stuck to the library, comparing many source books; then she took to typing it. She didn't rest at all. She would be spent from the workload, but if she rested, memories of Rao would seize her and she would drown in melancholy. Ragappa kept to himself, not uttering even one word more than was absolutely necessary. Though he was worried about his future, he simply attended to his chores without asking anything of her about them. His master's demise had brought about gloom in him too.

Four months thence, one Sunday evening, Karuna was done with her work. The typing work was accomplished 15 days previous to that. She had immediately attended to the task of checking for typographical and syntax errors thereafter. She had to retype 20 pages; she then arranged them chronologically. The publishers had asked her to pen a brief biography of Dr Rao's life and erudition, which was to be included in that volume. Her depiction of his life and work was endearing and clearer than an artist's painting. By the time she packed it neatly, sealed it with lac and wrote the publisher's address, it was 10 in the night. She reclined on the armchair. Unaware of herself, she wept. She hadn't wept through the four months of her work. The feeling that Rao was thereabouts and was engrossed in his work, had lent life to her existence. While she typed away, it seemed as if Rao was dictating the matter in her ears. While she penned the preface, she felt as if he dictated it, and she made note of it in shorthand seated before him. Now that all the work was accomplished, she felt a void. She made no effort to contain her tears. She wept for over one full hour. Then she walked up to the window. Outside, darkness congealed.

She slowly walked up to the front door. Ragappa was asleep in the living room. Not wanting to wake him up, she locked the door from outside and went for a walk. As it was a sparsely populated part of town, the lampposts were spaced much apart. She walked on in the dim light. Unintendedly, she walked up along the bund of the Kukkarahalli tank and sat on a stone bench in an arbour to her left. Soon, she recalled that she had visited here one dawn in the company of her Rao long back, on the eve of her return to her homeland, after submitting her thesis. Grieved by the need to leave him and return to her country, she had placed her head on his thigh and had wept. Rao had held her in an embrace. For a moment, that memory held charm. She permitted herself to immerse in that memory and became oblivious of her environs. After five minutes, she came to the present; along came the tears. She could sit there no more. She walked towards the college. Leaving the tank behind, she entered the college grounds. The trees in the grounds! After supper, they used to relax under one of those trees and discuss the tome they were working on. After the discussion, they would sit quiet for a while. On their way back, if it was dark, she would lead him by his hand. That memory deterred her from lingering there, and she walked in the direction of the college. The college stood firm as ever. For about 30 years, Rao had taught at this college. The pull of his scholasticism could be felt in the air that coursed thereabouts. She walked on. The library building to the left made its resplendent presence felt even in the darkness of the night. Karuna went up to it and stood facing it. It was in that building that they both had worked for over more than 16 years, and had brought out their tome. The methodology of their work, and Rao's posture as he sat in his chair and dictated to her, appeared before her eyes clearer than any real life experience. She couldn't bear with that memory even, and as she moved on, she felt spent. She went straight to her house. Though she lay on her cot, sleep did not come. It was in that room that Rao had breathed his last. Her mind replayed that event: *if Nagalakshmi were not visiting then, and I alone had cared for him, I would probably have seen to it that he was not emotionally charged and would live on 10 more years.* She couldn't sleep the entire night.

She got up at dawn and had coffee. She remained in the room till 8, after which she started for the post office to courier the parcel. The neighbouring professor, who was in his front yard, saw the parcel in her hand and asked, 'Going to the post office? Give it to me. I will have my attendant do it.'

'No. I will attend to it myself. But thank you,' she said and walked on.

5

While returning after couriering it, she felt bleak. What would she do henceforth? The main mission was accomplished. There remained the work of penning a few minor titles and some articles using the incidental information collected for the tome, but that could wait. Now, her mind was frightfully void. She had soon turned into a lonely person who had no relatives, and with no one to care for her. Reflecting as to who she could fall back upon, she was passing by the Ramaswamy circle when she spotted Prthvi. Desiring to speak to him, she called out to him. 'Where are you going? It is just 9:15 now.'

'To college. I have a special class.'

'It is okay to skip special class today. Come with me,' she neared him and held his hand. He held his head down in hesitation. 'Come on,' she led him by his hand. By the time they reached home, Ragappa was almost done with the cooking. 'You have not yet eaten, have you? Eat with me,' she said and kept conversation with him till Ragappa laid the plates.

'How is your aunt?'

'Over some days now, fever is unremitting. She is very weak, and is on sick leave.'

'Uncle?'

'He goes to the college for one or two hours. The rest of the time, he keeps aunt company.'

'Oh, that is why he has not paid a visit here of late. I, too, couldn't visit as I was busy here.' Ragappa had everything ready by then. She went in, laid two plates and called him. She had lunch with Prthvi beside her. After eating, she took him to Rao's room and showed him to the cot where his father slept, and then she sat on it. Pointing to the volumes of Rao's tome that were placed on a nearby table, she asked, 'Have you read those works of your father?'

'No.'

'Why?'

'I am a student of science. I have enrolled for B.Sc. this year.'

She smiled within herself in despair. The son has no interest in the literary achievements of his father, which he had accomplished for the sake of the erudite, towards which end he bequeathed his entire life. And the faculty of his son's academic pursuit is different! We say that our work is for our next generation. She asked herself as to what that generation was. It readily occurred to her mind that the tome was for the generations that would pursue the cultural history of India, and would not accrue to children just for reason of biological nexus. She watched Prthvi's face. It was like Nagalakshmi's. But his eyes and nose were like his father's. The son was fuller in body than his father though. His father's quest for knowledge would be lacking in him. He resembled his father in his posture while sitting, and also in the way he spoke. Karuna moved closer to him and said, 'Child, come place your head in my lap and lie down.' He held his head hung from hesitation. 'Don't hesitate. I am your mother too.' She tugged at his arm and pulled his head onto her thigh. She then held his face with both her hands and asked, 'Child, your mother suffered because of distancing from your father. Do you hold me in derision for that?'

'No.'

'Was it not because of me that your father did so?'

'But I was told that it was because of you that he could pen all these. My uncle and aunty have told me everything.'

Karuna's heart brimmed up. She bent over him and embraced him. For 10 minutes, she was immersed in that indescribable bliss and forgot herself.

When Prthvi started to leave, she took hold of his hand and said, 'Tell uncle that I will pay a visit soon. You keep visiting here.' By now Prthvi had shed some of his hesitation. 'Ok, I will visit,' he said, and walked away. She stood by the gate till he was out of her sight. When she came inside, the sleep that had eluded her yesterday now overtook her. She was fast asleep within 10 minutes of lying down.

When she got up at 5 in the evening, her mind was once again frightfully void. The memories of her time with Rao flooded her. If she were a mother, there would be some succour to fall back upon. Once she had desired to beget a baby. When they had visited Nandi, that desire had sprouted and grown into a mighty tree. If she had conceived then, she would have had a kid of eight or nine now. The emotional rapport with it would have checked her mind from getting depressed. Life would not have been awful thus. *I arrested the desire for motherhood. I erred*, she kept thinking. When she retired after supper, sleep eluded her. Her mind, that was incessantly engaged in work all these years, found it unnatural to be languorous. *If I were a mother, the tome would not be completed expediently. He would have been dead by the time the fourth volume was just half done. The tome is in fact the baby that we came together for, and we eventually conceived it. It has achieved fame and lives on. He is the father to it, and I the mother. Life is never so full as to bestow all and everything,* she consoled herself.

Tonight, too, she went on a walk. But every spot that she visited was redolent of past memories. Vis-à-vis those bygone situations, her current state seemed more and more frightful. She was back home in half an hour. *Where to live in this town? My partner is no more. The purpose I came here for stands fulfilled. Barring these two, I was not interested in getting acquainted with anyone, in socializing with anyone, and in earning the trust of anyone. I didn't have time for all that. Now I am a loner. Who is mine in this town? Who?* Soon, her hometown came to her mind. Though her parents had passed on, her brother was still alive. He was 50 now. His children would have grown up much. They might not even recognize her. There was no exchange of letters with her brother. Memories of him surfaced, and with an affection that was not felt hitherto. Deciding to apprise him of the developments, she soon walked up to her desk and started writing a letter to him. She was surprised when it ran into five pages. As she went on narrating it all, she was seized by emotion. In the end she wrote, 'I have, by now, achieved the mission that I had taken up. But in the void that has surfaced now, I yearn for your company. I will wait for your letter and then decide on coming over. I shall seek a career as a lecturer in some university there.'

Though she wanted to visit Raja's house, her mind was recalcitrant over the past three days. Mostly, she would simply lie down, without even caring to roll the bed and put it away. The fourth day Raja visited her house at 11. He had emaciated so much that his cheek bones had become very prominent.

'You had sent word with Prthvi that you would visit. You didn't. I got anxious about your health,' he said.

'Sit down. My spirits are at their nadir. Six days back, I sent the typed manuscript to the publisher. I wanted to visit over the last three days, but my legs would not cooperate. With a heavy heart, I just lay on this bed. How is Katyayani?'

'She is,' he said, and on his face was disappointment. 'She speaks alright, but if I am not by her even for a little while, she weeps. At nights she lies down, embracing me tightly. When fever is high, "Don't leave me," she babbles.'

They slowly discussed those issues. Then Karuna told him of her letter to her brother. 'You would be able to understand my mind. If my brother is still alive, and he asks me to come over, I will go. I have given a thought to everything else. There is a bank balance of decent credit. I will transfer it to Nagalakshmi's name. The royalty from the tome accrues to Prthvi. You take with you the furniture and household items from here. I will give a gratuity of 1,000 rupees to Ragappa and relieve him. You may want to engage him. The books in this house, this manuscript, and this typewriter, please pack them all well and parcel them to me. What residual research work he would have undertaken if alive, I will attend to it from my hometown, and spend whatever is left of my life there.'

'You pay a visit to your hometown. But can't you stay in my house and attend to these tasks?' asked Raja. At that very moment, a taxi drew up by the gate. Karuna got up to check. A dark complexioned, stout, robust man was approaching her. He only had a small leather bag in his hand. Karuna could not recognize him. When he neared her, he said in Sinhala, 'Didn't recognize me?' Karuna knew instantly and she held his hand. It was her brother. He said, 'I got your letter. I couldn't contain myself. I could get a flight ticket, so I started immediately. I have booked flight tickets for two from Madras to Colombo for tomorrow night. We have to leave here tonight.'

Karuna introduced him to Raja, 'He is my brother-in-law.' She could only take minimum luggage for the flight. Ragappa took to cooking for the guest. Leaving her brother home, she went with Raja to her bank in the waiting taxi. Though Raja protested, she retained 1,000 rupees and handed over the balance to him, asking him to give it to Nagalakshmi. From there, they went to Raja's house.

Katyayani's condition was graver than Karuna had thought. The lustre of her body had waned, and it seemed like parched white leather. She still spoke. Karuna conversed with her for over an hour and then went in to see Nagalakshmi. Holding her hands, she said, 'Now both of us are broken-hearted. Whatever my fault, you should pardon me.' Nagalakshmi did not know what to say. She simply wiped her tears.

When he was given 1,000 rupees, Ragappa's heart swelled from gratitude. Karuna bade farewell to the neighbouring professor and his family members.

When they both were seated in the train, Raja said, 'Please visit us some time.' Holding Prthvi's face in her hands and kissing his forehead, Karuna said, 'Notwithstanding the fact that you are a student of science, read your father's works once.'

When the train started moving, Karuna was wiping her tears. Raja was doing the same. Prthvi stood a mute witness. When they exited the railway platform, Raja's mind was ruminating on the events since Karuna's advent till date.

CHAPTER 26

1

When he could get no information about any descendants of the Srotri clan whatsoever, Srotri abandoned his efforts at tracking them. His mind now thought up something else. In about eight days, his mind fully endorsed that idea. When he shared it with her, an incensed Lakshmi said, 'Sheenappa, you are truly a mad one. Nobody in this world would go gaga like you do.' He said, '*Dharma*'s ways are very subtle, Lakshmi. You cannot grasp it from just the mores of the masses.' She kept seething despite his reply.

One Sunday afternoon while tutoring Cheeni in Vedas, Srotri said, 'Child, you have many times asked as to what ails my mind. I have now found a solution to it. It is a matter of subtle *dharma*. Unless you accord your hearty consent, I will do nothing of it.'

'Grandpa, have I ever contested anything you have said? Let me know what the matter is.'

Srotri hesitated for a minute, but he eventually spilled the episode of his birth in all detail. Cheeni was mystified. 'Look, I had, at first, thought of tracking Kittappa Srotri's descendants in Edatore or elsewhere, and hand over their share of the estate. I feel that I have no authority over even a brass cup of this estate. Given that we are not consanguineous to a certain pedigree, how may we beget the authority to enjoy its estate? If my occupation of a certain nest is illegitimate, as my grandson you are an equally illegitimate occupant of that nest too. The name Srotri does not pertain to us. Allegiance to a certain lineage is required for *upanayana*. We were initiated in the name of Kāṣyapa-gotra. We have assumed it in allegiance and faith, and are adhering to it. From the customs viewpoint, we may continue to express allegiance to Kāṣyapa-gotra. If we do not meet up with the descendants of Kittappa Srotri, we are left with the only alternative of donating all this to deserving beneficiaries.'

Cheeni contemplated for just two minutes. He understood what their fate would be if the entire estate were given away in donation. Still, the fact that such proposition came from his grandfather engendered in him respect for the subtleties of *dharma*. 'What you say is right. I am 17 now. Soon, I will land myself a career, and the three of us can somehow manage to live.'

The grandfather was happy to hear him say so. 'Your words are deserving of one who is versed in the Vedas. The moment we get to know that our assets are not ours, we should dispense with them. If we didn't do so, someone down the line will squander it the illegitimate way. We may not rest assured that they deserved to lose it, for in the process they would have resorted to anti-dharmic ways. And there is no loss greater than accumulating sins. I still believe that our accumulated sins and virtues will be on the lookout for a descendant of ours to relieve themselves. That apart, listen to my second proposition.'

Srotri stated his ultimate mission in life. 'I had started on a life of renunciation as far back as your father's wedding. His death caused me to revert to family responsibilities. A desire to take to *sanyāsa* has been alert in me all through the last eight years. After getting to know the secret of my birth, I am all the more determined. Though the concept that one shall strive to invigorate his lineage is no more relevant to me, I still hold it in reverence. I am 75, and you will soon be eighteen. Permit me to retire.'

Tears welled up in Cheeni's eyes. 'Grandpa, I readily consented to your first proposal. But what sin have I committed that you want to abandon me? It is but natural that you despise this estate. But should you distance yourself from your grandson?'

'I do not despise you. Child, I have led a life of a family man till now. In his last days, one should live according to the call of the age, should renounce everything, and should lose himself in meditating on the Supreme Self. To stay from aligning our objective, opinion and lifestyle in accordance with the evolvement in our life is to sin also. It is quite some time since I've attained the age to take to *sanyāsa*. I am on the verge of winding up my obligations as a family man. Only your consent remains. I would have taken to *sanyāsa* even if I had not got to know of the secret of my birth.'

Cheeni had no answer. His mind could grasp his grandfather's words, but his heart would not. He simply sat with a heavy heart. Srotri continued, 'I am not yet done with my obligation towards you. First, I should find you a suitable bride from a virtuous family and promote you to the next ashram. That, I will do. This year you will complete your intermediate. Deposit into your bank account 5,000 rupees so as to suffice for two more years' academics, and for your other effects till then. Though this money belongs to the Srotri family, by virtue of being its bailee I have strove to manage it. What you owe to me is to earn your degree in the coming two years, and lead a virtuous family life. There is two acres land in Hejjige in Lakshmi's name. It belongs to her. It is your responsibility to look after her all her life. Before her death, she is free to use it for any dharmic purpose as she thinks fit.'

The grandson spoke nothing. 'You have learnt the Vedas from me. Contemplate on it all. There is no need for haste at all.'

2

One day, Cheeni noticed what books his grandfather was mostly reading of late. He discovered that he had taken to studying *Sanyasopanishat*, *Vaikhanasasutra*, *Dharmasindhu* and *Jivanmuktiviveka* intently. Bits of peacock feather served as bookmarks at various sections. He had marked some *ślokas* in ink. Cheeni glanced over them. He had placed a bookmark at this *śloka* in Shankaracharya's commentary on *Bṛhadāraṇyaka-upanishat*:

> *Atha parivrāḍ vivarṇa vāsāmuṇḍō aparigrahaḥ|*
> *Śuciradrōhī bhaikṣaṇō brahma bhūyāya bhavatīti||*

Cheeni could well comprehend Sanskrit *ślokas* by now. At a certain place it said, 'In order to merit the eligibility to assume *sanyāsa*, one should perform *prajapati-yajña* and donate all his estate to the Brahmins, the poor and the helpless.' Elsewhere, it said, 'After leaving back his wife and children, he should live outside the villages. Shelterless, he should sleep beneath trees or in uninhabited houses, or wherever he is at sunset. Only in the monsoons he may stay at one place.' Cheeni would sigh at the thought of his 75-year-old homeless, drifting grandfather spending entire nights beneath trees.

'A *sanyasi* should collect *bhikṣa* from not more than seven houses that are not predesignated. Before giving him *bhikṣa*, water has to be sprinkled on his palms. Then food should be given. After giving food, water has to be again sprinkled.'

'He should never eat bellyful. He should eat just to keep afloat. On days when he gets food, he shall not rejoice. On days when he doesn't get food, he shall not feel depressed.'

'All that should be on him is a *kamaṇḍala*, one vessel to rinse his cloth, wooden footwear, a mat, and a ragged cloth?'

When he read the next marking, Cheeni's heart filled with grief. 'A *sanyasi* should sleep on a raised terrain. If he were to catch disease, he should not worry. He should not invite death. Neither should he love life. He should be in anticipation of his last living day as would a bonded labourer in anticipation of his release.'

Srotri had marked a section in the *Anushasana-parva* of the *Mahabharata*. Delineated there were the four types of *sanyāsa* viz. *kuṭichaka*, *bahūdaka*, *haṃsa* and *paramahaṃsa*. Srotri had marked the characteristics of a *paramahamsa*: '*Paramahamasa*s stay beneath trees, uninhabited houses or in cemeteries. They may wear clothes or may be naked. They are beyond the divide between *dharma–adharma*, truth–false, hygiene-unhygiene, etc. They treat gold, land and everything else as atman. They will accept *bhikṣa* from all the four *varṇa*s. The stipulations and prohibitions prescribed in the *śāstra*s are not applicable to them.'

As he read each detail of the lifestyle that his grandfather had decided to assume, Cheeni's mind filled with more and more grief. He had read about the fourth ashram, *sanyāsa*. He wasn't ignorant of its objectives and purpose, and of the ways of living of a recluse. But he could not put up with the prospect that his grandfather, who had tended to him with such great love, had determined to subject his aging body to such an austere living. He was not worried about his own fate consequent to abandonment by his grandfather.

One day, he took Lakshmi alone to the jasmine creeper in the backyard, and explained to her the details of the life of a recluse as enunciated in the treatises. Then he pleaded with her, 'You talk him out of it. If I take to a career, all three of us can live contentedly.'

Cheeni's description caused anxiety in her. 'If he takes me along, I will look after Sheenappa well. But he is set to go alone. He is a godly person. He has not sinned in his life. Is he not content with the virtues he has accumulated till now? Why then should he take to this? All the same, he is a wise man. We don't have the capability to advise him. But our heart will not concede,' she would bemoan.

Cheeni attended college as usual. His grandfather would not let him do any work even now; he continued with his kitchen chores. Now, he would tutor him in *dharmaśāstra* after supper daily. He would cite anecdotes from the lives of many a great sage, and characters from the Purāṇas. He would take hold of many a Sanskrit book and say, 'Read this sometime.' Seated facing his grandfather, whenever Cheeni listened to his staunch voice, his intellect would admit his words as righteous. But as he left home for college, his mind would grieve at the thought of his grandfather's imminent departure.

3

The news that Srotri was donating all his estate and taking to *sanyāsa* permeated every nook and corner of Nanjangud. His well-wishers met with him and enquired, 'What is the matter? Why this decision?' 'I am aged,' he would underplay, 'and it is my *dharma* to take to *sanyāsa*, nothing else. My grandson says he doesn't want these assets, so I am donating it.' Many began speaking to him in a tenor so as to convey to him that they were the only ones deserving of such donation. One or other of them would always be in attendance in Srotri's house. Cheeni had no doubt anymore about his grandfather's determination. His heart told him that it wouldn't be *dharma* on his part to impede upon his grandfather's proposed path of emancipation by just his love for him. Lakshmi was steeled from intermittent indoctrination in dharmic matters by Srotri himself all through.

One day in April, Srotri sent word for the school teacher Anantaram through Cheeni. He was a native of Chamarajanagar, and was settled in Nanjangud for the last 10 years. For about three or four years, he would serve in the local middle school, then he would seek favours from his higher-ups and get transferred to a nearby village so that he could commute daily from Nanjangud; and after a year or two, he would seek to be transferred back to Nanjangud. He was 50 now, and had five more years of service. He stayed in his own house in an extension of Nanjangud, and had acquired three acres of wet lands in Hullahalli. There was a special reason for Srotri to develop camaraderie with the teacher. He was quite learned in Sanskrit. A pious and tradition-honouring man that he was, he would seek out Srotri for clarifications regarding *dharmaśāstra*. Gladdened by his traits, Srotri would invite him to be one of the two designates at the annual death rites of his parents.

When Cheeni brought him along at 8, he greeted the teacher and said to Cheeni, 'Cheeni, we both will go for a stroll.' They leisurely walked past the temple and sat on a step of the bathing deck of the river. The teacher knew about Srotri's resolve. When he had got news of it, he had met Srotri and requested him in all humility and affection, 'You should not leave us.' But eventually he had concurred with Srotri, what with him being well-versed in *dharmaśāstra* himself. But he could not understand why he had decided to donate his estate.

After two minutes' silence, Srotri said, 'The reason for donating my estate is known only to Lakshmi and Cheeni. Today, I am sharing it with just you. There was really no need for sharing it with you, but I want a favour from you.'

'A favour? From me to you? It will not augur well for me if you request. Rather, you should ordain me,' said the teacher humbly, his hands folded.

'Listen to what I've got to say,' said Srotri and revealed the secret of his birth, his efforts at locating the descendants of Kittappa Srotri, and his musings of late. The teacher did not say a word for quite some time. Eventually, he spoke. 'I have known none in modern days who properly interprets the tenets of *dharma* as you do, and abides by them. I haven't the gall to say that your determination is incorrect.'

'I will lay bare before you another of my wishes. I cannot exit without instating my grandson in *gṛhasthāśrama*. You are a person totally worthy of trust. Please be magnanimous enough to give your last daughter, aged about 12 or 13, to my grandson. He has written his intermediate exams now. I have earmarked 5,000 rupees for his future academics. At times, I think that I better not draw even that 5,000 from the Srotri estate. But to deny him even that much would mean to detest and reject the Srotri estate. Why should I permit myself to such intemperate feelings? Besides, it would be against *dharma* to leave Cheeni in a quandary in the name of *dharma*. It would suffice for him to get a B.Sc. degree. I will be happy on all counts. It is your responsibility to see that your son-in-law completes his B.Sc. course and treads the righteous path. I have not held back anything from you.'

The teacher went into contemplation for about 10 minutes. Then he said, 'You said yours is Kāṣyapa-*gotra*, right?'

'I told you. I do not belong in the Srotri pedigree. My *upanayana* happened in allegiance to Kāṣyapa-*gotra*.'

'Get up. Let's go home. I consent to your proposal. Cheeni has inherited the qualities and virtues of his grandfather. It is my good luck to get such a fine son-in-law. I only have to go through the formality of asking my family.' He got up. Srotri was relieved.

The next morning, the teacher visited Srotri with his daughter's horoscope and compared it with Cheeni's. They matched fine. He asked Cheeni, 'Child, will you wed my daughter, Lalite?' He knew nothing about it. He just grunted assent. 'Your grandfather will also advise you so. We are all very happy about it. Will you wed her?' Cheeni looked at his grandfather. His face then became red from coyness.

Lalite was a very charming girl. As early as her thirteenth year, she was studying in high school. As per the norms of present day, she seemed too young for Cheeni, but they were a good match physically. Even though the wedding would be held soon, Srotri proposed that nuptials be postponed till after he was done with his B.Sc. By then, the bride would have graduated highschool. On an auspicious day in the first fortnight of the second lunar calendar month of the ensuing year, a simple wedding was held in the Nanjundeshvara temple as desired by Srotri. Cheeni became a *gṛhastha*.

Srotri paid visit to the lands owned by him and carefully studied the economic conditions of the sharecroppers. Most of them had nothing to fall back upon other than this. Most of those families would have to go without two square meals a day if he annulled their contracts. Srotri determined that there were none more deserving than those share croppers to receive the respective lands as donation. When he stated that he would take to *sanyāsa* after donating the lands to the respective farmers, each of them humbly fell at his feet. 'Master, I do not want the property of a godly man like you. You continue to be the master. We will work to raise crops to the maximum extent, give it to you, receive our share and live contentedly.' Srotri suitably convinced them all and returned home. In the company of Cheeni, he made deeds of the lands in favour of the respective farmers. A land measuring six acres was willed to an orphanage at Mysore. It was decided that the house they lived in shall serve as a free lodge for pilgrims. He got every deed drafted by a lawyer, signed them, had Cheeni sign them, went to the sub-registrar's office and got them all registered. Back home, he sighed in relief from getting clear of an excruciating yoke.

He had now to decide upon the date of his retreat. For assuming *sanyāsa*, there was the need for initiation by a guru. He was not sure in which place this would happen. Eventually, Srotri decided that he would leave this place on an auspicious day and go to Haridwar or Badri. He would discern an able guru there, and formally wrap up *gṛhasthāśrama* there.

The school teacher, Anantaram, had three daughters and two sons. The elder son was Cheeni's age. He commuted by train daily to a college in Mysore. The second had to write his highschool exams in the coming year. The teacher said to Srotri, 'Don't you worry. Son-in-law is on par with a son. Let Srinivasa commute to college in the company of my son. Until he is done with his undergraduate course and lands a career, he and Lakshmi shall stay with us. We will take good care of them as if they were family.'

Srotri was happy with that proposal. He sold the silver and gold that was in the house and donated it to the temple trust fund. The vessels, too, found their way to the temple kitchen.

Giving all his Sanskrit books to Cheeni, Srotri said, 'Child, reckon this as the invaluable estate inherited from your grandfather. By now I have imparted you quite some treatises. In the days to come, you take to adding to your knowledge by studying them on your own, and also by seeking guidance from learned scholars. Tomorrow, we have to vacate this house. Shift these books to your father-in-law's house tonight.'

It was decided that he would walk away from this place on the fifth day of the first fortnight of the third lunar month. Try as they might, Cheeni and Lakshmi could not contain their anguish. Lakshmi had resolved not to cry before her Sheenappa. Cheeni, too, tried not to cause gloom to his grandfather by bringing tears to his eyes on the eve of his departure. But they would isolate themselves and cry silently. Srotri calmly looked forward to the day of his retreat. Many people in Nanjangud invited him to visit them before leaving. He complied to their requests. The farmers brought their carts and took him to their village to give him milk and fruits. He heeded them all with a smile on his face.

On the day of his departure, a simple banquet was held for him in Anantaram's house. Other than the clothes he wore, he rolled two dhotis and one vessel in a towel, tied it to a bamboo staff, drew 100 rupees for train fare till Haridwar, and took leave of them. Anantaram's wife, his children and Cheeni's young wife cried volubly. He placated them all and left for the railway station. June it was, and it was drizzling since morning that day. The train was at 5 pm, and even in the rain, many people had assembled there to see him off. They surrounded him; everyone prostrated at his feet. At the moment when the train rolled in and he was about to board, Anantaram prostrated at Srotri's feet and pleaded, 'You were a guru to me. I will faithfully discharge the duty that you have entrusted upon me. Bless me.'

Cheeni, Lakshmi and Lalite prostrated at his feet. *Lead me from untruth to truth, from darkness to light, from death to immortality, om shantih shantih*, Srotri recited in mind as he serenely boarded the train. When the train moved, the people cried 'Hara Hara Mahadev' in unison. When his grandfather's face faded away, Cheeni's head reeled, he took hold of Lakshmi's hand, and slumped to the floor. His father-in-law, who was nearby, held him.

4

By the time the train touched Dalavai bridge, the drizzle increased. Srotri looked at the river through the window. The river flowed between trees that had luxuriously grown on both sides. Right from as far as he could remember, he had had his daily bath in that river till date. When he would be in low spirits, he had sat on her banks and overcome his boredom. This same river had claimed his son's life. But the grain that he had consumed all his life had come from his farms that were irrigated by this river too. The events of his life rolled past Srotri's eyes. He recalled his mother and Nanjunda Srotri. He imagined the contours of a Shyamadasa whom he had not seen. His wife Bhageerathamma, son Nanjunda, and daughter-in-law Katyayani appeared before his mind's eye. The thought of Katyayani froze his thoughts. It was 14 years since he had seen her! Where would she be now? Sadashiva Rao had told him that she was in Bangalore. He felt like seeing her once before relinquishing his worldly life and thought: *get down at Mysore, see Sadashiva Rao, get Katyayani's address from him, visit her in Bangalore, and undertake onward journey to Haridwar from there.* As he thought that the route to Haridwar was via Bangalore, the train rolled into Chamarajapura station. He stuck his baggage to the bamboo staff and alighted. It was still drizzling. Knowing that Sadashiva Rao would be in the professors' bungalow, he enquired the address and went there. Posting himself at the gate of a bungalow, he asked in a loud voice, 'Which is Dr Sadashiva Rao's bungalow?'

A person who was seated on a rattan chair by the main door neared him and said, 'He is not here. He passed away some eight months back.'

Srotri was grieved at the account. 'Where does his wife live? And his brother?'

'His first wife is with his brother. The second wife returned to her country. The brother lives in this city, in Lakshmipura.'

Srotri went tracing Raja's house as directed by him. The drizzle lived up to its name. Presently, the dhoti he wore was wet and dripping. He retrieved another dhoti from his bag and put it on his head. 'All this only a few more days. Then on, I shall not carry additional clothes even,' he recalled. Arriving in Lakshmipura, he made more enquiries. By the time he arrived at the door of Raja Rao's house, it was 7:30 pm. When he knocked the door, a tonsured widow appeared at the door and asked, 'Who are you looking for?'

'Tell them that it is Srinivasa Srotri from Nanjangud. A Katyayani is here, right?'

His voice drew the attention of Raja and he rushed from within. Prostrating at Srotri's feet, he said, 'You came alone? Where is your grandson? And the taxi?'

Srotri could not get the head or tail of it. 'I don't know a thing. I came here casually to meet with you.'

Raja led him to an inner room. A woman, frail of body, lay on the cot in terminal condition. 'She is Katyayani,' said Raja. Srotri could not believe his eyes. 'What happened?' he asked. 'First, you change. Your clothes are wet. I will tell you later.' He led him to the bathroom. Srotri took off his wet dhoti, squeeze-dried it, and wore the other dhoti that was less wet. Noticing, Raja offered to give him a dry dhoti, but Srotri refused. 'This will do,' he said and went to the room where Katyayani lay.

Katyayani was covered with blankets. Her body was truly scrawny. Her eyes remained shut, and her face was skeletal. Her breath was slow.

'What ailment?' Srotri asked again.

'Nothing that a physician can cure. She should have stayed with you without remarrying. But Providence willed something else. A conflict among *dharma*, *karma*, dos and don'ts goes on in her mind incessantly. No amount of efforts on our part could contain that. I will tell you the details later. The doctor said that she is likely to die tonight. This evening, she desired to see you and her son. I immediately dispatched a taxi. I am not sure if her son will visit. It is our good fortune that you came.'

'No. I think that he will surely come.'

'I have got to know of his atypical nature. While he studied at the government college, he got to know that she was his mother. She had even brought him here, to this house. So that there would be no more association with her, and probably out of disdain, he left that college and enrolled at another. You would know.'

Srotri was taken aback. It was impossible for him to even imagine that the reason for Cheeni changing colleges was this. He said, 'I surely did not know of this. He sought my permission to move to another college stating that the coaching was not good at the government college.'

Raja apprised Srotri of everything. 'She aborted thrice. She construed it as the effect of her sin. Eventually, when she was spurned even by her son, she lost all hope. It was probably then that her innards resolved to end it all. I am not sure he will come. At least you came. That is a great relief.' As he said this, tears welled up in Raja's eyes. 'I have done disservice to you. Had I known you, and were aware of your persona, I would not have wed her. You should pardon me,' he said, and prostrated at Srotri's feet.

'Providence willed thus. What is your fault in this?' Srotri lifted him up. Raja bent over Katyayani and said loudly in her ear, 'Your father-in-law Sri Srotri is here, look.' He said it again. The expression on her face said that she understood his words. Try as she might to open her eyes, she couldn't fully. 'Be seated, but place your feet on this bed,' said Raja. Srotri complied. Raja held Katyayani's hands and placed them on Srotri's feet. She knew what was happening, for there was a tear in her eyes.

A taxi drew up at the gates. Hearing it, Nagalakshmi, who was standing by the door of the room, rushed to look. Alighting from the taxi, Prthvi and Cheeni entered the house. Prthvi entered the room with Cheeni in tow. He was surprised to see his grandfather there.

'Come child. You should serve your mother at least now,' said Srotri. Cheeni stood by the cot. Srotri said, 'Sit by her side on the cot and hold her hand.' He complied. Katyayani's breath was laboured now. Raja said that it was because of the strain caused when he turned her on her side. Srotri dilated her eyelids with his fingers and said, 'No, it is not from strain. She is dying. Won't you call the doctor?'

'No use calling the doctor. She has no desire to live on. Three days ago, she indicated to the doctor not to visit anymore,' said Raja.

'If you have water of the Ganga, let me have it now. Even other pure water will do,' said Srotri. Nagalakshmi brought good water in a silver cup, and a silver spoon. 'Cheeni, feed this to your mother,' said Srotri. Cheeni's eyes welled up. His hands trembled. Srotri held Katyayani's mouth open. Cheeni fed her a spoonful of water. It went in.

For the next 10 minutes, her breathing continued to be laboured. Then it began to abate. Eventually it calmed: her breath calmed. The duality that had showed up in her life and had besieged her all through had now culminated in death.

5

Raja took to weeping incessantly. Prthvi and Nagalakshmi took to a corner, and were crying too. Srotri consoled them all. It was too late for cremation. Everyone seemed to have arrived at an unexpressed consensus not to share the news with anyone till morning. Folding the corpse's limbs and placing a knife there, Srotri led Raja by his hand, brought him to the veranda, and showed him to a chair. Nagalakshmi was seated behind the door in the room, and was grieving. Prthvi was crying. Cheeni sat to one side and was deep in thought. Though grief had rent his face, he was not weeping.

Consoling Raja, Srotri picked up a conversation with him to veer his mind from the grief. He enquired about the death of Sadashiva Rao in detail. Also, about his tome and his second wife. After relating it all, Raja asked, 'You just came by! Where were you bound to?' He could not believe it when Srotri said that he was bound for Haridwar or Badri to accept *sanyāsa*. Srotri explained him some things about the ways of *sanyāsa*. By then, it was two hours past midnight. The impulse of tears had abated and they were all listening to him. Not knowing what to say next, Srotri made a general query, 'What is your native place?'

'Bellur, but we all grew up in Kunigal, in our uncle's house.'

A question surfaced in Srotri's mind. He asked, 'Well, is there anyone by the family name Srotri in your place?

'Why?'

'They are our relatives. I am given to know that a certain Kittappa Srotri, a brother of my father, migrated from Nanjangud, some 80 or 90 years back. I do not know what happened of them.'

'Kittappa Srotri you said,' Raja raked his memory. 'I have heard that my grandfather's name is Kittappa. He was from thereabouts…Nanjangud. But I do not know if the family name is Srotri.' Nagalakshmi, who was behind the room's door, intervened, 'Yes, he was called Kittappa Srotri. I have heard my father pronounce so.'

Srotri was perplexed. He asked, 'What is your *gotra*?'

'Kāṣyapa-*gotra*.'

There was no more doubt in Srotri's mind. He sat frozen. Nagalakshmi said, 'Kittappa Srotri had four children. All died early except the second. My aunt was given in marriage to him. These two are his children.'

Srotri was dumbfounded again. His mind set to contemplate on the relationship of this family with him. But in his state, he could understand nothing. Unintentionally, he uttered, 'How imprudent of me!'

'Why, what happened?' asked Raja.

'Nothing, let's say.'

'But didn't you say you were imprudent?'

'Did I say that? Well, let me say it all. Kittappa Srotri's family had the rights to all my assets. My father deceitfully expelled them from the family. I got to know of this some eight months back. I made all efforts to track them since then. I could chance upon none. Thinking that I would fall to disgrace from holding assets there I was not entitled to, me and my grandson donated it all, including the house, a fortnight back. If I had got to know about you, I would have transferred it to you.'

Raja had got to know about the distinguished personality of Srotri from his brother. He had heard Katyayani mouth the same in her dreams. But he could never have imagined that consciousness about *dharma* would be of such a high order in him. For once, he intently regarded the man seated to his fore. He felt an unknown fear. He kept mum.

By then, crows heralded dawn. Srotri got up, went outside, glanced at the sky and re-entered. 'It is about 4 am. The drizzle has ceased. You take to the next tasks. I will leave.'

'Will you leave us all now? You just announced our novel relationship. You are fatherly to me,' said Raja.

'Yes, relationship may be perceived so. But to one who has taken to the path of *sanyāsa*, no relationships apply. I am really grieved to leave you thus. But I have resolved to be in Haridwar in four days.' He packed his dhoti, tucked the bag to the bamboo staff, and started to leave. Raja neared him to prostrate at his feet. 'You should not prostrate now,' said Srotri, and turning to Nagalakshmi, he said, 'I leave,' and just walked on. Cheeni was in a state of half sleep. Srotri went past the main door. Posted by the door, Raja kept watching him.

Srotri had trekked some half a furlong. The rains had caused damage to the power supply and all the streetlamps were off. He strove to identify the colour of the road in the darkness and headed for the railway station. At that moment, he heard Cheeni holler from behind, 'Grandpaaa!' Srotri held on. Nearing him, Cheeni said, 'I will not cry before you again. But tell me one thing.'

'What is it, child?'

'That dead woman is my mother. Her life took its own course and wound up somewhere. Should I attend to her death rites?'

Srotri stood silent for two minutes, his eyes closed. Then he said, 'Child, we have no authority to assess the sins and virtues of others. To assess the sins and virtues of parents is to sin. Our only duty is to discharge our obligations. You must attend to your mother's death rites with all devotion and faith. Tell your uncle that I said so. Perform them on the banks of Kapila.'

Cheeni stood his place.

'You go now. You have to attend to the cremation too,' said Srotri, and walked on.

GLOSSARY

Agni (90): *Sanctus ignis* raised to perform homa and yajña (both listed here).

Amarakośa (201): A metrical Sanskrit work that is a dictionary cum thesaurus of nouns and adjectives.

Ārati (20): The hallowed camphor/wick flame that is ceremoniously lustrated at an idol as part of worship rituals to the accompaniment of recitation of mantra-s.

Arundhati, the star (219): See Saptarṣi-maṇḍala listed here.

Ārṣeya tradition (248): The tradition initiated by the ancient ṛṣi-s (sages). The root word in ārṣeya is ṛṣi, as is phonetically obvious.

Āśrama: The four phases that mark one's lifespan as per the traditional Indian way of life:

- Brahmacarya: Pre-marital phase when academics is pursued.
- Gārhasthya: Married life. As the head of a full household, a **gṛhastha** provides victuals (see bhikṣa listed here) and other facilitation to brahmacāri-s (1 above) and sanyasi-s (4 below).
- Vānaprastha: Forestial exile in old age.
- **Sanyāsa:** Renunciation of the worldly ways and living as a recluse.

Aṣṭāṅgayoga (435): The eight-fold yoga system as propounded by sage Patanjali in his Pātañjala-yogasūtra: Yama, niyama, āsana, prāṇāyāma, pratyāhāra, dhyāna, dhāraṇa, and samādhi.

Āyurveda (11): Traditional Indian science of wellbeing.

Bhagavadgīta (12): The most holy and popular philosophical work of the Indian tradition. Part of the mighty epic, the Mahabharata, it is the conversation between the preceptor Kṛṣṇa and the pupil Arjuna on the war field.

Bhasma (224): The holy ash, collected from the pit of homa/yajña, used to anoint the forehead and certain parts of the arms and torso. It is a śaivite practice.

Bhikṣa (495): An offering to brahmacāri-s and sanyāsi-s (look under Āśrama listed here). These two classes are ordained to follow austerity, and are not to cook for themselves.

Bṛhadāraṇyaka (495): One among the famous ten Upanishad-s, it is the most protracted Upanishad, and is commented upon by many seers and scholars, including Ādi-śaṅkarācārya.

Candravaṃśa (417): The famous lunar dynasty referred to in the various Purāṇa-s, including the Vishnu- and Bhāgavata-Purāṇa.

Cūḍākarma (241): 8th under Saṃskāra listed here.

Dharma (17): One of the four puruṣārtha-s (life's primary pursuits). This word is not translatable to non-Indian languages. It can be roughly explained as the cosmic ethics or the cosmic sustenance of living.

Dharmachakra-mudra (42): One of the postures of Bhagavan Buddha.

Dharmarāya (455): Eldest among the five Pāṇḍava siblings in the epic Mahabharata authored by the sage Bhagavan Vedavyāsa, Dharmarāya is known for righteousness, truth, honesty, modesty, tolerance, and non-violence.

Dharmaśāstra (11): A lore that expounds on dharma (listed here) and its various aspects.

Dhoti (20): A Hindi word—a phonetic variation of the Sanskrit word dhotra (also known as vastra) which, in turn, is derived from the word dhauta (washed). It is an unstitched length of cloth measuring about four yards, draped around the waist in many designs, extending up to the feet.

Dhṛva, the star (219): The pole star.

Gāyatri-mantra (224): See Upanayana, 11th under Saṃskāra listed here.

Gobhila-smṛti (443): Authored by the sage Gobhila, it is one among the eighteen smṛti-s. Smṛti-s are Dharmaśāstra (listed here) treatises, which in turn are one among the fourteen vidyā-sthāna-s, the gamut of the traditional Indian study corpus.

Gṛhastha (205): 2nd under Āśrama listed here.

Gṛhasthadharma (115): Stipulations for a gṛhastha (listed here) so that he takes care of himself, his dependents, and the society by and large.

Gṛhasthāśrama (205): A.K.A Gārhasthya, it is the significant one among the four āśrama-s (listed here), and sustains the other three.

Homa (323): A ritual to invoke divine blessings by offering oblations (called *havis*) to desired deities in divine agni (listed here).

Idli (293): A popular south Indian steamed breakfast dish made from a batter of rice and black gram. It has a history of more than a thousand years.

Kaliyuga (50): The last of the four eras (yuga) as per Indian mythology, the previous three being kṛtayuga, tretāyuga, and dvāparayuga. Kaliyuga is supposed to be the worst era vis-à-vis the rest.

Kamaṇḍala (495): A small pitcher with a handle and spout, in which holy water is stored. It is one of the basic belongings of ṛṣi-s.

Lalitāsahasranāma (450): A panegyric hymn on Goddess Lalitā, the highest motherly goddess. It is part of Brahmāṇḍa-purāṇa, and is a conversation between sage Agastya and Lord Hayagreeva.

Mīmāṃsa (372): One among the six orthodox schools of the traditional Indian education. It focuses on Vedic practices in general, and particularly on rituals, their details and their benefits.

Mṛcchakaṭikam (33): A play authored by the great playwright Śūdraka, a king who is believed to have lived a hundred years.

Name of year (444): Many purāṇa-s (listed here) list out the names of the sixty lunar years (saṃvatsara). They are supposed to represent the sixty sons of the great sage Nārada.

Navarātra (189): A nine-day kṣātra (Look under varṇa listed here) festival where—alongside Gods—warfare arms, chariots, implements, and vehicles are worshipped.

Pallu (44): The decorative fringe of sari suspended over a shoulder after the rest of it is used up for draping. It is a Hindi word.

Pavitra (460): A projecting hoop for the ring-finger made from halfa grass, worn during rituals.

Purāṇa (11): Constitute a very big chunk of Sanskrit literature. Traditionally it is believed that all the purāṇa-s are authored by Vedavyāsa, the creator of the epic Mahabharata. Purāṇa-s are one among the fourteen vidyā-sthāna-s, the gamut of the traditional Indian study corpus.

Raṅgoli (20): A derivative of the word raṅgavalli, it is the attractive creeper-like (valli) freehand patterns drawn on a stage (raṅga). It is also laid in the front yards of houses, worship chambers etc. Rice flour, white granite powders, coloured powders, etc. are used.

Ṣaḍja (20): Is the primary note among the seven notes in Indian classical music, and goes by the phoneme sa. The etymology of the word is thus: The other six (ṣaḍ) notes originate (ja) here.

Saṃskāra: The sixteen rituals in the lifespan of an individual from conception till death:

- Garbhādāna: Conception
- Puṃsavana: Engendering a male issue
- Sīmantonnayana: Hair-parting
- Jātakarma: Birth rituals
- Nāmakaraṇa: Naming
- Niṣkramaṇa: First stepping over the sill of a door of the house
- Annaprāśana: First feeding of cooked food
- **Cūḍākarma**: Ritual tonsuring of the head in the third year of the male progeny when he has grown teeth and can utter words correctly. A small tuft is retained to the hind of the head.
- Karṇavedha: Piercing the earlobes
- Vidyārambha: Learning the alphabets
- **Upanayana:** Upa=near, nayana=leading viz. leading the boy towards the teacher/ values-of-life. It is also called Brahmopadeśa. Brahma means veda, and upadeśa means imparting. It is an occasion where the boy is taken into the folds of a teacher for such imparting. On the occasion, the initiated boy will be given a ceremonial dress, which he has to wear thenceforth throughout the tutelage. This dress includes a **yajñopavīta** (an orbicular set of threads suspended by the

left shoulder and passing underarm on the right side, and technically serving as an upper garment). Then on, he has to live on bhikṣa (listed here). Commencing this initiation, a person should perform **sandhyāvandana** viz., the worship (vandana) of the two cosmic temporal junctures (sandhyā) of each day viz., dawn and dusk. He shall recite the **Gāyatri-mantra** (a couplet) a certain number of times as customary. His curriculum is stipulated in much detail. He will graduate (see samāvartana, 14th below) after twelve years of such study.

- Vedārambha: Commencement of Vedic study
- Keshānta: Shaving the beard
- Samāvartana: Graduation viz. end of twelve years of gurukula learning. Presently he is a snātaka.
- Vivāha: Wedding
- Antyeṣṭhi: Cremation and other rituals performed at death. The fire for lighting the funeral pyre is sourced from the embers ritually given to him on his wedding day, and carefully preserved by him in a burning state in ashes all through his life thence. Twelve days of mourning (sūtaka) follows the cremation, during which period various rites are performed intermittently.

Sandhyāvandana (14): See Upanayana, 11th under Saṃskāra listed here.

Sanyāsa (322): 4th under Āśrama listed here.

Sāṅkhyakārikā (222): One of the principal texts of the sāṅkhya system of philosophy. It is a small work of less than eighty verses in a meter called ārya, and is penned by Īṣvarakṛṣṇa.

Saptarṣi-maṇḍala (219): The Ursa Major, believed to comprise the seven sages Vasiṣṭha, Marīchi, Pulastya, Pulaha, Atri, Āṅgirasa and Kratu. **Star Arundhati** exists close to star Vasiṣṭha (they are a married couple) in this constellation.

Śāstra (10): A body of knowledge that has some revelations (śaṃsana) and some prescriptions (śāsana). In a broad sense, a śāstra is any systematic body of science. In a traditional sense, it is the scriptures.

Sins and virtues (315): The Sanskrit word for *sin* is *pāpa*. There is no word in English for *puṇya*, which is exactly the opposite of *pāpa*. Just as one earns *pāpa/sin* by acts of vice, he earns *puṇya* by acts of virtue. Inevitably, the word *virtue* is used to mean *puṇya* too.

Śilpaśāstra (36): The science of sculpting, it is one among the four upa-veda-s (subsidiary Veda-s).

Śloka (300): A most popular and basic type of metre of 32 letters/ syllables. People largely use the term to refer to moral/devotional Sanskrit verses in any meter.

Sūryavaṃśa (417): A lineage (vaṃśa) that has Sun (sūrya) at the helm. Details of this lineage are available in various purāṇa-s (including Viṣṇu, Bhāgavata, and Matsya).

Tarka (372): Logic; systematic way of thinking. It was considered so profound that it was accorded a place among the six schools of Indian philosophy.

Tīrtha (20): This word takes on many prefixes and suffixes to mean as many things: Rivers, mountains, places of pilgrimage, shrines, sages, dharma conferences, etc. Commonly tīrtha means 'that which purifies.' It is used in this sense in this novel, and is a sip of consecrated water dealt into the palms of devotees after performance of worship/rituals.

Upanayana (261): 11th under Saṃskāra listed here.

Varṇa (496): Varṇa means social order, and there are four of them: Brāhma, Kṣātra, Vaiśya, and Śūdra. We find references to these in Vedic literature itself. As per the very etymology of the word varṇa, in the Vedic period, one could change allegiance to a varṇa of his choice. In the post-Vedic period, varṇa-s branched out, morphed to *castes*, and became assigned to birth.

Yajña (457): An elaborate ritual intended to eulogize and propitiate the deities by way of oblations through agni (listed here). Most yajña-s are performed in fire raised in three pits.

Yajñopavīta (61): See Upanayana, 11th under Saṃskāra listed here.

ACKNOWLEDGMENTS

For guidance in the matter of philosophical, historical, cultural, and literary aspects of the epics, classics, and the works of a writer like S.L. Bhyrappa, there is none other than the scholarly Dr. R. Ganesh, who is himself a philosopher, historian, artist, and a prolific litterateur. I have sought his help in delineating the concepts and terminologies of Indian philosophy, tradition, history, and culture that extensively feature in this novel (See *Translator's Note*). To thank him adequately is not in my capability.

I was not happy with my translation of a crucial paragraph in this novel, which expounded on history-literature nexus. I requested my good friend Dr. G.L. Krishna, a physician—more a medical scientist—who is well-read in philosophy and literature, to translate it for my proper understanding. Thanks to his benefaction, my understanding cleared, and I could express it satisfactorily. He has also helped me with the English meanings of words and phrases on ill health and traditional Indian therapeutics in the novel. I owe him a lot.

For understanding the Sanskrit verses in the novel, I have sought help from a young scholarly friend of mine, Sri B.N. Shashikiran. It has helped me in translating them effectively. I am much indebted to him.